Newes from the Dead

Being a true story of Anne Green

Hanged for infanticide
at Oxford Assizes in 1650

Restored to the world
and died again 1665

Newes from the Dead

Mary Hooper

Roaring Brook Press
New York

Text copyright © 2008 by Mary Hooper

Published by Roaring Brook Press
Roaring Brook Press is a division of
Holtzbrinck Publishing Holdings Limited Partnership
175 Fifth Avenue, New York, New York 10010
www.roaringbrookpress.com

First published in the U.K. by Random House Children's Books,
one of the publishers in The Random House Group Ltd.

Library of Congress Cataloging-in-Publication Data
Hooper, Mary, 1948-
Newes from the dead: being a true story of Anne Green,
hanged for infanticide at Oxford Assizes in 1650, restored
to the world and died again 1665 / Mary Hooper.—1st American ed.
p. cm.
Summary: In 1650, while Robert, a young medical student, steels himself
to assist with her dissection, twenty-two-year-old housemaid
Anne Green recalls her life as she lies in her coffin, presumed dead
after being hanged for murdering her child that was, in fact, stillborn.
ISBN-13: 978-1-59643-355-7
ISBN-10: 1-59643-355-8
1. Greene, Anne, b. 1628—Juvenile fiction. [1. Greene, Anne, b. 1628—Fiction.
2. Death—Fiction. 3. Household employees—Fiction. 4. Executions and
executioners—Fiction. 5. Pregnancy—Fiction. 6. Great Britain—
History—Stuarts, 1603-1714—Fiction.] I. Title.
PZ7.H7683New 2008
[Fic]—dc22
2007016591
1 3 5 7 9 10 8 6 4 2

Roaring Brook Press books are available for special promotions and premiums.
For details contact: Director of Special Markets, Holtzbrinck Publishers.

Book design by Robin Hoffmann | Brand X Studios
Printed in the United States of America

First American Edition May 2008

Contents

Part~1

Chapter ~ 1

I t is very dark when I wake. This isn't frightening in itself, because most of the year I rise in darkness, Sir Thomas insisting that as much of the house as possible be put in order before any of the family is about. It is the quality of the darkness that is strange; blacker than black, soft and close about me.

I go to turn my head toward the window, to see if any streaks of light can be seen in the sky, but my head doesn't move! I try again, and again. I lift my hand—or try to—but it doesn't want to obey me either.

It must be that I am deeply asleep, in some sort of trancelike state, and aware that I'm dreaming. I think I will just wait for it to pass so I may rise, dress, and go about my household duties.

———◆◈◆———

The waiting continues, and I feel nothing: neither cold nor warm, hungry nor replete. I just sense the blackness and soaring emptiness, but this is not too unpleasant. Some time later, though I cannot tell how long, I perceive movement across the backs of my eyes: four blurry white streaks, moving and gliding in the blackness. The streaks are feathery soft and remind me of doves, or of the soft, enveloping wings of angels. The blurry shapes dance across my eyelids, but when I try to stop them, to endeavor to focus on one and see if I can spy a shining halo or a gold harp, I find it impossible.

I would like it to be angels that I dream of, for I know that would be very lucky. The Reverend Coxeter told us that. He said that no matter whether you are a scullery wench or a lord in his castle, you are truly blessed if you dream of angels. I have tried to dream of them ever since I heard that, but have never succeeded.

Suddenly I remember something and want to scream with terror, and the blackness loses its velvety softness and takes on an aspect of such vast and unknown fears that the angels disappear. What I have remembered is this: the last time I saw the Reverend Coxeter 'twas not in church, but in a bleak yard in the icy rain, and he was entreating the Lord to have mercy on me, preserve my soul, and convey me quickly to paradise. Behind him had stood a great crowd of people, a man wearing a black hood, and a mighty wooden scaffold from which hung a heavy, knotted rope. And it was for me that all these were waiting, for I was . . . was about to be hanged.

A terrifying thought comes to me: *If this happened, am I now dead?*

No, I cannot be, for surely I can hear my heart thumping within me and echoing through my ears.

Then is this the state that they tell us about in the Bible? Is this purgatory?

I struggle to think, and recall that purgatory is said to be a painful state, with tortuous fires that cleanse the soul and bring it to righteousness. But how long does it last, this purgatory? A very long time, I think—thousands of years.

My state is not painful *now*, though, so perhaps it might not be too terrible to be in purgatory. If it just means lying here quietly in the dark, it might be quite bearable. There would be no rising at two in the morning on washing day to soak the linen, no more scrubbing of the kitchen range until my hands bleed, no more going without food for breaking a plate and being unable to sleep for hunger. No more of *that*, either—that which Geoffrey Reade sought. As I think on this, I feel a shadow pass over my soul and know, without being sure of the circumstances, that he is inexplicably connected to my fate.

I leave this thought atremble in the air and move on. Yes, I could, perhaps, bear purgatory. What I cannot bear . . . what I won't contemplate is . . . no, no! I won't let that thought in. But it comes anyway: *What I could not bear, dare not consider, is the possibility that I'm not dead, but merely occupying a coffin, having been buried alive.*

I'm of a sudden desperate to come out of the trance I must be in, for surely—oh, surely—I am still in the little bedroom I share with Susan, and only deeply asleep. I urge myself on. In my mind's eye I picture myself pushing back my coarse blanket, swinging my legs out of the bed, and rising up, but though the urge is there, though I think I can perceive my muscles trembling with the effort to work, nothing happens and no part of me moves.

I concentrate harder. Maybe sitting up is asking too much of my body. It will be enough if I can move my hand, feel what's around me: the straw mattress beneath me and the blanket on top. Once I know that I'm safe in my bed, I'll be content to lie here longer.

I realize then that instead of being in my usual sleeping position, curled up like a wood louse, I'm lying straight and still with my hands crossed over my breasts. But this is not the usual manner in which I go to sleep . . .

My limbs are not working, but my mind is going ahead, whirling on a dance, showing me images of the effigy in St. Mary's: a stone woman lying with her arms crossed over her cold stone body. Indeed! That's how they lay out the dead! I'm so disturbed by this image that for a moment I forget to breathe.

I open my eyes; close them again. It makes no difference to the quality of the darkness. In fact I don't know if I'm opening my eyes or just dreaming I am. Am I asleep or awake? Alive or dead? Am I already a cadaver?

My heart contracts with terror; there is a pain behind my eyes where I long to cry and a choking in my throat, but it seems that even crying is denied me. I begin to count to calm myself down. It is what I learned to do when Master Geoffrey was—but no, I cannot think on that yet.

I wonder if this state, this condition of mine, is punishment for what I have done, for they are very hard with all who commit sin now, and I have heard of women who have fornicated being tied on a ducking stool and dropped into a pond, and those who have stolen being whipped around the village behind a cart. I have never heard of anyone being buried alive, though.

I am very, very frightened. If I find out that I *am* buried, I'll claw at the wood that surrounds me, scratch the walls of my coffin, and break out. But what will I do *then*? If I'm a buried corpse, then I'm under six feet of earth and will never get free. Best to die quickly perhaps, to clamp my lips together, stop myself from drawing breath, and perish.

In the blackness behind my eyes I try to see the blurry shapes again and turn them into comforting angels, but I cannot. Instead, chunks of my life come crowding in, clamoring to be heard, asking that they be considered in order to make sense of what's happened to me.

———◆◆◆———

So to start. It seems to me that going to work for Sir Thomas Reade was the beginning of it all, for that was how I came to be acquainted with his grandson and heir, Master Geoffrey

Reade. His name evokes a terror, but I don't want to think why. Not yet. It is ahead of me though, a source of shadows in my head, waiting to be explored.

But surely not all my recollections of that household are painful? There must be some that are not, I think, and I scuttle through my mind, throwing up memories like fallen leaves, looking for the bright ones.

I have been working for the Reades since I was but a young child and, this titled family being the most noble in the area, 'tis thought a great honor to serve in their household. They own several estates in the county of Oxfordshire, and at first I worked for them at Barton Manor, a vast dwelling in Steeple Barton, the village where I was born. This village contains about a hundred people, who mostly work on the land, and is a small but ancient place with farms and cottages, bakers and blacksmiths. At one time it also contained a gracefully ordered church, but that was before Cromwell's men tore down its altar rails and broke its windows and pretty statues to turn it into a bare meeting house.

Being well taught by my ma as to cleaning, washing, and the making of soaps and scented waters, I began working at Barton Manor as a scullery maid. This meant that I was the lowest person in the household and had to heed the wishes of everyone, which—if two persons had opposing wishes—was sometimes very difficult. I soon got to know the ways of the Reades, however, learned how to walk softly about the house so as not to disturb them, to bob a neat curtsy, and to discourse with lowered head if addressed by a member of the family. I can remember some good days then, for life seemed easier in the old house, and we servants had an amount of freedom. In Maytime there was always a pole on the village green to be danced around with ribbands. In the summer we'd while away hours cherry-picking in the orchard and gathering soft fruit—raspberries, strawberries, and mulberries—eating as much as we collected in our baskets. Later in the year, when the harvest was in, there would be a dance in the servants' hall, with a fiddler paid for by Mr. Peakes, the butler, with his own money, and we'd have a merry time dancing most of the night. We always sang as we worked at fruit picking or scrubbing or scouring: old songs we'd learned from home and ballads that the pedlars sold, and so my first two years with the Reades, before the war started, passed quite pleasantly, for I was but a child then, and my wants were few.

The big house, however, Barton Manor, was burned to the ground during an early battle in the Civil War, and two of Sir Thomas's sons died during this skirmish, for they fought for King Charles—which was to say they fought for the losing side. When I think of our King Charles, he that was beheaded, I suddenly recall a bright memory that concerns that good man. On one particular day Lady Mary, Sir Thomas's wife, bade all the servants line up together in the great hall, saying she wished to speak to us on a matter of great importance. There were about twenty of us: cooks, housemaids, laundry maids, dairy maids, ostlers, footmen, butlers, and valets, and you can be sure that on that day we were all looking our neatest and best. Milady stood halfway up the stairs, where she could see everyone, and told us that two very important personages were coming to the house and everything had to be faultless for their visit. The house was to be seen at the peak of perfection, the evening meal was to consist of the rarest and most extravagant items, the musical entertainment to be the most delightful, the wines and sweetmeats the most delicious, and the whole household must work together to achieve this end.

"Every aspect of the house must be immaculate and we must fill our visitors with wonder," said Lady Mary. "We must show them that even in remote Oxfordshire we are able to be hospitable." However, she went on to say, all this perfection had to be achieved as if by magic, for—apart from the waiting men who would serve the food—the servants were not to be seen going about their duties at any time. If we *were* seen, we would be dismissed in an instant.

"Why should that be?" I asked one of the housemaids the following week as I flew between the innumerable jobs to be done before these feted guests arrived. "Why are we not to be seen?"

"It's not so much they must not see *us*," she said, "but we who must not see *them*."

"Why then, who are they?"

"You goose," she said, "'tis King Charles and Queen Henrietta who are coming. Did you not know that?"

I shook my head.

"But no one can know they are here, for there is money on their heads."

I must have looked at her stupidly because she added, "There's to be a war, haven't you heard? And it's to be called a civil war—that is, 'twill not be fought with France or Spain this time, but between ourselves and across our own lands. And the fight will be between those who are for the king, and those who are for parliament."

"And we are for the king?" I asked.

"Of course! King Charles holds Sir Thomas as his friend and ally, and because of this the king and queen have chosen our house to say their goodbyes to each other before Queen Henrietta goes to France to sell her jewels."

"Why is she doing that?" I had to ask, for I was as green as a sprout.

"To raise money for the king's cause," she said, and then lowered her voice. "But there are spies everywhere and no one is supposed to know of their visit."

And so the house was made ready. The tapestries were taken out, beaten, and re-hung, the wooden wainscoting hard-polished with beeswax, the portraits reglazed, the mirrors gilded. On the day of their coming, fires were lit in all the rooms, and the garden raided of its every flower so that great blossoming arrangements stood on each coffer and table.

It was late afternoon when the king arrived, and I stood in my little room at the very top of the house, looking out across the drive. I remember thinking that if no one was supposed to know of his visit, then why had he arrived in a carriage and eight, for such an imposing retinue was almost unknown in Oxfordshire, and Sir Thomas himself only traveled in a carriage and four. The king's coach—what I could see of it from my window on high—was painted shiny red and purple and was very grand. The horses—all grays—wore matching red and purple ribbons in their manes and tails, and the coachmen were in purple livery.

This retinue stopped at the marble-columned doorway, and when the king emerged from his carriage he stood for a few moments looking across at the knot garden, then stretched out his arms and yawned. I was surprised at this and strangely thrilled, for until then I'd not thought that kings were real people who might suffer cramps and tiredness, but were somehow above all that. I had even childishly supposed that a king and queen, being so important, would be larger than ordinary people, perhaps as big as giants.

The king looked around him as if surveying the countryside over which he still had domain, and then gazed at the house and looked up . . . upwards . . . and saw me at my window staring at him in wonder. I waved to him and I *think* he smiled at me (I will always think so), and then Sir Thomas came down the steps of the house, bowed low, clasped his arm, and they disappeared inside. I did not see him again, but heard the musicians playing most of the night and, after his departure the next day, was given two sugared plums that had been left over from the banquet.

I was very upset when he was beheaded last year, and sorry for his wife and poor children. It didn't seem at all proper to me that a king, God's chosen on Earth, should be put to death. I think many feel as I do, but we don't say so, for Cromwell has spies and the country is in his control now. Cromwell is not a bit like our tall and graceful king, who had elegant features and fine, curling hair and mustaches; Cromwell, they say, is short and stocky, with warts over his face, and I know I should be very frightened if I came face to face with him.

But not as frightened as I am now.

Chapter ~ 2

At 59 High Street, Oxford, in a large, cold room above the shop of Mr. Clarke, the apothecary, rested a corpse in a coffin. The room was bare apart from the trestle table it sat upon, although a meager collection of twigs and dried-out cones had been placed in the fireplace ready to be lit. The only person in the room apart from the corpse was Robert Matthews, a scholar of New College, Oxford.

Before arriving at the house of Mr. Clarke, Robert had been to the Eagle and Child to take a tankard of strong beer, and then another, for what he had just witnessed had fair turned his stomach.

He'd been to a public hanging before: two highwaymen who'd been hanged on a tree together, maggoty-headed, drunk, and laughing, and an old man who was so befuddled in his wits that he hadn't known which way was up, let alone what would happen when the noose tightened around his neck. The hanging of Anne Green had been different, though. The girl had been young and comely. Shapely, too, as the crowd had seen, for after taking off her gown and cloak and bequeathing them to her mother, Mistress Green had faced the cold and driving rain wearing just her undershift. The thin cotton of this garment, soaked by the rain, clung against her breasts and defined their shape. The men in the crowd had hardly known what attitude to take, wanting to show a seriousness but having a lusty curiosity for such a well-shaped young body. Anne's mother, a care-worn creature, had come closer and tried to cover her with a blanket, but had been ordered away by the surly hangman so that he could go about his duties unhindered, leaving Anne Green to be hanged in the cold and rain with only a cotton undershift between her and nakedness.

Robert glanced over to the coffin, which had been placed next to the window so that its contents could derive the most benefit from the morning's pale and unsatisfactory light. He was not generally squeamish, for he'd been a scholar at Oxford for a year, had seen drawn and quartered corpses as well as hangings and amputations, but there had been something intensely depressing about the girl and her death; about the way that she'd stood, trembling, pathetic, in the prison yard, looking around in some awe at the attention given her by the gathered crowd, her glance passing over them as she, perhaps, looked for a loved one.

And now, less than four hours later, her body lay in that flimsy parish coffin that stood on the trestle table before him, her life blood hardly cool within her. Had her soul yet departed? Was her ethereal presence nearby—or had she, being a murderess, been consigned to hell, already enduring its fires and eternal torments?

━━━◆◆◆◆◆━━━

Even though he'd stopped at the tavern, Robert was first to arrive at the apothecary's house; the physicians weren't due for another half-hour or so. Being early he could, he knew, have taken the best place right beside the coffin. He could. But even as he told himself to move closer, get as near as possible to where the great men would be working so that he might garner every scrap of intelligence, he hung back, surveying the trestle at a distance while trying to warm his hands inside the sleeves of his black gown.

Why did he feel like this? What was he so apprehensive about? Anne Green couldn't hurt him. A girl like that, tremulous on the scaffold, trembling with cold, couldn't hurt a fly whether she was dead or alive.

But she *had* hurt someone, he thought with a start. She was a murderess, had been found to be so by judge and jury, and thence had become one of the five hanged persons a year that the teaching establishments of Oxford were able to claim for dissection.

Robert forced himself to recall that early morning scene when Anne had appeared from the confines of the jail, supported by two burly prison officials. She'd tried to cling, weeping and shaking, to her mother, but had been roughly pulled away by the hangman. "I protest my innocence," she'd whispered, and her words had passed around the crowd. "May God in his wisdom prove me innocent of the charges against me."

Her speech was recorded by two pamphleteers who stood beside the scaffold, endeavoring to write in the rain. The pamphlets, Robert knew, would be published on the morrow with many a linguistic flourish added and perhaps even a poem, together with an etching of Anne praying beside the scaffold steps and calling upon God's mercy. These would be best sellers—for cases such as this, tales of fornication and murder, could hardly be got off the printing press quickly enough.

He had watched, horrified yet fascinated, while Anne Green climbed the ladder to the scaffold and the heavy noose was placed around her neck. Her final words had been, "May God convey me swiftly to paradise," but the last of these was hardly out of her mouth when the hangman shoved her off the ladder, and put an end to her and her prayers. Some young men—her brothers, perhaps—had rushed out of the crowd and, weeping freely, hung on her legs in order to hasten her death. One of them had lifted her body several times and pulled it down again with a sudden jerk, the sooner to break her neck and dispatch her out of her misery. After twenty minutes or so, a sergeant-at-arms had climbed the ladder and pounded several times on her breast with the butt-end of a musket, using some considerable violence, in order to drive the last remaining breaths from her body. After thirty minutes, when she was observed to neither twitch, breathe, nor move, her body had been cut down and pronounced dead by a prison official and a doctor.

So, Robert pondered, if Anne Green was neither bold nor fierce enough to hurt him in life, what was he frightened of? Did he truly think that now, *dead*, she might have taken on a more frightening aspect? That as a wraith she was capable of doing him harm? But what was it that Dr. Willis said about wraiths and ghosts? That they were nothing but creations of the imagination. That once the immortal spark was gone from someone, all that remained was a carcass.

Mr. Clarke's maidservant, a girl named Martha, with frizzy red hair and pale freckles, well-wrapped against the cold, came in and struck a tinder to spark the fire, then began lighting tapers around the room. These, however, did little to dispel the gloom of the December day.

"'Tis extreme cold," she said to Robert, rubbing her hands up and down her arms to warm them, "and the rain looks like turning to snow."

'Tis the year's midnight, Robert thought to himself, and glanced up at the sky, which was leaden and streaked ugly yellow. For sure it would snow, and then perhaps it would seem more like Christmas—although Cromwell had already decreed that there should be no dancing, carousing, or festooning of dwellings with greenery this year, but that people should simply offer up an extra prayer.

"A beggar died under St. Clement's bridge of cold and hunger," Martha went on. "At least, he began to die in St. Peter's parish, but the parishioners discovered him and carried him into St. Clement's to breathe his last there and so to save St. Peter's two shillin' for his burying!" She rolled her eyes to heaven. "That never used to happen with our king on the throne. If you ask me, people are acting meaner since Cromwell's been in charge. And now he's put a stop to mumming!" She seemed to check herself after saying this, looked over her shoulder, and put her finger to her lips.

Robert smiled and made the same gesture back. It didn't do for a citizen to speak against Cromwell—or to speak in support of the royal line, either. Why, only last week two fellows had been arrested in the Rainbow for drinking a health to young Charles, the dead king's son and contender for the throne.

Martha, obviously wanting to stop and gossip, pulled her shawl more tightly around her and nodded toward the coffin. "Take yon girl, for instance. There's talk of whether she was truly guilty or not, or whether her employer had a hand in seeing her found so."

Robert looked at her inquiringly, hoping she might say more, but she merely straightened up, pushed the hair out of her eyes, and considered him. "You're here with the gent'men from the college to see the cutting?" she asked, and when Robert nodded, added pertly, "Don't have much to say for yourself, do you?"

Robert swallowed nervously. She was pretty, but she was only Mr. Clarke's servant and so of very little consequence. There was no call for him to be timorous. He could offer her a pleasantry, comment on the foul weather, or wonder aloud where everyone else was. Nothing could be easier.

"W . . . w . . ." he began, and then cursed himself silently. W was one of his worst starts. He should have gone for a softer beginning. "M . . . m . . . mer . . ." he began again as Martha looked at him, head on one side. "M . . . m . . ."

Realization spread across her face, and she put her hand to her mouth and giggled behind her fingers. "Oh, I beg your pardon, sir," she said. "I didn't realize you were afflicted! But don't you strain yourself by trying to speak on my account. People say I talk enough for two anyway."

Robert swallowed and nodded at the girl. This was what always happened, and it wasn't just with pretty girls, either. He'd grow out of it, his father had said. But what if he didn't? What if he ended up a proper, qualified physician with a pronounced stammer? How would he attend to his patients and find out what was wrong with them? How was he going to be able to treat anyone if they giggled when he tried to ask what their symptoms were?

The church bells began tolling, and Martha counted on her fingers, listening for the number of strikes. "There! That's another soul hanged. A man this time. Pity he's not for the cutting instead of the young lass here."

They both glanced over at the coffin, and Robert gave a sudden shiver as a forgotten memory stirred in him. A coffin . . . yes. He could see in his mind another coffin—though not a parish box, but one fashioned from rich cherrywood with clasps and handles in gleaming brass. But whom had it contained—and why had he suddenly remembered it so vividly?

Chapter ~ 3

I search my mind for a prayer to help me through. *Though I walk through the valley of death, I will fear no evil.* But, oh, I'm in the valley of death now, and I *do* fear it, for it seems to me that being shut alive in a box and put into the earth is the most cruel and wicked thing that can ever happen to anyone. I swear I didn't do that wicked murder, and God knows my innocence.

How could I be brought to this? Thinking on the answer brings to mind my intention of recalling my life, and I let myself dwell on the hated name of Geoffrey Reade.

Master Geoffrey came into the household when he was fourteen, about the time his father perished and Sir Thomas made him his heir. He was a big lad even then; as tall as a man, and strong and muscular, with a lot of fair curls and sandy eyelashes. I think about his appearance now, just briefly, and cannot say if he was handsome or not. I know I had thought so at first, for he had dark eyes like shiny brown conkers, and they looked very well with his fair curls. But when I recall him now, his face is clouded by my more recent thoughts of him, and he appears ugly and defiled.

But I must put things straight in my mind; order my thoughts so that I don't lose my sanity. And the facts are these.

After Barton Manor was burned down in the war, the Reade household moved to Dun's Tew, which is a village a short way off, with a manor house and farm held by Sir Thomas. Dun's Tew Manor is a very large and noble house, with many suitable and convenient offices, including a laundry and pressing room, a dairy, still room, brewhouse, salting room, and ice house. All these rooms, however, meant more work for the servants, for whereas previously Lady Mary had elected to send out to have her pigs salted, her flower essences made, or her ale brewed, now all these tasks were done in the house. The manor-house grounds also contain a large dovecote, which holds six hundred doves a-calling and a-cooing to each other day and night, two lakes well stocked with fish, a big kitchen garden, and a farm that supplies milk and beef and mutton. With these the household is almost replete and hardly needs to look outside its gates for any other provision.

Things changed for all of us at Dun's Tew, however, for with all the extra work there was not so much gaiety to be had. And 'twas not just this, but the fact that Sir Thomas and Milady were much altered by the deaths of Master Geoffrey's father and uncle and the destruction of Barton Manor in the war, and became stricter and more remote from us.

Master Geoffrey stayed with us but briefly when he was fourteen, for he was soon sent away to be a scholar in London. We were a busy household, however, for other members of the family came and went: aunts, cousins, and grown-up nephews and nieces of Milady, so that there could be two or twenty of the family living there at any one time. We had a kindly old cook at first, Mrs. Norman, who treated me like her own, but when she developed a toothache, Sir Thomas said that she wasn't able to do her job properly and must go to the poorhouse. She was replaced by Mrs. Williams, who didn't much like me. She brought two other servants with her, and one of these was Susan, who was a housemaid and also her niece. Susan is my age but looks younger, for there's no shape to her, and she's as thin and flat as a pressing board. Her

face is flat, too, and scarce ever has any expression on it
but a peevish one.

Susan and I started friendly enough, but then I did
something that upset her, and she has hardly given me a
word since. This came about when we had two journeymen
barbers call at the house to cut the hair of Sir Thomas and
the other men of the household, and also to shave and bleed
them. The younger of these fellows, Tobias, had a merry eye,
and we soon fell to laughing and joking together. At the end
of the day I offered to read his palm and tell his fortune,
which Ma had taught me and which was merely a bit of fun.
But telling palms meant I had to hold his hand, and Susan
came upon me doing this at the scullery table and slammed
out of the room in a temper, which I was very amazed at.

I excused myself from Tobias and went after her, catch-
ing up with her on the back stairs and asking her to hold a
moment.

"Well might you ask me to hold a moment, Anne
Green," she said very crossly.

"What do you mean?"

"How dare you act the trollop with my suitor!"

"I did no such thing," I said, astonished, for although
Tobias was a merry fellow, he had a pink, round face and tiny
eyes within it, and I didn't find him the least bit handsome.

"I saw you hand-holding, and looking at him so wanton!"

"I was telling his fortune—nothing more," I protested.
"But I didn't know you were even acquainted with each
other."

"I knew him from my last position," she said sullenly. "We
were friends whenever he came to the house, and we . . . we
had an understanding."

"Oh," I said, for I'd seen no signs of such a thing.

"But because you've been acting so shameless with your giggles and wanton ways, he's hardly spoken to me all day."

"Well, I do beg pardon, I'm sure."

"'Tis too late now for the begging of pardons!"

"You should have told me that there was an arrangement between you."

She went red. "'Tis not an arrangement as such . . ."

"I will go and ask his pardon this minute and tell him that I was sorry to have caused a falling out between you."

This made her crosser than ever. "You will not do any such thing!" she said, and as she spoke gave me such a hard pinch on my arm, it later turned quite blue.

The next time Tobias and his brother called, about a month later, I stayed out of the way. Things did not go as Susan wished, however. I heard from Jacob the footman that Tobias had hardly spoken a word to her. This was no surprise to me, for to my mind he was a skipjack sort of fellow who would have a girl in every house. I tried to say this to Susan, but she wouldn't listen, and we were never friends again.

I got on well enough with the other servants, but Susan was the girl I had to work beside and also share a room with, so the fact that we didn't speak was troublesome. I say work *beside*, for we were both housemaids and could be called upon for most kitchen duties. But over the last good while, it had seemed to me that she'd been doing all the dainty work: the sugaring and the candying of flowers, the making of junkets and taffety tarts, the distilling of violets, and the mending of lace collars, while I was responsible for the rest: the salting of the swine, the skinning of the eels, and the morning ritual of emptying the chamber pots into the cesspit. The only cooking I'd been allowed to undertake of late was the making of calf's-head pie, and I believe that Mrs. Williams only let me do this because she knew that such a business wouldn't be to my taste, and that rinsing out the brains of the creature and cutting out its tongue would certainly turn my stomach.

✕ Mrs. Williams is not what she seems. The family thinks her an excellent and proficient cook, and indeed she always acts both humble and courteous when any of them is about, but they don't know her at other times, however, for I've marked many an occasion when she's been slatternly or dishonest. She takes her instruction from Mr. Peakes, but they are birds of a feather flocking together, and there are lewd goings-on between them, for I once surprised them in the brewhouse with his hand under her petticoats.

Not that I can think on that sort of matter while pretending to have the virtue of a maiden, however, for I must confess that I am that no longer. And here I think again about what happened concerning this and what it led to, and a dread comes over me. *Oh, let not me be alive and in the ground . . .*

Master Geoffrey. I must think now, carefully and truthfully, about whether I am to blame for anything of what came to pass.

When he was seventeen, he came back from his school in the early summer and was much changed, having lost his boisterousness and adopted the manners and costume of a man. A *man*, I say, and not a gentleman, for I believe I know how they are supposed to behave, and his manners were not conversant with that.

He began to flirt with me and to indulge in saucy conversation, which I supposed he had learned from his fellow scholars, and this led me into some confusion, for I was not sure of how to act in response. On the one hand, I was mindful of the deep gulf between us—he the master and I the servant—but on the other hand, there was something playful and pleasing about his manner toward me that was very appealing, especially as Mrs. Williams and Susan were acting so cold.

By the strangest coincidence, it was just about this time that I first became acquainted with John Taylor, a young and bluff fellow who was apprenticed to the blacksmith in the village.

When I picture John Taylor, my heart contracts with sorrow, for if I'd not been so trusting, so easy to fool, and so puffed up with my own vanity, then surely I wouldn't be lying here, recounting my downfall. If only I'd valued John for the good and decent man he was and not looked higher . . .

But I will think of him now, for he has a part to play in my story.

I had seen him in church before, and we had oft smiled at each other, but we began to be friends about the middle of May, on the occasion of one of our big wash days at the house. At these times Mrs. Williams took on extra girls, and so my sister, Jane, had come over from Steeple Barton the night before. Jane is younger than me and still living at home, for she is very headstrong, and not biddable enough to be a housemaid. She finds work enough to pay her way, however, for she tills the land in the spring and helps bring in the harvest, and is also able to turn her hand to glove-making, mending, sheep-minding, or whatever else might be called for. That morning we had to rise at two to begin heating the water, but I was mighty pleased to have her beside me, and she and I talked the whole time of happy days at home as we washed and starched and blued the linen.

Our ma birthed six children, but two had died as babes before Jane and I were born, and our brothers, Jacob and William, were both working as grooms on a big estate in Banbury, which, being some distance away, meant we hardly saw them. Jane had news of whom they were walking out with, however, and gossip from Steeple Barton, and although Mrs. Williams frowned at our chatter, she couldn't make much objection because we continued to work hard the whole time. Besides, she was pretty much occupied with the wash, and also not only with insuring that the four extra girls were fed, but with fiddling the accounts: marking down that we'd eaten meat for our dinner when we'd only had a dish of peas and some buttered eggs. (I found *this* out when I heard her whispering to Susan that she'd made two shillings on that week's accounting, so Susan was allowed to buy herself a ribband from the next pedlar who came to the door.)

When the first big sheets had been rinsed and wrung out hard, with Jane and I twisting them between us with all our strength, we folded them, loaded them in a basket, and carried this between us to the drying ground—the orchard at the front of the manor house—to hang them on bushes to dry. This being done, we were about to go back to the house to begin again, when there was a sudden yapping and yelping, and, before we could move, two puppies ran in under the front gate and, jumping and clawing, pulled our sheets onto the ground.

Jane and I shouted and hastened to snatch up the puppies, and would have thrown them back over the hedge (which is not such a tall one), when John Taylor came running around the corner, still wearing his blacksmith's apron and as red in the face as if he'd been supping ale and pickled oysters all night in the Barley Mow.

"Ladies! My apologies!" he cried. "I was minding them for my master, and they got out of their kennel and ran amok!"

I didn't reply, for I was staring in dismay at two of our best linen sheets, which now lay on the ground with mud and paw prints all over the fancy embroidered *R* lettering. John ran over to pick them up, but this made matters worse, and I could not but scream when I saw him do it, for his hands were black with soot from the forge.

"Oh, no! A hundred pardons!" he said, looking down at the new marks with surprise and dismay. Jane gave a frightened shriek, and I burst into tears, for I knew Mrs. Williams would be furiously angry with us.

John Taylor picked up the puppies by their scruffs and shook them, and seeing as Jane had joined me in weeping then, became flustered and confused and did not know how to deal with this situation at all. On questioning us, however, as to what he might do to make recompense, and discovering that it was Mrs. Williams I was afeared of, he arranged to have the two sheets taken back to his ma's house and have her wash and blue them again, then return them to the bushes so that no one would be any the wiser.

This he did, and because of this we became good friends. Sometimes—when Mrs. Williams was what she called "checking stock" with Mr. Peakes in the cellar—I would go out on the excuse of collecting eggs from the dovecote and call over the hedge to him, or sit in the nearest apple tree and play jests (one morning I imitated a robin's call and had him looking in the branches for the bird), for his smithy stands just outside our gates and he was there most days a-striking and a-twisting of iron, carrying on his blacksmith's trade.

Dearest John. I know now that a man must not be judged by his appearance and his means, but by how he treats others, and I wish with all my heart that I'd continued with him as my friend, and not been so stupid as to believe the lies that led to my downfall.

After I'd been sharing banter with John for some three weeks, and he'd made me a present of a little candlestick wrought in iron to go in the bedroom I shared with Susan, he came to ask Mr. Peakes's permission to walk back with me after church on a Sunday. As St. Mary's, however, is less than a stone's throw from the back door of the manor house, John and I would extend this to walking around the village together and once, when we found the door of the Barley Mow open, we went in and he bought me a small tankard of beer. I was very happy that afternoon, for the men in there were giving the two of us smiling and knowing glances, and old Tom Hawkes once referred to me as John's sweetheart, which pleased us both very much (though we didn't say a word about it).

Although the rest of the household would sometimes tease me about John, calling him my beau and making me blush by saying that blacksmiths were strong and lusty men that it took a deal to satisfy, neither Mrs. Williams nor Susan ever said a thing about our courtship, but always seemed busy when I returned from my walks with him; bent over an awkward bit of mending or deep in a whispered conversation. Even when John gave me the candlestick and, finding the stub of a candle, I lit it and stood it on our nest of drawers, Susan didn't say a word or even appear to notice.

It was about June, then, that Master Geoffrey returned from his studies and began acting strangely. At first it was jokes—crude jokes, when I was alone with him (for he seemed to have an instinct as to where I was working in the house and would come and seek me out). He would ask made-up riddles: what was the difference between a harlot and a pair of gloves? a beaver and a pock-marked whore? a prick and a burn? And of course I never knew the answers and so would repeat the question, which delighted him so immensely that he would ask me to say the words once again. It was then that I realized what was on his mind. And it was then that I should have stopped.

I did not, though, and from the riddles, which grew ever more outrageous and had me laughing and blushing, he moved on to paying me compliments. He'd say how rich my hair was, how blue my eyes, how shapely I appeared, how soft of skin.

"Dressed in silks and satins, Anne, you'd pass for a lady," he'd say.

I'd try to be modest, but couldn't help feeling flattered. "I'm sure I know my place, sir," I'd reply.

"But wouldn't you like that, Anne?" he would persist. "Wouldn't you like to wear a gown in the latest Paris fashion, and have servants of your own?"

"Yes, but I don't think that will happen, sir, so it's best not to even think about it."

"And you could have jewels in your hair and a neck-lace of sapphires to match your eyes! And it could all happen if you are a good and generous girl to me," he'd say, and I'd get on with whatever I was supposed to be doing and pretend not to know what he was talking about.

One morning, when I was sent to the dovecote to collect eggs, matters advanced between us. Egg-collecting is one of my favorite duties, for it's softly dark in the dovecote, and very warm and close, and the cooing of the doves surrounds you so that you feel you're in a nest of your own. I began stretching up to the boxes to collect the eggs within reach, and my trug was almost full when I heard a movement behind me and felt someone's hands on me in the darkness. I knew immediately that it must be Master Geoffrey, and I gave a scream of fright that startled the doves so much that, with a frantic beating of wings, many flew up and away.

"Hush, Anne," Master Geoffrey said, putting one hand about my waist and the other on my bosom. I was very affrighted then, for until that time I might have persuaded myself that although his manner was a little too familiar, it was mere words and nothing that I couldn't manage. Now, though, I knew exactly where his mind was set.

"I have to take the eggs back for a syllabub, sir," I said, and I lifted my trug up across my body and so shrugged off his hand.

"Just stay a little longer." He spoke softly, pleadingly. "You must call me Geoffrey."

"I cannot!" I said, shocked.

"And I shall call you Annie." He gave a little whistle, then sang under his breath, "Annie Green, Annie Green, the prettiest girl I've ever seen."

I should have pulled away then (I have heard of maid-servants bold enough to slap a man—even a gentleman—for getting too familiar), but I didn't. Instead, I am ashamed to say that I stayed to hear more.

"Annie Green, Annie Green, the prettiest girl I've ever seen," he repeated. "Annie Green, Annie Green, her kisses are like honey."

And so saying, he knocked my basket to one side (causing about five little eggs to smash on the floor) and placed his lips hard on mine.

I didn't move or push him away, for I was struck with astonishment and also—as I must be truthful at this time—took not a little pleasure in knowing that a young gentleman of such standing should find me attractive.

When, after a moment, I did break away, he spoke breathlessly. "Annie. I could raise you in this world. Make you a lady!"

"I don't know what you mean, sir," I said, very flustered.

"When my grandfather dies, I will come into the title and the estates and will be able to do anything I like."

"But how can that affect *me*, sir?"

"Why, it is then that I can marry you!"

I began to shake with giggles, for such a thing was so nonsensical that it could only be laughed at, but at the same time my heart was beating very fast. It was as if I could see a great treasure trunk opened before me full of gold, silver, glittering jewels, and ropes of pearls, which could all be mine for the taking.

"I mean it, Annie," he said earnestly. "I have a strong desire for you. Oh, such a strong desire! If you let me have what I want, then as soon as I get my title I'll see that you rise in the world. You can become mistress of this house."

I stopped giggling then, for I was dazzled by the dream of myself as Lady Anne of Dun's Tew, of commanding the staff, presiding over dances . . . and docking the wages of Mrs. Williams and Susan and dismissing them without a character.

But I was not so much of a jack pudding that I fell for this line of Master Geoffrey's straightaway. Instead I looked into my basket and began to rearrange the eggs. "Please don't trifle with the feelings of a poor servant girl, Master Geoffrey," I said, and I whisked past him, knowing my way better than he in the darkness and moving before he could make a grab for me again.

I didn't say anything to anyone about this, for I had no one to tell, but I made up my mind I would inform Jane and Ma of it on my next afternoon off and see what they had to say.

The following Sunday after church I was, to my deep shame, pert with John Taylor, saying that I was bored with village life and might seek amusement elsewhere, perhaps in Oxford or even London. I was encouraged in doing this naughty thing after seeing Master Geoffrey, from his position in the first pew of the church, turn around and give me a look—*such* a look that when Susan saw it and realized it was for me, she gasped aloud. She never said a word to me after, though, and I know she regretted that gasp as much as I couldn't help but take pleasure in it.

Oh, but I should not have done, and I should not have suffered, what came after. I should have stayed on the path of righteousness and kept my soul unsullied.

.

Chapter ~ 4

As the notes of the tolling bell died away, there came a stamping and a shouting from outside and, skirting around the coffin with as wide a margin as she could, Martha went to the window and looked down. Walking across to join her, Robert saw that this window overlooked the apothecary's herb garden and its tall fence, against which a collection of people had gathered. Shouts and loud thuds could be heard as they banged their fists and cudgels against the wooden gate, through which the body of Anne Green had lately been carried.

"See? They're trying to get in to rescue yon corpse!" Martha said with some satisfaction. "They want to give her a Christian burial."

"B . . . b . . . bu . . ." Robert tried. He wanted to say that although dissection might seem unpalatable—even barbaric—to the ordinary people, if bodies weren't cut up, how was a physician to understand how they functioned? How could a surgeon work without knowing the best place to make an incision for the stone, how to cut out a cancerous growth with minimum blood loss, or where to sever someone's gangrenous arm?

"They're fearful angry; they don't like this a-cutting up of bodies," Martha said.

"N . . . n . . ."

"An' it's always someone poor they cuts to pieces," she went on before Robert could get out a full word. "The *gentry* don't get flayed! Don't they ever commit murder? I vow they do!"

Robert gave up trying to speak and shrugged, thinking that what she said was true enough. The poor had precious few rights, and the bodies granted for dissection were always those of the lower classes; convicted felons whose families had neither the astuteness nor the necessary means to make a better offer to the hangman. Sometimes, there being no family to consider, the convicted man would sell himself to the dissectionist before he died and then drink away his body weight in ale and sack, for a corpse in good condition was worth a full two pounds. Three pounds, perhaps, if it was an exceptional one—as the fresh young corpse of Anne Green surely was.

There were noises in the hallway downstairs, and Martha's face brightened. She set one last candle in a holder, lit it, and went out. There was some laughter, a male voice was heard to say, "I swear I'd swing for those freckles, Martha!" and she replied, "Go to, young Master!" and came back into the room with her cheeks blushed pink. She was followed by two gowned scholars, both of whom Robert knew by sight and reputation. First, Edward Norreys from Christ Church College, followed by Christopher Wren from Wadham College. Wren, although only eighteen, was being hailed as something of a genius; he already had the degree of Bachelor of Arts and was held in high esteem by the masters both for his remarkable intelligence and also for his most beautifully precise drawings of body parts. Both of them wished Robert a civil good morning, but he only nodded and smiled by way of reply, G being another of his bad letters.

"As you see, good sirs, I've made the room all ready for you," Martha said with a curtsy, looking at Edward

rom under her lashes. Robert smiled to himself
ng at the fellow, could not but admire his style,
s affected the curling lovelocks of a Cavalier
and, with his old-style frilled shirts and plumed hat, cut a
dashing figure. It was said that he lined his study with oil
paintings and silk hangings, and even kept a harp in his
bedroom so that, in times of anxiety, a musician could
soothe him to sleep. "If you need aught, let me know,"
said Martha. "Some refreshments later, perhaps. Some
bread and cheese?"

"Thank you, Martha," Wren said, and Norreys
flicked her a coin. She caught this and curtsyed again
before she went out. Wren immediately drew closer to the
coffin, looking at it keenly, as if he could already see the
body through the wood.

Norreys stared out of the window. "Bit of a crowd
down there, but all seem to be of the lower classes—
whores and harlots, pimps and panders."

Just the dead girl's friends and relatives, Robert
thought, good citizens all, and glancing once more at the
coffin, he could almost feel their affection for her. If she
was his, he probably wouldn't want her dissected either.
He closed his eyes momentarily, trying to remember the
other coffin he'd recalled but dimly. Had he seen it in a
dream, perhaps? If so, it seemed an old and familiar
dream, one that had perhaps recurred over the years—but,
strangely, he couldn't recall it coming to mind in his waking hours before now.

"Perhaps peasants don't feel the cold," Norreys
mused. "Seems there's snow about to fall, but they're not
going to be put off."

Wren snorted. "Are *you* going to be put off, Norreys? I trust you're not going to faint during the dissection this time."

Norreys grinned. "No, indeed. I've been steeling myself for this, and I cut up two toads and a dog last week in readiness. I would have had a cat, too, but another fellow got to it before me."

"Y...you...you..." Robert began, and they turned to look at him. He wanted to say that Norreys might have had the body of the tramp under St. Clement's bridge if only he'd been quick enough. "Y...you..." He could feel his color rising; if he could just get a little further into the sentence, he might be all right. "Y...you...you..."

"Never mind, old chap," Wren said after a moment. "Must be blasted annoying."

"Bad enough for us," muttered Norreys, and they all laughed, Robert included.

Martha came back in carrying a shovel of hot coals, threw these onto the fire, then smiled at Norreys and went out again.

"I heard that it's damned cold in London," Wren said, walking up and down the room in an effort to warm his feet. "Even worse than here. There's such a hard frost that the Thames has frozen over and hucksters' tents have been erected on it. The ice was so solid that a coach and six was driven right across it without so much as a creak!"

Norreys drew a pen and bottle from inside his gown and frowned. "But how are we supposed to make notes when the ink is frozen?"

"Use a pencil!" Wren said, and he held up his pad of drawing paper. With his other hand he pinched the end of his nose. "And I tell you, good friends, I would rather have *this* weather for dissection than a stinking August." The others nodded agreement, and then all turned and looked once more toward the coffin, in which reposed the corpse of Anne Green, who would presently be sawn, dismembered, divided, cut, pared, sliced, peeled, and flayed. No part of her would go untouched, unseen, or unrecorded. Even her brain—Dr. Willis having a keen interest in cerebral tissue—would be exposed to the world, weighed, analyzed, pondered over, portrayed in charcoal, and eventually preserved in vinegar.

Robert took a deep breath. This was his first dissection—such was the paucity of bodies and the demand to attend their cutting that a scholar had to take his turn. He'd seen a pair of feet dissected, it was true—for these had been the only parts of a hanged man that his tutor had been able to obtain—but these would not count toward his degree. For this he had to witness two complete dissections and also carry out two himself, as well as directly cure three maladies completely unaided.

"Did either of you see the dispatching of this girl?" Wren asked. Robert nodded, but he could not, of course, give his observations.

"I missed that, *and* the trial," Wren went on. "Was she hanged for murder or theft?"

Norreys shrugged. "Who knows? All I heard that she was a common trull who was servicing her employer's grandson."

Wren asked who her employer was and Norreys answered that it was Sir Thomas Reade. "Who is rumored to be coming along to the dissection today," he added.

Robert listened to this with interest. He'd heard of Sir Thomas Reade, of course, and had even glimpsed him at various meetings of the city fathers, for not only was he a justice of the peace, but also a wealthy and influential landowner with vast estates nearby.

"But his grandson—young Geoffrey—is only sixteen or seventeen," Wren interposed.

"Aye," said Norreys with a broad smile. "I've heard it said that he's a forward youth."

"And he's also Sir Thomas's heir and close to the old man's heart."

Norreys nodded. "So young Geoffrey could have had his pick of fair wenches—why should he bother with a grubby servant?" He shrugged and added, "But I suppose she was near to hand."

"And one never has to try too hard with them," said Wren. "Though we should take care—that fellow Montgomery was expelled last year for attempting to ravish his housemaid, and now his father's cut off his allowance and he has to beg his bread at the Rainbow."

"So we mustn't get caught with our hands in the maid's milkchurn . . ."

They laughed at this retort, and Robert, eager to know more about Anne and the crime she'd committed but knowing the impossibility of asking, laughed with them, looking from one to the other and envying them the ease and precision of their speech. Once *he'd* spoken so; he'd been told that before he was breeched he used to make the household laugh with his prodigious use of words he didn't fully understand. Being an early reader and gaining access to his father's library, he'd memorized

woof

long pages of prose with which to entertain visitors. He couldn't remember those times now, though, those bab-bling, easy-speaking times, for something had happened in the intervening years that had thwarted his vocal cords, made them strangely unwilling to respond to his wishes, caused his words to choke in his throat and stutter on his tongue. Only in his head and in his reading was he lucid of speech—to the outside world he sounded like an idiot boy. And that, he thought, was what many people believed he was; even his father often lost patience and shouted at him, or tried to finish his sentences. His stepmother—well, she was tolerant enough but had more concern for her own eight younger children than to bother with the one that she'd taken on merely to gain a husband.

The fire caught at last, and the three students stood with their backs to it, surveying the coffin.

"When we have done, will what remains of her be buried?" Norreys asked, nodding toward the corpse of Anne Green, and Robert looked at him gratefully, for this was what he'd wanted to know.

Wren nodded. "If there's anything left then the family—that's probably them waiting outside—can claim it. Though often there's barely enough to make a dog's dinner."

There was a sudden noise from the crowd outside, a long-drawn-out wail of despair that went on for several moments, and Robert thought to himself that it could be Anne Green's mother, that bedraggled wretch of a woman who'd clung to Anne in the prison yard. Neither of the scholars commented on it, however, or showed that they'd even heard it.

Chapter ~ 5

S ummer continued, and I had some respite from Master Geoffrey's entreaties when he went to stay with his grandmother's family, who live in a great house called Brocket Hall, in Hertfordshire. 'Twas immense hot for two of those weeks, and we sweltered in the heat; indeed it became so very close that the cesspits stank day and night, the poultry died in their boxes, and we maids took to leaving off our heavy aprons and sometimes even our day dresses and sitting about in our shifts. We would only do this latter thing when we worked in the sewing room, however, and there was no risk of being seen by the men.

One sultry afternoon, Mrs. Williams talked at the door with a fellow who'd come around the back of the house wanting to buy old pans and dishes. She told everyone that she'd sold him a battered dish for scrap, but I knew 'twas not battered at all, but a good pewter one with a lid, and what was more, she'd hidden two live ducklings inside that could be fattened to sell. Very pleased with herself, she then took half a bottle of claret and Mr. Peakes, and went to the storeroom.

The other servants being employed elsewhere, I finished the work I was on, which was seaming pillowcases in the sewing room, and decided to go outside and find some flowers of feverfew to take with a little bread, for I had a headache from the heat. But first I had to put on my day gown—a patched and worn affair that I had bought second-hand from the rag market in Woodstock—and I retrieved this from the back of my chair and threw it up and over my head.

Oh, what a shock I had then, for I hadn't even known Master Geoffrey was back, and he'd come up on me so

Meow

stealthily that I hadn't heard his footsteps. "I saw you in your undersmock," he murmured, putting his arms around me, "and you looked quite delightful. I have long missed you, Annie! I yearn to have you in my arms and in my bed, and to kiss you all over."

I was at a disadvantage, for I was caught up inside my gown, which had tight sleeves and a sewn-in petticoat, but did my best to wriggle out of the situation I found myself in. "Please . . . sir," I said. "I am aware of the . . . the honor you do me . . . but . . ." As I was speaking, I had somehow forced my hand down the wrong arm, and now had to endeavor to tug it out again. I managed this, but as I did so the thin, over-washed material of the bodice ripped across, making me cry out with vexation.

"Desist!" he said. "I am mad for you, Annie, and I shall have you."

"Please, sir!" I was all of a dither, as worried about the tearing of my day gown (for I had only one other) as about what might happen with Master Geoffrey.

"Don't they teach you that you should obey your master with singleness of heart?" he murmured, his face pressed against my neck. "Don't you want to be raised in the world—to have a house and servants of your own?"

I did, of course I did, and just for a moment I hesitated, and he pressed home his advantage and also pressed something else, which frightened me and—I must admit to it—excited me at the same time. "I mean it, Annie," he said, very hoarse. "I shall love you and make you my own. I shall give you everything you want, and you can have a lady's maid and fine clothes and whatever your heart desires."

As he spoke, his hands ran frantically over my body,

touching my private parts, and I thought to myself that it was not so very much, this thing he wanted. Not if, in exchange, I might become a lady. And I did not think about how stupid I was being, or how I would face John Taylor again, or what would happen if Master Geoffrey was telling me lies, but instead stopped struggling and allowed him to push me back against the linen press and have his way with me. And that was my first time. The first time with him and the first time with anyone.

———❖❖❖———

Immediately following this, I became horrified at my lewd behavior, feeling myself only a step up from the meanest whores who, it is said, ply their trade under the bridges in Oxford. At this time, however, I truly believed that he cared for me and that I would sometime be mistress of Dun's Tew Manor, so I made up my mind that I must at least act honorably toward John Taylor and discourage him. I felt sad about this, because our little conversations, our jestings, the clasping of our hands as we walked the lanes (for 'twas all innocence between us) had become a warm and happy part of my life. However, I knew that if I wished to obtain all that I'd been promised by Master Geoffrey, then for propriety's sake I must disassociate myself from John. Accordingly, the following Sunday after church when he came up and offered me his arm as usual, I didn't take it, but instead said very seriously that I had some important matter to speak to him about.

"Oh, so formal, Miss Green!" he teased, and he took up my hand just the same and linked it through his. I noticed that his hands were scrubbed Sunday-pink and his nails were clean, and thought to myself that it must take no little effort every church day to get them like that, and just for me. This touched me deeply, but also made me feel very sad.

I was conscious that, just ahead of us at the lych-gate of the church, Sir Thomas, Lady Mary, and Master Geoffrey were speaking to the Reverend Coxeter and perhaps congratulating him on the length of the sermon, which had almost reached two hours that day. As I glanced toward them, Master Geoffrey turned and looked straight at me. His eyes took in John Taylor and were piercing, accusing. I felt myself becoming flustered. What if he knew that John Taylor had been courting me? What if he thought he was *bedding* me? For certain he would withdraw his promise to raise me in the world, and what I had endured through his attentions would all be for nothing.

"We must walk around to the back of the church," I said to John quickly, "and then I can tell you in private what I have to say."

He looked at me, surprised at my tone, but we walked together to the old church garden. Some of the manor house windows look onto this space, but I was not apprehensive of being seen, for since our churchwarden was killed in the war it has become a mass of overgrown trees, tangled briars, and weeds, and we were well hidden from anyone in the house who might have wished to spy on us.

We stopped by a fallen statue while I detached my Sunday-best tabby skirt from where it had got caught on a cage of brambles. Nearby I could hear children circling the church and singing, "Well ploughed, well sowed, well harrowed, well mowed—and all safely carted to the barn!"— for it would soon be harvest time, and they were practicing the songs.

"Is something wrong, Anne?" John asked.

"There is." I moistened my lips, but no words came. I'd not thought of how I should order the matter. I looked around, seeking inspiration but finding none. "It is just . . . just that I cannot allow our friendship to proceed any further," I said after some moments. "I hope you'll oblige me by your understanding."

He smiled at me, looking almost relieved. "You are jesting with me, sweeting."

I shook my head. "No, I'm not. I'm sorry for it, but I can no longer be your friend. I feel I must speak now, for already people are thinking of us as a couple."

"And should they not?" he said, sounding bewildered. "I thought you welcomed my friendship. I thought . . . well, I've thought all along that you and I make a fine pair."

"That's as may be," I said, which is what Mrs. Williams says and is to my mind meaningless and one of the most annoying phrases in the world.

"A fine pair," he repeated warmly, "and that in due course we'd—"

"Please don't say it!" I interrupted. "'Tis not to be."

"But why ever not?"

I shook my head, then swished my hand through the weeds and, pulling up a long stem of chicory, began tugging at the blue petals. I felt horrid and wicked and ashamed of myself. Poor John, a kindly fellow, to be treated so when he'd done nothing wrong. To have scrubbed his blacksmith's sooty hands and pared his nails for my sake, only to be cast aside.

"He loves you, he loves you not," said John, taking the stem from me. "Count with me, Anne. See whether or not I love you truly."

Oink

I straightaway dropped the stem, but he picked it up and began plucking the petals from one of the flowers. "You see—he loves you," he said as the last blue shape fluttered to the grass (although I think he had made it come out so). "And you love me, do you not?"

"No, I do not, nor ever shall." I swallowed through the dryness in my throat. "And therefore I must allow you the freedom to seek a sweetheart elsewhere."

He gave a hollow laugh, for there are precious few single girls in the village, and I suddenly thought of Susan, and how very much it would pain me if he began a courtship of her with her sullen little mouth and peevish face. And it was *then* that I realized I didn't want anyone else to have him, that indeed I loved him, and that even though I might become the mistress of a great manor house, I was going to have to make many sacrifices along the way. And this was the first.

"There's more to this than I can tell," he said, his voice low and gruff. "Is it that you've met someone else?"

I hurriedly shook my head. "No! Not at all."

"No one has been acting improperly toward you, have they?" he asked harshly, his hands clenched into fists. "For I would not hesitate to fight for you, Anne. Even if the fellow was twice my size."

"'Tis not that!" I said with haste.

"Could it be that you have your sights on someone higher placed than I?"

I shook my head, sweat standing on my brow, while the children's voices encircled us.

"For although I am only a jobbing blacksmith now, Joseph Parnell has promised to sell me the smithy when he is too old for the working of it, and that should be in only two years' time. And I already have a little money put aside for its purchase."

"'Tis not that," I said, and without thinking I tugged at another weed, which turned out to be a nettle and stung me badly across my palm. "'Tis just that I . . . I do not love you."

He was silent for a long while, then he said in a low voice, "Hearing that fair breaks my heart."

I did not reply and *could* not, for there seemed a lump in my throat as big as a dove's egg.

"Do you want me to go now?" he asked.

I nodded, but kept my face averted, for I could feel the tears brimming and feared that at any moment they would spill over. I had made my choice, though, done the deed, and knew there was nothing else for it. Even if I changed my mind, I was used goods now, and no decent man would have me.

"I will say one more thing," he said, his voice choked. "I'm a proud man, but would not hesitate to have you back if you thought you'd made a mistake."

"I have not," I said, shaking my head, "but I'm monstrous sorry if I've caused you pain." With that I turned away from him completely, and a moment later heard the thud of his footsteps and the brambles scratching at his best serge breeches as he stalked off. I took up a piece of the chicory leaf and, bruising it, rubbed it across my palm where I'd been stung, as Ma used to do on our cuts and bruises when we were little, but it didn't help the pain in my heart and the knowledge that I'd caused a strong man, a burly blacksmith, to have tears in his voice.

I stayed in the graveyard for some time, composing myself, and reflected that in some ways it was good that

Neigh

Susan and I didn't speak, because I wouldn't have to explain my discomposure to her or tell her that John Taylor and I were no longer walking out. I said nothing to anyone else, either, but the following day I asked young James, the boot boy, to take the candlestick that John had made me back to the smithy. When I asked him afterward what John Taylor had said, James informed me that he'd said nothing, but had thrown the candlestick the length of the smithy, then gone after it and kicked it into the street. That night I set my candle stub into a broken saucer again, and if Susan noticed that the candlestick was gone, she didn't say a word. I didn't say a word, either, about the fact that she'd bought a yellow silk ribband with the money from Mrs. Williams and trimmed her cap with it, but I was pleased to see that the color didn't suit her doughy complexion a bit.

How strange a fact it is that I lie here not knowing whether I'm dead or alive, and instead of reflecting on the strangeness of the universe and the pity of my situation, think instead of such a petty and inconsequential matter as the color of a silk ribband.

I try to clear my mind, and address again the matter of purgatory. If I'm there now, where are the fires that are supposed to burn and cleanse? I can feel nothing of them. Maybe I've not reached the stage that has the fires. How long before I get to these, then, and what will such heat feel like?

Ah, I remember now! The Reverend Coxeter once told us that the fires would be unbearable, for only then could our sins be burned away. But how can they be unbearable, when there is no option but to bear them? And how long will I have to endure them in order to burn away all *my* sins?

Chapter ~ 6

Five or six new scholars clattered noisily into the dissection room. Jacob's Coffee House had opened in the High Street only that week, and some of them had been out celebrating the end of term with dishes of coffee and mulled wine, and were somewhat the worse for the experience.

"Move over there, you lot!" came the shout from several of them.

"You've been warming your arses for long enough."

"Give someone else a chance!"

"Let the dogs see the rabbit!"

Robert and the others shifted to allow the newcomers to warm their hands at the fire and, once they were nominally heated, a hearty discussion ensued about the freshness and rarity of the corpse, its possible shapeliness, and who might be selected by the doctors to take notes or hand over instruments.

As they settled into their positions, a young boy, servant to one of the doctors, arrived with a heavy leather bag full of dissection tools, which he placed on the table.

"Don't you want to look at the corpse?" Norreys asked him, and jeered as the boy paled and ran.

One of the newcomers, a Christ Church man, began to dance a little jig, his gown swirling around him. As he danced, he sang a bawdy ditty from a new ballad sheet, a song about a girl with skin as soft as apricots who'd serviced half the young men in town. As he sang the chorus he pointed toward the coffin in which Anne Green lay, thrusting his hips forward at the end of each line.

Ribbit

He finished, and everyone roared with laughter, stamping on the rush-strewn floor and warming their feet at the same time. Robert laughed too, for he didn't want to be seen as a Bible-thumping Puritan, but he wished he hadn't. Wished he didn't think it necessary to laugh along with everyone else. Wished he could look solemn and explain why, tell them the poor girl had suffered enough without being ridiculed after her death.

"Was she hanged for whoredom, then?" one of the newcomers asked with interest. "I thought she was a murderess."

"Whore, murderess—much the same thing," said the scholar who had sung the song. "Though this one here is very pretty, by all accounts. 'With a skin as soft as apricots and her hair all tumbling down, O.'"

"Her skin won't be as pink as apricots now," Wren pointed out. "For rigor mortis will have begun setting in, and the blood will have faded back from the skin. She'll probably be yellow, tinged with blue."

"Maybe she will, Wren, but that wouldn't be so pretty to sing about," Norreys said.

Another of the newcomers shook his head decisively. "Not rigor mortis already, surely, for 'tis scarcely three hours since she was cut down."

"But 'tis damned cold and she may have *froze* into it!"

The crowd outside suddenly found their voices again and began banging on the fence, their shouts penetrating the room. A man's cry carried clearly—"Give us Anne's body! Give her back!"—and Robert felt certain that it was her brother, the fellow in a rough tweed coat who'd hung on to Anne's legs.

Two of the scholars exchanged glances and then moved away from the window, fearing that they might be recognized and set upon by the mob later.

"Well, rigor mortis or not, I've heard that she's passing fair," said Norreys. He tweaked the ear of one of the others. "Here's your first chance to see a woman undressed, eh, young Wilton?"

The gingery youth blushed. "'Twill not be my first!" he protested, to some jeers from the others. "I've seen my sister."

"A sister doesn't count," said Norreys. He grinned around at the rest, encouraging them to take up the jest. "And what's this we've heard about your mother moving into lodgings above yours, Wilton?" While the others jeered on cue, he added, "Is it to see that you don't waste your money on card games and whores?"

"Whores?" came a bellow. "He wouldn't know what way to hold one!"

"My mother is merely staying there while visiting her sister," Wilton said when the laughter died away.

"There'll be no chance of finding you with a naked woman in your rooms this term, then!"

Robert laughed along with everyone else, although he'd never had a naked woman in his rooms, either. Two weeks earlier, however, owing to a sudden determination to lose his virginity before his eighteenth birthday, he'd had carnal knowledge of one, and usefully enough, the whole procedure had taken place with hardly a word having to be exchanged. He'd spotted the woman—reasonably clean, with dyed-red hair and lustrous eyes—sitting on the parapet of Magdalen Bridge, which (so he'd been told) was one of the best places for the picking up of whores. He'd crossed the bridge very slowly, his stomach churning, and then walked back again, apprehensive about approaching her directly because a fellow in the mathematics department had had his face slapped and a lawsuit filed for taking liberties with a woman who was merely selling mousetraps.

This girl, however, was definitely a whore, because she'd asked him what he'd heard was the usual question—if he wanted to do business—and when he'd nodded, she'd motioned with her head that they were to go under the bridge. Once they were in the muddy darkness, there had been one awkward moment when she'd asked what he wanted and given him, at lightning speed, a selection of her possible actions and their various costs. He had not endeavored to speak, though, nor question the amounts, but instead had taken some coins from his pocket and pressed them into her palm. She'd counted these carefully, then deftly carried out what he presumed was the course of action covered by such an amount. So swift was this procedure, unfortunately, that all he could recall afterward was a swift realignment of body parts, a blur of movement, and a couple of seconds of delighted surprise—which led him to wonder whether the sum paid always equaled the pleasure obtained, and, if he was to pay double next time, whether twice the pleasure would ensue.

But thanks be to whores, he thought, for otherwise, being so afflicted, how could he even speak to a respectable girl, let alone get to know one well enough to perform that other matter?

◆•◆

Minutes passed, and Martha showed a new man into the room: a young surgeon by the name of Nathaniel Frisk, who was attending the dissection as an observer. He was thought well of by the physicians (despite being merely a surgeon and affiliated with the barbers) and attended as many dissections as possible.

A bench was brought into the room and placed behind the first row of standing students, so that those who came later would have a better view of what went on. As the scholars regrouped themselves, the fellow at the door shouted that they were to look lively, and after a moment the imposing figure of Sir William Petty came into the room, wearing a sleeveless scarlet cloak over a black gown and carrying rolled-up charts and a heavy medical book. He removed his tasseled cap and nodded to the assembled scholars, who in turn returned a deep and respectful bow, for Dr. Petty was quite a favorite. Twenty-seven years old, tall and good looking, with goose-gray eyes under brows that were thick and straight, he was, as every student there knew, marvelously good natured and affable. He had studied at Amsterdam, Utrecht, and Paris with men who were prime exponents of experimental science, had been made a Fellow of Brasenose College, and was tipped to become Professor of Anatomy. His only perceivable fault was a tendency to overeat.

He was followed into the room by John Clarke, the tall and weedy apothecary whose house they were in, lauded throughout Oxford as a fine chemist and expert beekeeper, and he and Dr. Petty immediately engaged in close conversation. Two minutes later Sir Thomas Reade appeared, wearing the outfit of a country gentleman: a heavy wool surcoat over checked breeches and high leather boots. He carried himself with some pomposity, and his red-blue nose and cheeks were crisscrossed in a mesh of broken veins.

Sir Thomas ignored the scholars but bowed in turn to Petty and Clarke (a shorter bow to Clarke, Robert noticed, for after all he was not a gentleman, but merely a shopkeeper), and they returned the courtesy.

"Are you here as a justice of the peace, Sir Thomas?" Mr. Clarke asked politely. "Or is dissection one of your interests?"

Sir Thomas shook his head. "The crime committed by this . . . this *woman* here affected my household," he said stoutly. "I am here to see justice done and this unsavory job carried through to its end."

"The corpse, one Anne Green, was a serving maid in Sir Thomas's house in the village of Dun's Tew," Mr. Clarke explained to Dr. Petty.

Sir Thomas nodded brusquely. "She was. And I rue the day I ever took her in, for she proved to be nothing but a scheming whore."

"Tsk . . . tsk," murmured Dr. Petty.

"And a murderess to boot," Sir Thomas added for good measure.

Dr. Petty raised his eyebrows. "She is dead now, Sir Thomas, so perhaps you may speak of her more appropriately."

But Sir Thomas merely made a short harrumphing noise and turned away, pushing himself into the first row of the scholars and making them shuffle along to accommodate him. Robert, feeling himself dwarfed by such a hefty bulk of tweed, turned and climbed onto the bench behind, leaving Sir Thomas standing foursquare in front of the coffin with his arms folded across his chest. Sometimes, Robert thought, a gentleman would faint on seeing a corpse dissected for the first time, but he didn't think Sir Thomas was going to suffer this indignity.

Dr. Petty removed his black and scarlet academic gowns, donned a bloodied white butcher's apron, and rolled up his sleeves. "Doctor Willis will be with us shortly," he said, "but in the meantime we will remove the corpse and place her on the table ready to begin work." He gestured to the nearest two youths, who happened to be Robert and Christopher Wren. "If you please, gentlemen."

Robert exchanged startled glances with Wren and, without saying a word, one went to the foot of the coffin and one to the head. They made a contrasting pair: Wren dark and stocky, Robert slight and very fair. Together, they lifted the wooden lid and exposed the body of Anne Green to the dissectionists.

Chapter ~ 7

Some strange thing has happened. I am still here, unmoving in the darkness, but the quality of this dark has changed and is now a strange black-gray. It is lighter, somehow. Am I ascending to heaven? No, that cannot be, for surely I've not yet been lying here hundreds upon hundreds of years—the length of time we were told purgatory would last. But perhaps that number of years *has* passed. Perhaps an age goes by in a moment when you're in purgatory. Perhaps all those incidents with John Taylor and with Master Geoffrey happened a thousand years hence. Oh, but I fear they did not, for I feel them close by and inside my head, as if they would devour me.

But as I cannot know if my endurance is about to end or only beginning, I will return to my story and recall how I was mightily relieved when, about the end of the summer, Master Geoffrey went back to continue his schooling. I did not welcome his attentions, nor ever had done, and felt that once he was out of the way I might not be constantly anxious and affrighted by what was going on between him and myself, and what might happen to me if Sir Thomas found out that we'd bedded. I would lose my job for certain, but worse than this, I feared the punishments I would have to suffer for being discovered to be of loose morals.

I sinned six times in all.

The first act, in the sewing room, was over very quickly, leaving me to ponder afterward how such a small and strange act could be so very important and worth so much. Wonder of wonders, that doing such a thing could obtain me riches! But I must have been distempered in my mind at the start of it, for I'd stupidly supposed that when Master Geoffrey said he'd reward me if I let him have his way, I'd only have to allow him to do it once. That first time, however, far from cooling his passions, seemed to inflame them, and soon he was trailing me around the house with his blood hot and his mind set on a jolt with me again.

The second time followed a week after the first and happened in the dairy. Lady Mary, who'd been laid low with some malady or other, had given word through her lady's maid that she had a fancy for a milk junket. Mrs. Williams and Susan being out at the weekly market in Stapleton, I thought to make this—or at least begin it—so had gone over to the farm in order to obtain milk fresh from the goat. I put a pan of it on the fire to warm, added rennet to make it curdle, then poured it into a dish to cool. I'd scraped a sugar loaf upon it and was about to grind cinnamon for the top when the far door leading from the kitchen garden opened, and Master Geoffrey came through. Straightaway I hid myself behind a pillar and waited, quiet as a mouse, for him to go out again.

But he was looking for me—and indeed had found me, for a flounce of my skirt was showing around the pillar.

"I see you and have got you now, Annie Green!" he said, and then with no more ado he fell on me, endeavoring to get one hand down my bodice and the other into my petticoats.

"Please, sir!" I said, trying to back away from him, for although the dairy was at the far end of the kitchen, it was only separated from it by a tiled wall and anyone might have seen us. "Please, sir, don't!"

"Go to it with your please sirs!" he said. "You are as hot as I, and don't deny it!"

"If anyone sees . . ."

"If anyone sees, they will not dare say a word, for they know I am to be master of this house. And a master's wishes must always be obeyed!"

I wriggled away from him and darted around the table, and indeed 'twould have been almost farcical to see us, with me circling the room and him in hot pursuit, already fumbling with his breeches.

"Annie. Annie! Don't you want to be mistress here?" he asked. "Have you already forgotten everything that will be yours?"

I didn't say anything, for I'd only just realized how green I'd been, and that the act would probably have to be endured many more times in order to keep him satisfied. And whenever would I get what I'd been promised? For although Sir Thomas was upwards of sixty years of age, he was in robust good health and did not seem about to roll over and leave his lands and fortune to Master Geoffrey just yet. Wondering then what would become of me, I began to wish with all my heart that I'd not submitted in the first place. We are told often enough when we begin work as maids that gentlemen may try and take advantage of us, and we must therefore be sober in our discourse and never gay, so that they may not think we are open to levity. But—oh, stupid girl—I'd certainly been frivolous with Master Geoffrey, and from this he'd deduced that I'd be persuaded to lie with him.

I stopped going mulberry bush around the table then, knowing that my protests were useless, and stood against the cold stone sink, waiting. I only counted to seven before the act was finished, but sometime during this, my dish of junket got knocked onto the floor, so that when Mrs. Williams returned and heard of Lady Mary's request, she scolded me for not having had the intelligence to obtain the goat's milk from the farm earlier.

The third act happened early one day in Master Geoffrey's bed, when I'd been sent in with his morning washing water. He has a stately bedroom, with ewer and basin of silver, two mirror glasses, and a vast feather bed with four posts hung about with costly drapes. I don't usually carry the washing water around and hoped that he'd be asleep—indeed, I removed my shoes and tiptoed across the thick carpet in bare feet—but he seemed to know it was me, for his eyes sprang open the moment I set down the jug on the washstand. He was out of bed in an instant, took five strides across the room, picked me up, threw me onto the bed, and drew the curtains around us. When George, his manservant, came in a moment after, he told him he must leave and come back in ten minutes.

Of course, George didn't know who was behind the drapes with Master Geoffrey, but he knew *someone* was, and spread the tale downstairs. The servants began gossiping and speculating and, knowing it must be someone in the household, before long had all deduced it was me, although I never admitted it. Instead of teasing me, though, as they had about John Taylor, they were quite mean in their comments. Mr. Peakes said that no good would come of it; Mrs. Williams, pinch-faced, said that that was as may be, but I needn't start putting on airs and graces; another said that when a youth was Master Geoffrey's age, *anyone* would do, and one of the menservants winked at me and said that if there was aught left over, could he have a share. I began to feel bitterly

horse

ashamed of our association, which I could not even justify by saying that I loved him—for which emotion, I believe, many such similar sins of the flesh might be forgiven.

The fourth time with Master Geoffrey happened over by the carp lake. I'd cast the fishing nets onto the water and only then discovered, by him coming up behind me quietly over the thick grass, that he'd followed me out there. Seeing I was less than willing to do what he wanted, he tickled me until I was doubled up with mirth and pushed me into some myrtle bushes, swearing on his mother's life that he was devoted to me and would make me mistress of all I could see. Indeed, he said he would make me queen of England, too, if he'd been able.

The fifth time—oh God, I swear I didn't want this or encourage it in any way—the fifth was in the churchyard amid the tombstones, where the ground swarms with souls and spirits and surely 'tis a profanity to carry out such an act.

The churchyard. Am I there now, still breathing but under the earth? Oh, I pray not, for I swear that nothing I have ever done in my life has been wicked enough for that fate to befall me.

The sixth and final time occurred on the stairs in the dark, after he'd worn me down and made me weary enough to scream at his continual pleadings, saying things such as he loved me entirely and couldn't carry on without easement, and that I was being cruel and selfish to deny him this one thing before he went back to school. It was over very quickly, but I felt so bad afterward that I told him I didn't wish to go on with it when he returned, no matter what he might promise. He insisted, however, that it must and would continue in December, when he returned to the house.

"For seeing as you've lost your maidenhead, how does it matter whether or not you do it with me?" he asked.

I had looked at him, not discerning his meaning.

"For your maidenhead wouldn't come back even if you were to keep your legs together until the day you die!"

I turned away from these crude words, not wanting to hear more.

"And a fellow will always know, even though some jades try and fake their virginity. So you may as well be nice to me, Annie, for I am your only hope." He ran his hand up my arm and tucked it inside the puffed sleeve of my blouse, pressing his fingers into me hard. "'Twould not be a clever idea to turn your back on me now."

"You may be right, sir, but indeed I wish you had not started it!" I burst out.

"*I* start it?" he asked. "I wouldn't say that was the case, Annie. It could be said that you led me on with your giggles and blushes and your unseeming language."

My face flamed, but I had no reply to this, and knew that aught I said would be twisted and shaped to suit his own ends. I began to cry and after looking at me askance for a moment—for we were still on the stairs and mighty close to the door of his mother's room—he pulled five silver shillings out of his pocket and pressed them into my hand.

"Here. Stop your women's weeping," he said, "and buy yourself something fancy to wear with this."

I'd stared at the money in awe and not a little consternation, for five shillings was the most money I'd seen altogether in my life, and near equal to my year's wages after my livery is taken off.

"You must spend it on something splendid to wear," he said, "for when I raise you up you'll be required to dress as a great lady, and this can be the start of your wardrobe."

I'm ashamed to say that these silver coins were enough to turn my head, and I took them from him, knowing they were enough to buy me a very handsome gown or two or even three second-hand ones, and after this we parted and said no more. I was most happy and relieved to see him go back to school, however, and I resolved that, come what may, I would not succumb on his return.

There being nowhere in Dun's Tew to spend such an amount of money, on my afternoon off (with Mrs. Williams being busy in the cellars with Mr. Peakes), I took a ride on one of the carts going into nearby Woodstock, which is a fine and fashionable town. Here in a shop in the High Street I purchased—not a gown, but a most beautiful bodice embroidered all over with silver thread and embellished with pearls. I did not have a skirt to match it in beauty—nor indeed any occasion to ever wear such an item—but I kept it wrapped in tissue paper under my mattress and sometimes took it out and looked at it. I told no one about it, for I'd already been chastised by Mrs. Williams for wearing a red petticoat on a Sunday and knew the bodice wasn't a suitable thing for a maidservant to own.

I never wore it. The last time I saw it was in prison, when I handed it over to Ma and then went to meet the hangman.

Chapter ~ 8

As the coffin lid was removed, Robert found his hands were shaking and that he was unable to look directly upon the corpse, although for what reason he couldn't say. Perhaps he feared that the girl might have taken on a terrible aspect, her face contorted and her eyes starting from their sockets. Perhaps it was that he didn't know whether she lay in the coffin in her undersmock, or naked—and that if the latter, he feared the sight of her might induce some fellows to sniggering, or to make lewd jokes that even the presence of Dr. Petty might not prevent. But then, he reasoned, Dr. Petty would probably cut her clothes off before they started the dissection, so that sooner or later she *would* be naked before them all. And more than that, for very soon they would see not just her skin, but her flesh, her muscles, her bones, and her very heart. No, he thought, it was something to do with that other coffin, the one that remained elusive to him. Despite being recalled but hazily, it was a matter so sensitive, it almost hurt him to think of it.

But when Robert finally forced himself to look at the body of Anne Green (for they had not bothered to dignify her corpse by wrapping it in a shroud), he saw nothing too gruesome. The girl still wore the stained and wet undersmock she'd been hanged in, and although her hair was in damp strands, her face, streaked with tears and dirt, seemed in repose. The flesh of her arms and legs was creamy white—as white as the cheap cloth that lined the coffin—her face was somewhat pink—due to, perhaps, the breaking of blood vessels—and the only strange and jarring aspect of her appearance was that the great knotted rope by which she had been throttled was still around her neck.

As the lid was placed on the floor, there was a movement from the scholars as they craned and peered into the coffin.

"You may remove the corpse," Dr. Petty said.

Robert swallowed the bile that had risen in his throat, thinking to himself that strong beer too early in the morning should be left to more experienced constitutions.

"You take the top half," Wren instructed him.

Robert nodded, then slid his hands under the dead girl's shoulders. As they lifted her, the hangman's rope slid toward the floor, jerking her neck and, for a ghoulish moment, making it look as if her head had nodded.

"She moved!" Norreys said in alarm, and there was a collective gasp from the assembled students. Dr. Petty, engaged in unrolling a chart, glanced over and smiled slightly. "My dear boys," he said, "I can assure you that she did not move. She has been dead these three hours and more."

"She is certainly dead," another confirmed with a slightly nervous laugh. "She hung over half an hour on the scaffold. And her family swung on her legs to hurry her end."

"Until the jailer told them to stop for fear the rope would break!" another added.

Robert opened his mouth to add something of his own but then thought better of it. No matter, for one of the scholars had seen the same thing and was speaking his lines. "I saw someone batter her breast with the butt of a musket to help her on her way."

Dr. Petty nodded. "She is undeniably not of this world." An ironic smile played across his lips. "Even now she may be knocking at the door of heaven."

Dr. Petty's charts had been unrolled and put up on the wall behind him. One depicted a skeleton, every bone down to the smallest precisely labeled; another showed the muscles in the body, red and livid; the final one was a depiction of a human head, the front of its skull removed to show an approximate replication of the whorls, cavities, and coils within the crater of the brain.

The dissection tools—knives, saws, gimlets and pliers, brass probes, pincers, curved needles, syringes, long-handled scissors, and a range of small knives with blades as sharp as razors—had been removed from the bag and stood at the ready. And, although a corpse was not expected to bleed much, wadding had been provided, and there was a pile of it at the head of the table. As a further precaution, Martha came in with a pail full of sawdust brought in from a nearby coffin maker's and threw handfuls of it onto the floor. She stole a quick glance at the corpse as she went out, shuddered dramatically, and then looked at Norreys to see if he was looking at *her*.

The crowd outside in the High Street seemed quieter now, for a small detachment of soldiers had arrived and were rough-handling anyone foolhardy enough to get too close to the fence. Robert wondered to himself how Anne's mother—and her younger sister, had it been, who'd been near her in the prison yard?—were faring. Were they still waiting out there in the sleet with the others, or had they gone home to mourn?

As Dr. Petty and Mr. Clarke conversed in low tones about who should take responsibility for which part of the body and in what order, the scholars either spoke among themselves or just stood and stared first at the charts and then at Anne Green, trying to work out for themselves the positioning of some of her interior organs. Robert stared too, and fell into a kind of reverie in the staring, trying to remember more details of that other coffin and who'd been lying inside it.

The fellow next in line, young Wilton, nudged him, making him start. "Were you at her trial?" he asked.

Robert shook his head, and Wilton directed his speech behind his hand so that Sir Thomas could not overhear. "The whole business of the trial and hanging was a strange one," he confided. "And an unjust one, it seems to me."

Robert looked at him intently, for he knew Wilton to be a fellow who took a deep interest in the politics of the day. It was rumored, too, that he'd kept faith with the Levelers at one time, until the last rebel band of these fellows had been rounded up in Burford the previous year and their leaders shot.

"*He*"—Wilton nodded toward Sir Thomas and lowered his voice—"had too big a hand in it."

Robert was anxious to hear more but, curling his lip with frustration, knew that it was well nigh impossible for him to pose the question.

Sir Thomas suddenly spoke up, his voice brusque and impatient. "Will it be *much* longer to wait? When are you going to start the business?"

Dr. Petty pulled out a pocket watch, which the students regarded with a great deal of interest. "We are waiting for Doctor Willis. I believe he had an important laboratory experiment already booked for this morning."

Robert wondered what this was and if it might be something innovative and radical—like the recently posited notion from Dr. Willis that catarrh did not pass into the nostrils from the brain, as had always been presumed. He thought of the experiment *he* was currently running, which involved a chicken and a constant supply of eggs, the contents of which were examined and logged a certain number of days after they'd been laid. The chicken, whom he'd named Scarlett on account of her red feathers, lived in his lodgings with him, ate scraps, and provided him with quite congenial company, for (to his surprise) Robert had found that he could talk to her almost normally and with rarely a stammer. He let her out into the yard every morning for regular liaisons with a rooster, and so far no one had noticed her presence in his room; although the students were forbidden to keep grayhounds, ferrets, or hawks, a chicken appeared to be beyond this censure.

At last there came the sound of footsteps hurrying along the passageway and Martha's voice was heard to say, "Just along here, sir, if you would be so kind," and a moment later Dr. Robert Willis came into the room wearing a wool cloak, which he discarded at the door to reveal a stained black gown. Although not as charming a figure as Dr. Petty—for Dr. Willis was plain, stocky, and had hair as red and bristly as a pig's—his intense intelligence, plus his avowed intention to unlock the secrets of man's mind, was causing immense interest in his work both with the Oxford students and in the general scientific world. He had recently written a treatise on sadness, saying, controversially, that it was a complicated distemper of the brain and heart and not a melancholic humor at all. Robert felt himself lucky to be at Oxford with such a brilliant physician, and profoundly pleased that his first dissection would be conducted by him and Dr. Petty.

"Good morning, gentlemen, and my apologies for keeping you waiting," Dr. Willis said, bowing to all corners of the room.

He went directly to the cadaver and walked up and down the table, surveying it with a keen eye. He slouched as he walked, Robert noted, and did not have the bearing of a gentleman or person of quality. He was certainly a gentleman in the true meaning of the word, however, for he had long treated the poor without payment.

"This is the murderess? She seems a very mild one." He caught up one of Anne Green's hands and examined it. "She was a housemaid?"

"Indeed," said Mr. Clarke, the apothecary. "A housemaid who was found guilty of murder, although she maintained she was . . ." He suddenly caught the eye of Sir Thomas, and his voice faded away.

"*She* maintained?" inquired Sir Thomas. "Are you saying, sir, that the word of a whoring housemaid should be taken above that of judge and jury? Are you saying that the law of the land was not properly implemented and that twelve good and educated men were wrong in their judgement of her?"

Everyone in the room waited for a response.

"Not exactly," Mr. Clarke said at last. "It's just that she maintained her innocence until the end and—"

"Have you ever known a convicted felon who did *not* proclaim his innocence?" demanded Sir Thomas.

Mr. Clarke, who could be easily cowed, shook his head.

"Fortunately, we are not concerned with the girl's guilt or innocence now," interrupted Dr. Petty, "for it's obviously too late to discuss the finer points of the accusation. No, we are here with the express wish of improving our understanding of the functioning of the human body."

"Then I suggest you get on with it!" said Sir Thomas.

"Indeed," said Dr. Willis. "The fresher the body, the more we shall learn."

Sir Thomas nodded. "Quite. Quite. Even without the murder charge, the new laws state that fornication may be an offense punishable by death, so the jade has got what she deserved."

"But who was it that she fornicated with?" Wilton whispered to Robert. "Should he not also be culpable?"

Robert, although rather startled by this thought, found himself nodding.

"There has been some skulduggery here, you may depend on it . . ." said Wilton.

Dr. Willis picked up a whalebone rod tipped with silver and twirled it in his hand. "Shall I begin?"

"If only you would, sir!" came from Sir Thomas.

Dr. Willis moved forward and, watched closely by everyone in the room, tapped the tip of the rod against Anne Green's breastbone.

A tiny sound escaped from her mouth.

Only Robert heard it. At least, he *thought* he'd heard a faint noise, like the far end of a sigh, but with the press of people around couldn't be perfectly sure of the direction from which it had come.

He stared at Anne Green, pale, silent, and immobile on the table; her life force extinguished over four hours ago and dead as a flitch of bacon. Of course he hadn't heard anything. But . . . He suddenly shivered so violently that Wilton gave him a concerned look. He saw, clearer than before, that *other* coffin. He saw another corpse, a young woman about the same age as Anne but tranquil and serene in her death, wearing a white ruffled nightgown, with dark curls showing at each side of a white cap. There were candles standing at the corners of the table, and a sweet, high scent perfumed the room. Incense, he thought to himself—although it had been banned from churches and it was a while since he'd last smelled its fragrance.

Wilton gently pinched his arm. "You've gone as pale as a wraith, good fellow. Are you all right?"

Robert formed his mouth into a *yes* and nodded his thanks. He pulled himself back from his reverie, paid attention to Dr. Willis.

"I am about to dissect the corpse of a woman," the doctor said. "She appears in good condition and was not suffering from any malady before her demise. With your permission, gentlemen"—he made a flourish toward Petty and Clarke—"I intend to make the first incision under her ribs and then open up her chest cavity to reveal her heart."

But as Dr. Petty and Mr. Clarke bowed back, another sound came from Anne: a faint rattling noise. It was a noise, Robert thought, more generally made by a corpse breathing its last than by one that had been pronounced dead some hours ago.

This time, most of the room heard it, and although the medical men did not seem unduly disturbed, the scholars gasped, and Sir Thomas Reade took a step backward, looking affrighted.

"'Tis nothing, merely the last breath she took, coming back from her lungs," Dr. Petty said calmly. "I have heard such a thing before."

"I know what to do," said a fellow standing on the bench, and he did no more than jump up onto the table and stamp down hard on Anne's chest and neck. "That will see her off!"

Robert and several other scholars gave a cry at this violation, and Dr. Willis ordered him off the table. "That was unnecessarily brutal and could have harmed our specimen," he said brusquely.

The fellow looked put out. "I merely sought to help, sir."

"Then please do not," came the stern reply.

Dr. Petty picked up Anne's limp hand and felt around her wrist. "There is no pulse here and no sign of life," he said. "I suggest we proceed with the dissection forthwith."

Chapter ~ 9

Such a pain! Such a pain of a sudden came upon me, as if someone had hammered across my breasts and my neck and my rib cage. And there was no way of expressing it nor of screaming out with the agony of it, so I had to contain it within me, and thus it seemed so much worse.

For a time (a moment? a hundred years? a thousand?) I could not think of anything but this pain, and then gradually, very gradually, it diminished. When it allowed thought to come in, I wondered to myself if this was the beginning of the torment I would have to endure to enable me to progress through purgatory. In that case, perhaps I should not fear it, but welcome it. It did not continue, however, and once the first agony was gone I felt nothing but a dull ache right across my body.

———•◦•◦•———

At the start of the cider-making season I had my afternoon off and walked home to see my ma, only to discover a terrible thing; a thing which I had felt in my heart, but which I had pushed away as being too dreadful to consider.

My home village is about three miles from Dun's Tew. 'Tis a pleasant enough walk over fields and cart tracks, though 'tis a sadness to see the ruins of Barton Manor, now all tumbled and near disappeared under brambles and briars. On crossing the common I met some of my old neighbors picking the last blackberries, and also saw our family's two sheep, Bramble and Bracken, grazing peacefully near where the maypole used to stand. All was just as I remembered and how I like to recall it—although since I've been working for the Reades I've never visited my home without thinking of how small it is, and how humble. And indeed I thought it then, for 'tis but two rooms, one down and one up—this latter reached by a ladder—also an outhouse where the chickens live and are joined in winter by the sheep and, if Pa has had the money to buy one that year, a pig. There's no glass in the cottage windows up or down, and the wooden shutters, which do their best to keep the wind out, also serve to keep out the light, so in winter it's necessary to burn a tallow candle even by day. In our downstairs room there's a wide hearth containing a spit, cauldron, and kettle, but there's no bread oven, so Ma buys her daily loaf at the baker's, and is thereby allowed to take her own pies and pastries along to be baked in his big oven. The room has not much furniture but is homely, with two benches, a table, and an oak coffer that stores linen and trenchers and so on. 'Tis passing sufficient, for there's only Jane living at home now, and Pa is not often there, nor ever has been, for he labors long on the land and takes on extra work whenever he can and for whatever master. 'Tis long been his ambition to buy a cow, and they don't come cheap.

I know that Ma is not a clever woman when it comes to book learning—she has not had a day's schooling in her life and cannot even write her name—but there are certain things she knows about, for I'd not been long inside the door before she put aside the piece of lace she was making and looked me over carefully.

"You're pale of face and have rings about your eyes," she said. "Are you with child?"

I protested that I was not, even though I had not seen my courses for nigh on two months.

"Are you sure, Anne?"

I began shaking my head but she said, "I know the signs! Have you lain with a man? Don't lie to your own ma!"

Of course, I did no more than burst into tears and say that I had.

"Is it your young man's? Is it John Taylor the blacksmith's child?" she asked, for I'd not been home since the beginning of July, and at that time John and I had been seeing each other regularly.

I didn't reply to this, for I was too ashamed, and she must have felt pity for me for she reached over and took my hand. "Well, you needn't take on so," she said. "Many girls anticipate their wedding and you'll not be the first. We can fix a date now, and when the child comes early, no one will say a word."

I still did not speak.

"Take heart, my girl," she said, squeezing my hand. "'Tis not what I wanted for you, but the Reverend Belchard will be sure to marry you, and we'll give you a little feasting." She paused. "Where will you live, though? What sort of dwelling can John Taylor provide?"

I continued weeping. "I've not set eyes on John Taylor these past three months," I said between sobs, which was not exactly true, for I knew exactly where he stood in church and out of the corner of my eye had oft seen his strong and upright figure, face resolutely turned to the front with never a glance toward our servants' pew at the back of the church. I would stare at what I could see of his head, note how his black hair touched his Sunday-white collar and went in a soft curl over it, and wish with all my heart that I had not given in to Master Geoffrey.

Ma gasped. "'Tis *not* John Taylor's child?"

I shook my head.

She dropped the hand that she'd been holding so tenderly. "Someone else is the father? Oh, Anne, for shame! Who have you been a-tumbling with?"

I cried harder then and couldn't look at her, indeed was so very much ashamed of myself that eventually she relented and, putting her arms around me, promised that she wouldn't reproach or chastise me if I told her the truth. So I told her about Master Geoffrey and how he'd been so friendly and easy with me, how he'd promised me gold and silver and the tenure of Dun's Tew Manor if only I'd lie with him, and how eventually I'd been persuaded.

She shook her head with each sentence I uttered. "Oh, Anne, you simple girl," she'd said, sighing again and again. "To think you'd fall for such false and honeyed words."

"But he's a gentleman," I protested, "and I thought 'twould be well enough to trust him."

"The gent'men are the very worst." She looked at me closely, then slipped her hand onto my belly to feel the shape of it. "When did this start with him?"

"About the first hay-making," I said, for I remembered that there had been revels in the village on that very hot summer day and morris men dancing on the green, despite the new rulings that there should not be such tomfoolery.

"And when did your terms cease?"

I told her, and she calculated that I was perhaps three months with child.

"But all is not lost if we're quick," she said, "for there are certain plants and herbs which are said to bring down a woman's courses." She stood up and took her shawl. "We must visit the cunning woman at once and find out what they are."

———◆◆◆◆———

I should have been back at Dun's Tew by five o'clock, for Lady Mary was having a musical evening, and there was a deal of dainty sweetmeats to be prepared for it, but we decided that, my absence being noticed, I would say that Ma had been taken ill and that I'd had to stay with her until Jane came home. Ma and I then went together to the cunning woman's hut, which was on the common, close to the hoarstones where the goblins were said to be buried. For the excursion I wore Ma's old cloak and had a shawl close around my head, for I didn't want to be recognized going to such a place.

There are those who say that the cunning woman is a witch, but I don't think she is; she's just an old and bent woman who lives with three cats and a lame fox. Her hovel has a stamped-earth floor and a hole in the roof to let the smoke out, and she has only one chair and a planked bed to call her own—surely if she was a witch the devil would have seen to it that she had more comfortable surroundings? She said that I was with child for sure, and, judging from my tear-streaked face that I did not wish to be, picked hyssop and sage from the profusion of herbs that grew around her cottage in tangled skeins and pounded them together in some agrimony water, which she then bottled. She told me not to take more than a scanty amount of the hyssop mixture—a bare spoonful at a time—for the herb's powers were so strong that an overdose could lead to poisoning. She also gave me a jar containing a decoction of the leaves and berries of the bay tree, saying that I should add this to a bowl of hot water and sit in it, for it was a sure remedy for a woman in distress. Ma paid by giving her a chicken and promising another come Christmas, and this seemed to satisfy her.

I went home with Ma, and she boiled some water over the fire and sat me in a washing bowl containing the bay mixture (for of course there was not the privacy to do such a thing at Dun's Tew), and Jane, who'd been out earning money bird-scaring in the fields, came in by and by and laughed heartily to see me placed so in the bowl. I explained to her what was wrong, however, and swore her to secrecy—for Jane loves to gossip—and she went very quiet and serious. She listened to my tale but did not seem impressed with aught that Master Geoffrey had promised any more than Ma had been, even though I said I'd have taken care to raise them, too, and had Jane to come and live with me as my companion. As I said these words, however, they struck me as false, mere fancies, and I wondered how I ever could have believed them.

I sat in the water nigh on an hour but nothing happened, not so much as a gripe or a cramp, and afterward I dressed myself and took the hyssop cordial back to Dun's Tew to drink before I went to bed. The cunning woman had said that I should stay close within the house after taking it and be prepared with clean rags to stem the flow that would ensue, so I couldn't sleep that night for worrying about how bad the pains would be and how I'd keep the matter a secret from Susan. In the end, however, nothing happened, and my undersheet stayed unsullied.

In the morning I took another spoonful of the cordial, and then another, but was scared to take more because of what she'd said of its power. When, a day later, it was clear that it wasn't going to work, I poured the rest of the mixture away and threw the bottle into the midden.

I was at a loss then, and thought about getting a message to Ma but decided against it, not wanting to make her anxious. After more sleepless nights I decided that there was nothing else for it but to carry on as usual and, should my condition begin to show, lace my stomacher and bodice tighter and try to be patient until Master Geoffrey came back at the beginning of December. He would know what to do, I told myself. He was young, but had been educated to deal with such vexing questions, so would surely order things and see that everything was well. Perhaps he'd pay for me to go away and give birth in London, where no one knew me and where, I'd heard, these matters were not of such great import. Lodgings there would not be difficult to obtain, and the child and I could live there quietly until such time as my seducer came into his inheritance. For at that time part of me still believed that he who had caused my condition would support and help me, and that I wouldn't be left to bear things on my own.

Thinking on the future, then, I felt that all was not lost, and tried to put the matter to the back of my mind, content in the fact that Master Geoffrey was away and that I would not have to put up with his pleadings and fumblings for the next good while.

———◆◆◆———

As I related, people speak of the cunning woman of Steeple Barton as being of the devil's brood, but I'm sure she's not. A more powerful witch, to my mind, is Mrs. Williams, for in the days following my visit home it seemed to me that she was always speaking of childbirth and pregnancy—seemingly innocently, but with one eye upon me to ascertain my reactions.

One tale in particular was a favorite: the story of Sara Freeman, a girl from a nearby village who'd died after a long and painful struggle to give birth, for it was said that her bones were too narrow to let the child pass through. She'd been buried swiftly, for it was a hot summer, and then a day later a village crone, walking through the churchyard, had heard the faint crying of a baby. Thinking it a ghost, she'd fled the place, but then some sense had come to her and she'd returned and reported to the cleric what she'd heard. Already fearing some catastrophe, he called for the gravediggers, and the coffin was exhumed. When its lid was lifted, they found it contained not only Sara Freeman, but also the body of an infant, newly born and newly dead, for it seemed that, after burial, Sara had remained alive long enough to give birth.

Mrs. Williams would oft recall her, and tell of another woman some years before who was said to have been delivered of thirty rabbits, and yet another whose path had been crossed by a hare and who'd borne a child with a hare-shotten lip. She told of women who'd died in travail, and those who'd birthed children conjoined, and said that there was no telling what ill creatures might be born now, for God was grievously displeased with those who'd beheaded his anointed king, and this was his way of punishing them.

"The world is turned on its head now," she said one morning when I was at the salting table in the scullery. "And all we can do is pray that God will not choose to punish *us* for Cromwell's great sin."

I didn't speak, for I was concentrating on the job I was doing, which was rubbing salt into a dead sow's skin, the better to preserve the animal over winter. 'Twas nasty work, for every so often the salt crystals would get into a cut or graze on my hands and cause me to wince.

"So we must carry out our jobs quietly and well in the station in which he has placed us," she went on piously.

"Amen," Susan said. She was chopping hard-boiled eggs for a garnish, and I knew without looking that she had a righteous expression on her flat face.

Mrs. Williams, who had been watching me critically for some moments, suddenly said, "Anne, you have dressed your hair differently this morning."

"Have I?" I asked, although I knew full well that I had set my cap farther back on my head and waved the front part of my hair so that it fell curly around my ears. I had seen girls in Woodstock with their hair dressed so, and it had looked very well on them.

"Indeed you have. And the manner of your hair is not in keeping with your position—haven't I just been saying that it does not behove us to try and rise above our stations?"

"You have." I nodded. The smell of the eggs rose and hit me, and I was hard pressed not to gag at it.

"Well, then, 'tis not seemly that you should primp yourself up. You're only a housemaid and should know your place."

I didn't reply, but noticed Susan glancing at me slyly to see how I was taking this.

"The fashioning of your hair that way makes you look saucy and impudent," went on Mrs. Williams, "so go upstairs now, comb out your curls, and properly put your cap on your head."

I went, of course, and was glad to get out of the egg-stinking room for a moment and rinse the salt off my hands, but I made sure that I pulled in my stomach and held myself tall as I walked out.

I didn't know how much they knew or if they'd guessed my condition, but, aware that Susan had taken to staring at me as I undressed, I always turned away from her before taking off my gown at night. What I feared most was that it would be detected that I was with child before Master Geoffrey came back, for I would be dismissed of an instant. And how would I then be able to approach him?

With Mrs. Williams's awful tales fresh in my mind I began to dream horrid dreams of giving birth to an infant that had no limbs, or of not delivering a child at all, but a silver fish. I never ever had a dream where the babe that was born to me was pink and plump and full of contentment. Not ever.

I began to pray fervently that God would forgive me my fornication and bless me so that I'd see my courses again. Even as I prayed, however, I knew it to be unlikely that he would forgive, especially as, wickedly, I now looked for any weakness or ill health in Sir Thomas, signs that he was going to die so that Master Geoffrey might all the sooner come into his inheritance. I saw none, however, and he continued as robust as ever.

About a month after I'd been to the cunning woman, I had a dreadful shock, and as they say that a shock can cause a woman to miscarry a child, I did hope for this (may God forgive me), but it was not to be.

This shock started off as seeming to be favorable news, for we heard that Master Geoffrey was returning briefly to Dun's Tew. This was earlier than I'd anticipated and would enable me to see him the sooner, tell him of the trouble I was in, and have his help in the resolving of it. When, however, we were at our dinner in the servants' hall two days before he arrived, Mrs. Williams landed a substantial game pie on the table and said, "Well, whatever news do you think I heard this morning from Lady Mary?"

Everyone looked at her, for we all loved hearing intimacies about the Reades, whom we knew just as well as—and indeed saw more of than—our own families.

When she had everyone's attention she went on, "There is to be a special supper on Saturday for Master Geoffrey, and what do you think the family is celebrating?"

Thinking it was his birthday or that he'd had some success with his studies, I didn't pay much attention, but looked eagerly toward the great pie, for after two days of sickness I was suddenly hungry.

"It concerns a certain young lady," Mrs. Williams said, cutting through the pastry.

A young lady. I heard these words and at first didn't register their import.

"Such a lovely young lady, so Lady Mary told me," Mrs. Williams went on, deftly slicing and scooping. "Sixteen years old and heiress to a vast fortune."

I went cold. As cold and still as I am now, for I knew then where this story was heading.

"Oh!" everyone cried, and, "There's a fine thing!"

"Are she and Master Geoffrey already betrothed?" someone asked.

"They are! Or will be after the supper," Mrs. Williams said, "for Lady Mary told me that a ring has been made from her own mother's emeralds. Spiced peas, Mr. Peakes?"

Several of the servants around the table began exclaiming, and I knew some were looking at me, but I said nothing. I stared down at my plate and did no more than begin to count the number of peas I could see there. *Betrothed.* Oh, then I was truly lost.

We were all served. We lowered our heads, and Mr. Peakes said grace.

Susan trilled "Amen!" merrily, then cried, "Oh, how romantic! Master Geoffrey and—what's the lucky girl's name?"

"Her name is Clementine," said Mrs. Williams. "Miss Clementine de Millet. When do you suppose they met? And when did he propose?"

"'Tis of no account when they met," said Jacob dourly, "for most likely this agreement was forged between the families years back. 'Tis always that way for the nobility."

"Not so," corrected Mrs. Williams. "Lady Mary said 'twas a love match."

"Aye. He loves her money," said Jacob.

I burst out with a snort of laughter that was close to tears, and everyone turned to look at me and then looked away. I knew how their tongues would wag the moment I disappeared to bed.

"'Tis excellent news for Master Geoffrey and the family. Don't you think so, Anne?" Mrs. Williams asked.

I opened my mouth and then shut it again. I swallowed. I began re-counting the peas. I knew I mustn't speak in case I began to cry, for then everyone would guess my secret.

I didn't care about him. Oh, not a jot. I didn't care if he was betrothed to someone named Clementine, I didn't even care that I wasn't going to be the lady of Dun's Tew Manor. What I *did* care about was what was growing in my belly and what would happen to me when everyone found out.

"Our Master Geoffrey!" said Susan, more animated than I'd ever seen her. "There'll be young ladies aplenty who'll be breaking their hearts when they hear the news that he's betrothed."

"That's as may be," said Mrs. Williams, "but they'd be silly young ladies if they believed that he'd ever choose one of nobility who was not favored by his family."

"Indeed!" chimed Susan.

Mrs. Williams looked at me slyly. "Not eating your pie, Anne? Don't say you've lost your appetite again."

"No, indeed not," I stuttered, and I forced down the food and sat there for the rest of the meal, and again as we sat mending stockings after, while such a deal of bibble-babble ensued about when the wedding might be and whether we might be issued new gloves and caps for the occasion, while pretending all the time that nothing they said was of the least concern to me.

That night I had my worst dream ever. I dreamed that I was trying to birth a monstrous strange tree with twisting, gnarled branches that snaked outside my body and tried to strangle me. I knew that I was dreaming, but was no less terrified for this, and tried my utmost to make myself wake up, pinching my arms with my fingers and trying to force my eyelids open. When I eventually did wake, there were tears wet on my cheeks and my heart was beating as fast as that of a dove.

It was still dark in our room, and I whispered across to Susan to ask if it was near morning, for I was fair desperate to speak to someone—even her—and be reassured that I was safe and back in the real world. She didn't reply, though, just turned sharply in her bed with a squeak of the springs and an angry, impatient noise, which I took to mean that she was cross that I'd woken her with my tossing and turning.

———◆◆◆◆———

Remembering that dream, that night, and how I'd endeavored to force open my eyelids and wake, I try to exert a mighty effort of will to do the same thing again. If I managed it once, then why can't I manage it now?

Because, reason tells me, I was merely asleep then.

Now I am dead.

But I try nonetheless, and vow that I will keep on trying until the darkness consumes me . . .

Kbert's heart thumped. That other corpse. *Had* it been a dream? It seemed very like one, a dream that faded as fast as recalled, drifting away as cloudy and insubstantial as chimney smoke. He closed his eyes. *Think*. A room, a coffin, and he there—yes, he—but as a child. Where had he been, though? And who was the corpse?

Dr. Willis glanced about the room. Two years older than Dr. Petty, he was, it seemed, going to take overall charge of proceedings. "I agree we should begin," he declared. "Would you take the pointer," he said, handing the rod to Norreys, "and as I cut into the corpse and locate the organs, point to where they are on the wall chart for the benefit of those unsure as to their whereabouts."

Norreys gave a short bow and went to the other side of the coffin, where he smirked around at the rest of the scholars, pleased to have been chosen. Robert nodded back to him, thinking that Wilton was more *his* sort of fellow; someone with whom one might go for a row on the river, play cards, down ale, or snort over the latest college gossip. But why would a fellow like Wilton bother with someone like *him*? Someone who couldn't even speak properly?

"Wren will make accurate drawings for us," Dr. Petty said, and Wren, who had taken up his drawing pad, nodded.

The scholars pressed together, closer to the coffin, and Robert found himself so near Sir Thomas Reade that he was able to feel the big man twitching, fuming, and bristling with impatience. But they could not begin cutting yet, Robert knew, for it was usual for the leading doctor to quote some words from Galen before he started to open the body, making the claim that human dissection might be unpalatable to some, but was essential for the furtherance of medical knowledge.

Accordingly, with silence in the room apart from the bronchial breathing of Sir Thomas and an occasional shout from the crowd outside, Dr. Willis began: "The work of this day is to open the way into the Practice of Anatomy and into the knowledge of man's body . . . to care and ease the distempers that befall it, and to show proud man that his most mysterious and complicated energy is nothing to the compounded mysteries within the very fabric of man itself."

The scholars nodded sagely, taking in every word, for Dr. Willis was an excellent orator. As the doctor spoke, Robert stared at the woman lying before them, trying to forget her similarity to another figure at another time. He tried instead to view her as a practice piece, someone who hadn't actually lived at all, so that the shock of seeing her dissected wouldn't be too great. He'd been told what to expect and braced himself for that first cut to the stomach, the stink of viscera, the tumbling out of the guts, and the strange and unnatural sight and sounds of a body's inner organs being pulled into view. To think that this woman, just a few hours ago, had been a cogent human being: living, breathing, loving, hating. To think that those arms had clasped her mother in a final embrace, that that mouth had spoken, bidding goodbye to the cold world, and her eyes had looked upon the same doleful scene of hangman, tree, and noose as *he* had. Now she was just a lump of flesh.

So where had the part that animated Anne Green gone? Was it still somewhere inside her body, or had it left for a higher plane? If still within, would it escape and fly away when the doctors cut into her? Should the window be opened for such a purpose?

Robert had seen four deaths at close quarters, although in three of these he'd arrived just too late and the only duty he'd been able to perform was the closing of the corpse's eyelids. At no time, however, had he noticed any sort of spirit or presence coming from the body. Was the soul something one could see? he wondered.

There was a sudden and very loud scream from outside. "I want to see her!" came the cry, and it was repeated twice more.

Robert started. I want to see her. *I want to see her.*

And of a sudden he remembered. Twenty big steps down the stairs at home, on each step a word, a comforting echo in his head.

I
want
to
see
her.

These words, repeated four times each, had brought him down to stand outside the drawing room of their home in Somerset.

I want to see her. He knew that, as a small child, he'd been saying these words a long time. Two or three days or more, for he could almost taste them in his mouth.

I want to see her. But he wasn't allowed to see her because she was busy. She was resting. She had gone out. She was sleeping.

His mother.

I want to see her. He'd slept at last with those words on his lips and in his head, and woken when the rest of the household was asleep. And then he'd climbed out of the bed he shared with his nurse and come down the stairs to the library, somehow knowing—had he heard a whisper of it during the day?—that this was where she would be.

He remembered now the way he'd pushed open the door to flickering candlelight and a table bearing a cherry-wood coffin. He recalled now how tall wax candles had stood guarding each corner of the coffin, their light reflected off its polished wood. He saw again the mirror, portraits, and tapestries hung about with black drapes, and his family's coat of arms, proud with lions and castles, draped across the window shutters.

He remembered staring at the scene for some moments, trying to work out in his child's mind what it meant, and then pulling a chair across the room and clambering onto the table to see inside the box.

And *there* was the woman he'd so much wanted to see. There was his mother, her face ivory, her dark hair waxed, wearing a gown and cap of frothy white lace. Her eyes were closed, and her hands clasped at her breast with a Bible placed between them.

I want to see her! He gave an involuntary gasp and was aware of Dr. Petty turning to glance at him, no doubt thinking he was feeling nervous about the dissection.

My father hadn't told me, he thought. When I asked to see her, they said she was busy at some household task or was resting or unwell, and all the time she was a dead corpse in her coffin.

And when he'd discovered her that night in the drawing room, what happened next? He couldn't quite say. He remembered touching her cheek and feeling it cold, and then could remember no more. But later, when he was a little older and had asked his father about the death of his mother, he'd been told that she'd died abroad, of a strange disease. And then, very quickly, his father had married again and his mother had been talked of no more.

Dr. Willis's voice rose again. "For the end of anatomy is knowledge of each part, why it exists, for what purpose is it necessary and what is its use."

Sir Thomas Reade sighed impatiently, and Wilton looked at Robert and raised his eyebrows. Robert gave a slight smile back.

They had thought to protect him, perhaps. Or maybe his stepmother was jealous of the other woman's memory. He would ask his father again, now. Ask him for the truth about the death of his mother.

Taking a deep breath, he tried to dismiss the matter from his mind, and concentrated once more upon the body of Anne Green, his eyes taking in each part of her. From healthy peasant stock, she was of excellent stature, her legs long, her body shapely, her arms full and muscular. Her face was fair: a curved, full-lipped mouth, a straight nose, her eyelids now a translucent violet. She was fair and she was dead—and her death had been untimely. She should, he thought, have lived to provide a home for a man who loved her, and together they should have bred a houseful of milk-maids and sheep farmers. Her last view should not have been of a hangman, but of her cottage fire sixty years hence. Those eyes of hers should have finally closed on—

Those eyes! As Robert's gaze rested on Anne's face, his reverie ceased and he became shocked and fearful, for her eyelids had seemed to flicker, as if there was life still within her body.

Shaken, his belly churning, he stared at Anne's face until his gaze blurred—but did not see movement again. Should he say something? He almost smiled at this. What was the point of trying to speak? By the time he got his words out, Anne would be in pieces.

Robert nudged Wilton to signal to him that he should look at Anne. If there *was* anything amiss, let him see it too. Only let someone else see it! Robert frowned, nodded, indicated with little jerky movements what he was trying to convey, but Wilton just looked at him, puzzled, and then turned back to gaze reverently at the two doctors.

There!

Robert had seen the eye movement again; the smallest flicker from within her, like a hearth fire which, although put out hours before, suddenly gleams within with a tiny glow-worm brightness. Oh, he must speak! He must speak now or die in the attempt. Before he could consider its delivery, the word *"Sir!"* came from him fast as the retort of a gun. Every eye in the room turned to stare at him, and his face grew hot.

"What is it?" Dr. Willis asked, frowning.

Dr. Petty looked at Robert with concern. "Are you feeling unwell?"

Robert shook his head. He stepped forward and pointed to Anne's face; to her left eyelid. "Moo . . . moo . . ."

There was a snigger behind him. He heard someone say in a low voice, "'Tis Buttercup the cow," and there was some stifled laughter.

"*Movement?*" Dr. Petty asked. "Eye movement?"

Robert nodded violently, then pointed at his face and made twitching movements with his own eyelid much more violent than those Anne had made. "Eye moo . . . moo . . . movement!" he confirmed.

Gasps broke out around the room, a chorus of disbelief. Robert heard the singing scholar say, "The fellow's been drinking for sure."

"Either that or he's fallen in love with the wench and doesn't want her touched," came the reply.

There was a bellow from Sir Thomas Reade. "What is all this? What the devil's happening now?"

"Has anyone got a hand mirror?" Dr. Petty asked. He turned to Mr. Clarke. "You, sir?"

The apothecary shook his head. "There's one in the hall, but 'tis the size of a door."

Dr. Petty bent over Anne. "We need a small mirror to see if she breathes."

"There's not such an object in the house!"

Dr. Willis edged around the table, frowning down at the corpse and bending low over her. "There's no need for any mirror, surely. Her chest is not rising and falling. She does *not* breathe."

Mr. Clarke took up Anne's limp wrist and felt around it. "No. And I feel no pulse," he said. He replaced her arm and it fell off the table, dangling, blue-tinged white.

The three doctors turned to look at Robert, who was still watching Anne's face intently. "Are you absolutely sure you saw movement?" Dr. Willis asked.

Robert nodded vehemently, his mouth forming the word *yes* several times over. Already he doubted himself, though. Had he imagined it? It was snowing quite hard now, and the light in the room was thin and pale; the beer he'd taken had been strong, and he'd stayed up late the night before writing detailed comments and suppositions concerning the contents of Scarlett's latest eggs. Perhaps, feeling pity for the girl . . . perhaps, being confused with the wonder of that other, newly remembered, corpse, he'd allowed himself to be deceived into thinking there were still signs of life within Anne Green.

"Carry on, sir!" Sir Thomas roared.

"This is most unusual. But we must be completely sure," said Dr. Petty, sounding a trace distracted.

"Just put her out of her misery!" said Sir Thomas. He gestured to the fellow who had stamped on Anne's chest before. "Come," he invited, nodding toward the corpse. "Help her on her way again. Let's dispel any argument about whether she lives or no."

The fellow hesitated. His lips twitched nervously as he looked to the physicians for guidance.

"No, you will not!" Dr. Willis said. "Stay where you are, sir!"

"Doctor Willis and I are in charge of this dissection," Dr. Petty reminded Sir Thomas.

"So what in the devil's name is the matter with all of you?" Sir Thomas asked, exasperated. "She has departed this mortal life. She was dead when she was cut down and she's dead still. Just look at her lying there and then tell me there's any doubt about it."

The students shuffled their feet, exchanging alarmed and excited glances. What a thing it would be to talk about later, Robert thought. To discuss—if one was able—with fellow scholars in taverns.

"You doctors make a fuss about obtaining cadavers to cut up, and now that you've got one, you're treating it with as much reverence as you would your own mother!" Sir Thomas bristled.

"Just a few moments longer, sir," said Dr. Petty calmly.

"You've had your moments—now get on with the job you're here for!"

No one responded to this, but on an impulse, thinking it looked uncomfortable, Robert stepped off the bench, leaned over for Anne's dangling arm, and replaced it gently on the table across her breast. It was icy cold to his touch, and he shuddered at it. He *must* have been mistaken. There could not still be life within this cadaver. She was a dead thing, all animation gone and as cold as stone.

Dr. Petty stared at the corpse for a long moment, puzzled, shaking his head. "We should, perhaps, ask Dr. Bathurst for his opinion."

"Someone could go to Brasenose for him," said Mr. Clarke. But no one offered.

Suddenly Wilton shouted out. "God's teeth! Her eye *did* move. I just saw it!"

Sir Thomas Reade gave a cry of anger, and there was a thud as the body of Nathaniel Frisk, the surgeon, slumped to the ground in a faint.

The two doctors exchanged glances. "Was it a nervous twitch you saw," Dr. Willis asked, "like that of a chicken when its throat's cut?"

"I've seen a headless chicken run across the common, sir!" one of the scholars said, and there was some uneasy laughter.

"Dammit, the girl was hanging in the prison yard from seven-thirty until eight of the clock!" Sir Thomas said in an explosion of rage. "She was hanged by the neck until dead, as the law required. A doctor certified her dead."

Robert shouted something unintelligible. It was meant to be the word *Again!* but that didn't matter, for this time everyone could see Anne's eyelids trembling, both of them; the thin, lilac-hued skin quivering as if straining to open upon the world.

There were loud cries, gasps, and a general consternation in the room; Robert found that his whole body was shaking with fear and excitement. Sir Thomas gave a roar and stepped toward Anne's body, his hands raised as if he would strangle her himself. Norreys, whom Robert had heard was secretly a Catholic, fell to his knees and made the sign of the cross. "Oh, glory!" he cried. "She lives!"

At any other time the scholars would have been aghast at this flagrant display of popery; now they scarcely noticed. Everyone looked to the two doctors.

Dr. Willis said, "There is the hand of God in this."

And he and Dr. Petty put down their dissection instruments.

Chapter ~ 11

The morning after the announcement of Master Geoffrey's betrothal, I went over to Home Farm to collect some duck eggs. I was crossing the driveway on my way back, my basket full, when I heard the sound of horses' hooves and wheels on the road outside and turned to see a pretty blue and white carriage coming through the gates with two bay horses afront, lifting their legs in an elegant trot.

I knew who must be inside the carriage and could easily have slipped around the house and gone in through one of the back doors, but was caught by an intense longing to see the person who alighted. Hesitating too long, I then had to move behind the laurel hedge and conceal myself from the arrivals.

The coach circled the drive and stopped at the front door, then the footman jumped down and lowered the steps. Master Geoffrey got out and turned to help someone else down, and I held my breath, fixed and staring as if my life depended on it. In a moment Miss Clementine de Millet appeared. I had some small comfort in seeing that she wasn't beautiful, for she had an olive skin and a long thin nose, which was pushed into the air as if she detected a bad smell. She was small and delicate, however, and dressed very finely in a blue flowered dress and, over it, a yellow taffeta cloak lined in the same blue. Her dress was of a design I'd seen in Woodstock, with a ruching at the front showing an abundance of yellow petticoats, and as she lifted it slightly in order to climb down the steps I saw that she had dainty blue-leather mules.

Master Geoffrey made a great show of helping her from the carriage and offering her his arm to walk to the house, as if she was a wisp of a creature who could not proceed unsupported. As they strolled across the drive, I saw him point in a genteel manner to various things, such as the huge maple tree, the herd of dairy cows, and the pretty aspect of the church spire between the poplar trees, and I dare say he was speaking of his family's wealth in the owning of such an estate. He also pointed to the dovecote, and I wondered what he was saying about it. Not, I determined, that it was a place in which he'd begged and implored a housemaid to give up her chaste ways and lie with him.

The two of them hesitated a moment at the foot of the marble steps that led into the house and looked over to the farm, and I felt a moment's fear that they would take a turn around the grounds and discover me behind the hedge, but Miss de Millet's lady-in-waiting was close behind them, and the footman with her luggage, and so they went in.

I stayed behind the hedge for some while, trying to compose myself and still the thumping of my heart. It was true, then. He really was betrothed. And it was then that I knew myself to be as stupid as a quince pudding, for in spite of what Ma and Jane had said, in spite of every sensible part of me knowing it could *not* be true, all this time I'd been secretly telling myself that Master Geoffrey might have played fair; that he loved me and in time would raise me.

I, mistress of Dun's Tew? I thought of the dainty girl I'd just seen in her elegant gown and blue-leather mules, then looked down at my sturdy feet in their wooden pattens, at my stained apron, at my chapped and begrimed hands with their bitten nails. No, of course I would never be a mistress, no, not even of a rag shop or a brewhouse!

I became full of misery then and fell to weeping, wondering how I was going to survive. I wished myself dead and Master Geoffrey too, cursing him and praying that he would be struck down by the falling sickness and die most horribly. I could not bring myself to go into the house, for my face was red and blotched (and I knew that the rest of the servants would be sure to deduce what I'd been crying about), so I left my basket outside the back door and took myself across the yard and into the dovecote. Here I climbed a stepladder into the darkness and squeezed myself onto a wooden platform to sit among the cooing birds, the droppings, the feathers, and the scraps of down floating on the air. Once there, well hidden, I felt I could have stayed forever, for to my simple way of thinking it seemed that the doves would look after me, and would not deceive and trick me as Master Geoffrey had; that I could trust them more than I should ever have trusted him.

After some time, though, I stopped weeping, grew cold, and began to fear what they'd be saying at the house about me, so was too frightened *not* to return. I went back very solemn, anxious about how I might be punished for my disappearance, but the house was in such a tipsy-topsy state with preparations for Master Geoffrey's betrothal supper that my disappearance had hardly been noticed. I was brought down with melancholy, however, and when I was sent to the herb patch for pungent herbs to stuff a goose that afternoon, I could not help but look across to the smithy and recall the washing day when I'd first begun speaking to John Taylor. I missed him greatly at that time, and was so unhappy that the dishonorable notion came upon me that I might bring myself into his favor again, and lie with him, and pretend that the child I carried was his own.

He was not to be seen over the road, however, and thankfully such a wicked idea was soon gone from my head. Yet I shed more tears thinking of John's kindnesses to me, and his gentleness, and how wicked I'd been to cast him off so cruelly when he had truly cared for me.

My situation seeming to have no solution, when I returned to the kitchen I didn't protest when Mrs. Williams said I was to scour out all the slop buckets and chamber pots, for it seemed fitting to my mood and situation that I should be set such a horrid job—and even seeing that Susan had been set to the pretty task of making spun-sugar nests to go over candied apricots for the party did not make my disposition worse. Nothing could do that.

Everyone was eager for news of the new young lady's arrival, and Patience, who was maid to Lady Mary, told us that she'd seen Miss de Millet at dinner that noon. She reported that she was a pretty, fresh young thing and had been wearing costly jewels, although her complexion was rather brown and her nose slightly on the long side.

"She seemed very ladylike, though," she said. "She eats very dainty with her fork and knows just how to act. And I heard them say that she embroiders so neatly and with such fine stitches that the end result is like a painting."

"What was she wearing?" asked Susan.

"A satin dress with an embroidered bodice and a line of ribbon knots all down the back," Patience answered. "And it was in a flame color, which they said, being orange, was a play on the name of Clementine."

All the female servants drew breath at the wit of this device, which did not strike me as clever at all, however, especially with her brown complexion.

"And does Master Geoffrey dote on her?" Mrs. Williams asked.

"Oh, yes, he does!" Patience replied. "And 'tis nice to see him so, for I've sometimes thought him a selfish young man."

"Does he carry out little duties?" Susan wanted to know.

Patience nodded. "He looked after her fan and shawl, and led her to the table and saw her seated, and altogether acted as if he was very much in love with her, paying her little compliments and the like."

Jacob gave a snort of derision, which pleased me, but the women gave him a cold look and said that he shouldn't be so scathing, and 'twould be a good thing if all men were more mannerly. Susan cried, "What a pretty sight they must be together!" and glanced at me as she said it.

Later that day I determined that I must appeal to Master Geoffrey and tell him of my situation, for if I was not to end up in the parish workhouse I would soon be in dire need of a place to lay my head. I wished that I had some money put by and need *not* appeal to him, but as I sent most of what I earned home to Ma, I had only a few pence to call my own. My only possessions were my clothes—I could sell my bodice, of course—and the wedding ring of my grandma, although this would not fetch much, for it was but poor gold and had worn as thin as a hair over the years.

Speaking to Master Geoffrey alone was, I knew, going to be monstrous difficult, for it was only the footmen who served dinner and the ladies' maids who were allowed about the house when visitors were within. I was, however, determined to try, for what would become of me if I did not?

The guests arrived (including, so we heard, Miss de Millet's parents), and supper was served at seven o'clock. It had not been possible for me to get anywhere near Master Geoffrey before this, for most of the afternoon he'd been in the library deep in conversation with Sir Thomas, and someone had seen a gowned man of the law arrive bearing parchment and seals, which Mr. Peakes had said was sure to be something to do with the marriage settlement. After the family and guests had eaten supper, we servants cleared away and washed the dishes, so by the time eleven o'clock came, I was dropping with tiredness and also felt ill, which I thought was likely to be nerves because of what I knew I must do. Susan went to bed, as did most of the other staff, so that in the end the only servants sitting up were those who waited on their master's or mistress's coming to bed. This didn't look like being for some time, however, for a group of fiddlers had come to the house, and some of the company had moved from the dining room to the great hall, and were dancing.

I went to bed, but crept out of the room when Susan was asleep and sat on the servants' stairs listening to the music and gaiety from downstairs. If I'd known then what was going to happen and the intentions of the Reade family toward me, then I believe I would not have sat there so patient. I believe I would have gone down those stairs into the great hall and spoken my piece in front of everyone. Oh, what a disturbance I could have caused if only I'd been brave enough! Miss de Millet's face would have shown stunned disbelief, Master Geoffrey's would have been red and horror-struck, his grandmother would have had a shrieking fit, and his grandfather would have roared with rage. What a harum-scarum cockfight I could have caused in the great hall that night!

But of course I didn't dare do any such thing, but stayed on the stairs and every now and again, when I heard a door open, ran to my bedroom and hid until I felt it was safe to go out again. I believe I fell asleep at some time, for when I woke there was no noise from downstairs and it seemed that the merrymaking had ceased. It felt safe, therefore, to go through the baize door into the family's quarters and onto the bedroom landing, and to creep along in the shadows until I came to Master Geoffrey's room, where a faint line of light under the door told me that his candle was still burning.

I pressed my ear against his door, shaking with cold and fright. I knew, of course, that Miss de Millet wouldn't be in there—*her* body would be held sacred until they were married—but I feared that his valet might still be in attendance. All I could hear, though, was Master Geoffrey humming, and I felt angry when I heard this, for it seemed to me to be the hum of a contented man who has everything planned and neat in his life and cares nothing about what unhappiness he might have caused along the way of it.

I tapped on the door, but so tentative was I that he didn't hear it. I tapped again, then gently pushed at the door and peered around it, ready to turn tail and run if I had to. It opened a little, and I saw Master Geoffrey at the washstand pouring himself a glass of water from a jug. He wore only a nightcap, had nothing on beside to hide his nakedness, and cut such a comical figure that I might have laughed at him had I been there for any other reason.

I tiptoed into the room. "Master Geoffrey . . ." I began, and he jumped, turned, and saw me, and attempted to hide his private parts with the water jug. Why he did this I had no idea, for every other time I'd seen him he'd been only too anxious to have them on display.

"Out!" was the first word he said to me. As if I was a cur, or a cat to be chased off the soused herrings.

"Sir, I am most anxious to speak to you—"

"Out, I say!" he said in a harsh whisper. "At once!"

"Sir, I . . ."

He looked at me with great disdain. "Are you so hot, woman, that you have to come to my room and lay siege to me?"

I was astonished and outraged at this, but before I could give him a reply I heard the handle of the door to the adjoining room rattling, as if someone had put a hand upon it, and in my imagination saw Sir Thomas coming in, perhaps to acquaint his son with the results of some conversation he'd had with Miss de Millet's father. I immediately reversed the two steps I'd taken in and, very shaken, backed out of the room as quickly and silently as I'd entered.

The next morning we were up at five o'clock as usual, although I could barely drag myself out of bed for weariness. My only hope of speaking to Master Geoffrey, I knew, was to catch him in his room. Accordingly, after doing my morning chores, I put a washing jug to one side and hid it in the buttery. Later, after the warm water for the family had been sent up and when Mrs. Williams was occupied elsewhere, I took up the jug and carried it to Master Geoffrey's room. If anyone had seen me, they would merely have thought I was bringing him fresh water.

The curtains around his bed hung open, but he was still asleep, and as I looked on his sleeping form I was filled with a hatred such as the Bible says we never should feel, e'en toward our greatest enemies. Oh, I'd been stupid and I'd been lewd, but those were my only sins; Master Geoffrey's were surely much worse, for he had cruelly used and deceived me, taken advantage of his position as Sir Thomas's heir, and got me with child.

With this at the forefront of my mind, I became bold enough to shake his shoulder. "Sir," I said. "Master Geoffrey . . ."

He must have recognized my voice, for he immediately turned away and burrowed further into the bed.

"Master Geoffrey. I must speak with you."

There was no reply.

I called him again, and again. Desperately, I shook him more harshly and moved the drapes around the bed to cause a draught. At last he opened his eyes.

"What is it you want?" he asked coldly, every trace of the sweet-talking flattery, every one of the wheedling phrases he'd used before now disappeared.

"I need to speak to you most urgently," I said.

"How dare you come to my room!"

"I came because I am desperate, sir. I am in an impossible situation."

"Get out now, or I'll call George and have you thrown out. 'Tis disgraceful you should beard a fellow in his room in this way."

"But, sir, I beg you." He closed his eyes and seemed about to go back to sleep, so I shook his shoulder again. "Sir, I must tell you that I am in a certain condition. I . . . I am with child."

There was a moment's silence, then, opening both eyes and seeming immediately to be fully awake, he said, "Then 'tis not mine."

I stared at him, stunned, for in spite of my low opinion of him, I'd never considered that he might deny he was the father, nor hardly thought that a gentleman might do such a thing. At that moment, so much did I hate him that if I'd had a knife in my hand, I would have run him through with it and taken the consequences. "But I have not lain with another man!" I said, astonished.

He did not say a word.

"I never have! You must believe me!"

But he had gone back to being a stone again, his eyes tight shut, his face set stern, his mouth a hard line. I tried again and again to garner some response from him, but could not. In the end, frightened of being discovered there, I had no recourse but to leave.

I returned to my duties, not speaking with anyone but doing as I was bid without question, my mind running frantically in all directions. Should I leave the household now, before it was discovered that I was with child, or should I remain and get a little money put by? Should I return home? Would my father, who is not known for either his patience or his tolerance, allow me to stay with them, or would he insist I go into a workhouse? What would I do when the child was born? Perhaps, I thought grimly, I would swaddle it, bring it to the house, and leave it on the doorstep with Master Geoffrey's name on it.

———◆◆◆◆———

He was to leave Dun's Tew that same afternoon, for I heard that Miss de Millet was taking him as far as Oxford in her carriage, where he would stay one night and then catch the coach back to London. But I had obviously given him a fright with my words, for he appeared in the servants' quarters about midday saying he had a gold angel that Miss Clementine's parents had left for the waiting staff. (I was in the dairy straining the buttermilk and became so anxious on seeing him there that I quite forgot to put salt in the butter, so that after two days it went rancid.)

After speaking to Mr. Peakes and giving him the money for distribution to the servants, he came to the dairy and, standing by the door in a casual attitude, said in a low voice, "There are ways to order these things. You must get rid of the child."

"'Tis too late for that," I said, my hands trembling as I held the muslin taut. "And besides, I have tried."

"Then you have not tried hard enough."

I didn't reply.

"How do I know that you haven't got yourself with child deliberately so as to obtain money from me?"

"Begging your pardon, sir," I said, "but I cannot get myself with child on my own."

"You knew what you were doing well enough! 'Twas not your first time."

I didn't answer this, for I was too angry to control myself and felt that I might begin weeping. Either that or strike out at him.

"If you tell anyone that 'tis mine—"

"It *is* yours!" I burst out. "As God is my witness, it is your child!"

"Then I'll deny it. My family—my grandfather—will never believe you."

I sighed when he said this, for I knew he spoke truly. Sir Thomas doted on him and would be bound to take his side whatever the circumstances. "And besides, I will get George and some of the menservants to say that they have also lain with you."

Oh, how I loathed him then! And how it tormented me knowing that I carried his offspring within me. Struggling to keep from weeping, I scraped the butter onto the marble tile and began to form it into a block with the wooden spades. "If you shame me like that," I said in a low voice, "then may you be cursed for your lies, and may God reveal you for the wicked devil you are."

He replied immediately, "I will tell them that you cursed me, and you will be taken away for a witch!"

I turned on him angrily. "If they would take me from here then they cannot come quickly enough, for I rue the day I ever came through your door!" I said, and as I spoke I formed the butter into an oblong, then gave it such a mighty bang with one of the spades that soft drops of yellow spattered up into the air and fell onto the marble. I closed my eyes in despair for a moment, and when I opened them he'd gone.

I wondered after if I should have spoken to him soft and pretended I cared for him, for that might have been a better way. I should have used honeyed words and sweet talk, and assured him that his betrothal to Miss de Millet would not alter things between us, and I would still allow his liberties. Then, when he was won over and confident of my fidelity, I could have told him of the child and asked for his help. I did not do any of those things, however, and later spent many hours cursing my temper.

Now, though, I know that whatever I'd said to him, it wouldn't have changed things.

I make one more effort to open my eyes, straining to see what's about me in the darkness, but it does me no good, for I am nowhere . . .

Chapter ~ 12

For a moment everything halted. The doctors and scholars who surrounded the corpse formed a tableau around Anne Green, whose body seemed rapt between heaven and Earth. She neither lived, nor was she wholly dead.

Robert gazed at Anne unwaveringly. He knew that something strange, something problematic and metaphysical was happening. A choice was being presented to the physicians: they could decide to give her succor, or assist in her peaceful passing.

Suddenly the scene reanimated. The doctors began moving into place around the body, the scholars crowded forward. Nathaniel Frisk was pulled into a corner and left, slumped sideways, to recover on his own as best he could.

"We must help her breathe," Dr. Petty said urgently.

"I agree," Dr. Willis said. "Shall we sit her up? Warm her?"

"*What?!*" roared Sir Thomas Reade.

"Chafe her legs, perhaps," suggested Mr. Clarke.

"*Hold!*"

A voice rang out from the back of the room, and Robert turned to see a figure in clerical black, his white collar and tall hat marking him out as a Puritan.

"Now we shall have fun," Wilton said.

Robert looked at him inquiringly.

"Puritans cannot tolerate anything upsetting the rightful order of things," he whispered. "The man has wandered in to watch a dissection, and instead found a resurrection."

The Puritan's right hand was raised, finger pointing up like that of an avenging angel. "Hold, I say. That woman belongs to God, and God alone! You will not take her back from him!"

Chapter ~ 13

A month later I was still at Dun's Tew Manor, lacing myself into my bodice and stomacher each morning and pulling them a little tighter betimes. I'd not left the Reades' household, for a lethargy seemed to have come over me so that I had neither the energy to leave, nor the courage to go home and face my father. I knew I should have told Ma of my situation, or at least got a message to her, for it was probable that she thought the cunning woman's cordial had been effective, but I did not wish to cause her any more distress. As well as this, I could not have faced the walk back to my village, for my legs ached mightily and I was constantly weary.

I could not decide how to act or what to do. Having been instructed and ordered all my life, I now longed for someone to command me in this. I felt I was waiting for something to happen—but what this thing was, I didn't know. Perhaps it was for someone to discover I was with child and help me, or for Master Geoffrey to return, own to his obligations, and give me a little money to aid me, or even to summon the strength to open the door of the house, walk out, and keep on walking—for I knew I wouldn't be the first young woman to cross to a parish where she wasn't known and beg aid for herself and her unborn child. In the meantime I went about my duties and tried not to think too much about my situation. With some little effort, I was able to pretend to myself that it wasn't happening.

I hardly spoke to the other servants. On the fifth of November the household celebrated Gunpowder Plot Day and we were allowed to have a bonfire in the evening, but

I didn't care to be present. I began to be called Mistress Nose-in-Air by some, and knew that they were gossiping about me, but couldn't bring myself to care. Now that I had a *great* concern in my life I marveled at the trivial things that had occupied me before, at how much I'd fretted about an uncompleted job, a torn petticoat, or a missing gewgaw, whereas now these trivialities hardly touched me, and I would go for several days with a piece of lace hanging from my gown or my hair awry.

My undoing came on the first day of December, however, for this day Mrs. Williams set me to work in the brewhouse stirring a great quantity of malt in a barrel. This was feverish hard work and backbreaking, and the smell of the barley was cloying and sickening to my stomach besides. I stirred and stirred with the great wooden paddle until my back felt almost broken, and only paused at dinnertime, when Mr. Peakes sent in half a loaf and a chunk of cheese for me. After I'd eaten, I began stirring again—for every so often Mrs. Williams would look in on me to make sure I wasn't slacking—and it was then that I began to get the pains.

At first I was full of joy, for these were low-down pains in my belly, as if my courses were beginning anew, so I felt that my prayers might have been answered. The cramps grew more severe, however, and I went out to the far privy, which was some distance off across the yard, and there came from me a quantity of liquid which did not seem to be urine and was, I thought (for I remember being told so by Ma), that certain watery substance that women lose when they are about to give birth. I became very anxious then, for I knew I had not gone full term with the child and wondered what it meant and if I was about to bleed to death.

I sat on the privy, still and anxious, and after a bit the pains seemed to pass. I went back into the brewhouse and stood for a while leaning on the paddle, and once, when Mrs. Williams passed by, pretended to stir the malt. After perhaps an hour the pains started again though, worse than before, and I went again to the house of office.

As the surges grew worse and came closer together, I became terrified, for I knew that delivering a child was hazardous, and without a midwife or anyone in attendance I might die. I tried to cast my mind back to the birth of a neighbor's child that I'd attended with Ma, although I'd only been eleven years old then and could barely remember how things had been ordered. My duty had merely been to fetch warm water and sponge the woman's face and hands, and I'd never once looked below at her private parts, nor wanted to, just been glad that this was the province of the midwife. *That* neighbor had had a bed to lie on, however, and old remedies to aid her safe delivery. She'd had a piece of jasper tied to her thigh, warming broths to sustain her, linen sheets beneath her, and gossips and goodwives to comfort her.

In the privy, I had none of these. And I know now that no woman should go through the perils of childbirth unaided, for it sets you in such a deal of terror that you almost lose your wits.

I undid my stomacher and removed my skirt, but after that could not think how I should conduct myself: should I stand or sit, or perhaps lie on the floor—although this was dirty and covered with blown-in leaves and other rubbish. I was afraid, though, that if I sat on the only available place, which was the privy itself, then the child might come from me and fall into the mire before I could catch it.

As the sun went down it got much colder, and I had not a shawl with me, nor a candle to see what I was doing, and I feared that someone might come into the adjoining privy and hear my moans and cries. I wondered how long my labor would last and thought of tales I'd heard from Mrs. Williams, one of a woman five days in labor, and another who'd been unable to give birth at all because the child had been lying across her belly instead of head down, so both mother and babe had died. I began to sob in fear then, and wanted my ma there, and wished even for Mrs. Williams or Susan to come and aid me. I thought about getting myself back to the house, but at this stage knew it would have been beyond me to walk across the cobbles. Those twenty yards might as well have been twenty miles.

In the end the pains got so bad that I picked up one of the sticks from the floor and bit it to stop myself from screaming out. And then the pains came all the time, with no gap between them to pause and think about what was happening, and I wanted to scream but could not even find the breath or the space to do so. My body felt it was being ripped, and I fell onto the ground and writhed about, and somehow found myself on my back with my legs against the privy door and at last, with one mighty effort, pushed the child within me out and onto the ground.

I had one short moment of blessed relief, and then I looked down at the child to see how it fared and was immediately filled with horror, for it was very small and blue in color, with a waxlike substance over its body. Maybe I should have picked it up—and I have heard of shepherds who will breathe into a dead lamb's mouth to revive it—but in truth I was terrified of the sight of it, for it seemed such a frightening and unfamiliar thing, and not like any babe I had ever seen, nor hardly human at all. And even while I looked down at it the pains began again, and I knew I had to expel the afterbirth, and this, thankfully, came out from me quickly with a gush of blood.

I lay there after, shivering and crying, and all the time I watched the child that I had given birth to, and it neither moved nor breathed. It was only as long as a man's hand and its features were indefinite, although I could see it should have been born male. It looked very pitiful lying there so raw and cold and, though I couldn't bring myself to take it up and hold it, I tore a strip of linen from my petticoat and wrapped it around its body so that it wouldn't lie quite naked on the ground.

All this while I had been lying on the floor in a mess of blood, leaves, and debris, my mind a blur of confusion. I couldn't think of how I was going to order things. *What was I to do with the child?* Once I'd had a puppy dog that had died, and my pa had dug a hole and buried it in the garden. Would I have the strength to dig a hole on my own, I wondered, with the ground froze so hard? Besides, shouldn't this child have some little sanctity? It had never drawn breath, but surely it should be due more reverence than a puppy dog. Perhaps, I thought, I would hide it for now, then on the morrow, when I was feeling stronger, take it to a little spot in the churchyard and find a place to lay it down.

At this point someone came over to the privy next to mine—one of the men, for I heard him whistling—and I wondered whether to call out and ask for help, or for a woman to be sent to me. I did not, however, for I was thinking that it might be possible for me to hide all the evidence of what had happened so that it would not be discovered I'd ever been with child, and thus could go on as before.

Accordingly I sat there as still as a fallen pippin and did not make a sound, and when the fellow had gone, pushed the dead infant to the back of the privy and took up leaves and other material to cover it, for I was resolved by then to go back the next day and take its corpse into the graveyard. I'd wrap its body in a decent piece of cloth—I thought of my pretty bodice—say a prayer over it, and perhaps in the summer I'd plant a pansy or a daisy over where it lay in the ground, for they say that children like the friendly faces of these flowers. Thinking then on the poor dead babe (unwanted by anyone on Earth, which I believe was why it had died), I began to cry again but weakly, like a kitten cries, for I had hardly any strength left to do more.

When this ceased, I tidied myself as well as I could, shook out my skirt and put it back on, then resolved to go back in the house and hide myself away in my bedroom. When I came to stand, however, I discovered that my legs were as unsteady as sea legs, and I staggered and fell down again, and had to drag myself up and lean on the wall for some moments. When I felt ready to set off, I opened the privy door and took several deep breaths of frosty air before making my way across the cobbles in the darkness, shuffling my feet like some old woman.

At length I found myself at a back door of the house and, as I opened the door onto candlelight and warmth, felt immense relief at being among the living again; thankful that I had not perished giving birth but had come through my ordeal. I could not go and be churched as did other happy mothers, but I resolved that next Sunday I'd say a private prayer of thanks for my life, and another for the soul of the child who'd not lived.

Slow and timorous of step, I walked along the hall toward the back stairs, touching my palm against the wall every now and again to steady myself. As I did so, Susan came hurrying toward me, looking agitated.

"Why, wherever have you been? We've searched everywhere in the house for you!" I was surprised at this speech, which was more words than Susan had spoken to me in months. Before I had a chance to reply, however, she gave a scream. "But what disorder you're in. What's happened? Have you had an accident?"

I should have said yes, that I'd fallen outside or that a passing carriage had struck me in the dark, but I was not thinking properly or quickly enough.

A torch on the wall suddenly flared then, enabling her to see my appearance more clearly, and her face registered horror. "Why, Anne Green, whatever have you done?"

"Susan," I began tentatively, and I took a step toward her, holding out my hand in entreaty, whereupon she screamed and moved away, staring at it in horror, for there was blood on it. "I can explain," I said, though I had scarce thought of what I was going to say. "Give me a moment. Let me tell you . . ."

"No!" she said, seeming genuinely fearful.

"I've done nothing wrong," I protested.

"Mrs. Williams!" she screamed at the top of her voice. "Mrs. Williams—come here quickly!"

"No," I said. "Please don't . . ."

But Mrs. Williams hurried through within moments and, looking me up and down, seemed to take in the situation straightaway. She said with a gasp, "I *thought* you were with child. Didn't I say that, Susan? You've just given birth, haven't you?"

Susan gave a scream of horror.

"That's right, isn't it? But where's the child?" Mrs. Williams asked, looking up and down the hallway as if I might have concealed it there.

I took a step, swayed, and almost fell over.

"You must tell us where it is," Mrs. Williams demanded. "You must tell us now."

I stared at her. This was not what I'd planned.

"Everyone will find out about it. You'll not be able to keep it to yourself," she said, and indeed I could see through to the kitchen, where Mr. Peakes and the other servants were, and they'd stopped going about the business of preparing supper and were looking at us with curiosity. I knew then that I wasn't going to be able to keep what had occurred a secret—I'd not the strength to begin the construction of a story that would cover my present appearance and demeanor. Besides . . . oh, besides, I felt I'd been alone in this long enough and needed to share with someone all that I'd been through, to unburden myself to someone who'd help.

"Now, where have you left the child?" she asked again.

"'Tis in the privy . . ." I answered up obediently.

"The *privy*? It's still there?" On a nod from me, Mrs. Williams patted Susan on the shoulder. "Go out there with a candle and a shawl and bring the babe inside, for 'tis a bitter cold night and e'en a bastard child deserves warmth and succor." Addressing me, she added, "Why, whatever were you thinking of, leaving a newborn babe outside?"

I know I should have told her the truth of it then, but could not because my body had begun to shake and my teeth to chatter violently. As Susan hurried off, Mrs. Williams put her arm about me, led me into the kitchen, and sat me down close to the fire, and this unusual and unexpected kindness on her part so affected me that I began to weep and could not stop.

"Now," she said, beckoning to Mr. Peakes with some urgency, "you must tell us who the father is, and tell us truly, and we will try to help you."

But before I could consider what I should say to this, there was a scream from outside. A terrible scream. And I knew that Susan had discovered the infant's corpse.

A moment later she came running in, crashing through the door, her hands raised, high and shaking, as if she was trying to dislodge what she'd just seen from her mind and body.

Mrs. Williams stood and gaped at her.

"The babe is dead!" she shrieked. "Dead and on the floor in the dirt!"

Mrs. Williams uttered a cry of horror. Mr. Peakes and the rest of the servants stood staring and gasping.

I was terribly affrighted and didn't know what to do next, bar continue weeping.

"You killed it, Anne Green, didn't you?" Susan said. "You went and killed it so that no one would find out about it!"

"Oh, you wicked creature!" said Mrs. Williams, and there was no kindness in her voice then. She looked at me as if I'd crawled out of hell and still bore the marks of the devil on my skin.

"I did not . . . did not kill it!" I said, choking on my sobs. "I gave birth to it out there, but it never drew breath. On my mother's life I promise that it didn't breathe."

No one spoke, but Susan screamed again, high-pitched. "What a sight! I never want to see the like again!"

"I didn't kill my own child!" I protested, tears running down my face. "That would be wicked—the devil's work. No girl could do such a thing as that!"

Mr. Peakes stepped forward. "That's enough said. 'Tis the first I've heard of this, but 'tis a bad business, a *terrible* business."

"I suspected . . . I thought all along she was with child," Mrs. Williams said.

"But I didn't—" I began.

Mr. Peakes stopped me. "Before you say any more, Anne, Sir Thomas will have to be told of this."

"No! Please . . ."

"Indeed he will. And it will have to be investigated properly, for a dead child is a shocking thing, whatever the cause."

I think I lost consciousness then, for the kitchen swayed around me, and I fell into a welcome blackness where I did not have to think more. The last thing I heard was Susan screaming, "Oh, I'll never forget the sight of it as long as I live!"

When I opened my eyes, Mrs. Williams was waving a singed bunch of rosemary under my nose, and the smoke from it was in my eyes and mouth, making me cough.

"She's back with us now," she said. "Back and can answer to the wicked deed she's done."

I coughed again, rubbing my eyes, and when I fully came to was alarmed to discover that Sir Thomas and Lady Mary had been summoned to the kitchen and stood there in front of me. I was so disquieted by this that I felt my head swim and was like to have fainted again, except that Mr. Peakes was holding a cordial to my lips and telling me to take sips of it. This drink restored me somewhat, but did not lessen my terror, for I'd never seen both my master and mistress together in the kitchens before, and to know that I was the one who'd caused them to be there was most alarming.

"She's back with us, sir," said Mr. Peakes.

Sir Thomas bent down until his florid face was just inches from mine. "What is this terrible, *shocking* tale I've heard?" he asked, while Lady Mary, who was wearing a bolero fashioned from white doves' feathers sewn onto silk, stood a little behind him. She looked, I thought, most indignant at finding herself in the domicile of her servants. "Answer me, girl."

"And you must tell Sir Thomas the truth, mind," Mr. Peakes said.

"Or it will surely be the worse for you," Mrs. Williams added.

I merely blinked around at them. I saw that, apart from these, all the other servants were grouped at the far end of the kitchen, watching us intently, and that work on the family's supper had stopped completely. The only sound was the rhythmical clanging of the wheel in the fireplace where the dog ran to turn a pig on the spit.

"You have had a *child* . . . in the privy?" Sir Thomas asked. "Can this shocking thing be true?"

I didn't reply, and Mrs. Williams said, "'Tis true indeed, sir. Susan found the dead infant concealed under some leaves."

Sir Thomas addressed the room. "And did any of you here know that she was with child?"

Everyone shook their heads.

"Although I had my suspicions," Mrs. Williams said roundly, "because she's a secretive jade. Though it's not something as you can ask a girl who's unmarried."

"I thought she was!" Susan called over, very self-righteous. "For she's been mighty private when she's been getting dressed of a morning."

"Then all this should have been reported to Mr. Peakes," said Sir Thomas, "and he would have told me, and arrangements could have been made for her admittance to a suitable establishment." He cleared his throat. "And the child is dead, you say?"

"I have been out and looked myself, sir," Mrs. Williams said. "'Tis stone dead right enough."

Sir Thomas looked at me sternly. "How did it come to die, pray? What hand did you have to play in the poor unfortunate's demise?"

I found my voice. "Please, sir, it was dead-born," I said. "It didn't draw breath at all."

Lady Mary shuddered, and the dove-feather jacket shivered and trembled. "Such a thing," she sighed. "Here. Here in my house."

"Is this true?" Sir Thomas asked me. "Did you not have a hand in its death?"

I shook my head. "Of course not, sir. Oh, never!"

"But tell me who is the father of this child," he went on, extending his arm around the room as he spoke. "Who is the lewd fellow you have been fornicating with?"

I know now that if I had named someone in the village or said it was a fellow I had met with but briefly, a passing pedlar, then things might have gone better for me; Sir Thomas might have believed that the child had been born dead and dealt with the matter privately. However, a strong urge within me made me want to tell him the truth. And, as I must be honest at this time for the sake of my soul, 'twas not just for truth's sake that I spoke, but more that his grandson should be brought to answer for the part he'd played in my disgrace.

"Answer me, girl," Sir Thomas repeated. "Who *is* the coarse fellow?"

"'Twas your grandson," I answered then, as brave as I could. "'Twas Master Geoffrey who got me with child."

Chapter 14

As one, the room turned and stared at the black-hatted figure at the back of the room. "On whose authority do you speak, sir?" Dr. Petty asked him.

"On the highest authority, sir, for I am God's deputy in this world," replied the Puritan.

"He has many deputies," Dr. Petty said mildly, his eyes still fixed on Anne Green, alert for any further movement.

"And you might say that I and my colleagues are also God's deputies," put in Dr. Willis, "for we heal, cure, and restore to health as the Lord did when he was upon Earth."

"But only God Almighty can say whether someone should live or die."

"Exactly!" Sir Thomas shouted with immense satisfaction, applauding the Puritan. "We must not go against God, or against the law of the land, for it has been cited that Anne Green should be hanged by the neck until dead."

"Indeed," said Dr. Willis. "A duty which has already been performed."

"And once dead, she should stay dead." As Sir Thomas addressed the doctors, his voice took on a patronizing tone. "It has *not* been cited that she should be resurrected, or that such a thing may ever be attempted."

"I believe that my colleagues and I are working through the Almighty," said Dr. Willis after a moment. "If he grants us the power to cause this woman to live, then it will be his will."

"But I say that a doctor has already certified her dead!" cried Sir Thomas, and his voice was a bluster and a harrumph and a roar. "And I say again, sir, that you must get on with what you're here for!"

The doctors took scant notice of him, but Mr. Clarke, aware that Sir Thomas had far-reaching powers and might take it upon himself to close his shop if he was so minded, glanced at him nervously.

Dr. Petty again took up the corpse's hand. "Anne," he said. "If you can hear me, squeeze my fingers."

Everyone in the room looked keenly at Dr. Petty's face, watching for any shade of change upon it. He repeated the question once more, before shaking his head and concluding quietly, "She does not respond."

Robert felt his heart fall. He wanted her to be alive. He wanted a miracle.

"She does not respond because she is not there," said the Puritan. He looked up piously toward the ceiling and beyond it. "She is already approaching the gates of heaven. You must let her go though. You must not try and restrain her."

"You see!" said Sir Thomas. "This commendable fellow knows. This true and godly man knows one should not attempt such a thing. The woman does not respond because she is dead! This is clear to anyone but a fool."

The doctors remained unmoved. "Get Ralph Bathurst!" Dr. Willis said abruptly. "Someone go for Doctor Bathurst. He should be here."

The scholars shuffled their feet. Not one of them wanted to go to Brasenose College to find Dr. Bathurst, for they knew that if they did so, they might lose their position at the table and perhaps miss seeing something momentous, something marvelous and significant. The scholar closest to the door, however, was pushed outside and told to go and find him.

Robert stared intently at Anne's corpse. What was it that made her so different from the other dead bodies whose deaths he'd attended? He thought of these: an ancient waterman who'd drowned in the Isis, his corpse bloated and swollen; a beggar so ingrained with dirt that his skin appeared as black as the rags he wore; a porter at college; an old woman killed when her carriage had overturned. None, to his mind, had been like Anne. Somehow her corpse still seemed to contain a spark . . . a kind of faint animation. Was that because her soul was still within her, or because she was still young and had died before her rightful time? Was it, perhaps, because she was innocent of the crime she was said to have committed?

And what of that other corpse—his mother? He longed for the leisure of a moment to think again of the journey down the stairs he'd made as a child, but Anne Green's body lay before him and he knew that that time was not now.

Sir Thomas left his place and walked to the window, blowing in his hands to try and warm them. He looked briefly at the crowd outside, then seemed to check himself and edged back.

"*He*, you see," Wilton said in a low voice, nodding toward Sir Thomas, "made quite sure that the girl was found guilty. You know why?"

Robert shook his head, trying to make up for his lack of speech by his interest and questioning expression.

"Why? Because he recently negotiated a fine marriage for his grandson—the one who is said to have got Anne with child."

Robert looked at Wilton, startled. "Sh . . . sh . . . she . . . ?"

"Didn't you know she bore a child?"

Robert shook his head.

"He wanted to make certain that Anne didn't live to tell the world that his grandson was responsible," Wilton continued. "Sir Thomas Reade is a powerful and wealthy man. What he seeks, he obtains. His word is law."

Robert, desperate to know, dropped his voice to no more than a whisper. He also found it easier to speak that way. "Who . . . d . . . d . . . did . . . she . . ." he began, and then, not wanting to say the word *murder*, mimed someone being garrotted.

"'Twas hardly murder!" Wilton burst out, rather louder than he had meant to. "'Twas infanticide."

"Infanticide?" Robert's mouth formed the word as he stared at Wilton.

"Not even that! The midwife at the trial said the child was hardly formed and but nine inches long. The girl had miscarried. 'Twas nothing but a stillbirth!"

"So the midwife said!" put in a scholar who stood close behind them, his face and tone declaring what he thought of the honesty of that band of women.

"There was no reason for her to lie," said Wilton, for his mother was both a midwife and a purveyor of herbs and cures. "Hearken to this: do you know that infanticide stands alone as the only law where the accused is guilty until proven innocent?"

The scholar shrugged, uncaring, but Robert shook his head, intrigued.

"Infanticide is a cruel law that only applies to the lower classes," Wilton continued. "When was one of the aristocracy last hanged for such a crime? Can you tell me that?"

Robert was about to attempt another question, but Sir Thomas resumed his place just in front of them, and he thought better of it. So she was hanged for infanticide, he thought, astonished. Why, if every woman whose premature child had died was found guilty of such a crime, then the gallows would be straining under the weight of them all.

If there was any justice in the world, this woman would live . . .

Chapter ~ 15

It was Lady Mary who fainted then, falling onto the floor in a flurry of doves' feathers. Sir Thomas struck me hard around the face so that I rocked backward on the chair. "You wicked girl!" he cried. "May God forgive you for such a terrible lie!"

Some of the servants ran to help Lady Mary, and Mrs. Williams put a light to the charred bunch of rosemary and waved it under her nose. When she had come to somewhat, Mr. Peakes and Patience picked her up and carried her between them out of the kitchen.

No one said a word. My fellow servants, all of whom might well have suspected Master Geoffrey of being the father of the child, remained mute. (Although I own I mustn't be too hard on them, for there is precious little other work in the village if they lose their positions at the manor house.)

"You must refute those words," Sir Thomas said, trembling with anger. "And may God forgive you for saying such a thing about my boy."

I didn't speak, for I was shocked and dizzy from the blow, also half distracted by what had happened to me.

Sir Thomas came toward me saying he would *make* me tell the truth, and at this point Mrs. Williams stepped in and said that she wished to beg his pardon, but in her opinion quiet words might do more good than hard knocks. Sir Thomas backed off from me then, breathing hard, saying that he rued the day I ever came to work for him and that he'd known e'en then from my wanton looks that I was going to cause trouble within his house.

Mr. Peakes returned. "Now, Miss Anne," he said with some semblance of concern (and indeed he has never been cruel to me), "you must tell us the truth about this child and how it came to die."

"I swear that it didn't die—for it never lived!" I looked around me, desperately seeking a kind face. "You must believe me! I would not ever kill a newborn babe—they are helpless, innocent things and least deserve to die of any of us."

"Would you not even think to kill it if you wished to conceal its birth?" asked Mr. Peakes.

I shook my head. "Never, sir. On my mother's life I promise you that it never drew breath. It was an early child and should not have been born. I birthed it, and it was very small and looked blue from the start."

"Ask her again who is the father," Sir Thomas said brusquely. "And tell her that she must speak the truth this time or suffer the consequences."

Mr. Peakes asked the question, but I didn't answer. I knew that my reward for the truth would be another blow, and I was not brave enough for that.

"You must tell us, Anne," Mr. Peakes tried again. "It will be best for you in the end."

"But I *have* told you the truth." I shot a look at Sir Thomas and felt my mouth dry up with fear and my voice catch in my throat so that I stammered. "B . . . b . . . but I dare not say it again."

"If you will not speak here," Sir Thomas said, "then you must answer for your actions in court."

In court. I didn't really know what these words meant, what they might conceal, so he might as well have said that I should answer for my actions in a field or in the marketplace. Some of the servants, though, gave a gasp, and must have realized the seriousness of my situation.

"And there in court you shall answer truthfully and before God!"

There was another long silence before Mrs. Williams asked in a troubled voice, "Shall she be taken there tonight, sir?"

"No, but at first light in the morning," Sir Thomas said. "And she must be locked in the icehouse overnight so that she doesn't escape."

"Locked in all night?" I asked, my voice shaking, for 'tis cold as charity in the icehouse, and besides, I've always been afeard of the darkness and knew that there were no windows there—no, not even a crack where the moon might shine through.

"And in the icehouse, sir?" Mr. Peakes added after a moment.

Sir Thomas nodded. "For she cannot be trusted. None of you are safe in your beds while she is close by."

Everyone continued staring at me, and I began to be very frightened. "But what will happen to me?"

"Tomorrow you will go to Oxford, to the prison," Sir Thomas said with no little pleasure in his voice, "and in time you'll stand trial at the assize court for your crime."

"W . . . w . . . what crime?"

"Are you dull of wit as well as wicked? For the crime of murder."

"But I never did murder!"

"That will be for the judge and jury to decide. And if you dare say again that your foul fornication was with the innocent boy who is the heir of this house, then I shall add slander to that charge."

I began weeping, as did some of the other female servants. Mr. Peakes coughed and said in a low voice, "And what should we do with the dead child, sir?"

"It will be needed as evidence," Sir Thomas answered. "I charge you with the task of taking a cloth and wrapping it ready to travel to Oxford with this . . . this murderess here." He got out his pocket watch. "I shall send horses to the prison governor tonight and ask that the cart be here at first light. In the meantime you must see that she doesn't escape."

"Sir," Mr. Peakes said, bowing a little, "the icehouse is very cold. She may perish out there."

"It would be as well if she did," came the reply. "Rather that a body should freeze to death than stand and answer to the foul charge of murder."

"She . . . she may maliciously spoil the meat stuffs there," Mr. Peakes said with a ghost of a glance at me not to speak. "I think, sir, if you will allow it . . . the cellars here may suffice. I shall see to it that she doesn't escape."

"Very well," Sir Thomas said dismissively. "I leave it to you, Peakes."

He went out and I curled myself up on the chair, my arms tight around my legs. I continued weeping and would not look at anyone even when they spoke to me, for I felt ill and wretched and bitterly ashamed of everything that had happened. Susan didn't venture near, but Jacob and some of the women came close by and tried to say some comforting things, although none were able to give me any solace. After a while I was given soup and a bowl of hot potatoes, and after eating these I was led down into the cellars. The thought of being left in darkness terrified me, but a moment after Mr. Peakes locked the door it was opened again and someone—I didn't see who—put in my warm cloak, also an undersmock and some clean petticoats, which I was pleased to change into. They also left a lit candle.

After I'd dressed myself, I sat on the floor and rocked backward and forward in an effort to warm and comfort myself. It was fearsome cold (although not as cold as it would have been in the icehouse), and I was unable to sleep, being too scared of the shapes and shadows, the faint noises from around the house, and the skittering and scattering of the rats to close my eyes. More than this, I had an ache in my belly and my heart and could not stop weeping, for I was in a deal of fright thinking of the morning and what it might bring, and how I could let my dear family know what had happened.

Very early the next morning Mr. Peakes unlocked the cellar door, and Susan came in with a bowl of hot oatmeal pottage and a glass of small beer on a tray. She didn't speak and looked away from me, embarrassed, when she put it down, but I saw that the pottage had some plump raisins in it, and the thought came to me that she must have added these herself. I wanted to speak with her then, tell her everything that had happened, and explain how I'd come to such a fall, but of course it was much too late for me to try to make a friend of her. I pressed her hand by way of saying thank you, but could do no more.

"Now, Anne," Mr. Peakes said when she had hurried away, "you must eat up quickly and make yourself ready for the cart that will take you to Oxford."

I began trembling. "Am I really to go to court then, and to jail, as Sir Thomas said?" I asked, for I had been comforting myself with the idea that this might have been an empty threat, something said in the heat of a moment—for my father has such a temper—that might be forgotten about in the morning.

"I fear that you are, Anne."

"And what will happen to me?"

"You will go before the court and be tried, and they will decide whether or not you are guilty of killing your child."

"But you have my word that I am not!" I said straight off.

"Then that's what you must tell the jury."

"But what if they decide that I *have* done such a thing?"

"Then . . . then you will have to answer for it. They will"—but he did not speak of the worst thing that could happen, although he must have known it all along— "they will perhaps brand you on the arm. Or put you in the stocks for a time. You must prepare yourself to be brave."

I did not speak for a while, for I was fair famished and intent on eating every bit of the pottage.

"Sir Thomas is fearful angry," Mr. Peakes said when I'd finished.

I nodded. "But 'tis mostly because I said Master Geoffrey was the father of the child, is it not?"

Mr. Peakes cleared his throat, seeming to be uncomfortable. "If . . . you . . ." he began slowly. "If you were to name another man as the father of the child, then matters might improve. But if you persist with saying that the infant is of Master Geoffrey's begetting, then things could go very bad. Sir Thomas is what's known as a justice of the peace, which is a high office of the law."

"Name another man as the father?" I asked. "But you've told me that I must speak the truth!"

He didn't reply for some time, then said, "Think on this and know what's on Sir Thomas's mind. If the family of Miss de Willet hears of your accusation, then the marriage that has been negotiated between her and Master Geoffrey will be annulled and the Reade family disgraced. The liaison between two great families will fall asunder. Do you want that on your conscience?"

"Then what are you saying?" I asked in disbelief. "That I should lie?"

"Well," he said slowly, "what if, instead, you told the court that you didn't know who was the father of the child. That you had lain with half a dozen men and couldn't tell who was responsible."

"I could not!" I said, horrified. "'Tis not true, and I would not bring such shame on myself or my family."

"Then name one other only. Name your erstwhile suitor: John Taylor the blacksmith."

"I could not do that, either!"

Mr. Peakes looked at me gravely. "Just think on't, Anne: if you named John Taylor as the father, then Sir Thomas might relent and deal with the matter himself. You might not need to go to court."

"But it isn't true!" How could I name John! Why, he and I had only ever held hands. Besides . . . besides, I loved him, and would not besmirch his life to save mine.

"Name him and 'twill not be so bad," Mr. Peakes went on, "for all that will happen is that he'll be hauled before the magistrates and be made to marry you. And Sir Thomas will drop the charge of murder."

"No!" I said. "And anyway, John Taylor wouldn't ever marry me. He hates me now." And with this I fell to weeping again and wouldn't be comforted.

A little bit later, while it was still dark, Mrs. Williams came down and said that the cart and two of the sheriff's men were here from the prison to take me away. She'd done up all my possessions: some undersmocks, a tabby skirt, three jackets, my Sunday gown, and a day dress. There was also the precious, hateful, silver-threaded bodice, which they must have found under my mattress. "I have given you some foodstuffs," she said, "and Susan has found a comb and mirror of yours, and a gold ring and some ribbons, and we have put them all in a pocket here." She rolled everything into a tidy bundle, which she tucked under my arm and bade me take care of, then she took my hand and, squeezing it hard, wished me Godspeed.

I thanked her, and thought of that which had kept me awake and crying all last night. "How will I let my ma know?" I asked. "How will my family learn what's happened?"

"You may rest easy on that," Mrs. Williams said. "Susan is to go to your cottage in Steeple Barton straight after she's finished her morning duties, and she'll relate to them all that's occurred."

"And tell them I didn't do it!" I cried, and Mrs. Williams nodded and turned away, for she didn't seem able to look me in the eye. I didn't feel then that I hated her or Susan, for it seemed to me that they both regretted what they'd put in motion by taking the matter to Sir Thomas.

A shout came that I was to get outside and look sharpish about it, and I stood, all of a shake, and Mr. Peakes offered me his arm to help me up the stairs. Together we walked through the kitchens while the rest of the servants paused in their morning duties to wish me luck, and some of the women (perhaps having more foresight than I about what was going to happen) fell to weeping. I found myself stopping and saying silly and comforting things to them, such as I was all right, and would be sure to be back with them before too long. And it reminded me of when Lily Grove the scullery maid had got married to a carrier two years before, and Mr. Peakes had led her through the kitchens and everyone had pressed flowers into her hands and given her little trinkets for luck (although these had not worked, for she had died giving birth to her first child).

Two men were waiting at the back door, and at first they looked at me very stern and spoke gruffly when asking my name, but afterward seemed to relent when they saw that I wasn't going to resist. I climbed into the back of the cart with some help from Mr. Peakes, sat on the floor of it with my bundle, and one of the drivers climbed in after and clasped my legs together with an iron manacle and some chains, the way I'd seen highwaymen and the like pictured in the news sheets. Once secured, I crawled into a corner of the cart, huddled into my cloak, and prayed that the journey to Oxford would be quick. I was pitifully ignorant of the ways of the law at that time, for I thought that the matter might be settled that afternoon; that the jury would be there waiting and, when they realized that I was not a murderess, release me. I looked in fear for Sir Thomas or Lady Mary to come out, but they did not, and I cannot say that I was glad about anything on that morning, but I was glad about this.

Mr. Peakes gave me some money wrapped in a paper that he said was my wages, and we were just about to set off when he shouted to the drivers to wait a while for he'd just remembered something, and, going back to the house, came out again with a small bundle wrapped in a rough linen dish clout. I thought this must contain something that I'd forgotten, and so I held up my hands to receive it. Mr. Peakes shook his head at me and handed the bundle to the driver, who placed it under his seat. I realized then that it was the dead infant, and was struck with mortification and pity.

It was scarce light by the time the cart trundled out of the manor house gates, but there were already people in the lane outside going about their morning duties. I shrank back and hung my head so that my hood covered my face, fearing they might realize that it was a prison cart and follow the usual custom of shouting after it, or of throwing old vegetables and other rubbish at whoever was being borne away. I least wanted to draw attention to myself right *there*.

To my horror, however, as the cart turned at the corner of Cow Lane to go toward Oxford, John Taylor came by on his way to work and hailed the driver to ask who was aboard, saying it was news to him that there were knaves and thieves about these parts.

I prayed with all my heart that the driver might urge the horse on without replying or John might not wait upon his words, but God was not listening, for the driver paused to adjust his cape about him and John stood his ground.

"No thieves, but one murderess," came the reply.

"A murderess!" John asked, astonished. "Someone from this village?"

"Aye."

With my eyes tight shut I heard him walk two steps closer to the back of the cart to see if he could discern who was there. All he would have seen of me, however, was a huddled black shape. "A *murderess*?" he repeated. "From where does she come?"

"From the manor house."

The carter whipped up the horse, and I heard John Taylor ask, "And by what name goes this murderess?"

But just then the horse began moving and the wheels of the cart turned on the gravel, and I don't know if John Taylor heard the reply that came, or even if one was uttered. I pictured him standing in the lane looking perplexed, his hands on his hips, and I ached to look at him and see his dear face once more. I did not do this, however, for I was too ashamed and, besides, feared to see the repugnance and disgust that would be writ on his features when he found out it was me.

There followed a miserable journey. I was jogged and jostled about on the floor of the cart and became bruised and sore, and it was so fiercesome cold that even with my cloak tight about me I shivered. We went over a crossroads where a highwayman (so I heard my drivers say) hung on a gibbet, and I could not resist looking at the sight, which was terrible indeed, for the flesh of the person was near all gone so that it was a mere man of bone who hung there in an iron cage, with a bird of prey perched on his skull.

We went through the villages of Gylmpton and Wootton without anyone hardly noticing the cart, but at Woodstock we stopped so that the men could take refreshment at the Feathers, leaving me chained to a stave in the back. I curled up very small again then, and remained still, so that anyone seeing me would have thought I was just a bundle of rags. I heard some passing children talking of whether there was a person in the cart, and one of them jumped in the back and kicked me. I still didn't stir, however, for I knew it would be the worse for me if I was discovered.

When the two drivers came back, they were merry from the ale, and, laughing as they whipped up the horse, thought they would have some sport by shouting to passersby what it was they carried to Oxford City. They thus began calling, in the manner of tradesmen shouting their wares, "What ho—a murderess!" and "Look sharp for a murderess!" At Yarnton a group of villagers heard them and began to run after the cart, shouting that I should be hanged forthwith, so that I became frightened that they would pluck me out right then and hang me from the nearest tree. They beat on the back of the cart with branches, and clanged pots and pans, and threw stones, and one came right up with a sharpened stick and gave me a hard poke through the bars of the cart. This tore right through my clothes and lacerated my arm, but I still did not move or utter a sound.

The journey to Oxford was perhaps twenty miles. We covered this in five hours, and it was terrible and wearisome all the way, and muddy, too, for the wheels of the cart went into potholes and puddles and splashed up water so that I was fair soaked with mud by the time we neared Oxford. I did not weep, however—I had wept so much in the past day and night that I could weep no more. I just sat as still as a stone, infinitely weary and sick to my soul, trying to brace myself for whatever should come next.

As we entered the city of Oxford and the horse began to labor up a hill, the drivers shouted back to me that I should stir myself, for the end of the journey was in sight. I peeped out from under the hood of my cloak and saw at the top of the hill a hideous and forbidding old castle, and I knew that here lay my destiny.

Chapter ~ 16

"What next?" Dr. Petty asked his colleagues with some urgency to his voice. "What ought we to do?"

"*Should* we do anything?" Dr. Willis replied. "We will not dissect her at present, of course. Perhaps we should just . . . leave her."

"Let nature take its course?" asked Mr. Clarke.

"Exactly."

No! Robert wanted to shout. Don't leave it to the healing power of nature, in case nature chooses *not* to heal.

Dr. Petty put his hand to Anne's cheek, where the rope had rubbed and caused abrasions to her skin. "But . . . don't you agree that we may intervene a little?" he asked. "Assist nature?"

"I wonder if that would be ethical," Dr. Willis answered, sounding concerned. "Isn't the Puritan correct? Wouldn't anything we do be deemed as interfering with the will of God?"

Dr. Petty shrugged. "But God—or whoever," he couldn't resist adding, for it was known that he was a doubter, "has chosen to leave signs of life within this woman, so surely it would be going against his wishes if we *didn't* aid her?"

"Excuse me, sirs," one of the scholars said, "but on the gibbet she asked that God in his wisdom should prove her innocence to the world."

"Indeed she did," said Dr. Willis, his face clearing. "And mayhap this is God's way of answering such a request."

"And we are but his assistants," said Dr. Petty. He spoke with a slight mocking tone to his voice, but Dr. Willis didn't seem to notice.

"Is rigor mortis set in?" Mr. Clarke asked after a moment.

Dr. Petty felt along Anne's arms. "Difficult to tell whether it's rigor mortis or she's frozen solid. It's so damned cold in here." He gestured to the back row of the scholars, where the one who had sung and danced earlier stood. "You. Kindly go and fetch more coals."

The scholar went out, reluctantly, and Wren turned to his pad of paper and began drawing a picture of Anne's recumbent body. Robert, suddenly feeling an immense frustration at the uncertainty, the indecision, the *slowness* of what was occurring, stepped forward. He didn't think of the unreliability of his speech, merely of a desperate desire to move things on; to take away that blasphemous and odious noose, that dread reminder of death.

"T . . . t . . . t . . . take r . . . r . . . r . . . ?" he suggested. He tried again with the *r*, then gave up and made gestures with his hands to show what he meant.

Dr. Petty nodded. "There would be no harm in that."

"And then we will see what Bathurst has to say," said Dr. Willis.

Robert stepped forward, his hands shaking slightly. He touched Anne's head, felt the cold roundness of her skull, the hard roundels of her spine, the matted dampness of her hair. His fingers caught at a knot, and as he gently lifted her head from the table and felt the slackened muscles beneath the skin at the nape of her neck, he saw that she'd tied back her dark hair with a red ribband. This was damp and bedraggled, but the sight of it touched him. He could not help but picture her in her prison cell early that morning, preparing herself for death and tying her hair back in one last feminine and practical gesture. *The pity of it. The very pity of her death—especially if she had been innocent.*

But perhaps she was not going to suffer death. Suddenly he was overcome with some emotion that he barely understood, and his vision blurred. Blinking hard, he maneuvered the heavy noose over Anne's chin and up over her face, then dropped it. It landed on the floor, scattering sawdust in all directions.

Sir Thomas gave a loud and exasperated sigh. "I have never before witnessed such a farrago. I'm going straight to the prison governor."

Dr. Petty leaned over and laid a gentle and restraining hand on his arm. "Just allow us a few more moments, sir. We must make completely sure that this young woman—"

"I've already allowed you a few damn moments!" Sir Thomas pulled out a pocket watch golder and grander than Dr. Petty's. "I've been here near on fifty minutes and not a thing has been done—you haven't even started the cutting. I'm going to the prison governor now to discover the ruling on these things. If necessary, I'll have this jade hauled back to the prison yard and re-hanged."

"And I shall come with you, sir!" called the Puritan at the back of the room. "'Tis going against the law of the land that these men should mess with corpses. She cannot be dead one moment and alive the next!"

The atmostphere grew tense as the two of them left the room. Frisk, who had hauled himself to his feet, was leaning on the wall looking pale, and the only sound in the room came from Norreys, who, although not now on his knees, was muttering what sounded suspiciously like a Roman Catholic prayer. Robert hoped, for his sake, that there were no fervent anti-papists present.

The singing scholar came back with a scuttle containing hot coals and threw these onto the fire, which flared up immediately. A moment after, Dr. Ralph Bathurst hurried in with snowflakes dotting his cloak and his arms full of glass jars. A slender, clever man who wrote verse in French and Latin, he had personally been hit hard by the Civil War, for six of his twelve brothers had been killed fighting for the Royalists. Calm and sociable, he tried to retain an equable disposition at all times, and, together with Drs. Petty and Willis, was an enthusiastic member of the small group of natural scientists who met regularly in Oxford.

"I was on my way here and was nearly bowled over at the door by Sir Thomas Reade hurrying from the building!" He looked around the room at the rapt faces. "But whatever's going on?"

He was told by a chorus of voices and fell to marveling, then placed the jars in a row along the windowsill. "I brought these jars to receive the woman's vital organs for preservation," he said, "but possibly they won't be needed." He nodded outside. "There's a mob down there waiting to claim her body. If they hear of this, I fear they'll break the doors down."

"Then we must *not* let them hear of it until the matter is decided one way or the other," said Dr. Willis.

Dr. Bathurst looked down at Anne, touched her cheek, bent over to check if he could hear breathing. "But the whole story is almost unbelievable. Several of you saw it, you say?"

"*All* of us saw her eyelid move," said Dr. Petty.

"It has moved twice!" Wilton interjected, and Robert looked at him gratefully. "And before that she seemed to croak in the back of her throat."

"There may be nothing in it," Dr. Bathurst said. "It may be certain fluids and humors moving about her body—but, if you both agree, I think we must give her a chance."

Both doctors nodded, and Dr. Petty glanced at the scholars. "I'm inclined to the view that we should treat this as a lesson," he said. "It may be disappointing to some that there's no body to dissect, but scholars can take instruction just the same."

"Indeed," said Dr. Bathurst. "So perhaps we should first ascertain which of her humors might be wrongly balanced." He looked at the students standing before him. "What are the vital forces in the body, young sirs? And which of these four may be out of kilter in this young woman?"

But no one was willing to venture an opinion on which element might be lacking, or in excess, in the body before them.

After several moments' silence Dr. Petty asked, "So what should we do to help to restore her to the world?" He spread his hands. "And this question is also for me and my fellow doctors, for to my knowledge such a thing has never happened before."

Indecision clouded the room.

"Cut pigeons in half and apply them to her feet?" Norreys suggested, but this being a method regarded as rather old fashioned, all three doctors shook their heads.

A powdered burned swallow and the drippings from a roasted swan evoked similar responses.

"A cordial, perhaps?" said Dr. Willis. "Surely a restorative cordial could do no harm."

"A cordial might be in order . . . perhaps cinnamon and sorrel mixed with rainwater?" Dr. Petty bent down so that his face was very close to Anne's own, and placed his fingers on her lips, pushing them open to reveal small white teeth. "Although her teeth are so hard clenched," he went on, "that 'twill be difficult to pour any such liquid into her mouth."

"Her fists are also tight shut," Dr. Willis said, lifting her right arm. "Each finger is turned inward." He replaced the arm. "Can you move your hand, Anne?" he asked the still form.

Robert held his breath, but nothing about her stirred.

"What should we do?" Dr. Petty asked. He pounded his hand into his fist. "We must do *something*!"

"Take blood?" Dr. Willis suggested.

"Of course!" said Dr. Bathurst, and the medical men nodded as one. Blood-letting was generally regarded as mandatory in all cases where a prognosis was in doubt.

Robert heard a movement in the corridor outside, and he looked toward the door anxiously, fearing that at any moment Sir Thomas would return with the hangman close behind. It was merely the lighter step of Martha, however, who came in with a glass of ale to help revive Nathaniel Frisk.

"I'd like someone to take notes for us," Dr. Petty said, and on Robert quickly raising his hand, went on, "for until we are certain that Anne Green is entirely dead, we must treat her as a normal patient. Someone, perhaps, who's recovering from the ministrations of some blundering surgeon." His eye caught that of Nathaniel Frisk, and he checked himself. "I do beg your pardon, sir."

"No offense taken, sir," said Frisk weakly.

"We must treat her as a recovering patient," Dr Petty went on. "One who needs constant monitoring and care."

Robert nodded and took out his notepad. "I . . . I . . . I . . ." he began, and then gave up and merely held the notebook and a sharpened pencil aloft and gave a confirming nod.

Dr. Petty consulted his watch, then handed it to Robert. "The time is now eleven fifteen. Start with that."

Chapter~17

This soft and enclosing blackness where I can feel neither heat nor chill, hunger nor thirst, is indeed preferable to the circumstances in which I next found myself, which was the jail at Oxford Castle. I had been thrown into a big dark space more like a pit than a room. It was circular in shape, with high-up windows that had bars across them but no glass, so that the wind constantly swirled around and in and out and made a ghostly moaning sound that frightened me at night and stopped me from sleeping.

Not that I *could* sleep easily. I found no comfort there: not a mattress, a plank, nor even straw to lie on, for most of the inmates slept either directly on the foul floor or on the stone seating ledge that ran around the outer limits of the room. This hard ledge was cold and inhospitable, but, if you could but secure yourself a place on it, was preferable to the floor, which was damp with slime and gritty underfoot.

But I am jumping ahead of myself. On being rough-handled into the jail, the first thing to assault my senses had been the fetid smell. At home with Ma I'd lived constantly with the hot stink of livestock, but this stench was much worse than that and made me retch, for 'twas a fusion of smells which—I know now—consisted of human excrement, rotting limbs, untreated sores, and the foul miasma of squalor, degradation, and despair. It also held the stench of death, for three days after I'd been admitted, a crone wearing heavy leg irons who'd been hunched into a far corner was found to be dead—and to have been dead for some days, too, for when they went to move her, it was discovered that her legs had quite rotted away from her body.

When, that first day, I became a little more used to this stink and was able to stop retching, I dragged myself (for I still wore manacles) to a space on the ledge and looked around me. What I saw was like a scene from hell—only that hell is hot and this was wintry cold—for some forty souls were crammed into this room, either sitting around with their faces full of despair, or walking about raving and railing against whatever had brought them here. Some inmates seemed utterly mad; one woman spoke high-pitched and sobbed in a child's voice, another did nothing but gibber like a strange animal and run up and down in the channel where we relieved ourselves, and one man spent most of the day against the wall, standing on his head.

I was terrified, of course. Though I had hardly known before that such a thing as a jail existed, nor at all what it would be like, I never could have imagined it would be as foul and offensive as this. For some time I sat in a dark corner, clutching my bundle of clothes to me without moving or drawing attention to myself, for I thought it best to observe the inmates going about and see how things were done and if there was a certain way to behave.

I quickly realized, however, that there was no pattern to the day and no set of rules to follow, for all was just confusion and beastliness. People shuffled about, dragging their manacles behind them, or sat, heads drooping, seemingly owned by misery. A continual wailing filled the air, and occasionally there would be a scuffle and one man would half-heartedly wrestle another to the ground, but generally they seemed too cold, ill, and disheartened to bother with anything, as if the very effort of keeping themselves alive in such a place was trial enough.

It was bitter cold, and though there was a brazier in the center of the room wherein burned a few sticks, it was surrounded by so many trying to glean its meager warmth that it could not easily be seen, and I did not even discover its existence on that first day. There was no outside space to use, and it became apparent that everyone was incarcerated continually, with no respite from the foulness that surrounded them, and never a breath of good fresh air. The only space where the outside world could be seen was through the high windows, which afforded tiny, oblong views of sludge-gray sky way over our heads, and a barred grill in one of the walls, which opened onto a pathway through the castle, enabling inmates to beg alms from visitors as they walked through the grounds. When anyone passed, a beseeching and a crying would come from every nearby prisoner. "Sire, spare a little food!"; "I beg you, madam, I am dying!"; "I have three children and a babe to feed!" they would variously plead (for there were, indeed, several poor children placed among us).

I found that a small amount of old straw had been placed here and there along the concrete ledge, but when, that first night, I went to take some to sleep on, I soon discovered that each paltry clump had been bought and paid for by a prisoner, who would as soon stab you through the heart as have you take it from him.

Some time after the sun went down, perhaps about five o'clock, just as I was fearing that we were going to be left in the dark all night, a few torches were lit and put to the wall, and then one of the turnkeys came around with a great basket of dark bread and began to throw it to us, joking that we were all performing dogs and must catch it. Indeed, everyone saw to it that they *did* catch it, because to miss would have meant it falling onto the floor, which was coated with filth, dung beetles, and dead lice.

I jumped for a roll when he threw one my way, for I was very hungry. This amused the turnkey to no end, and he began to roar with laughter, saying it was quite a thing to see a murderess jumping for her bread—but that I must have done many a good jump in my time. I hardly knew what he meant, but the jeering and hooting from some of the men told me that he'd been making a lewd joke. Some of them looked at me strangely after this, and I knew that they were wondering who I'd killed and if it was perhaps my sweetheart. I did not speak to them, however, or ever tell the truth but to one person, for I thought it better that they should think I was a murderess, for then they might be a-feared of me and leave me alone.

The bread was dark and solid, but I began to gnaw at it, and then remembered that Mrs. Williams had given me some food. I opened this paper and found some slices of ham, a decent-sized piece of cheese, a green marchpane cake, and an apple. I stared at the apple, and then clutched it to me and began to weep, for it was a little red apple from the tree at the very front of the orchard that overlooks the lane and—it being an early fruiter—I had probably picked it with my own hands that summer, sitting in the tree's branches and calling over the fence to John Taylor at the forge. I'd been happy then, but had not realized it. Oh, how I yearned for that time again so I could order my life differently!

But through my tears I could smell the delicious aroma of the cheese, so dried my eyes on a corner of my skirt and, when I looked up, was surprised to see myself surrounded by six or seven men and women, all staring hungrily at my food.

"Do you not want that, mistress?" one asked.

"Can you spare a little?"

"It is several months since I had a bit o' meat."

"I'm fair starved, so I am . . ."

I was torn by pity for them and greed for myself, for I knew that if all that was to be provided was black bread, I'd soon be in dire need of more nourishment. As I hesitated, however, each put a hand out and looked at me with such pleading eyes that I could do no less than place a small amount of food into each one.

Of course, as soon as the rest of the room saw what was going on, they flocked around me like the doves when I threw grain, and I had to tuck the apple up my sleeve and quickly stuff the rest of the food in my mouth or would have found myself with none at all. And so, barring the apple, by the end of that first day my food was all gone.

I didn't sleep a bit that night, for I couldn't secure a place on the ledge and had to lie on the floor, and there was never a moment when someone wasn't wailing, screaming, pleading to be let out, or begging for rope to hang themselves and be done with the place. As well as this there came horrid little noises as the rats pattered along the floor or the occasional splash as they entered the open sewer and began to eat whatever they found there. I was terrified that if I closed my eyes, one might creep up and begin to gnaw at my finger or toe.

I spent most of that night thinking on the scrap of babe that I'd birthed and found it hard to rid myself of the image of it rolled, tiny and stiff, in its linen shroud. I also wondered with horror if I might have unthinkingly killed it by neglecting it. If I'd picked it up and rocked it, or cleared its mouth, might it have lived? I could not envisage myself doing either of those things, however, for whenever I thought of handling it, it made me near shudder with dread. I couldn't think that I ever would have loved such a little creature, although I pitied it with all my heart.

The following morning there was more black bread to eat, and some thin and foul gruel, and at this time I was approached by a prisoner I did not think I'd seen the previous day. She was a woman I judged to be of around thirty years of age, not too shabby in her dress and wearing a passably clean white apron and cap. Her hair was frowsy and colored red, and she had some fleabites on her face, but she was not unattractive, with large and very dark eyes. She asked if I'd brought any food from home and, if so, if I had a scrap to spare.

I shook my head. "I'm sorry but I have not, for it all went last night," I said—although I still had my red apple up my sleeve.

"No matter," she said, sitting down beside me. "How did you like your first night in the jail?"

"I did not like it one bit," I said and, feeling my bottom lip begin to tremble, knew that I was about to weep again. "How do you bear to stay here? I can't see how I'll survive in such a place."

"'Tis not too bad for me," she said, "for I gets myself out of this animal den at night."

"You go home?" I asked, looking at her in astonishment.

"No, dear," she said. "But I go to a gentleman's cell of an evening, and there I sleeps the night on a good feather mattress."

I forgot my tears. "How do you do that?"

"I'm a nightwalker, dear," she answered. I must have looked at her uncomprehendingly, for she added, "A trug-moldy. A whore."

"Oh," I said, much shocked, for I had not met any woman of her occupation before, and she sounded so very bold about it.

"They picked me plying my trade under Magdalen Bridge, so while I waits to be sentenced, I does a little work here and there to keep my hand in."

"But where are the gentlemen's cells?" I asked, looking around.

"They're on the floor above," she said, and went on confidentially, "There are all sorts there: famous and rich highwaymen, and gents who turn tricks with playing cards, and also a couple of merchants who are accused of stealing from each other. And all are very willing to pay for a lady's company of a night."

"They have their own cells?"

"They do indeed! And some of these are nicer than my own lodgings at home, for they has pictures and hangings brought in, and food sent from the tavern, and one of the highwaymen even has his own four-poster bed. You may obtain anything here if you has the money to pay for it." She looked at me questioningly. "But you don't seem the regu-lar sort of prisoner, and I sees you aren't of my persuasion, so why are you here in Oxford's finest?"

I sighed and, there being precious little else to do, began to recount the story of Master Geoffrey and my downfall. And I finished by telling her, *swearing* to her, that the child was stillborn and never drew breath. "But for all that, they still say I'm a murderess!"

She took my hand and squeezed it. "Never fear, my dear, the truth will come out at the trial, for when you has a chance to speak you must say exactly what happened. And when the judge and jury realize that you're a truthful and honest girl, then they're sure to release you straightaway."

"But when do you think that will be?"

"Well, the judge travels about the country, but I've been told that he'll arrive here before Christmas. About the thirteenth of December, so they say."

"How far off is that?"

We worked out that it was nearly two weeks hence, which realization filled me with acute misery. To think I had two weeks incarcerated here before I could come before the judge, tell him I'd done nothing wrong, and be released. I didn't even consider that my liberation might not happen.

"If you wish, I can find you a nice gentleman protector," my new friend—whose name was Rebecca—said, "and then at least you'd sleep comfortable well at night." She gave a knowing little smile and added, "Or you would sleep well after you'd done the business with him!"

"I could not," I said, shaking my head. "I was persuaded to sleep with Master Geoffrey, and it has led to my ruin. I'll never lie with another man until I'm wed. I'm certain of that."

She looked at me consideringly. "After you've been here a few days, you may change your mind."

"I shall not!" I said, then added more gently (for I had a mind to keep Rebecca as a friend, whatever her occupation might be), "But thank you for asking me."

I found out that she'd come to Oxford some eight years before, when the king had brought his court from London for safety before the war. "I was but fifteen then," she said. "I was a beauty, with long black hair, which I wore in ringlets right down my back, and my eyes very dark and lustrous—as brown as yours are blue. My eyes!" she went on. "Oh, men wrote verse about them, saying they bade them come to bed." She sighed. "I had several admirers among the young men of the court, and they paid for my lodging and bought me dresses and pearls. Once I even had a pretty pink carriage drawn by a white horse."

"And what happened?"

"Then the war came to Oxford and all the men went into battle, the king was captured, and the city went over to parliament. But even at the start there was not so much rollicking fun to be had here as in London in the early days."

"Was there truly not?" I asked, for I had heard as much from the ballads.

"And now 'tis all different—everything is run by Puritans and they're all for stopping everyone's fun."

"And have you been a nightwalker all that time?" I asked.

She nodded. "But only for gentlemen," she said. "I wouldn't take a farmer or a laboring man. I have some clerical gents, one man who's a magistrate—and many an Oxford scholar keen to lose his virginity!" She began to laugh. "They know where their member is, but don't know what to do with it. Why, a young gent I had a few weeks back was so scared he was struck silent the whole time and could scarce e'en manage to thank me after."

I looked at her, marveling. "But . . . but do you not continually find yourself in a certain condition?"

She shook her head. "I do not, for there are secrets to the game which are known to all ladies of the night."

"And what are those?"

"I take a daily cordial of tansy and pennyroyal, which I was told to do by a mountebank in London, to keep my terms regular," she confided. "And as well as that, one or two of my regular gents, not wishing to find themselves with bastards to despoil their family names, have taken to wearing a device made from a pig's bladder, which they wear over their member."

I blushed to hear such talk, although wished that Master Geoffrey had used such a device.

"But if you are not to try for a gentleman yourself, then we must endeavor to improve your position here. Do you have any money?"

I nodded and, trusting her completely, for she had been so open with me, brought out from my pocket the fold of paper that Mr. Peakes had given me the day before.

Only one day before, I thought in disbelief, I'd bade goodbye to my fellow servants in Dun's Tew and heard John Taylor's voice for the last time. Thinking on this, a pretty conceit formed in my head: that if, on hearing him speak, I'd revealed myself in the back of the cart and asked for his aid, then perhaps he would have reached into the cart to rescue me. He might have struck off my leg irons on his anvil, thrown me over a horse, and carried me away to safety.

I felt my eyes fill with tears at this sentimental and silly notion, and Rebecca had to shake my arm gently to stir me. "How much money have you there?" she asked, and when we counted it, found that there was three shillings and four pence.

"You are a made woman! With this you can send out for some warm things, hire a mattress, buy some better food, and even have a little tipple of brandy to warm you of an evening. And what clothes have you?"

I unrolled my bundle and showed her, and her eyes rounded in admiration at the sight of the bodice, which she offered to sell for me. I turned her down, however, for I felt I had riches enough with my three shillings and fourpence, and should keep the bodice for another occasion. "You must guard that, for it's worth a deal of money," she said. "And when you need to sell it, I'll get you a good price."

I thanked her kindly and said I would remember her words, and she offered to go and speak to the turnkeys and bargain with them for whatever I wanted. We debated how I should spend my money, and I was happy to discover that I'd be able to rent a mattress stuffed with straw, a pair of fur gloves and a woolen tippet, some candles and a candlestick, and still have enough left over to buy food for several days. Another discussion led to us deciding that I'd dine later that day on oysters and boiled ham, and of course I invited her to share these delicacies with me. I felt a good deal better while these discussions were going on, for, although still cold and frightened, I was very content that my situation would shortly improve.

I waited while Rebecca went to speak first to the turnkeys and then—for she sent a message to say so—to the prison bailiff to pay what was owed and to organize the delivery of some of the items. She warned me that she drove a hard bargain so this could take some time, but said she'd be back well before midday and hoped to have the boiled ham with her. She suggested that we drink a couple of measures of spiced wine with it in order to heat our bellies, and I thought this a most agreeable proposal.

It was about midday when a turnkey brought the bread, but Rebecca hadn't returned. It got later and later, and as I sat watching the darkness creep down the walls, it finally dawned on me that she wasn't coming back at all. I'd been cheated out of my money! I'd been taken for a fool, and Rebecca—or whatever her real name might be—was probably even now in one of the private rooms upstairs, drinking a toast to her good fortune.

Later that evening I spoke to a watchman and tried to make a complaint against her, only to discover that she was not a prisoner at all, but a well-known trickster who would bribe a turnkey now and again to let her into the jail so that she might prey on gullible newcomers.

I spent that night in devastating loneliness, feeling that I had not a friend in the world and might die of cold, hunger, and misery, and no one would care. I thought of my ma and pa, and my sister, Jane, and my brothers, and wondered what they were all doing; how they would have heard the news; and what they thought of me. In that very low time I felt that even they had forsaken me.

I was woken—for I eventually slept, despite everything—by someone shaking my shoulder. Opening my eyes, I found my sister standing beside me holding her nose, her face horror-struck at the surroundings in which she found herself. For a moment I thought that I must be dreaming, but then I looked past her and saw my ma there, too, looking around, as frightened as a fawn, and immediately jumped up and threw myself upon them, hugging them both.

We wept many tears together, and Jane and Ma could not desist from looking about them and shuddering and bewailing my situation, and saying how could I stand it and that I'd surely run mad in such a place. And while they were speaking, a prisoner was relieving himself in the kennel, another was gnawing at a dead rat, the man who stood on his head was happily doing so again, and yet another, covered in sores, was skipping around naked—so that it did indeed look like Bedlam, and I was dreadfully ashamed to have caused Ma and Jane to come there.

They told me they'd started off from Steeple Barton on farmer Smith's turnip cart at three o'clock that morning, and my poor dear mother, exhausted from the journey and the shock, looked as though she'd aged twenty years. They wanted to know all that had happened to me, and what was expected to happen, and this I told them and could not hold back my tears as I did so, being so very thankful to have them there.

"But who will speak up for you at the trial?" Ma asked, after I'd told them all.

I said I didn't know.

"Should you not have someone on your side, to give their opinion of you?" asked Jane.

Ma nodded. "Or otherwise Sir Thomas will have it all his own way, and being a man of the law, he will take his advantage."

I thought for a moment. "But 'twill be known from the size of the babe that 'twas not full-term. And the gentlemen of the jury will be on my side, for they'll discern that I was telling the truth and surely feel pity for someone so deceived."

"But as you said, they are *gentlemen* of the jury," Ma explained, "landed gentry all, and probably kin to Sir Thomas for all we know. They will naturally be on his side, Anne, for they are of his persuasion."

I frowned, thinking on this.

"And just suppose . . ." she went on with a tremor in her voice, "you *are* found guilty, what then?"

"But I will not be—for I didn't kill the child!" I said. "And even if the jury should go against me, then surely the judge will not."

Ma said nothing more, but turned away and could not speak.

Sadly, they only had an hour with me while farmer Smith took his turnips to the market and then came to collect them from the prison for their return, but before they left, Jane gave me seven pence, which I knew was all her savings, and Ma gave me a whole chicken, which she'd roasted on the spit the previous day, and also two silver shillings.

"'Tis from your father and 'tis his cow money, Anne, so use it well," she said, pressing it into my hand. This was the first word I'd had of my father, for I'd been scared to ask after him in case he'd disowned me, and hearing now that he'd sent me his precious cow money touched me deeply.

I took them both to the iron door of the prison, where we said our goodbyes, and they promised to visit me again before the trial. They wept pitifully as they left, and so did I. To see them going off into the freezing fog of the morning, knowing I was the cause of all their sorrows, fair broke my heart.

Chapter ~ 18

R obert turned to a new section of his notebook and wrote:

> *Saturday, 14 December 1650*
> *11.15 a.m. — The dissection of the body of Anne*
> *Green was halted on her eye being seen to*
> *move by several of the assembled scholars.*

He looked at this note and then changed the word *eye* to *eyelid*, for Dr. Petty was known to be a pedant for precise language.

Having decided to bleed their patient, the doctors sent for a bowl and tourniquet; as, providentially, they were working above an apothecary's shop, these items were located just down the stairs. They also called upon Martha to obtain some extra candles and two large cushions, these latter enabling the corpse to be placed in a semi-upright position.

Anne Green, reclining on pillows, looked less like a cadaver and more like a person — though the trembling of her eyelid had ceased, and there was absolutely no animation about her at all. Robert glanced out the window at the mob; he was sure he could pick out Anne's mother. How utterly bewildered she'd be to see Anne sitting up and being bled, just as if she were alive.

Perhaps, by fair means or foul, she *was* alive.

His heart quickened as he thought of foul means, for a horrifying thought had just occurred to him: maybe Anne Green was a witch. Maybe she had foiled the hangman and secured her life by the use of magic—and without stopping to consider the soundness of such an action, his eyes moved over her body, looking for teats at which a familiar might have suckled.

He could see none. And then he scolded himself, because this was the middle of the seventeenth century, and he was a student at the most forward-thinking institute for learning in the country. A mere five years ago, the Puritan Matthew Hopkins had instituted witch hunts all over the rural Southeast and been instrumental in the hanging of nearly three hundred alleged witches, but Hopkins had since been discredited—and they were now, surely, living in more enlightened times, when a woman might grow old and bent without being accused of consorting with the devil. Besides, the comely person of Anne Green did not in any way fit that description.

Dr. Willis applied a tourniquet just below Anne's shoulder. This was tightened, a small incision made in her fleshy upper arm, and the bleeding bowl held underneath.

A short moment passed, during which time everyone in the room held their breath, then a drop of blood was seen at the site of the cut. This grew larger, then formed into a ragged line that slowly trickled down Anne's arm and into the bowl beneath. Wren let out a cheer, echoed by several of the other scholars, and Robert wrote with shaking hand:

> *11.20 a.m.—Anne Green's arm was lanced and she was seen to give blood to an approximate amount of*

"Not so fast with your cheering, boys," Dr. Bathurst said. "I have seen dead corpses bleed before now."

Wilton frowned and asked, "Is it true, sir, that a corpse bleeds when it is in the presence of its killer?" and just then—at that precise moment—Sir Thomas strode into the room at the head of a small party consisting of the Puritan, Mr. Stegg the prison governor, a legal scribe, and a uniformed sergeant at arms. There was a murmur of astonishment from the rest of the room, loaded glances were exchanged, and the scholars shuffled around to allow the new party access to the corpse.

"Are you bleeding her, Dr. Willis?" asked the scribe, surveying the body on the table with amazement. "How so? Since when does one bleed a dead corpse?"

"When one suspects she may not be entirely dead," Dr. Willis answered, with scarcely a glance at the deputation.

"You must stop this nonsense at once," said Sir Thomas. "Tell them, Stegg! Order them to stop."

Mr. Stegg scratched his head, but no one else moved. Every person present continued to stare at Anne's arm as her lifeblood, its color showing bright in the dull-hued room, trickled into the metal bowl until it was a quarter full. A strip of linen was then wrapped around her arm, and the bleeding stopped.

Robert wrote *approximately five fluid ounces* in the space left in his notes.

"I think we will apply a clyster next!" Dr. Petty said, with some levity to his voice. "This will bring heat and warmth to her bowels and may have some significant effect."

"Dammit, sir, I tell you that you will *not* do such a thing!" Sir Thomas shouted. He gestured around at the prison officials. "Can't someone stop all this? What does a person have to do to make this madness cease?"

The Puritan stepped forward. "The very idea that you should attempt to raise the dead is improper and profane." He extended his arms in preacherly pose. "Every man and woman has a time to be born and a time to die. It is not meet to interfere with the holy scheme of things. Man should not be raised again."

Dr. Willis looked at him keenly. "What of the raising of Lazarus? His time to die had come, but Jesus raised him up once more."

"Do you dare to compare your works to those of the Lord, sir?"

"I believe the Lord said afterward that Lazarus had merely been sleeping," Mr. Clarke said and, over an anguished cry of "Blasphemy!" from the Puritan, hurriedly addressed Dr. Petty: "What do you require for the clyster, sir? I shall go downstairs and obtain whatever's necessary."

"Something mild. Hot rainwater, perhaps, with a little pepper or warming spices in it?" Dr. Petty mused. "What think you, Robert?"

Dr. Willis nodded his agreement. "And—while you're in your stock cupboard, John—perhaps we should have some cantharides to try and produce blistering."

As Mr. Clarke went off, Dr. Petty put his fingers to the neck of Anne Green and felt around for a pulse. "Perhaps . . . perhaps . . ." he said, shaking his head doubtfully.

"Though if I feel anything, it is so faint as to hardly be there at all."

Robert wrote: *11.30 a.m. — Faint pulse?*

"Observe the color of her face, however," Dr. Petty suddenly said with some excitement, studying Anne's cheeks closely. "She grows pinker, surely . . ."

"Damn you for your ignorance!" Sir Thomas shouted, making everyone start. "Am I to understand that you are going to act outside the law and will continue to try and resurrect this woman?"

"Yes," said Dr. Petty curtly. "And 'twould be better if you just left us to it and stopped causing these constant interruptions."

"Please remember, sir, that these rooms are our domain," said Dr. Willis.

"But the law is mine!"

Footsteps sounded along the corridor, and two fellows of Christ Church ran into the room. They had dressed hurriedly, for one was without his gown and the other still struggling into his at the door.

"We heard the rumor!" the first said.

"Is it true?"

"Does the hanged woman truly live?" asked the first, incredulously. "There are whispers of it about the quad."

The face of Sir Thomas showed total rage. "See what's happening? All and sundry will prattle of this, and 'twill become a freak show! You are using this woman for your own ends."

"Not so, sir," Dr. Petty said mildly.

"You are using her to endeavor to increase your fortune!"

This last remark was ignored, and the two new fellows took their places around the body of Anne Green, staring at her with a still and silent absorption.

"Her feet are extreme cold," Dr. Bathurst said to his fellows. "While the clyster is being prepared, perhaps we could anoint them with spirit of turpentine. 'Twill make the skin hot, and she may feel the benefit."

"Indeed." Dr. Willis nodded. "And her legs and arms should be rubbed to increase the circulation of her blood to her extremities."

"Very well," Sir Thomas suddenly roared, "then let her live!"

At this strange and unexpected change of heart, the medical men turned to stare at him.

"And as soon as she is on her feet—nay, as soon as she can answer to her rightful name—then I will see to it that she is taken back to the prison yard and re-hanged. And this time I will personally insure that the matter is carried out with no opportunity for error. Even if I have to knot the rope and push her off the damned gibbet myself!"

There was a pause, and then Dr. Petty corrected him. "You will *not* take her, sir."

"For we shall see that you do not," said Dr. Willis. "And if by some miracle we do cause her to live again, and she thrives, then we shall put her on the witness stand, and all shall hear the truth of it: the reason why, when a woman has clearly miscarried a child which was but nine inches long, she should be found guilty of murder."

Sir Thomas seemed about to say something else, but then choked on his words and clutched at his chest. For several moments he seemed to find it difficult to draw breath, and although Dr. Petty called for a chair to be brought so that he might examine him, Sir Thomas would have none of it. "None . . . none . . . of you bloody quacks here will lay a finger on me!" he croaked, backing away.

Dr. Petty bowed. "As you wish, sir."

"Do not think I shall allow you to continue with this," Sir Thomas railed when he had gathered a little more strength. "I shall return here with greater authority . . . I shall call upon Cromwell himself to judge whether this . . . this profane act should be . . . be . . ."

But he had gone a strange yellow color—as yellow as his teeth, someone was later to report—and seemed to find it difficult to say more. He backed out of the room, his feet shuffling as if he could barely move them along the ground, his eyes always on Anne Green. The Puritan, protesting once more that the revival of corpses was ungodly work, left at the same time, supporting Sir Thomas on his slow progress down the corridor.

Mr. Stegg, the prison governor, approached the doctors with deference, for earlier that year Dr. Petty had saved his wife from choking to death on a cherry stone. "Good gentlemen all, I feel this is none of my business," he said expansively. "The girl was hanged, she was dead, and there's an end to it. What happens now is naught to do with me."

"Wise words, sir," Dr. Willis said, giving him a short bow from the other side of the body.

"So if you'll excuse me, I'll return to my duties." Nudging the scribe, he bowed toward the doctors, and both men turned away.

"But hold one moment," Dr. Willis said. "If you wish to cooperate with the divine providence that may have saved this woman, then perhaps you would do so by contacting the court usher and asking him that a reprieve may be granted until such time as she is recovered—if this be God's will—and an official pardon obtained for her."

"At your service, sir." The scribe nodded. "I'll do it myself," he added as he left the room, for he had fallen foul of Sir Thomas's temper in the past and was pleased to have this occasion to thwart him.

—◆•✦•◆—

Spirit of turpentine was applied to the soles of Anne's feet, and these, and her arms and legs, were rubbed vigorously. In spite of each of the doctors by turn using considerable energy to try and ignite a warmth, however, her feet and limbs remained as if frozen.

The students fell back, disappointed. Robert wrote:

11.45 a.m.—Anne Green's feet were painted with turpentine and her legs and arms rubbed with vigor. These attentions did not appear to make any difference.

The enema was mixed and applied.

12 noon—A clyster of hot rainwater and spices was applied to the bowels of Anne Green to increase the warmth of her privities. She gave no reaction.

Dr. Petty gave a cry of exasperation. "We must have definite proof she is alive—and quickly!"

"Quite so," said Dr. Willis, "or I fear Sir Thomas, on recovering from his ague, will use his influence to have her taken out of our care."

Dr. Bathurst approached the corpse and took up her hand. "Anne Green!" he called urgently. "Anne! Do you hear us?"

"Can you speak?" asked Mr. Clarke.

"Give a sign that you are alive—squeeze my hand or open your eyes!" urged Dr. Petty.

There was no reaction.

12.20 p.m.—She was called to know whether she could either hear or speak. She did not move her hand nor open her eye to command, however.

"What do you say to giving her a cordial?" asked Dr. Petty.

Dr. Willis nodded eagerly. "One with restorative properties."

"Barley julep?" suggested Mr. Clarke, and this was obtained.

12.25 p.m.—Drs. Petty and Willis, by gradual force, unclenched Anne Green's teeth. A quantity of barley julep was poured down her throat, but the swallowing action could not be produced, and most of the liquid was seen to run out the sides of her mouth.

The doctors and students observed this solemnly and in silence. Robert felt quite ill with disappointment.

Three fellows of Brasenose appeared, bristling with curiosity, having heard of what was going on. Nineteen people were now crowded into the room, not including the corpse.

"She does not hear us, and she does not swallow," Dr. Willis sighed. "She appears to have no reflexes at all. What now?"

There was another long silence. "Perhaps the signs of life we observed were mere reactions of the nerves after death," said Dr. Bathurst, somewhat reluctantly.

The others shook their heads unknowingly, then Mr. Clarke suddenly clicked his fingers together and dashed out of the room. He returned a moment later with a long quill feather.

"She is to mark her name?" Dr. Petty asked with an effort at a smile.

Mr. Clarke shook his head, holding the quill aloft. "One last thing to try . . . with your permission . . ."

Understanding what he meant, Drs. Bathurst and Willis between them managed to unclench Anne Green's teeth once more, and Mr. Clarke inserted the long feather to tickle the back of her throat.

As one, the scholars and doctors leaned forward and held their breath. For a moment nothing happened, and then her limp body suddenly convulsed with a cough.

A thrill of excitement ran around the room.

"Again!" urged Dr. Willis, and the feather was inserted once more, to the same effect.

There were some gasps, several cheers, and muted applause from a dozen pairs of gloved hands. Robert, his hand shaking with excitement, wrote:

12.30 p.m. — Mr. Clarke obtained a feather. Anne Green's teeth were unclenched and the back of her throat stimulated. She coughed three times.

Let her live on, Robert thought to himself. She *must* live . . .

Chapter ~ 19

What a short story mine seems, for it's as though only minutes have passed since I awoke into this strange state. I've tried, several times, to see the angels again, to open my eyes (or to somehow see them, miraculously, through my eyelids) and feel the comfort of their presence in the black that surrounds me, but they do not appear. I wonder if I merely invented them to be a comfort to my troubled mind.

I survived my time in Oxford Jail because I truly believed that I only had to endure a certain number of days before the judge arrived and discovered me innocent.

I was prepared for the fact that I might be charged with fornication and was also prepared—indeed, almost willing—to take my chastisement for this, whether it was to be ducked, put into the stocks, or whipped behind a cart. After I'd endured this, I thought, then I'd endeavor to put the terrors I'd suffered behind me. I'd go home and live quietly with Ma and Pa until I was no longer a subject of gossip, then try to obtain a position as a laundress or glove maker, so that I wouldn't be a burden to them. If I could, I'd find work in my own village, for I didn't ever intend to go into service in a big house again. *Hold the family you work for in high regard,* I'd been told throughout my life. *Obey your master with singleness of heart, for a good master will care for you like your own father.* But who'd ever cared about me there, in the Reade household?

And one day, perhaps—or so I still dreamed—a kind young man might come along who I could trust, and I'd tell him all that had happened, and he'd still want to marry me.

I tried not to think too much about this, however. I couldn't believe in my heart that a good and true man would ever want me, and that as certain as the wolf is in the dog, he'd flee when he got breath of the ill luck and scandal that had been visited upon me.

Ma and Jane came to visit me again and, arriving on a day when my spirits were at a particularly low ebb, were able to cheer me somewhat. They brought some fresh bread with them, and a whole cheese and some cooked potatoes, and Jane also brought two pretty combs for my hair and a wash ball she'd made herself from pink soapwort, and these dainty things thrilled my heart. They brought news from home, too, for Bramble and Bracken were due to lamb after Christmas, and told me that the chickens had been frighted by a fox and had stopped laying; also that the cunning woman had treated Jacob Twister for a growth in his stomach and cured him completely (although I could not but show some disbelief at this). I listened eagerly to these stories of the outside world, but, once told, they flitted through my head like shadows, none seeming true or real. My only reality was the jail and getting through my time within it, minute by foul minute.

Every day I asked the turnkeys the date, and as it crept so slowly toward the fifteenth, I tried to temper my impatience, telling myself that the judge might have been held up on his journey and that I'd only had *her*—the whore's— word for when he was due. That very day, however, on Friday the thirteenth day of December, we prisoners were roused early in the morning, and the turnkeys spread the word that on this day the judge would hear the cases of those of us who'd not yet been charged.

After we'd eaten the foul slop that passed for breakfast, Mr. Stegg, the prison governor, came down and read out some twenty names, including mine, and those called were herded and manacled together and presently led in a staggering, ragged procession out of the door I'd entered through two weeks before. This was the first time I'd been outside in all those days and, dazzled by the light, I wanted to stand and look about me and breathe in the fresh, frosty air. I dared not pause for more than a moment, however, or would have found myself upturned and dragged along by the others. I had just a few seconds to stare at the sky, and saw it was very soft and gray, tinged with pink, and the clouds drawn across it seemed like thin, translucent silk. There was but one tree to be seen, and although this was without leaves, frost had rimed its upper branches so that it sparkled in the chill air. And indeed everything about that small view of the world seemed different and heightened and beautiful after the darkness and stench of the jail.

We were taken across a mound of grass white with hoarfrost and then led to another part of the castle where the court was to meet, into a dim space named an anteroom. The judge was breakfasting, we were told by a man called an usher, and when he'd eaten and drunk all he wanted, then he would hear our cases. There was a wit among us by the name of Michael Lee, a footpad, small and shrunken and eaten up with scurvy, who, on hearing this, threw a shilling across to the usher and asked him to go and buy a decent bottle of brandy for the judge to have with his breakfast, because he would as soon have him merry as sober.

We waited a goodly time and there was not much talking among us, for, whether it was our first time or no, we were all afeared of what punishment we might receive and whether this might be accomplished quickly so that we could be out of jail for Christmas.

Michael Lee was called first. His irons were knocked off so that he was no longer chained to the rest of us, and he was pushed up the stairs that led to the courtroom. After only about ten minutes we heard a faint roar and some applause, and then he was pushed back into our room and manacled again.

We asked him how he'd fared, and he replied pretty well. He'd been sentenced to be branded on the cheek, and he professed he was content with this, for it was his third offense and he might have been hanged. He was more troubled than he cared to admit, however, and touched his cheek over and over, muttering that it was nothing at all, 'twould be over very quickly, he would make sure he was in his cups so he wouldn't feel a thing, and so on. In the end the others told him to quiet his mouth.

Another man went in then, accused of fraud. He was found guilty and sentenced to be sent to the Americas. They called an old widow woman next, who came back weeping, saying she'd been ordered to stay in the prison until someone paid the three shillings she owed her grocer, and she felt she might never see her home again.

There came another wait, and those of us who had not yet been called were a-twitching with the worry of it all. While we waited, I tidied my hair back as best I could with the combs that Jane had given me (although it felt lank and foul and was running with fleas), and tried to rub some spots of dirt from my gown, for I didn't want to appear frowsy and lackadaisical. *Cleanliness is next to godliness,* it says in a text on the wall of the dairy, which was sewn by Lady Mary's own hand. If I looked clean, I wondered, would I appear more innocent? Was a maid who wore grimy clothes more likely to have killed her own babe?

At last an usher of the court came and called "Anne Green!" in a loud voice, and, although I had been waiting and looking forward to this moment for many days, when I heard that call of my name I felt a coldness and a terror go through me and became extreme afraid.

My manacles were struck off, and I'd just a moment to rub the smarting places on my legs where the bracelets had rubbed and blistered before I was pushed up the stairs by a uniformed sergeant at arms, who then followed me up and stood behind me all the while to prevent my escape.

My first impression of the courtroom was that we were in a church, for it was a tall and well-ordered space, with dark wooden paneling and windows all around. In this room were a great many seats and benches, and on these a number of people were seated. I've seen pictures of a play performed in a theater, and it reminded me something of this, for although the seats were at different angles, they faced toward one thing, and that thing was the little wooden box in which I was standing.

My legs were light and frail without the irons on them, and such was my apprehension of what was to come that I felt myself swaying and had to grip the edge of the box in order to stay upright. Once steady, I began hesitantly to look around me and saw, to my great horror, Sir Thomas and Lady Reade sitting very close and both staring at me with stone-cold eyes. Behind them the people seemed all of a blur, for my eyes were out of sorts having so much light after so long. I saw several of my fellow servants from the house, however, and my dear ma and pa dressed in their Sunday best, and my two brothers, who must have come from Banbury, and others whom I could not concentrate on or give name to just then, for I felt light in the head and full of wonder as to how I had ended up there.

To my right were seated two rows of gentlemen I took to be the jury, looking pompous and severe enough to make me tremble anew, and several legal gentlemen in wigs and gowns, and a lot more, I think, from the university, some with purple gowns, and some younger men who were perhaps scholars, with black gowns over their suits and an air of anticipation about them.

And all there to see me.

I began to sway and might have fallen if the sergeant at arms had not gripped my arm firmly, telling me in a harsh voice to keep my place. A man in a steel-colored wig, who was named Dr. Gray, then stood up and began to speak. He asked my name and where I was born and I told him, but I had to repeat this twice more, for he said he could barely hear me. And as I spoke, everything I said was written down by two scribes, who were sitting on low seats scribbling and scratching away with their quill pens.

I was asked to swear on the Holy Bible that I would speak the absolute truth, so help me God, which I did, and someone addressed me crossly, saying that I really must speak louder or they could not proceed, and when I looked up to where the voice had come from, I saw the judge for the first time. He was in velvet robes with fur at the edges and had a great waved mane of white hair. I found out later that his name was Judge Unton Croke, although I had to call him "my lord" whenever I addressed him.

Dr. Gray called the names of the men of the jury one by one, and said they were all gentlemen and would stand as jurors for his highness Oliver Cromwell, Lord Protector of the Commonwealth of England, Scotland, and Ireland, and I looked around fearfully in case *he* should be there too, but it did not appear he was. After calling out their names, Dr. Gray said that I could object to any of the jury if I wished, but I didn't really understand what was meant by this, so said to him that I thought they'd do well enough, thank you kindly.

Someone stood, unrolled a parchment, and read out the charge against me, which was that on the first day of December in the year of Our Lord 1650 I had sought to cover the sin of fornication with a greater sin, namely I had most unnaturally and barbarously murdered my child so that it would not be discovered that I had conceived a bastard. And he asked if I pleaded guilty to this charge, or not guilty.

And I said not guilty, and he corrected me, "Not guilty, *my lord*," and I repeated this.

And then things began to happen very quickly. Various people stood up in the courtroom and said different things, some of which I didn't understand, and others went into another wooden box similar to mine and were spoken to by Dr. Gray or the judge and asked questions. And at some time Dr. Gray asked me if I'd known all along that I was with child.

I said that yes, I had thought that I was, and he then inquired how long it had been since my courses had ceased. This question embarrassed me somewhat, but I replied as sensibly as I could that I thought they had ceased about five or six months previous to my giving birth. Dr. Gray wanted to know if I'd informed my employers of my condition so that arrangements could be made for my lying-in, and I said I had not. And when he heard this, he said I had therefore concealed my condition from the world.

I began to weep and said I had not, for I had told my mother, and also told the father of the child.

"And who is the father?" asked Dr. Gray.

I took a breath, and was about answer up with the name of Master Geoffrey, when Sir Thomas stood up.

"I object," he said. "How is the naming of the father of this poor dead infant relevant to this case?"

Dr. Gray said, "It may be—for perhaps its father had a hand in its demise."

"But whatever she says, this girl's word cannot be believed. Being caught out in her foul deed, she may name someone out of spite."

"But I say it may be a way of discerning her intentions," Dr. Gray answered. "Was she about to be married to the man in question, perhaps?"

"She was not," Sir Thomas said. "And besides, she is nothing but a lying whore and always has been!"

I'm pleased to recall that there was a gasp of horror across the court at these spiteful words, and Sir Thomas was told to apologize to the judge for uttering them. He did so, but grudgingly, and I felt very much disquieted after.

I was asked about my travail in the house of office and how long I'd stayed there, and also if I'd picked up the child after I'd birthed it and tried to aid its breathing in any way.

I hesitated, longing to say that I *had* done something to help it, but, remembering that I was on an oath to speak the truth, did not dare. "The child was pale and still," I replied haltingly, "and made neither sound nor movement, so I did not touch it."

"But how did you know without a shadow of doubt that it was dead?" the judge asked me.

"I knew it, my lord, for it was too small to have ever lived," I said, and these simple words sounded strange and unnatural to my own ears, and I began to be afeared that no one would believe me.

A midwife was brought up to the stand who said she'd been working for seventeen years and had attended hundreds of births, and they asked if she'd examined the body of my dead babe and what was her opinion of it. I held my breath here and could not look at her for fear of what she was going to say, but to my relief she answered up with conviction that in her opinion the child was not viable, for it was but nine inches long and hardly formed.

"It was formed enough for it to be seen that it was a male child, however," Dr. Gray pointed out, and she admitted that this was correct. Someone else in the court asked if a certain test had been carried out to ascertain whether the lungs of the dead child had ever held air, and it was answered that it had not.

The midwife left the stand, and the judge addressed me. "Were you very frightened when you knew you were with child?" he asked.

"Yes, my lord." I nodded. "For I knew the punishments that could be afforded me."

"So did you ever seek to rid yourself of the burden of it?"

I felt my cheeks flush.

"Remember that you have put your hand on the book containing God's word, and sworn to tell the truth before him," he warned.

I hung my head. "Yes, I . . . I once took a cordial prescribed by a cunning woman," I said, and heard a little stir in the court. He asked when this was, and I told him the truth of it.

"And—this cordial having not brought about the change you required, what arrangements did you make for your confinement?"

"I did not make any, my lord."

"So it might be presumed from this that you did not ever intend the child to live?"

I heard a murmuring from the court.

"And that you sought to hide the sin of your fornication with the greater one of murder."

"I never did, my lord!"

"But you admit the sin of the flesh?"

I nodded. "But I was tricked into sinning with false promises!" I said, and thought again to give Master Geoffrey's name. When I looked up, however, I saw Sir Thomas glaring at me, shaking his head as much as to say, *You dare to say* . . . and I did not dare.

Next Sir Thomas went into the witness box to speak, and gave his name and a great list of all his titles, like Lord of the Manors of Beedon, Appleford, Barton, and a great many other places, and said that he was granted M.A. at Middle Temple and had served as High Sheriff of Berkshire, Oxfordshire, and elsewhere, and these accreditations went on for so long that I lost track of why we were being told of them. When he'd finished, Dr. Gray asked if he was the employer of the accused, Anne Green, and what he thought of my character.

"She is a maid in my employ," he said, "but until recently I had no idea of what type of a woman she was." Beside him, Lady Mary's eyes were closed as if she didn't want to see too much, and her hands clasped as if in prayer.

"And what sort of a woman is she, sir?" asked Dr. Gray.

"The very lowest kind," said Sir Thomas. "I was shocked and revolted to find that one of my own maidservants had been acting so lewdly, for I believed that I kept a Christian household."

"Quite, sir," said Dr. Gray.

"But since that . . . that *woman* was arrested, I've heard that she'd been making herself available to any man who came a-calling, whether he be barber, blacksmith, or baker. She's brought shame upon my house and my good name with her loose and vulgar ways."

"I have not been loose!" I cried out. "Or only with one. And before I lay with him, I was unblemished."

"So you say, madam," said Sir Thomas dismissively.

"You may ask my fellow servants," I said to the judge. "Ask them of my character."

The judge made a gesture toward the open court, as much as to say *Did anyone there want to speak for me*, but there was naught but silence. I was sad at this, but with Sir Thomas standing in front so puffed up and haughty, which of them was going to speak and say well of me and be cast onto the streets for their pains? Besides, so solemn and daunting was the air of the court that a mere servant would hardly have dared get to his feet, let alone have spoken.

"Have you anything to say in mitigation?" Dr. Gray asked me next, and I did not understand what this meant and must have looked a buffoon, for he added, "Is there anything you want to say which might lessen your culpability? For instance, perhaps you overlaid the child, or stopped its breathing for just a moment because it was crying, and so by mistake it died."

"I did not!" I answered indignantly.

He bowed to the judge. "I therefore conclude the case."

The judge spoke to the jury, telling them that they should now decide whether I spoke the truth or not, and they all got up and went into a huddle on the back bench, speaking together for ten minutes or so. And all this time I stood in the box hanging my head—for I could not look out upon those gathered there, and was scarce able to draw breath for the terror of my situation.

When at last the twelve men regained their seats, the nearest of their number stood up. I looked toward him, and as I did so there came a harsh cough from Sir Thomas, and I swear that the juryman's eyes flickered toward his. The apprehension came to me then that all was not going to go well for me.

The juryman said, "We have reached our verdict, my lord."

"And is it the verdict of you all?" said the judge.

"It is."

The judge asked, "How do you find the defendant, Anne Green: guilty or not guilty of murder?"

"Guilty, my lord."

There was a gasp in the room, and I let the words settle into my brain. I recall screaming, then, "'Tis not true!

May God be my witness I did not kill my child!" and I saw my mother on her feet, also crying out.

"Silence!" Dr. Gray said.

"I will now pass sentence," said the judge when all was quiet again, and there was a pause before a tiny sound crossed the room: no more than a soft intake of breath from all assembled there.

Bewildered to know what could have caused this, for he had not yet said what the sentence was, I looked to the judge and saw that he had placed a square of black silk foursquare upon his long white wig.

"Anne Green," he said solemnly, "you have been found guilty of infanticide—that is, the murder of your child—and I therefore sentence you to be taken to the castle yard and there hanged by the neck until dead."

I stared ahead, uncomprehending.

"You should spend the rest of your time on this Earth praying for forgiveness for the monstrous sin you have committed, and may the Lord have mercy on your soul."

The sergeant at arms beside me stepped forward and asked, "When should the sentence be carried out, my lord?"

"Tomorrow morning at seven thirty," the judge answered.

I looked at him blankly, for I could scarce understand what had been ordered.

"You are dismissed," he said to me, and called for the next case to be brought in.

As the sergeant at arms pushed me toward the stairs, I was aware of one more thing happening: of a smart gentleman (wearing the tasselled cap of a learned man and a long red silk waistcoat over a black cloak) standing and making a plea that my corpse, after hanging, should be granted to the university's medical department so that it might be dissected for the furtherance of medical knowledge.

And I heard my mother's screams at this before I was pushed downstairs and re-shackled.

Chapter 20

By one o'clock there were twenty-five people in the dissection room, and by one thirty, thirty-one. All were male but for Anne Green, and the room was no longer cold, but stuffy, and smelled of moist wool cloaks, stale tobacco, and damp hair. Everyone being hungry, a flagon of ale was sent for, and Martha, who had only anticipated a dozen for dinner, appeared with woefully inadequate portions of bread, cheese, and sliced meats and placed them on a folding butler's table in the corridor just outside the room. The doctors hoped that some of the onlookers might, on seeing the paucity of the food, go and take their dinner in the nearby Rainbow, but no one seemed inclined to do so.

Throughout this time, Robert continued with his note-taking.

12.45 p.m. — The patient was bled again, and four ounces of blood flowed freely into the metal bowl.

12.55 p.m. — Her legs were bound with linen strips to try and encourage the flow of blood to them.

1.00 p.m. — The sore and bruised place on her neck (where rubbed by the hangman's noose) was oiled in order to soothe it.

1.15 p.m.—Her hands were chafed to warm and stimulate them.

1.25 p.m.—Hot stones were placed beneath her feet.

1.40 p.m.—A plaister of sheep dung and pitch was mixed and applied to her breast to endeavor to warm her heart.

Anne Green's response to all these attentions was to flutter her eyelids tremulously, but so quickly did this happen that those who were paying attention to another part of her body missed it. A pulse, however, had been detected by Dr. Petty, who was said to have sensitive fingers, but not by Dr. Willis. Dr. Bathurst was undecided as to whether or not he could feel anything.

Robert recorded the ministrations carefully, willing her to live with every fiber of his being. He vowed to himself that she was not—could not be—guilty of murder.

A notice had been received from the offices of the prison granting the woman named Anne Green a temporary reprieve, and this had been nailed to the wall behind where they worked, in case Sir Thomas should try to remove her.

"If we *can* revive her, you know what this will do for Oxford, don't you?" Dr. Willis said to Dr. Petty. He spoke in a low voice, but Robert, standing close by, was privy to their words.

"We will obtain more fresh corpses, perhaps," came the answer. "That will be an excellent good thing."

Dr. Willis nodded. "But as well as that . . ."

Dr. Petty didn't reply, for he was wondering whether to apply another plaister above Anne's heart and what materials he should use to make it.

"Why, people will flock here!" Dr. Willis went on. "Oxford will become a holy city. They'll make a shrine of the place!"

"They may." Dr. Petty nodded.

"They will! The people of England have passed through the abyss that was the Civil War and are looking for proof of God. This housemaid may be regarded as a messenger from him, to prove his existence."

With Dr. Petty looking unmoved, he went on earnestly, "William, this woman called on God to prove her innocence to the world. If she lives, then he has heard and saved her."

Dr. Petty smiled. "Perhaps."

"It can only be a most excellent thing for us!"

"Yes, this could make our reputations. If she survives, then word will spread across the world of our success."

"Our success through Christ," Dr. Willis reminded him piously. "What we've done through his good graces."

"But what," Dr. Bathurst interceded, "if the girl persists in this present state; this condition where she seems neither fully dead nor completely alive?"

The medical men exchanged glances.

"For I have heard," Dr. Bathurst continued, "of someone who slept for a hundred years and didn't speak or move in all that time."

The other two smiled. "That's but a fairy tale!" said Dr. Petty.

"Well, perhaps not a hundred years, but a very great number," Dr. Bathurst assured them. "He was in a trance or a sleep and couldn't be waked from it. About sixty years, I believe it was, before he finally died."

"Well, if Anne Green decides to play Sleeping Beauty with us," said Dr. Willis, "they will still flock to Oxford!" He paused. "What if, though, she has no soul when she recovers? What if she is merely some form of wraith?"

The others exchanged concerned looks but did not reply.

Robert, after being privy to these conversations and prompted by further calls from the crowd outside, prepared himself to speak by breathing in deeply several times. Rehearsing in his head what he was to say, and pointing first outside and then at Anne in order to illustrate his speech, he asked, "M . . . m . . . m . . . mother?"

"She is not a mother," Dr. Petty said, glancing at him. "For that was the charge against her. That she had—"

Robert shook his head, pointed to Anne again, and then outside. "Her . . . her . . . her . . . m . . . m . . ."

"I think he means her mother is waiting outside in this foul weather," Dr. Bathurst said.

"That's something we should think on," said Dr. Petty. "Should we fetch the woman here? Should her family be witness to this miracle? This near-miracle," he amended.

Robert nodded vehemently, concerned about Anne's family, but just as concerned about her opening her eyes and finding herself on a dissection table surrounded by doctors wearing bloodied aprons and wielding instruments, with ne'er a familiar face nearby.

"I say they shouldn't come in yet," Dr. Willis declared, after thinking a moment. "Suppose she doesn't survive? It would be cruel to raise hopes that might well prove unfounded."

Dr. Bathurst lowered his voice slightly. "And suppose she lives, but runs mad? What then?"

"Indeed." Dr. Petty sighed as he considered this. "We must remember that her family will only be simple folk, and this may be more than they can comprehend."

Dr. Willis nodded. "They've seen her hanged and pronounced dead . . . and then to find that she is suddenly *not* dead . . ."

"They will think her an angel!" said Dr. Bathurst.

"'Tis enough to make even a wise man consider his sanity," said Dr. Petty. He turned to Robert. "Perhaps we should keep things within this room for now, and then tomorrow morning, if she still lives . . ."

"They'll continue waiting outside," Dr. Bathurst said. "They'll wait there until they receive what remains of her."

Robert felt a stab of disappointment. He'd wanted to—not, alas, tell the family himself—but to witness them being told. He'd wanted to share their joy.

"Tomorrow," Dr. Willis said to Robert, and he nodded.

A man wearing black entered the room. He was elaborately dressed, however, and his tall hat was decorated with braid, loops of ribbon, and a gold buckle, so it was immediately apparent that he had no truck with the Puritans.

"Is it true?" he was heard to say excitedly as he squeezed through the crowd. "Is it really true? They're talking about it all over."

"'Tis true—but get to the back," someone called to him.

"And there's no room to wear that hat in here!"

The doctors looked at each other. "And as for the news staying within the room . . ." remarked Dr. Petty with some irony.

At eight o'clock that evening the doctors finally packed up their instruments. The mob waiting in the street had dwindled, so they'd been told, to a core of about eight, and these few had obtained a covered cart from somewhere and settled themselves in it for the night, prepared to wait as long as they had to to obtain Anne's remains and give them a Christian burial.

Anne Green had been put through every medical procedure known to man, and had neither fully come around nor declined further. Her heart was beating more strongly, certainly; each doctor had now felt a pulse at her wrist and throat. Various cordials had been poured into her mouth, her face was now pinker and appeared more swollen, her throat had turned blue and purple with bruising, and traces of sweat had appeared under her arms. As a crowning proof, the doctors had obtained a small mirror, and Anne's breath had clouded it as evidence of air within her. In total, forty-six people had passed through the dissection room. Now all except the doctors, Christopher Wren, and Robert had gone home.

As he folded up his notebook Robert looked out of the window at the cart, its canvas covering showing the soft glow of candlelight within, and wondered if any news of Anne had reached her family. Assuming that she still lived, he intended to be there the next morning when they were told.

But first they had to get her through the night.

"She ought to be moved to a proper bed," Dr. Petty said. "How can she get a good night's sleep on a dissection table?"

"She should certainly be kept as warm as possible overnight," Dr. Willis said. "If she's allowed to get cold again it may undo all the good we've done."

At that moment Martha came in collecting beakers and bowls. She was yawning broadly, for her day had started at five that morning and she wanted to go to her bed. Dr. Petty's eyes fell on her, and he addressed Mr. Clarke.

"Your maid—does she live on the premises?" he asked.

Mr. Clarke nodded. "She has a small room at the end of the corridor."

"With her own bed?"

"Indeed," came the startled reply.

"Would she mind . . . ?" began Dr. Petty, then whispered the rest of the sentence in the apothecary's ear. Mr. Clarke shrugged; he appeared doubtful.

Nevertheless, a gently appeasing expression spread over Dr. Petty's face. "Martha," he began tentatively, "we have it in mind to give you a bedfellow."

Martha's jaw dropped. She'd been propositioned several times by scholars, but never by one of the doctors. And never in so open a fashion.

"Well, sir . . ." she began, blushing.

"No, fear not, not that!" said Dr. Petty hastily. "We are anxious for our patient here, and want to make sure she stays warm overnight. We wondered if we could prevail upon you to—"

Martha gave a short scream. "Never! What—lie with a dead corpse?"

"She's not dead," Wren said gently. "Merely . . . sleeping."

"You can be of *great* help to us," said Dr. Petty. "It may make all the difference to whether she lives or dies."

"When this case is being written of in the annals of medical history, then your name will be mentioned as being of particular significance," said Dr. Willis.

"And we will see to it that you receive the sum of five shillings," added Dr. Petty.

Robert looked at Martha's face and saw her expression falter and waver, going from fear and near-tearfulness to a kind of reluctant eagerness. "What would I have to do?" she asked.

"Keep her warm, that's all."

"Perhaps sleep with an arm about her."

"If you could manage to rub her limbs a little . . ."

Martha gulped and nodded. "I'll try, sirs," she said. "I'll try."

Chapter ~ 21

As I go over these remembrances in my head, I seem to hear the low murmur of voices. Is it a conversation, or one person on his own? Certainly I can hear a man's voice. Am I then nearing the gates of heaven? Perhaps St. Peter is approaching, offering blessings—or perhaps 'tis the devil, come to seek his own. But I am innocent! The devil will surely know this and dare not take me.

The low murmuring ceases, and I immediately lose the sense of when I heard it. A moment ago? Ten years past? Did I imagine or dream it?

But my life is almost told, and I bring myself back to my last day on Earth, where, early in the morning, I sat on a stool in the condemned cell, my hands reaching toward a few sticks burning in the grate. The flames that rose from these glittered as merry and bright as flames always do, for they didn't know that they were burning in the room of one whose last moments were approaching, one who would shortly be hanged by the neck until dead.

I'd dismissed the cleric who wanted to save my soul, for he and I had fallen to disagreement over my refusal to confess I was guilty of murder, or to ask God's forgiveness for such a thing. He'd insisted that judge and jury had found me guilty, and I'd insisted that, nevertheless, I had not committed any such crime. In the end, frustrated almost to the point of tears at my stubbornness, he had left, saying he'd return the next morning to accompany me to the prison yard, for the sight of the scaffold led many an obstinate person to confess their wickedness and, at the last, throw themselves on God's mercy.

I had asked for a fire to be built in my cell, which was granted to me as my last wish, and sat before it going over my life, as I do now in this black and eerie netherworld in which I find myself. And I wondered then—and wonder still—on the strangeness of life, and how the circumstances had occurred that led to my downfall, and if they might have been avoided by my having had a natal chart cast (as I've heard that the gentry do) showing what harsh planets were overhead. I might then have anticipated my coming disgrace and perhaps prevented such a thing.

During that long night I hadn't felt so much affrighted as weary and disbelieving, for it seemed that I must have some part in a mummers' play or be acting out a ballad. Surely 'twas not possible that I was in jail and condemned to hang on the morrow? Where had my life fled? How had it happened so?

At six o'clock a turnkey came in with my breakfast, which, as it was my last, was red herrings, anchovies, and fresh-baked bread. I felt hungry and was pleased to see such things, but as soon as I put them in my mouth they turned to ashes and refused to be swallowed, so I had to discard them.

At seven o'clock my sister, mother, and father were allowed into my cell, and my heart leaped with joy to see them—but fell again as I remembered what they were there for. We wept and held each other, and it seemed to me the first time we had ever done such a thing, for we weren't a family given much to the linking of arms or the kissing of cheeks. Even my father shed tears, which made me exceedingly sorrowful.

My mother, who is ever a sensible woman, recovered first and said that I should now prepare myself and try to have as respectable a death as possible, for she wouldn't like to think of me going wailing and screaming to meet my maker in front of the crowd that would be gathered outside in the yard. And I said that I'd do my best to compose myself and go with grace to meet him.

"But it surely won't come to that—for it must be seen that a mistake's been made," said Jane, a tone of yearning in her voice. "A pardon will come for sure!"

My mother shook her head. "We mustn't think on that. Who in the world would be trying to obtain a reprieve for us? No, 'tis only the gentry who can make representation to the law and get things changed." She took my hand and held it tightly. "We must prepare ourselves for the worst, Anne."

"Although afterward I intend to pursue the whoreson young master of that house and lay your death at his feet!" my father said with some anger. "Yes, e'en if I have to go to Northumberland or whatever fartling place they've hid him."

"Stay," my mother said. "What good would that do?"

"'Tis what a father *should* do!"

My mother sighed. "So I'd be left without a husband as well as without a daughter? And then where would I be?"

"Tush!" went my father, muttering under his breath.

"Where are my brothers?" I asked after a moment.

"They'll be there in the yard," said Ma, "and more neighbors and friends from home as well."

My heart felt like a stone. "And all coming to see me die . . ."

"Not only for that," Ma said soothingly, "but to be with you at your last. To support and pray for you, and to help guide your soul to paradise."

I began weeping. "My soul may not get there, for my body . . . my body will be cut into pieces!"

"Hush," Ma said. "I have spoken to the doctor, and he's promised to take the utmost care of your body and to treat it with respect. And . . . and . . ." But she turned away here with a sob, and couldn't continue.

"When you're brought home and put in the church-yard, I'll put flowers on your grave every day!" Jane said, and then she too burst out crying.

————◆•◆◆•◆————

And so the minutes went on, and with each of them my mood changed: first fear and trembling, then bewilderment and disbelief, then sorrow, then railing against my fate, and then a return to fear again. And by and by the cleric came in and spoke to my mother and father and knelt with them in prayer, and again addressed me, although of course I still would not admit guilt, for which he seemed very sorry.

Jane washed my face for me and brushed out my hair, and had brought a red ribband, which color she said I must wear to show that I was brave, and with this we tied back my hair so that it would be out of the way of the hangman's noose and not get caught up. And the four of them kept asking how I was feeling, and if I would be strong, and each time I answered yes, although indeed I didn't feel well or strong, but just wanted the whole matter over with, for being dead could surely not be as bad as waiting to die and seeing your family suffer beside you.

I was worried about how they would be after, for my ma and pa looked very old and sad, and I tried to speak to Jane to tell her to mind them well and be a good daughter, but each time I got three words into the saying of this I'd break down and be unable to finish saying what I had started. During this time all of us were crying and shivering by turn, for the fire had gone out and it was a cold and dark gray morning, with sleet dripping from the sky, and it truly felt as if the end of the world was nigh.

I knew it was near my time when the prison governor came in with a sergeant at arms. Both spoke to me quite kindly and said that I had nothing to fear, I'd feel no pain and die quickly. And the soldier said that when I was pushed off the ladder, my father and brothers should hang on my legs if they had a mind to, for that would speed my end. The governor asked what were my worldly goods, and to whom did I wish to leave them, and I told him of all my clothes, including the bodice, and said that I wished to leave them to my mother to do with as she thought fit. He asked me to disrobe so that my clothes would not be spoiled, and I undressed down to my shift and gave my gown and cloak to Ma, although I was exceeding cold.

"'Tis time to go," the governor said, on hearing the clock strike. "If you please, mistress . . ."

"Oh, give us just a little longer," pleaded my ma, holding on to me tightly and looking at me with something like hunger in her expression.

He shook his head. "We have two hangings today," he said, "and this is listed to be the first."

"Then, by your leave, let our Anne be the second," Pa begged. "Allow us a little more time together."

The governor shook his head. "'Twill be easier now—the waiting is the worst part, and the crowd outside will have grown in an hour's time." He regarded me with some sympathy. "'Tis more of an ordeal when it's a big crowd.

More 'prentices to shout and throw rubbish."

And so it was determined that I should go, and I kissed my family with a passion. My manacles were knocked off, and the governor led me outside, telling me to put my hand on his shoulder to help support myself, for every part of me was trembling so violently I would otherwise have fallen. He led me along an open passageway and into the prison yard, which was bleak and desolate, with not so much as a blade of grass, a tuffet of green moss, or a bird to be seen, but just ugly gray stone buildings running with rain and a strange and eerie feeling of anticipation in the air, as if the world was holding its breath.

The scaffold rose in front of me and, seeing the ugly reality of it, I swayed and almost fell, but the governor and sergeant caught me between them and held me upright. Standing beside this crude wooden structure, I looked around me and saw that the crowd consisted of perhaps eighty people. These included my brothers, some gowned scholars, learned men of the university, merchants, townspeople, the two carters who'd brought me in, the Reverend Coxeter, a governess from a dame school I once attended, several old neighbors, the squire from Steeple Barton, and also a group of my fellow servants from Dun's Tew. Indeed it seemed very marvelous to me that almost everyone I'd ever known in my life was collected before me, and I was able to pick out each of their faces as if they were portraits in the long gallery at the manor house. I saw Sir Thomas there too, and quickly turned away, for within his countenance I could see the hated face of Master Geoffrey.

As I turned from Sir Thomas my eyes alighted on John

Taylor, and for a brief moment my heart again leaped with joy, for his face was neither accusing nor vengeful but was filled with compassion. This gave me some small peace, for it told me that he'd forgiven me and that, at some passing time, he had even loved me. I smiled at him, though my head was swimming and I felt as if I was in a strange daydream, for 'twas the most curious thing to think that in a short moment I would cease to exist.

Beside the gibbet stood the hangman, wearing heavy clothes and a blanket against the weather, also a leather facemask so that he would not be recognized after. He was big and burly, looking very like the bogeyman that your ma tells you will come after you if you sin. And so he had.

"You must now kneel and make your peace with God," said the cleric, and he bade me kneel down beside the scaffold. The Reverend Coxeter pushed his way through the crowd and knelt with me too, and close by were the scribes, holding their parchments under their capes to shield them from the rain and waiting to hear what I had to say. First the two clerical gentlemen and I sang a psalm together, which was number twenty-three and which I knew from long ago; then he asked me if I would confess my sins, for I had not much time now before I entered into Christ's kingdom and came face to face with the Lord God.

This was a truly mighty thought and filled me with awe, and I could not but glance up to the solid gray sky and think about what he might be like and how he might receive me. I urged my mind upward while the rain pattered down on my face, but was offered no trace of the heaven beyond.

"You must now confess all," said the cleric.

"I will, and truly," I answered up. "I am guilty of the

wicked sin of fornication."

"Anything more?" he asked, urging me with his eyes to say what he wanted to hear.

I nodded. "I am guilty of causing my family suffering."

"And of what else?"

"Nothing of any consequence," I said. I hesitated and then made brave to answer, "And I would not be guilty of aught, except that I was led into sin in the house of my employer, Sir Thomas Reade."

Alarm spread across the cleric's face at this, and I wondered if his living came under the authority of Sir Thomas. He shook his head sorrowfully. "Then may our Lord God forgive you all your sins and allow you to enter into the next world without shame," he said, and offered me his hand to help me to my feet.

I began to tremble so frightfully that Ma ran forward and tried to put a blanket over my bare shoulders and embrace me again, but the hangman pushed her away, saying it would hinder things. She had a length of cord with her, which she requested should be tied around the bottom of my shift for modesty's sake, and he allowed her to do this. He gave me a hood, which he ordered me to put over my head, but my fingers were shaking so violently that they wouldn't do my bidding, and the cleric had to fasten it for me. Just before he closed the flap that went across my eyes, I looked across to my ma so that her dear face would be the last that I saw, and wanted to smile at her but could not, for I was sick with fear down to my very bones.

The hangman put a heavy coil of rope over me and around my neck, and bade me go up the ladder, which stood beside the gibbet. I climbed seven steps, feeling it shaking beneath me, while the icy rain fell on my bare shoulders and trickled down the front of my shift. I braced myself for lewd shouts, or for rotten fruit to be thrown, but these did not come. I heard, though, a scream from Jane and some cries of protest from my family, and several other voices in the crowd shouting, "Shame!" although I didn't know whether these meant shame on me for the crime I was accused of, or shame at my wretched fate.

I felt the hangman reach above my head and fix the rope that was to hang me, and someone—I believe it was one of the scribes—called to ask if I had any last words.

"I protest my innocence," I said, although my voice was so choked that I don't know if I was heard aright, "and I ask that God in his wisdom should let the world know this."

"Anything else?"

"Only that all maidens who are tempted from the path of virtue should think on me and be persuaded against such a course. And I pray that my death be quick and my family not suffer too much after."

I began saying, "And may God convey me swiftly—" but before I could add the words "to paradise", felt a violent push at my back and fell forward off the ladder. The noose around my neck tightened, and though I'd been told that—in order to make my passing all the quicker—I must try not to breathe, I found that this was impossible and, panicking, could not help but struggle to rasp in a minute amount of air through a throat now horribly constricted by the ring of rough rope. I'd wanted to make my last thoughts simple and wholesome, but there was no room for thoughts of any kind, for my senses were immediately assailed by a pain of such intensity that my head became filled with a searing white light.

I hung for a moment, suspended, felt my legs jerk and, unbidden, my body convulse, shudder, and twist in the air so that it seemed that I was flying twixt heaven and Earth, then knew no more until I came into this drear darkness.

Chapter ~ 22

Robert, back in his lodgings, couldn't sleep. Scarlett, too, seemed fretful, and instead of perching quietly on the wooden railing that ran along the balcony abutting Robert's room, could be heard skittering up and down on the planks of its floor, pecking sharply at the occasional wood louse that appeared from out of the sodden wood or a blade of grass that had grown through the knotholes.

Thoughts of corpses floated through Robert's mind. Anne Green, and that other, dreamlike one. His mother. To think that he'd recalled his mother when he hadn't even known he'd ever seen her!

There were many answers to be sought to many questions, but his chief anxiety at that hour, that midnight hour when all ills and suspicions can seem overwhelming, was Anne Green. He somehow felt a responsibility for her well-being. Was Martha keeping watch over her? Would she call Mr. Clarke if she felt her charge was in danger? How would a housemaid know such a thing? Suppose Anne passed away in the night just for want of warmth, a rousing cordial, or because her heart had faltered at a critical moment and had not been stimulated?

I want to see her.

Robert leaped out of bed. It wouldn't hurt to check up on her, he thought. He'd find a way in to her for sure — the apothecary's dwelling was one of a number of shops in the High Street that had interconnecting rooms, and all shared a backyard privy.

On retiring the previous night, Robert had, in view of the extreme chill of his room and the lateness of the hour, gone to bed in all his clothes, so only had to don his hat and shoes to be ready. He took his heavy cloak from the hook on the door as he went out and, going across the balcony, threw Scarlett a scrap of hard bread.

Fifteen minutes later, treading quietly, or as quietly as possible on the creaking oak floorboards, Robert made his way along the corridor that led to Martha's room in Mr. Clarke's house in the High Street. He hadn't been challenged on his way, for it was now near two o'clock in the morning and the whole of Oxford was asleep. Neither crier, night-soil man, whore, nor late-night reveler had been encountered on his short journey.

He heard a fierce snoring coming from Martha's room, and upon entering, Robert almost tripped over the recumbent body of Martha herself on the floor, wrapped up in what appeared to be a velvet curtain. He wasn't surprised at this: Martha obviously hadn't relished the thought of sleeping with such ghoulish company and had decided to leave the bed to Anne. This probably wouldn't have been discovered, for in the morning Martha would have been up and about before any of the doctors arrived, eager to claim her five shillings.

The fire in the room had been banked up in order to last until morning but was now only glowing, and Robert, stepping over Martha's form and lifting his candlestick so that the light would fall onto Anne's face, approached the bed with trepidation. Looking down at her still form, however, he noted with relief that her face held the same tranquil expression, as if she slept in peace. He placed the candlestick on the night table, picked up one of her hands to count her pulse, then bent his ear to her mouth to note her breathing. When he straightened up he was smiling slightly to himself, thinking her improved; her breathing was significantly deeper and her hands were less clenched than before. She seemed a little warmer, too, in spite of Martha's failure as a bedfellow.

"I thought you might have died," Robert said to her in a low voice. "I couldn't sleep, so I decided I'd come along and see how you fared." As with Scarlett, he found himself speaking to her quite normally. Perhaps, he thought with something approaching levity, that was the answer: to try and see everyone as innocuous as a chicken or a cadaver. *They* weren't about to laugh at him or try to complete his sentences.

He brought a chair close to the bed and sat upon it, staring at Anne. It wouldn't hurt to talk to her, he thought. He'd been told once—by Dr. Bathurst, if he remembered rightly—that hearing was the first and last faculty a human possessed, so perhaps speaking to her would somehow penetrate the lower levels of her consciousness. Besides, he found that he wanted to speak to her for his own sake; it would be a delight to address a pretty young woman and to know she wasn't going to stare at him as if he was a lunatic, or giggle behind her fingers.

"Are you going to live, Anne Green?" he asked and then, more reflectively, "And where have you been while you haven't been living . . . when you haven't been here?" Boldly, he took up her hand and stroked it. "You had many visitors yesterday. Scores of people came to stare. And today, later today, if you thrive, there'll be more. They sent a horse to London last night to inform some very important doctors. They'll come. Indeed, Cromwell himself may come when he hears of these happenings."

Anne drew in a slightly deeper breath, which caught in her throat and made a soft growling sound. Robert felt her pulse; was her heart beating a little faster?

He paused and tucked a strand of hair behind her ear. "I dare say, if you knew how many men have been staring at you, you'd ask for a mirror and brush and want to arrange your locks." He glanced toward the sleeping form of Martha. "Perhaps Martha could be prevailed upon to help brush your hair. Or maybe wash your face, for 'tis still stained with tears from . . . from before, and they've poured several herbal preparations into your mouth, which have turned your lips and chin quite green."

Anne Green slept on. Sleeping Beauty, Robert thought. Suppose she never woke? "Yesterday, watching over you, I remembered something else. A part of my past and another cadaver. But not one that I have remembered before—'twas my mother."

How odd, he thought, that he'd discovered such a thing after so many years. No wonder Dr. Willis's chief goal was to try and discover the secrets of the brain. It was surely a treasure house of miracles and marvels.

"I was but a child, you see, and they hadn't let me see her for days; they made excuses to prevent it. But the more they stopped me from seeing her, the more I yearned to do so. In the middle of the night, therefore, I rose and went to seek her." He paused. "But when I found

her, she was in a coffin, ready to be buried on the morrow.
And then . . . then I can remember climbing onto the table,
looking at her lying there in her nightdress, and wanting
to touch her . . ." He frowned, screwing up his face with
the effort of trying to remember. "And I *did* touch her—
but don't recall what happened after."

There was movement behind him. "You were discovered with her body by one of the household, I should
think," came a voice, and Robert turned in alarm to see
Dr. Willis standing in the doorway, the shadow thrown by
his candle shivering on the wall behind him. "And then
you were picked up and carried off to your nurse, and in
the morning they told you it had all been nothing but a
bad dream and you must forget about it."

Robert got to his feet. "F . . . f . . . f . . . for . . . g . . .
give m . . ." he began.

Dr. Willis raised a hand. "Please," he said. "It's I who
should ask your forgiveness for startling you. I decided to
check on our patient and, hearing a voice, crept along here
in order to discover what was afoot."

"I . . . I . . . I . . ." Robert began.

"And strangely, found you speaking to her quite
lucidly," Dr. Willis continued. "Although, if I may be so
bold, you normally have difficulty even saying your
name, do you not?"

Robert nodded.

"This is a very curious phenomenon," Dr. Willis said
thoughtfully. "I myself have recently observed several
children who, although stammering so badly that others
could not make sense of them, were able to speak easily to
their cat or dog."

Robert smiled. "Ch . . . ch . . . chicken!" he said, pointing at himself and then close to the ground at a chicken's height.

Dr. Willis nodded. "So," he said, "one day I may be able to investigate which part of the brain could cause such an anomaly. One day such mysteries may be revealed." He stared at Anne. "One day . . ."

Robert sat down again as Dr. Willis put his candlestick on the windowsill, then positioned himself comfortably on the end of the bed. "I struggle to understand certain disorders of the brain," he confided. "How some patients become terrified of cats or frogs for no particular reason, or feel compelled to carry out the same task over and over again. Why a man should of a sudden lapse into melancholy, or a woman fall to the ground in a fit and beat her hands upon the ground until they are bloody. All these seem to me to be disorders of the brain. And that may be to say, the soul."

Robert stared at him, wishing he had his notebook.

"And as for our patient," the doctor went on, indicating Anne Green, "she may survive, but we must pray to God that her soul is not lost."

Robert looked at him questioningly.

"If she died, even for an instant, her spirit may have left her body and be unable to find its way back."

Remembering what had been said at lectures, Robert looked at Dr. Willis inquiringly and pointed to his head.

"Is the soul in the brain, you ask?" Dr. Willis shrugged. "I wonder sometimes if it's not either in the brain or the heart, but is fluttering around outside us. We don't know, cannot tell. My great fear is that this girl's soul has flown and will not come back . . . that if and when she awakes, she'll be but a specter. A living form without a soul."

Robert shook his head. Such a thought was unbearable, almost incomprehensible.

Dr. Willis reached over and gripped his arm. "But as to you," he said, "I heard what you were saying to our wench here, and have to tell you that I believe I know the cause of your impediment."

Robert looked at him, startled.

"I believe that severe trauma in a child's life can cause him to develop a stammer. I don't begin to understand why, but sometimes a shock makes us internalize our feelings—we swallow them, in other words, and develop a reluctance to articulate anything. Do you know if you spoke normally at one time?"

Robert nodded, greatly intrigued.

"Perhaps, then, you began your wretched speech patterning after the shock of seeing your mother in her coffin."

"P . . . per . . . per . . ." Robert began.

"And if you can now come to terms with what you saw all those years ago, perhaps discover the truth of it from your father, it may improve. It won't happen in a day, but . . ."

Robert's eyes gleamed with excitement. "Th . . . th . . ." He took another breath. "Th . . . th . . . thank you."

Dr. Willis smiled at him. "So, to our charge here," he said, indicating Anne. "Shall we try and warm her a little more, seeing as Martha has proved less than reliable?"

Robert nodded. He wanted to say how elated he felt; how immensely grateful he was to Dr. Willis for his advice; how he wouldn't rest now until he'd overcome his disability. But of course he could not say any of that. Or not yet.

⁂

Charged up by his memories and his enthusiasm over the task in hand, Robert still sat at Anne's bedside, awake and alert, as dawn broke the next morning. Dr. Willis had gone home two hours before, leaving instructions for the patient's pulse to be taken regularly and, if anything untoward occurred, to wake Martha immediately and send her to him with a message. "Keep talking to our patient, if you will," he'd said to Robert, "and, toward dawn, mix a little of the geneva in the flask with rainwater and try to get her to swallow it. One of us should be with you by eight o'clock." He paused, and a wry smile crossed his lips. "If only to make sure that Sir Thomas Reade doesn't get in and endeavor to steal her away."

By dawn, Robert had told Anne of every incident in his life and had hardly a thing left to say. He stood up, went to the window, and stretched, trying—and failing—to make out the dark shape of the cart outside the gate. No streaks of light could yet be seen in the sky, but, feeling that the morning was not far off, he decided to give Anne the cordial specified by Dr. Willis. Accordingly, after rubbing her arms to stimulate and warm her blood, he prepared the drink, poured a little of it into a beaker, and gently lifted up her head. He remembered Dr. Willis's fears about Anne lacking a soul and suffered a moment's alarm, which made him falter, disturbed. What would someone without a soul be like? Dumb, dull, and unresponsive? A foul fiend? A lunatic?

He forgot his fears as soon as he touched the beaker to Anne's mouth, however, for her lips parted slightly on contact. This had not happened any time before and was astonishing and significant. "Here's something for you to drink," he murmured, startled, "and you may take more later, if you wish." Her lips again moved, and he stared at them, transfixed. "Perhaps . . . perhaps you'd like a warming posset with butter and spices, or a chicken off the spit, or some syllabub," he babbled. "I dare say your fare in prison has been truly foul—I hear tell that prisoners are reduced to eating week-old bread."

His hand shaking slightly, he tipped a little more of the cordial into Anne's mouth and saw, to his excitement, that her throat moved with the swallowing reflex. This also had not been encountered the previous day.

"'Twas well done, Anne!" he encouraged her. "A little more?"

On these commonplace words her lids fluttered, then suddenly rose to reveal sea-blue eyes, which fixed on Robert. He gasped with shock and, staring at her with a mixture of alarm and delight, let her head fall back on the pillow and stepped away from the bed.

Anne's lips parted again, and she whispered, her voice sounding faint, old, and cracked, "May God convey me swiftly to paradise . . ."

Part ~ 2

Chapter ~ 23

I feel my eyelids flutter up and then my eyes move slowly around the room several times, as if they can't remember how to focus or where to direct themselves. After a short moment, however, they alight on a figure in the room sitting beside me, who, when I look with keener eye, turns out to be the fair-headed young fellow I'd briefly seen in the crowd at my hanging, close by to the gibbet. He'd looked at me then with great concern in his eyes, and I'd tried to smile at him. But why can I still see him? Am I still suspended, my head in the hangman's noose—or am I somehow viewing him from heaven? And why is he staring at me, too, with something like awe and disbelief writ across his face?

My eyes move around to take in my surroundings, and I discover that I'm in a small room with pale walls that are stained and blotched with damp in several places. The roof slopes, and there are shutters at the window, their green paint peeling to reveal the bare wood beneath. The stub of a candle burns on the windowsill, and a faint light comes from outside, telling me 'tis either dawn or dusk. There's little in the way of furnishings apart from the bed I'm lying on, a nightstand, coffer, and several hooks from which hang a few tousled clothes. To my mind it's a servant's room. But not the room in Dun's Tew that I share with Susan, nor any room I've been in before. If this is heaven, I think, then 'tis passing strange that it should be so similar to Earth. Am I still to be a servant, then, in the nether life? Should I not be an angel or a spirit creature?

When I think on this, something in my mind makes a connection. "May God convey me swiftly to paradise," I try to say, but though my lips move I hardly make a sound, for my throat feels thick and parched.

The youth beside me gasps. He takes my hand, seemingly to comfort me. "I . . . I . . . it . . . it's . . ." he begins, and then he stops and takes a deep breath. He tries to speak again, fails, then pounds his fist into his palm as if he's angry with himself. He sits for another moment staring at me with disbelief, as if I might vanish like a street huckster's monkey, and then stands up and takes three steps across the floor. He immediately retraces these and sits down again, shaking his head. "C . . . c . . . can't," he mutters. "Can't go."

I wonder if he's mad, or if he's part of heaven or hell. Or—I have a sudden new thought—maybe I'm not in either of those places, a last-minute reprieve having arrived and prevented my hanging. No, that cannot be. I can remember my last moments: Ma's face, the scream from Jane, my final words, and the hard thump on my back as I was pushed off the ladder. Am I in limbo? Is limbo, then, a servant's bedroom?

My head begins to swim as if I've imbibed too much ale. "May God convey me swiftly to paradise," I mouth again, for this seems like a charm against the darkness and, besides, is all I can think of to say.

There is a sudden scream from someone lying on the floor of the bedroom, and when I look down there's a girl there, all wrapped around in fabric. Her hair is tousled and frizzy, her face puffy from sleep. "She's alive!" she screams. "The corpse speaks!" Still wrapped up, she moves on her backside toward the door as if she wants to get as far away from us as she can. "Oh Lord, she spoke!"

I look at her in some surprise, thinking that if anyone should be frightened, it should be I, waking from a night fright in this unfamiliar place among strangers and all unknowing about how I came to be here.

"I . . . it . . . it . . ." the youth begins, and he is talking to her now.

She darts a look at him. "I stayed with her some of the night, sir!" she says. "*Most* of it, I should say—till just before you came in. I went on the floor to give her more room. Oh, you won't tell the other gents, will you?"

He shakes his head.

"Shall I go for Mr. Clarke?" she asks, not taking her eyes off me as she unwraps herself.

He nods and makes some strange forward looping movements with his hands.

"And the other doctors?" she asks.

He nods emphatically and vigorously, as much as to say that yes, everyone must come, and she disappears harum-scarum down the corridor.

He stares back at me, draws a breath, closes his eyes an instant. "D . . . d . . . don't . . . don't . . . be frightened," he says, and he takes my hand in his. "'Twill . . . b . . . be . . . all right." There is another pause, and after a further deep breath he goes on, "Y . . . you . . . you . . ." He speaks carefully, pointing to me as he says the word. "*You* h . . . h . . . have been saved."

I consider this. *I have been saved.* But from what, exactly? You can't be saved from heaven, so it must be that I've been saved from hell.

"You did not die," he says, and then frowns and repeats, "You did not die. Or . . . or perhaps you did. B . . . but now, certainly, you are not dead."

What am I, then? I ask silently.

"You . . . you are still in the world of the living. D . . . d . . . do you understand?"

I continue to stare at him and discover I am shivering all over with cold. I look down at myself and find that I'm wrapped in a coarse blanket, and looking underneath this, discover a horrid and soiled undersmock. No, I think, I do *not* understand. I remember the long dream I'd had where I'd been alive but trapped in the ghastly darkness of my grave. What had come of that?

As I lie staring at him, my mind a perfect turmoil of wondering, he takes off his cloak and tucks it around me. I am suddenly conscious of an overwhelming thirst but, strangely, can't think of the right words to ask for what I want. I open my mouth and point inside, and then, exhausted with the effort of that, I feel my lids flutter down. Every part of me aches, I realize. My limbs, my breasts, my belly, my back—my throat and neck most of all.

"Y . . . you . . . you're thirsty," he says. "You want water? Some beer? Milk?"

I open my eyes and nod to any of these, and he gets up, and then sits down again. "I . . . I can't leave yet," he says. "Your grasp on life is too tenuous. W . . . will you take a little more of this geneva?" I shake my head, for the spirit is coarse and fiery, and what I long for is something soothing and warm.

"The doctors will be here soon, and then I'll go and mix you something else. S . . . something hot against the day, perhaps." He opens the window shutter a little wider, and a morning light falls into the room. "'Tis snowing again, and monstrous cold." He smiles at me. "B . . . but I should tell you that my name is Robert Matthews and I am a scholar of New College, Oxford. And I . . . I'm very pleased to make your acquaintance, Anne Green."

I want to smile a little, for he sounds so strange and formal, and besides, a gentleman of his standing is out of place in a servant's room.

"W . . . we are in Oxford at the house of Mr. Clarke, the apothecary," he says. He glances outside. "Your mother," he begins, and I feel a jolt of shock that he should speak of my ma. "Your mother and others of your family, I believe, are waiting just a little way off."

I close my eyes again and feel tears seep from under my lids. Although I can't say what has happened to me, I do know that I long to see my ma.

"As soon as the doctors arrive, we'll send a message to your family to let them know that you live."

I live! I wriggle my fingers and open and close my eyes several times, just to ensure that I can. Just to prove to myself that I am not under the ground.

How strange it all is. My head swims, and I struggle to understand. Did it all happen? Did the jail and the trial and the hanging really occur, or have I imagined the whole episode in a dream? I put my hand up to my neck and fit the open span of my fingers around it. No, I believe it really happened, for I can feel bruising there, and some swelling and pain. I move my fingers higher and feel the sore patch on my face, which seems grazed with blood.

"All . . . all the damage to your face comes from where the rope bruised you," Robert says. "I . . . is it sore? When Mr. Clarke comes he'll let us have some wintergreen."

I nod, satisfied, and, feeling myself drifting toward sleep, strain to stay awake, for if I sleep then I might return to that dark and drear place I was in before, that mysterious place where the shadow of death lingered.

I feel Robert's fingers at my neck, pressing gently. After a moment he says, "Your pulse is regular and strong. Dr. Willis will be very pleased with you; as will the others."

He says something more, and his words fade and fall into my head, drifting along like twigs in a brook as sleep advances and retreats by turn.

In spite of my endeavors, I believe that I sleep for a while, for when I open my eyes the light in the room is pinker. I hear voices, and two gowned gentlemen come into the room side by side, both looking toward me eagerly. I want to get up and curtsy to them, but I know that I would fall down in a heap if I tried to do such a thing, for I have scarce the strength to open and close my eyes, let alone bend my legs in obeisance.

"Is this true?" one of them asks as he enters the room.

"She has opened her eyes? Spoken?" asks the other.

"Sh . . . sh . . . she . . ." Robert begins several times, and then sighs impatiently.

"'Tis no matter," the first says to him, very kindly. He approaches the bed and takes up my wrist. "Now, don't be afeared, my dear," he says to me. "I'm Doctor Willis, and I'm just going to count your heartbeats."

"We can see from her color alone how she's improved!" says the other, who is a handsome man and strong of feature. He peers at me and smiles. "I'm Doctor Petty. Now, don't be frightened. You're doing very well."

Dr. Willis counts under his breath, looking at the watch he holds in his other hand. "Excellent!" he says. He puts his hand into mine. "Now, my dear young lady," he asks, "can you wriggle your toes and squeeze my fingers?"

Obediently, I do both these things—and I can't help smiling as I do them, for he looks so very amazed as he watches me.

"Merciful Lord!" he says, and of a sudden he slips down onto his knees beside the bed, his hands folded together and his head bowed. I'm surprised at this, for I'd thought him to be a physician and not a cleric—but perhaps he's both. "Our prayers have been answered," he says. "Thank you, Lord, for sparing her life and for allowing us, your servants, to act through you. And thank you for restoring her soul to her."

Conscious that he is praying for me, I think it meet to whisper, "And may God convey me swiftly to paradise."

They smile and look at each other. "Those were her last words!" Dr. Willis says.

"A . . . and her f . . . f . . . first," adds Robert.

"But we don't want that now," says Dr. Petty to me. "We rather hope that God does *not* convey you swiftly to paradise, my dear, for if he does, he will undo all the good we've done."

Dr. Willis gets up from his knees in such a hurry that he stands on his gown and tears it. That will be a difficult tear for a servant to repair, I think, for the fabric's old and the threads are pulled. "William, William!" he says. "This is a great day. A miraculous day. A day when we have witnessed his divine intervention with our own eyes."

Dr. Petty nods thoughtfully. "Yes," he says. "Or . . ." He looks at the other with one eyebrow raised. "Or perhaps the hangman's noose had a faulty knot and didn't press where it should have done to dispatch its victim."

Dr. Willis gives no indication of having heard this. "Today the bells of heaven will ring out in joy!"

"And the bells of Christ Church, if I have anything to do with it," adds Dr. Petty.

———◆◈◆———

The girl who had been sleeping on the floor of the room— I hear her being called Martha—rattles out the grate and lays and lights a fire, and another man comes in carrying a bleeding bowl and some cloths. He is introduced to me as Mr. Clarke, the apothecary whose house we are in. Next to arrive is a tall man with two assistants; he is Dr. Bathurst. All stand around and gaze at me, marveling and exclaiming by turn. Robert is sent down to the herb garden to see if there's any wintergreen growing fresh, but it's not the season, so he comes back with dried leaves from the shop, which are quickly made into a balm and applied to my throat and neck. Mr. Clarke goes to get the best honey from his lavender bees, and Martha is told to add three spoonfuls of this to some warm milk. She and Robert then lift my head gently so that I can drink it, and it soothes my throat most excellently.

Two more gentlemen arrive who are said to be masters at the university. They are told of my progress, my heartbeat, and my breathing, and they join the little group around my bed. Martha is instructed to go to the baker's for a fresh loaf of white bread and then crumb the inside of this and sop it into warm milk for me. I need nourishment, they say, for I have been through a great ordeal.

"To heaven and back!" says one of the masters.

"I'll go when I can find the time," Martha says, and Mr. Clarke looks at her most severely, telling her that the day will be a busy one and she must be prepared to work hard. She whispers something in his ear and he nods, then solicits some coins from the two doctors and presses these into her hand.

I'm bled into a bowl, my forehead is soothed with oils, and one or other of the men there takes my pulse, looks into my mouth, or just stands and stares at me. I marvel greatly at my circumstances; at how one moment I can be in the meanest jail among rogues and vagabonds with not a friend in the world, and the next be treated with as much deference as a queen.

"Is there anything you want?" Dr. Petty asks, his words drifting into my thoughts. "Or is any part of you in pain?"

With my fingers I point to my tongue, which feels strange and is numb at the tip. I frown a little; I can think the words I want to say, but not speak them. This must, I think, be a little like the trouble that afflicts Robert.

Three men look into my mouth and examine the part of my tongue I'm pointing to.

"It's been bitten," one says.

"But is not furry . . ."

"I think you must have chewed on it when you were hanging," says the third.

The apothecary looks in my mouth also. "And to treat it . . . perhaps a salve made from the green fruit of the blackberry? 'Tis more usually employed for ulcers in the mouth, but 'twill do, I think."

The others nod agreement. Robert is sent down to the shop to choose the ingredients and returns to say the assistant has them and will compound them into a paste.

My mind is set on what Robert promised earlier, and when he comes close I signal to him and point outside. He knows what I mean.

"H . . . h . . . her f . . . f . . . family," he says to the others.

"Of course!" says Dr. Willis.

"At this moment!" cries Dr. Petty, and they decide between themselves that he, Dr. Willis, and Robert will go to tell them that I'm alive. On the way out, Dr. Petty speaks to Martha, who is bent over the fire and looking agitated, her hair still frowsy. She nods but sighs when he's gone and looks at me rather crossly.

In a moment or two she brings up a bowl of warm water from downstairs and, asking the other gentlemen if they'll kindly wait outside for a moment, produces a chamber pot from under the bed. Ascertaining that I don't want to use this, she replaces it and then takes a muslin cloth, dampens it in the bowl of water, and, rubbing a morsel of soap on this, wipes me all over, being very gentle around my sore face and neck. She removes the bedraggled red ribband, brushes my hair, and brings out a pink ribband to tie back my tresses. Finally she goes to the coffer and gets out a worn cotton nightdress, which she changes for the stained undersmock I'm wearing. I can't think of what to say or how to thank her for all these ministrations, so merely smile at her gratefully and squeeze her hand.

She seems to unbend a little and smiles back. "You look better now," she nods. "Indeed, for a dead corpse you look a great deal alive."

I return the smile. *A dead corpse,* I think. I close my eyes for a moment to wonder about all the things that are happening, and why they are doing so. And when my mind clears a little, I reach some kind of an understanding and believe I know the truth of it. And the truth is this: *I was hanged, but did not die.*

Chapter ~ 24

may have slept again for a moment after that, for when I wake I feel more certain about what's happening and more accepting of it—although I still cannot understand such a thing. I look anxiously for my family, but they do not appear, and I'm in a fright of concern about them, for they'll surely never believe what has happened. Besides, my pa is not used to conversing with gentlemen and may have taken himself off in a fright on their approach.

Three more men from the university come into the room to look me over. Two of these fall to their knees and pray by my bedside to give thanks to God for my deliverance. Unsure of how to compose myself but knowing I must show a serious countenance, I close my eyes while they are doing this and press my hands together in an attitude of prayer. "May God convey me swiftly to paradise . . ." I whisper, and they smile at me and look wondering.

Martha complains about her bedroom being hardly big enough for such goings-on, and it's decided that I should be moved to Mr. Clarke's room. Accordingly, a witty and waggish fellow, one who came in with Dr. Bathurst, picks me up bodily, bedstuffs and all, and takes me to Mr. Clarke's own bedroom farther down the corridor. Here I am queen indeed, for I'm placed in a proper wooden tester, with gold and magenta hangings at the head and a deep feather mattress. The room is paneled, a quilted silk carpet sits on the floor, and paintings hang on the walls: two large ones depicting highland beasts, and smaller paintings of herbs and flowers. I've not been in such a room before—or only to clean—and feel anxious about it, for I have put Mr.

Clarke out of his own bed. He, however, seems extreme happy to have me there and says to the others, "I am a made man. We are all made men!"—by which I understand that they'll receive recognition for what has occurred.

One other thing goes with me into Mr. Clarke's room: the coffin that they tell me I was placed in after my hanging. This is propped up by the window with its lid standing beside it, and gives me the horrors whenever I look upon it.

Robert and the others are away a long time, and I begin to wonder if my parents might have gone home. I find out later, however, that the doctors had difficulty in making them understand what had happened, for my pa refused to believe it at first, thinking that they had come from Sir Thomas and were playing some cruel trick on them.

Martha brings a bowl of bread and milk, and I eat it in little mouthfuls, for it pains my throat to swallow. At last I hear noises: lots of footsteps in the hall and the voices of the two doctors floating out loud and cheerful as they shepherd everyone up the stairs, and I become very excited.

"In here now! In here!" Mr. Clarke calls, and in they troop: the doctors first, and then Ma, Pa, Jane, and my two brothers, all silent, awkward, and awestruck, which I know is because none of them has been a visitor to such a house before.

I smile, but don't know what to say to them; for that one single godly sentence I have in my head is not altogether appropriate.

"Well!" Ma says, staring at me with her hand pressed to her mouth. "Well!"

Jane takes two steps into the room, looks around at the furnishings, and her jaw drops. Pa and my brothers whip off their old felt hats and stand awkwardly, bowing around at the gentlemen gathered there. Jane sees what they're doing and begins curtsying and, strangely, gives a curtsy to me as well.

This makes me laugh and she laughs too, which makes things easier.

I struggle to sit up and hold out my arms to Ma but find myself weak as a kitten and fall back on the pillows. Ma comes to me then, and holds me, and we weep for a considerable time. After this I kiss everyone, then Ma and Jane take up positions by my bed while Pa and my brothers go out into the hall in order to leave more space for the gentry.

———◆·•◆•·◆———

Finding that I'm still unable to speak, the doctors apply a plaister to my throat, which warms it greatly, and after I've eaten a second bowl of bread and milk I find myself able to say a few words, but croakily. I say *Thank you*, first, and *Hello* to some visitors, and then I say the names of all my family, which pleases them enormously, and 'tis like when an infant babbles for the first time. It pleases the doctors, too, for Robert tells me later that some of them feared for my sanity until they heard me begin to speak. After this the words arrive all the time. I do not speak to anyone to ask what I long to, however, which is for news of John Taylor. Has he heard that I've survived? Does he care enough to visit me and accept my apologies?

———◆·•◆•·◆———

Two youths arrive who are scholars with Robert. "Ah," says Dr. Petty cheerily (and indeed everyone is very cheerful). "Here come a couple of fellows who are the very flowers of the nobility and gentry of the kingdom!"

The scholars bow around them, and Ma and Jane curtsy once more.

"Congratulations on your newborn patient!" they say, greeting Robert with a punch to the arm.

"G . . . good morning," he says to them, and they all hoot and ask him whether he's in his cups that he can speak so well.

He says, "No, not at all," very carefully, and then grins, delighted.

They both then gather around and gape at me as if I'm a sideshow at the May fair.

"We saw you yesterday in your shift, madam!" one says, winking at me. He is fine and dandy, with long, curling hair and a ruffle of lace at his throat. When Martha comes in he winks at her also and makes her blush, which makes me long to tell her not to believe any such sweet talk from him, for he's a master and she a servant, and I know from my own experience that any coupling would not prove a happy one.

Another of the scholars wants to make a drawing of me and retires to one side of the bed with a pad of paper. "I made two when I thought you were dead, and this will complete the set," he says.

More and more people arrive, and the one who was drawing me has his position taken by an elderly gentleman who brings his own shooting stick to sit upon. A hackney carriage comes from Cambridge containing some medical men, and they say some from London may come on the morrow.

"And all to see you," Dr. Petty says.

"And this is just the start of it," says Dr. Willis.

The new medical men stand at the end of my bed, stare at me, and marvel, and then look at my coffin and say that such a thing has never happened before and that I was indeed fortunate to have been *nearly* dissected by such learned men, for others might not have been able to revive me.

I hear Dr. Willis say, "Of course, we have no idea when the light of life goes out and the soul departs . . ."

"Or when the quick become dead," adds Dr. Petty, and there is general agreement in the room that this is true.

The two scholars go off to the coffeehouse and are quickly replaced by double that number. Shortly after this, a messenger brings word that two great ladies have come all the way from Windsor and wish to set eyes on me.

This causes quite a little stir in the room. I have my hair combed out once more (Jane makes an effort to curl it), and a walkway is made through the people so that these two ladies—Dr. Willis says that both are countesses—may approach me while everyone else stays at a respectful distance. The room goes silent as they arrive and so do I, for I can scarce believe that I am the purpose of their visit. They are finely dressed in velvet gowns, one in maroon and one in dark green, with fur-trimmed cloaks over, and when they throw their hoods back, their hair is dressed in ringlets, with pearls threaded through. Ma sinks into a deep curtsy, but Jane has forgotten to do so, and I see her out of the corner of my eye, her jaw hanging loose in wonder.

"Is it really true, my dear?" the maroon gown asks. "Were you hanged yesterday?"

I nod, feeling shy.

"And what was it like before you were awoken by the doctors? Can you remember where you were?"

I shake my head, and their faces fall.

"Nothing?" they ask. "You can't remember a thing?"

"I . . . I was just in darkness," I answer.

"But surely you must have seen *something*," the green gown asks, and she pouts her lips a little.

"Was it something very private and personal?" says the other. "For we are simply agog to know!"

The green lowers her voice. "Someone we know who suffered a fit and nearly died said she'd seen a vision of paradise, and it was all hot sun, green pastures, and silver rivers, as beautiful as could be . . ."

I nod slowly, wondering if I could have seen such things and forgotten about them after.

"Angels!" says the maroon. "Some people on point of death say that they've seen angels with flowing white wings and silver harps."

I nod more eagerly. "I believe I did see some angels," I say, remembering the blurry shapes that had passed across my vision in the darkness. "Four of them, walking together."

Their eyes light up. "I knew it!" green gown says.

"She may be a prophetess!"

I don't know what this is, but I nod, and before I can help myself am agreeing with them that I'd seen all sorts of things: strange wild beasts walking with lambs, rivers of silver, flying cherubs, and all manner of heavenly creatures together in a glorious garden in which an abundance of sweet-smelling flowers grew.

When the ladies leave, much pleased with me, Dr. Petty and Dr. Willis clear the room for a short while, saying that I need some rest. Everyone goes out, even Ma and Jane, then Dr. Petty sits on the bed and takes my hand. "Now,

Anne," he says, "I want you to tell me exactly what you saw when you were in that other place—before you awoke and found yourself in Martha's bedroom."

I feel myself blush.

"And you must tell us the truth, mind," says Dr. Willis, speaking very seriously and kindly.

I lie back on my pillows. "I think I *did* see angels."

"What were they like?" Dr. Willis asks.

"They were somewhat blurred," I say, "but seemed very much like angels."

Dr. Petty gives me a reproachful look. "Anne . . . ?"

I look away.

"And what of the strange wild beasts and the cherubs?" asks Dr. Willis.

My head drops. "Perhaps I didn't see them. But I thought . . . thought that was what the ladies wished to hear."

"Oh, they did, certainly," says Dr. Willis.

"But you mustn't be tempted to say such things," Dr. Petty says, "for on such a flimsy basis, whole religions can be formed. Some would need no more excuse to put you at the head of the Church, like Mother Mary, and a web of mummery and superstition formed about you."

Dr. Willis looks as if he regrets there not being any angels or silver streams. "The shapes you saw were probably those forms we all see under our closed eyelids," he says with a sigh.

The next visitors who arrive—two elderly and very learned gentlemen from Cambridge, in plush coats and plumed hats—I am more reticent with. I hardly say a word (for anyway, my throat is paining me), but Jane chatters like a jackdaw, smiling as she recounts the family's joy, and weeping copiously while she tells of our previous sufferings. The gentlemen are most sympathetic and give me a gold angel as they get up to leave. It must be used, they say, to purchase whatever is necessary for my complete recovery.

This is treasure indeed, for 'tis worth ten whole shillings. The family comes around the bed to marvel at the very goldness of the coin, and Jane bites it to make sure 'tis not counterfeit.

I find that I am more at ease in the grand bed now. I know that I have not, but I begin to feel that I've done something particular and special to be so lauded. Only two things prevent me from being truly happy: firstly, I fear that Sir Thomas may arrive at any time and take me to be hanged again; secondly, there is someone that I long to see and beg forgiveness from.

There are more arrivals. Dr. Willis brings a fellow to me. "This man is from Mr. Burdet, the printer, and he is to write up a pamphlet about you," he says, "so you must tell him truthfully whatever you can remember. And no more!" he adds.

I nod, and the fellow brings a chair and sits down beside the bed. People jostle all around him, so he asks Jane to hold his bottle of ink, then takes out a quill and a pad of paper. "'Twill make an excellent good story," he says to me. "An *improving* story wherein people may learn that good can triumph, and that justice may be found on Earth as well as in paradise."

"And what will it be called?" Jane asks him.

"*Newes from the Dead,*" he says. "For your sister here was dead and now is not. And she brings us news from that other world."

I look toward the doctors with some unease.

"We'll start with the angels," says the scribe. "The Countess of Wimborne says that you saw angels . . ."

Embarrassed, I shake my head.

"'Twas all a misunderstanding," says Dr. Petty.

The fellow frowns, rather disappointed. "Let me have your prayers, then, Mistress Green, for I must record your own words to the Lord. 'Tis said that when you awoke here, you began speaking at exactly the point where you left off on the gibbet."

I glance toward Robert, who is nodding at me. "When I awoke I found myself saying, 'May God convey me swiftly to paradise . . .'"

"Which were indeed her last words as she was hanged," says Dr. Petty.

Dr. Willis approaches the bed. "It was as if Mistress Green were a clock whose weights had been taken off a while, and afterward hung on again."

"Wise words, sir," says the scribe, and he writes them down. He asks me how often I attend church and I am about to reply, when there is a stir outside in the corridor and a little 'prentice boy runs in, pushing through the people. He works at a carpenter's, I think, for he wears a dusty brown apron down to the ground, and pale sawdust frosts his hair and eyebrows.

"Whatever is it?" Dr. Willis asks.

"Please, sir," puffs the apprentice, "Mr. Parker said I should come and tell you the news. He just heard from the Reade house, see. Got 'structions to go there straight."

"Who has? What do you mean, boy?" asks Dr. Petty.

"Mr. Parker," answers the boy, panting some, "says I must tell you he has been instructed to go over to Dun's Tew and measure for a coffin. A coffin for Sir Thomas Reade, who has upped and died!"

"Sir Thomas? *Dead?*" inquires Dr. Willis in a shocked voice.

There is a moment's silence, and someone calls, "Oh, behold God's providence!" and several men fall to their knees and begin praying aloud. As for me, I'd long wished him dead and at first wonder, with some guilt, if my wishes have worked a curse on him (but this guilt does not last long).

The scribe looks astonished for a moment, then I hear him murmur, "Excellent . . . excellent," before the nib of his pen begins scratching along the pad again. "Behold God's providence . . ." I hear him mutter under his breath.

Chapter ~ 25

I have slept well, or so the physicians who surround me declare, and my voice is sounder, the swelling and bruising to my neck much improved, and my heartbeat strong. I have even managed to stand for just a moment, before being overcome with a fit of dizziness. My brothers have had to return to their workplace, but Jane, Ma, and Pa are close by, and last night Jane and Ma shared my bed with me.

I feel leaden in my body, but my mind whirls away like a snowflake and notions and images run through my head, as many, varied, and entwined as ribbands on a maypole. Why have I been saved? What is meant by such an occurrence? Can it be true—as I was told by one gentleman visitor—that God means to begin a new religious order through me? I sincerely hope it is not. I don't feel able to lead such an order, to seek followers, or e'en know how I would address them.

I think about Sir Thomas's death and (although I own it wicked of me) feel mighty content about it, being unable to spare a thought for his grieving widow or his surviving family. How selfish a person I have become—but how very strange it is that he should die while I should live!

<hr>

The scholars are about my bed early and half fill the room, for their masters have set them a task to write a poem about my situation, and there is much laughter as they try out their lines (although some I cannot understand a word of, they being written in a language they say is Latin). Master Wren's produces laughter, for no one can tell what it means, and

Dr. Petty says to him, "By the Lord, Christopher, you had better look to your other talents rather than poesy."

By the time the clock strikes ten o'clock the scholars half fill the room, and they are shooed out by Dr. Willis to attend lectures. Robert puts down his papers—as well as writing the poem, he has been recording my treatments—comes to me and presses my hand. "I . . . I . . . I fear you will have a tiring day," he says. "It seems that the whole w . . . world are on their way to see you."

"'Tis of no matter," I say, for I am enjoying my reign as queen. I do not even have to speak much, but merely lie in the feather bed and smile graciously as people kiss my hand. I think 'tis the best and easiest employment I have ever had.

I thank Robert again for his ministrations, and some moments later the first of that day's proper visitors arrive: a group of clerical gentlemen who wish to pray at my bedside. They are joined by a deputation of apothecaries, a gentleman I am told is Cromwell's deputy in Oxford, and a party of scientific men who have just arrived on the coach from London and have not e'en stopped at the tavern for refreshment. After these, a finely dressed lady arrives with two maids accompanying her, her gown tricked out with so many petticoats that it takes up the space of six men. While she is still laying her hands on me and mouthing softly, "Oh, my dear, how you have suffered . . ." a swarthy woman and her daughter come in and scare her away. It appears that they are fairground people, and they ask if they can buy my nightdress to cut into squares and sell as lucky charms.

I think this an excellent idea and apply to Dr. Petty for permission, but he refuses.

"We will not have people making money out of such gewgaws," he says.

"Isn't that rather hard, William?" Mr. Clarke asks.

"Maybe. But such things are hocum-pocum nonsense and have no place in the practice of medicine," says Dr. Petty. "They are just in it to make money."

"But will we not make money from what we have achieved with the girl?"

"No, we will not," says Dr. Petty in a low voice. "We will make more: we will make our reputations."

Martha is busying herself and has heard some of this conversation. "Anyway," she says, "'tis my old nightdress and not lucky at all."

This matter with the fairground women has given Dr. Willis an idea, however. The doctors speak together and, the room being full to bursting again, it is cleared of all visitors, Dr. Willis saying that this is so that I may take sustenance and have certain medical observations made.

When just my family is left, Dr. Willis explains that as news of me spreads farther afield, the number of people coming to see me will increase. "And I fear we may not be able to admit them all to see Anne—this house just cannot contain them," he says.

"Do you want her to come home now, then?" Ma asks, somewhat faintly, and I know she is envisaging a parade of finely dressed gentry treading the path to our little cottage.

Dr. Willis shakes his head. "She must stay with us for a few more days yet—perhaps a week—until we are sure of her complete recovery. But to help us all, we intend to restrict those coming to see her by charging them a fee."

"Like a show at the May fair?" Jane asks.

"No, young mistress, like a proper scientific display, such as the universities put on from time to time."

"The poorer sort will thus stay away, but the quality will not be refused," says Dr. Petty.

"We will charge one shilling," says Dr. Willis, "and in a short time—mark my words—we will have enough to pay for all the medicines used on Anne, for our attendance at her bedside, and for the legal fees that will be needed to obtain her a full pardon."

"And what's left after will go some way toward her marriage portion," says Dr. Bathurst kindly, "for every girl should have a dowry of some sort."

My family says nothing to this last, but I know that they are wondering who ever would take me.

The day proceeds with my father standing at the door holding a wooden box Mr. Clarke has obtained and rattling this as people walk up the passage. They place their shillings in it without question (some give more), for a sign has been put downstairs in the shop warning of the charge, and those unwilling to pay do not venture up the stairs.

I am surprised at how quickly Pa falls into his role; "Come see Anne Green, the miracle woman!" he calls like a mountebank. "The woman that was hanged and lived to tell the tale! Come and see proof of God's mighty providence!" And sometimes, if the people are very grand, Jane goes over to greet them at the doorway, brings them to my bedside, and affects an introduction with much flimflam and curtsying.

Dinner is at noon, and straight after this I receive a further small deputation of gentlemen from London, who speak at long and boring length to Dr. Willis and Dr. Petty, then come and stand at the foot of my bed and shake their heads at me. I try to be alert so that they may see that I'm fully recovered, but my eyelids are beginning to droop with tiredness when I hear a discussion at the bedroom door and a voice pleading to be let in to see me without payment.

A male voice says, "For on hearing the news I threw off my apron, jumped on the horse I was shoeing, and rode here without a pause."

"I'm sorry, sir," I hear my pa answer. "'Tis a shilling for all and sundry."

"But I did not think to put money in my pocket, man!" the voice says urgently. "Do let me pass!"

Fully awake once more, I stare over the heads of the medical gentlemen and can just see the top of a battered felt hat.

"I'll bring a shilling to you directly! Just let me see her now."

"I'm sorry, sir, but I'm going to have to turn you away," my father says, then adds jovially, "Indeed, I would lose my job if I let you in without payment."

I hear a soft swear word and a sigh of exasperation, then comes the rustle of gowns and the clack of leather shoes as more visitors walk down the corridor. There is a clink as their money goes in the box.

Jane is sitting cross-legged on the bed sewing some gloves. "Who was that who spoke then—the man without a shilling?" I ask her with some urgency. "Go quickly and see!"

She nods at me but doesn't move fast enough for my liking, so that I have to ask the medical men to kindly shift to one side to enable me to see around them and to the doorway.

But no one stands there now, besides three Puritan women looking like crows in their black moiré gowns.

"Go after that man!" I say to Jane, pushing her off the bed. "Quickly!"

She goes. But doesn't have to go far, because the man in question has heard my voice, turned back, and now waits in the doorway.

He takes off his hat and stands awkwardly, staring at me. He's still in his working clothes with a soot-streaked face, grimy arms, and hair caught back in a band. He has not, today, scrubbed his hands or cleaned his fingernails.

I call, "Let him in, Pa!" and John Taylor comes toward me slowly.

We stare at each other. There's much to say, but that cannot be started yet. Instead I say softly, "Fie, John Taylor, am I not even worth a shilling?"

"Nay," he answers, "but you are worth silver and gold to me."

And I look at him and know that my life story can begin again, as if I am newly born, and count myself as both the most cursed woman, and the most fortunate, that ever was on this Earth.

Author's ~ Note

I first came across the story of Anne Green in 2004 while listening to a program on BBC's Radio Four. A panel was discussing the way in which women throughout the ages have been prosecuted for infanticide—the murder of a baby—when they had actually suffered a stillbirth or (if the child had lived a short while) a crib death. Anne's case was mentioned, the story told of how she was hanged for infanticide and subsequently revived, and I was gripped. Her death and revival have been documented many times over the years from the point of view of the doctors who were instrumental in her revival, but I wanted to write the story from Anne's perspective. Naturally, therefore, although the main thrust of the story is absolutely true, all the conversations and trivia are from my imagination.

Anne was a serving maid in the house of Sir Thomas Reade in 1650 and thus could have been present when Charles I visited the house to say his last goodbyes to Queen Henrietta some years previous to this. The present owners of the manor house in Dun's Tew kindly allowed me access to the buildings and grounds, and although these have been much altered over the years, the huge dovecote still remains. There was also a trace of the old outside privies for the servants, presumably still in the same place as the ones that had existed in Anne's day.

Sir Thomas's heir, Geoffrey Reade, was sixteen or seventeen at the time of Anne's hanging, but was spirited out of the county before her trial and was not heard of again. Sir Thomas's displeasure at his grandson's actions was, perhaps, illustrated by the fact that under the terms of his will, Geoffrey Reade only received a farm in Northampton, when he might have been expected to receive considerably more of the lands and great manors owned by the family. Sir Thomas was said to have been present at Anne's dissection, but was taken ill and died three days after her revival, which was seen as further proof of Anne's innocence and God's judgment.

Anne, following the stillbirth, was described as miserably ill and weak, and the conditions in Oxford Jail were said to be "indescribable . . . with lack of sanitation, warmth, and lighting." She would have had no one to speak for her during the trial. A law passed in 1624 prosecuted women (in practice, intended to apply only to unmarried girls of the lower class) whose babies had died, unless they could "make proof of one witness at the least, that the child whose death was concealed was born dead."

The four doctors present at the dissection had their reputations made as a result of Anne's case, although Christopher Wren's involvement only became known a few years ago, when his poem was discovered among thirty others written by the young Oxford undergraduates present. Among these is also a poem written by one Robert Matthews, Fellow of New College, and this was my starting point for the character of Robert, although I have no way of knowing if he had a stammer. It is said that Dr. Willis had one, however, and ruminated on the cause of it.

Anne recovered very well from her ordeal, and her fame spread widely through the sale of pamphlets entitled "Newes from the Dead," telling her story and giving speeches and prayers said to have been dictated by her. The original pamphlet with this title is included after this Author's Note. Pamphleteers, as they were called, were the equivalent of newspaper journalists today. There were three or four such leaflets published and sold, and Anne's ordeal made a great story. The information given in them differs according to what approach its writers wanted to take; one includes the scholars' poems (which haven't been included owing to their obscure language), another gives prayers that Anne is said to have written herself, one says Anne saw angels, another says she saw none. One can only imagine the sensation they caused at the time.

Generally, the people of the country felt that what had happened to her was God's miraculous way of saying she was innocent. The money collected at the apothecary's door from the hundreds who flocked to see her was used to pay for her pardon, and she became something of a celebrity, traveling up and down the country with her coffin and appearing in taverns and at fairs. She married soon after the event: the records merely say, "Anne Green of Steeple Barton married John Taylor of Dun's Tew on the 29th May 1651," so I am guessing that she knew John beforehand, probably from when she worked for Sir Thomas in Dun's Tew. The couple were not married in Steeple Barton, however (Anne's home village), but in the larger church at Tadmarton, which lies a little farther north. Perhaps the rector was unwilling to be a part of the fuss and excitement that would be bound to have accompanied such an event? However, Anne went on to have three children, and died in 1665.

What saved her from death? The instrument of hanging in those days was merely a noose from a tree or scaffold, without a trapdoor beneath, so the victim would have suffocated to death rather than have their neck broken, and the knot that should have pressed into Anne's throat may have been incorrectly placed. Perhaps most significant is the fact that on that day, 14 December 1650, it was fiercely cold, and it has been suggested that her suspended animation was due to something similar to cryogenic preservation, where the brain is frozen and thus prevented from being starved of oxygen.

Newes from the Dead.

OR

A TRUE AND EXACT

Narration of the miraculous
deliverance of

ANNE GREENE,

Who being Executed at OXFORD De-
cemb. 14. 1650. afterwards revived; and
by the care of certain Phyſitians there,
is now perfectly recovered.

Together with the manner of her Suffering, and the
particular meanes uſed for her Recovery.

Written by a Scholler in OXFORD for the
Satisfaction of a friend, who deſired to be
informed concerning the truth
of the buſineſſe.

Whereunto are prefixed certain Poems, caſually
written upon that Subject.

OXFORD,
Printed by *LEONARD LICHFIELD*, for
Tho. Robinson. A·D. 1651.

Newes from the Dead.

THere happened lately in this Citty a very rare and remarkeable accident, which being varioully and falfely reported amongft the vulgar (as in fuch cafes it is ufuall) to the end that none may be deceived, and that fo fignall an act of Gods mercy and providence may never be forgotten, I have here faithfully recorded it, according to the Information I have received from thofe that were the chiefe Inftruments in bringing this great worke to perfection.

In the houfe of Sir *Thomas Read* at *Duns-Tew* in *Oxford-ſhire*,there lived a maid named *Anne Greene*,born at *Steeple-Barton*,in the fame County, being about 22.yeares of age, of a middle ftature, ftrong, flefhie, and of an indifferent good feature ; who being (as fhe faid) often follicited by faire promifes and other amorous enticements of Mr *Jeffery Read* Grand-child to the faid Sir *Thomas*,a youth of about 16. or 17. yeares of age, but of a forward growth and ftature, at laft confented to fatisfie his unlawfull pleafure. By which act (as it afterward appeared) fhe conceived,and was delivered of a man-child:which being never made knowne, and the Infant found dead in the houfe of office, caufed a

B   fufpition,

fufpition, that fhe being the mother had murthered it, and throwne it there on purpofe to conceale both it and her fhame together. Thereupon fhe was immediately taken into examination, and carried before feverall Juftices of the peace in the Countrey: and foone after,in an extreame cold and rainy day, fent unto *Oxford* Gaole, where having paffed about three weekes more in continuall affrights and terrours, in a place as comfortleffe as her condition, fhe was at a Seffions held in *Oxford*, arraigned , condemned, and on Saturday the 14. of *December* laft, brought forth to the place of execution : where after finging of a Pfalme, and fomething faid in juftification of her felf, as to the faĉt for which fhe was to fuffer, and touching the lewdneffe of the Family wherein fhe lately lived, fhe was turn'd off the Ladder,hanging by the neck for the fpace of almoft half an houre, fome of her friends in the mean time thumping her on the breaft, others hanging with all their weight upon her legges; fometimes lifting her up,and then pulling her downe againe with a fuddaine jerke, thereby the fooner to difpatch her out of her paine : infomuch that the Under-Sheriffe fearing leſt thereby they fhould breake the rope, forbad them to do fo any longer. At length when every one thought fhe was dead, the body being taken downe, and put into a Coffin, was carried thence into a private houfe, where fome Phyfitians had appointed to make a Diffeĉtion . The Coffin being opened,fhe was obferved to breath , and in breathing (the paffage of her throat being ftreightned) obfcurely to ruttle: which being perceived by a lufty fellow that ftood by, he (thinking to do an aĉt of charity in ridding her out of the fmall reliques of a pain-full life) ftamped feverall times on her breaft and fto-mack with all the force he could. Immediately after, there came in Dr *Petty* our Anatomy-Profeffor, and Mr *Thomas Willis* of *Chrift-Church*,at whofe comming, which was about 9. a clock in the morning, fhe yet perfifted to ruttle as before, laying all this while ftretched out in the coffin

in

in a cold roome and feafon of the yeare. They perceiving
fome life in her, as well for humanity as their Profeffion-
fake,fell prefently to act in order to her recovery.Firft, having caufed her to be held up in the Coffin,they wrench-
ed open her teeth, which were faft fet , and powred into
her mouth fome hot and cordiall fpirits ; whereupon fhee
ruttled more than before,and feemed obfcurely to cough:
then they opened her hands (her fingers alfo being ftif-
ly bent) and orderd fome to rub and chafe the extreame
parts of her body,which they continued for about a quarter of an houre;oft,in the meane time,powring in a fpoon-
full or two of the cordiall water; and befides tickling her
throat with a feather , at which fhe opened her eyes , but
fhut them againe prefently.As foone as they perceived any
heat in her extreme parts , they thought of letting her
bloud: and no fooner was her arme bound for that purpofe,
but fhe fuddenly bent it, as if it had beene contracted by a
fit of the Convulfion: the veine being opened,fhe bled a-
bout five ounces, and that fo freely that it could not ea-
fily be ftopped. All this while her pulfe was very low, but
otherwife not much amiffe. Her arme being bound up a-
gaine, and now and then a little cordiall water powr'd
downe her throat, they continued rubbing her in feverall
places,caufed Ligatures to be made in her armes and leggs,
and then ordered her to be laid in a bed well warmed:then
they caufed her neck, and alfo her temples to be annointed
with confortative oyles and fpirits, and fo likewife the bot-
toms of her feet, and upon this fhe began to open her eyes
and to move the lower parts of her body. About this
time came in Mr *Bathurft* of *Trinity* Colledge , and
Mr *Clerke* of *Magdalen* Colledge, whofe advice and endeavours were then and all the time afterwards concurrent
with thofe of the other two above mentioned. Then they
applyed a plaifter to her breifts, and ordered an heating
odoriferous Clyfter to be caft up in her body, to give heat
and warmth to her bowels : after that,they perfwaded a

woman

woman to goe into bed to her, and to lye very clofe to her, and gently to keep rubbing of her. After all which fhee feemd about noone to be in a fweat. Her face alfo began fomewhat to fwell and to looke very red on that fide on which the knot of the halter had been faftned.

Whilft the Phyfitians were thus bufie in recovering her to life, the Underfheriffe was folliciting the Governour and the reft of the Juftices of Peace for the obtaining her Repreive, that in cafe fhe fhould for that prefent be recovered fully to life, fhee might not bee had back againe to Execution. Whereupon thofe worthy Gentlemen, confidering what had happened, weighing all circumftances, they readily apprehended the hand of God in her prefervation, and being willing rather to co-operate with divine providence in faving her, then to o-verftraine juftice by condemning her to double fhame & fufferings, they were pleas'd to grant her a Repreive until fuch time as her Pardon might be compleatly obtained.

All this while fhe had no fooner opened her eyes but prefently fhe fhut them againe, and being call'd upon to try whether fhee could heare or fpeake, there appeared no figne that fhe could doe either. Soone after, they made tryall againe: bidding her, if fhee underftood them, to move her hand, or open her eyes. Whereupon fhee obfcurely opened her eyes. The Phyfitians fearing leaft her face might fwell more and more, and a Feaver come upon her, by reafon of the former fuffocation, took frō her right arm about nine ounces more of blood, and then ordered her a Julep, and other cordiall things to be adminiftred upon occafion, and fo left her for that night: and about 2 houres after fhe begun to fpeak many words intelligible.

On Sunday the 15 about 8. in the morning they return'd, and found her much amended, being able to an-fwer to any queftion propounded unto her. Shee then complained of her throat, (but not much of any other part) whereunto they ordered a Cataplafme to be applyed,

ed:then she complaining of drought,a Julep was offered her,which she first took with difficulty,& at last refus'd: warm beere being given her,she disrelished it,bnt of cold she drank and thanked them.

All this while she lay often sighing and talking to her selfe,as if she had bin still to suffer.About noone she felt an extreame sorenesse in her breast and sides, but there appeared nothing discoloured or like a Contusion. That night they orderd her a Clyster,and a Cataplasme to be applied to her breast and sides,with other means to prevent what evil might ensue by reason of contus'd blood, and so left her to rest.About 9 of the clock she laughed and talked merrily,looking fresh and of a good colour: being a litle feverish, her tongue not furd nor clammy.

Munday the 16,they found that shee had taken some rest,and her feaver not much encreas'd : they then tooke from her left arme about 6 ounces of blood more: she fainted not,but talked very cheerfully,complaining some what of her neck,stomack, and throat.

But before they let her bloud,having first caused all to depart the room except those Gentelemen that were of theFaculty,they asked her of her sense and apprehension during the time of her suffering: shee answered,that after shee put off some of her clothes , bequeathing them to her Mother (which was early in the morning before her execution) and heard some one say that one of the prisoners was lett out of the chaine to put her to death , shee remembered nothing at all that had beene done unto her : and that shee knew not when her fetters were knock'd off, or how she came out of prison, or that she had bin upon the Gallows, neither could she remember that any Psalm had bin sung,or that she said any thing there:notwithstanding those that were present do testifie that she spake very sensibly: onely about a fortnight after, she seemed to remember something of a fellow wrapt up in a blanket, which indeed. was the habit of her Executioner.   It

It is obfervable alfo, that when fhe came to her felfe againe, fhe fell into the like fpeeches as fhe had ufed in prifon before the execution: feeming there to go on where fhe had fo long time left off;like to a Clock whofe weights had been taken off a while, and afterwards hung on againe.

That night fhe was fomented about the fides and other contufed places, her neck being very fore, efpecially on the right fide, where it was all black, and began to blifter: there appeared alfo divers fpots of fettled bloud on her right cheek.

Tuefday the 17. in the morning they found her pulfe flow, but very unequall : her tongue not very dry nor rough : the night before fhe flept well; in the morning fhe arofe, but her head was fo light that fhe could hardly ftand upright: fhe now complained of paine beneath the pit of her ftomack : fhe complained alfo of a deadneffe in the tipp of her tongue, thinking fhe had bitten it in the time of her fuffering: fhe call'd this day for fome bread, which fhe did eat, being firft toafted and moiftned in beare. At night when they vifited her againe, the paine of her neck and throat was decreafed : the fpots of fettled bloud about her cheek and neck leffened, but the deadneffe of her tongue ftill remained. That night fhe flept 6. or 7. houres : and on the 18. in the morning had no feaver; her pulfe was much amended; all Symptomes leffened ; the paines in her breift feemed to defcend into the region of the belly,being (as 'twas conceived) not in the bowells, but onely in the mufculous outward parts.

The 19. fhe was up, and did eat part of a chick. All fymptomes decreafed : yet could fhe not goe, without the help of fomewhat to uphold her. Her neck ftill fore, but mending. The deadneffe of her Tongue leffened. That night fhe flept well. About foure or five daies after, being hard frosty weather, there appeared a blackneſſe over the lower part of her right arme, and upon her flankes on the ſame ſide: which by degrees waxed yellow, and in foure or five dayes vaniſhed.

By this time, the care of the Phyſitians was well over. The paines in her Breiſt and ſide when ſhe drew in her breath, as alſo the inequality of the pulſe (which cauſed a ſuſpition of a contuſion and extravaſated bloud ſpilt on the Lungs) being now fully ceaſed. The deadneſſe of her tongue and foreneſſe of her neck quite gone. There remained onely a giddineſſe in her head when ſhe walked or ſtirred her body, which in a ſhort time likewiſe left her. And now being able to walke about the Towne, eate, drink, and ſleepe, as well as before this accident had befallen her, ſhe had liberty to repaire (and is ſince gone) unto her friends in the Country; taking away with her the Coffin whereinſhe lay, as a Trophey of this her wonderfull preſervation.

Thus, within the ſpace of a Moneth, was ſhe wholly Recovered: and in the ſame Roome where her Body was to have beene diſſected for the ſatisfaction of a few, ſhe became a greater wonder, being reviv'd, to the ſatisfaction of multitudes that flocked thither daily to ſee her.

One thing more I had almoſt forgotten; that when the numbers of people ſtill preſſing into the houſe began to be too impetuous, and the Phyſitians had obtained of the Governour to have a Guard plac'd at the doore; yet becauſe thoſe of the better ſort could not altogether be denied admiſſion, they thought it a ſeaſonable opportunity, for the maid's behalfe, to invite them either to exerciſe their Charity, or at leſt to pay for their Curioſity. And therefore (themſelves firſt leading the way) they commended it to thoſe that came

in

in,to give every one what they pleas'd,her Father being there ready to receive it. After a few daies the Governor (a Gentleman as much to be belov'd for his Courtesie, as he is honour'd for his Prudence) coming himselfe to see her,did not onely contribute to her in a liberall manner,but also improved his charity with many pertinent and wholsome Instructions. By this meanes there was gathered for her to the summe of many pounds: whereby not only the Apothecaries Bill , and other necessaries for her Dyet and lodging were discharged , but some overplus remained towards the suing out of her Pardon.

And now, having done with the Sufferings , and the Cure,it will not be amisse to looke back , and take a Review of the Cause of them,or matter of fact for which shee suffered: which (as I have said) was the supposed murther of her own Infant.

There are two things, very considerable , alleaged on her behalfe,and that many seem to cleere her Innocence as to that businesse.

The first is,that the Child was abortive or stillborne, and consequently not capable of being murthered. The other,that she did not certainely know that shee was with child,and that it fell from her unawares as she was in the house of office.

As for the first,it is evident that the child was very unperfect, being not above a span in length, and the sexe hardly to be distinguished: so that it rather seemed a lumpe of flesh then a well and duly formed Infant. The Midwife said also, that it had no haire , and that she did not beleive that ever it had life. Besides,her fellow-servants doe testifie,that she had certaine Issues for about a month before she miscarried,which were of that nature (Physitians say) as are not consistent with the vitality of a child: the eruption of which Issues came

in

on her after fhee had violently labour'd in skreening of malt. Laftly, it is not likely that the Child was vitall, the mifchance happening not above 17. weekes after the time of her conception.

For the 2. that fhee might not know certainly that fhee was with child, it is not improbable : for fhee was not 10. weekes without the ufuall Courfes of women, before fhee had thofe continuall Iffues which lafted for a Moneth together: which long and great Evacuation might make her judge, that it was nothing elfe but a flux of thofe humors which for ten weekes before had been fuppreffed; And that the child which fell from her unawares, was nothing but a lump of the fame matter coagulated. As for the paine, it muft needs be different in fuch cafes from that which accompanies the timely fruit of the wombe: and by reafon of thofe Iffues coming from her, for fo long continued a time before fhee could not have thofe throwes & paffions at the time of her abortion, as women in travaile are fubject unto.

Adde to all this, that at her Tryall fhee ingenuoufly confeffed as much as was alledged by the witneffes: and continued in the fame affertions, not only before, but at her Execution, the laft fuppofed minute of her life; and the very firft words, after fhee came to her felfe againe (which certainly were not fpoken with defigne, or purpofe to deceive) confirmed the fame.

There is yet one thing more which hath beene taken notice of by fome, as to the Maid's defence; That her Grand Profecutor Sir *Thomas Read* died within three dayes after her Execution; even almoft as foone as the probability of her reviving could be well confirmed to him. But becaufe he was an old man, and fuch Events are not too rafhly to be commented on, I fhall not make ufe of that obfervation.

C   It

It may perhaps be expected by some (and 'tis pitty I can give them no better satisfaction) that I should here relate some fine story (like those of *Orpheus* or *Æneas* in the Poëts) of what visions this maid saw in the other world ; what cœlestiall musicke , or hellish howling she heard; what spirits she conversed with,and what Revelations she brought backe with her, concerning the Present Times,or the events of things to come. But for such matters the Ballad-makers must rest contented : since she(as you have heard) was so farre from knowing any thing whilst she was dead, that she remembred not what had happened to her even when she was yet alive. Her spirits, at that time, being either so fixed or benummed with feare, as not to admit of any new Impressions ; or otherwise so turbulent and unquiet, as presently to discompose and obliterate them. As we often see it fares with men that are buzz'd in the head with drinke,or transported with madnesse, who,though they seeme sensible enough of every present object that moves them,yet after they recover can owne but little of what they did or said before.

Having here done with the Story, I cannot but reflect upon the generous attempt of those Gentlemen that freely undertooke, and have soe happily performed the Cure. That whilst they missed the opportunity of improving their knowledge in the dissection of a Dead body, they advanced their fame by restoring to the world a Living one : who now (deservedly) accounts it her happinesse to have fallen into such courteous and skilfull hands:not only for their successefull endeavours used in her Recovery, but for being a meanes to vindicate her from that foule staine of Murther, which, in most mens judgements (and, perhaps, Heaven it selfe also bearing witnesse) was so harshly charged upon her.

FINIS.

Bibliography

Burdet, W. *A Wonder of Wonders,* being a faithful narrative and true relation of one Anne Green. Oxford, 13 January 1651. Source of image on page v.

Fuller, Thomas. *History of the Worthies of England: "Sir Thomas Reade, Knight."* London, 1811.

Hewes, Gordon W. *Human Anatomy at Oxford in 1650: The role of future members of the Royal Society.* Paper given at the Conference on the History and Philosophy of Science, 28 April 1980.

Hughes, J. Trevor. *Miraculous Deliverance of Anne Green: An Oxford case of resuscitation in the 17th Century.* British Medical Journal, 285, 1982.

Oxford Dictionary of National Biography. Entries for Ralph Bathurst, Anne Green, William Petty, Robert Willis, and Christopher Wren. Oxford: Oxford University Press, 2004.

Pears, Iain. *An Instance of the Fingerpost.* New York: Vintage, 1998.

Petty, William. Ed. 6th *Marquis of Lansdowne. The Petty Papers.* William Petty's own notes on the case. London, 1924.

Plot, Robert. *The Natural History of Oxfordshire.* Oxford, 1677.

Robinson, Tho. "Newes from the Dead, or a True and Exact Narration of the Miraculous Deliverance of Anne Green." Leonard Lichfield, 1651.

Walsham, Alexandra. *Providence in Early Modern England.* Oxford: The Clarendon Press, 1999.

Wood, Anthony A. *The Life and times of Anthony A. Wood Antiquary of Oxford 1632-1695.* Oxford Historical Society.

Wrighton, Keith. *English Society 1580-1680.* London: Routledge, 2004.

Zimmer, Carl. *Soul Made Flesh: Thomas Willis, the Discovery of the Brain and How It Changed the World.* London: Heinemann, 2004.

National Archives. "Oxford Circuit Assizes from 1627." www.nationalarchives.gov.UK

MAGIC TREE HOUSE®
Super Edition #1

Danger in the
Darkest Hour

BY MARY POPE OSBORNE
ILLUSTRATED BY SAL MURDOCCA

A STEPPING STONE BOOK™
Random House 🏠 New York

Text copyright © 2015 by Mary Pope Osborne
Jacket art and interior illustrations copyright © 2015 by Sal Murdocca

War pigeons photo: © Bettmann/CORBIS
Enigma machine photo: © DIZ Muenchen GmbH, Sueddeutsche Zeitung Photo/Alamy
Westland Lysander photo: MAC1/Shutterstock.com
Anne Frank photo: © Pictorial Press Ltd/Alamy

Visit us on the Web!
randomhousekids.com
MagicTreeHouse.com

Educators and librarians, for a variety of teaching tools, visit us at
RHTeachersLibrarians.com

Library of Congress Cataloging-in-Publication Data
Osborne, Mary Pope.
Danger in the darkest hour / Mary Pope Osborne. — Magic tree house super edition.
pages cm.
Summary: "The magic tree house has taken Jack and Annie back in time to England in 1944. England is fighting for its life in World War II. Before long, Jack and Annie find themselves parachuting into Normandy, France, behind enemy lines. The date is June 5. Will the brave brother and sister team be able to make a difference during one of the darkest times in history?" —Provided by publisher.
ISBN 978-0-553-49772-4 (trade) — ISBN 978-0-553-49773-1 (lib. bdg.) — ISBN 978-0-553-49774-8 (ebook)
1. World War, 1939–1945—Campaigns—France—Normandy—Juvenile fiction. [1. World War, 1939–1945—Campaigns—France—Normandy—Fiction. 2. Time travel—Fiction. 3. Magic—Fiction. 4. Brothers and sisters—Fiction.] I. Title.
PZ7.O81167Dan 2015 [Fic]—dc23 2014021739

Printed in the United States of America

10 9 8 7 6 5 4 3 2 1

This book has been officially leveled by using the F&P Text Level Gradient™ Leveling System.

In memory of my father,
Colonel William P. Pope,
who fought in World War II

CONTENTS

PROLOGUE

One summer day in Frog Creek, Pennsylvania, a mysterious tree house appeared in the woods. It was filled with books. A boy named Jack and his sister, Annie, found the tree house and soon discovered that it was magic. They could go to any time and place in history just by pointing to a picture in one of the books. While they were gone, no time at all passed back in Frog Creek.

Jack and Annie eventually found out that the tree house belonged to Morgan le Fay, a magical librarian from the legendary realm of Camelot. They have since traveled on many adventures in the magic tree house and completed many missions for both Morgan le Fay and her friend Merlin the magician. Teddy and Kathleen, two young enchanters from Camelot, have sometimes helped Jack and Annie in both big and small ways.

Now Jack and Annie are about to receive an unexpected call for help. . . .

ONE

COMMANDO

"Jack!" Annie shouted from the front yard.

Jack looked up from his book. Tired from a soccer game, he was lying on his bed, reading about volcanoes on Mars. Late-afternoon shadows stretched across his room.

"Jack! *JACK!*"

Jack stood up and crossed to the window. Annie was standing by her bike. A towel was draped around her neck; her hair was wet from swimming in the lake. She was looking up at the sky as if she was searching for something.

"What do you want?" Jack called through the screen.

"Come down!" she called. "Help me look."

"Look for what?" said Jack.

"Just come! You won't believe it!" said Annie.

Jack sighed. He marked his place in his book and went downstairs to the front porch. "This better be good," he said. "I was in the middle of a book."

Annie was still looking up at the sky. "Where did he go?" she said.

"Where did *who* go?" said Jack.

Annie didn't answer. She walked to the edge of the yard and kept looking. "Oh, darn, I don't see him!"

"See who?" said Jack. "What are you talking about?"

"The pigeon!" said Annie.

Jack stared at Annie for a moment. "Seriously?" he said. "You're looking for a *pigeon*?"

"Yes!"

"You called me away from my book to see a *pigeon*?" said Jack.

"Yes! Help me find him!" Annie said.

Jack rolled his eyes and stepped into the yard. He looked up at the hazy sky.

"He was following me. He swooped down near my head," said Annie, still looking in every direction. "I don't see him now. Where could he have gone?"

"What's the big deal?" said Jack. "We see pigeons every day."

"Not like this one," said Annie. "When I was getting on my bike at the lake, I heard a loud cooing. I looked up—he was sitting on a branch, and he looked straight into my eyes. He was super-intelligent, I could tell."

"Are you sure you weren't out in the sun too long?" asked Jack.

"I'm serious," said Annie. "He had these intense staring eyes. I talked to him, like I said 'hi,' and then he took off. I thought, *okay, so much for that*. But then I started riding home and he flew in front of me—right across my path!"

"How do you know it was the same pigeon?" asked Jack.

"I just know. He circled above me all the way home!" said Annie. "He even swooped down a couple more times. But I don't see him now. . . . I don't see him at all. . . ." Her voice trailed off as she looked up at the sky and around the yard.

"Well, that's enough pigeon-hunting for me," said Jack. "I'm heading back to my book." He turned to go inside.

"Ahh! I see him! I see him!" Annie whispered.

Jack stopped. "Where?"

"There!" Annie pointed to a plump pigeon perched on a bird feeder that was hanging from a maple tree. She stepped toward him. The pigeon didn't move. She stepped closer and closer. The bird still didn't move. "Oh, wow, Jack. You won't believe this—I didn't see it until now."

"What? See what?" said Jack.

"Oh, wow, oh, wow," Annie whispered.

Jack walked slowly toward Annie. When he reached her side, he stopped and stared at the bird, too. It was an ordinary-looking pigeon: smoky gray with black stripes on his wings and iridescent-green neck feathers. His amber-colored eyes stared at Jack.

"Look at his leg," Annie whispered.

Attached to one of the pigeon's spindly legs was a tiny red canister. "Whoa," whispered Jack. "I think he's a carrier pigeon."

"A carrier pigeon?" said Annie.

"Yeah, they carried messages to people a long time ago," said Jack. "There used to be lots of them, but not anymore."

"Why not?" Annie asked.

"They're not needed anymore," said Jack. "Not with technology like the Internet and cell phones."

The pigeon made a low cooing sound.

"Why did he follow you?" said Jack. "And where'd he come from?"

Annie took a deep breath. "I know where he came from. I just figured it out," she said.

"Where?"

"Another time," said Annie. "A time before the Internet and cell phones."

Jack's heart skipped a beat. "You think?"

"I *know*," said Annie. "And the message is for us!" She moved a step closer toward the pigeon. But the bird flapped his wings and took off from the feeder. Then he soared out of their yard and up the street, disappearing into the trees of the Frog Creek woods.

"Let's go!" cried Annie.

"Wait, I'll get my pack." Jack bolted into the house, grabbed his backpack from the hallway, and hurried outside.

Jack and Annie raced up the sidewalk. They crossed the street and ran into the woods. As they weaved in and out of dark-green shadows, the late-summer air smelled of sun-dried wood and fallen pine needles. Birds called lazily from the treetops.

Finally they stopped at the base of the tallest oak.

"Of course," said Annie.

She grabbed the rope ladder that dangled from the treetop and started up. Jack followed and they both scrambled inside the magic tree house. Golden sunlight lit the stacks of books and the shimmering *M* in the floor.

"Of course," said Jack.

A soft cooing sound came from the window. The carrier pigeon was pacing on the windowsill.

"Of course a million times," said Annie, laughing. "Don't fly away. I won't hurt you, I promise."

The pigeon stopped pacing and stared at her with his amber eyes.

"I can take that message from you now," Annie whispered, "if you don't mind."

"He doesn't mind," said Jack. "He's a professional."

"Right," said Annie. The pigeon was very still as Annie reached out and gently opened the lid of the red canister attached to his leg. She pulled out a tiny scroll. Then she snapped the lid shut and unrolled the piece of paper.

Annie and Jack looked at the writing together. It wasn't elegant like Merlin's or Morgan le Fay's writing—it was the scrawl of a kid's handwriting. Jack looked at the signature. "It's from Teddy," he said.

"Uh-oh," said Annie. "What happened? Did he goof up again?"

"I'll bet he did," said Jack. They both laughed. The apprentice sorcerer from Camelot often made them laugh. Sometimes he made big mistakes when he tried to do magic. Many of the mistakes were funny, but a few had been terrible.

Annie read the letter aloud:

Dear Jack and Annie,
    I sent Commando to find you.

"Commando?" Jack interrupted. "That's a funny name for a Camelot pigeon."

"Yeah, it sounds like a tough army guy," Annie said. She kept reading:

> Kathleen and I are working with the forces of good in one of the darkest hours of history. And we need your help. Please come to Glastonbury, England. Right now.
>
> Your friend,
> Teddy

"I can't wait to see Teddy and Kathleen," said Annie.

"Yeah," said Jack. He was especially excited to see Kathleen, a brilliant and beautiful young enchantress from Camelot. "But what does Teddy mean—'one of the darkest hours of history'?"

Annie shrugged.

The pigeon made a low cooing sound.

"Commando wants us to hurry," said Annie.

"Okay. Let's go," Jack said. He took another deep breath and pointed to the words *Glastonbury*,

England on the tiny piece of paper. "I wish we could go there."

The wind started to blow.

The tree house started to spin.

It spun faster and faster.

Then everything was still.

Absolutely still.

TWO

TOP-SECRET

Commando cooed as if saying good-bye. Then he flapped his wings and flew out of the tree house. He disappeared into the misty gray twilight.

"Thanks, Commando!" Annie called after him.

"Well, I guess we're here," said Jack, shivering in the chilly air. "But our clothes didn't change. I wonder why."

The tree house had landed in the branches of a tall maple tree. Through the haze, Jack and Annie could see ducks floating on a pond and sheep grazing in a meadow bordered by hedgerows. Beyond the hedges were broken-down buildings— stone pillars and crumbling archways. There was no sign of people.

"It looks ancient," said Annie. "Is Glastonbury part of Camelot?"

"I don't know," said Jack.

"This looks sort of like Camelot," said Annie.

"Yeah, the *ruins* of Camelot," said Jack.

"Teddy! Kathleen!" Annie called.

There was no answer.

"Let's go look for them," said Jack.

Jack grabbed his backpack. He and Annie climbed down the rope ladder. They stepped onto the wet grass and started across the meadow. Rounding a hedge, they came upon the remains of what had once been a huge church. The roof-less building had tall ivy-covered walls and grand arches made of stone blocks.

"Cheerio, friends!" A teenage boy strode through one of the arches. The boy wore an old-fashioned flight suit, gloves, and a tight-fitting leather helmet. He carried a khaki duffel bag.

"Teddy!" cried Annie. She and Jack hurried to the young enchanter of Camelot. Teddy put down his bag, and they all hugged.

"I am glad Commando found you!" said Teddy. "He is quite a smashing soldier, you know."

"Who? The pigeon?" said Annie.

"Yes. Commando is a member of the National Pigeon Service," said Teddy.

Jack and Annie giggled. "You're kidding, right?" said Jack.

"Not at all," said Teddy. "Pigeon breeders have given over two hundred thousand pigeons to the British military to carry messages throughout Europe. Commando has been on dozens of missions. The missions were all in *this* time, of course. He needed the tree house to take him to *your* time."

"So what *is* this time?" asked Jack.

"It is June fourth, 1944," said Teddy. "And you have landed in Glastonbury, England. It is the site of one of the great monasteries of Europe.

"Teddy put down his bag, and they all hugged."

You can still see an ancient tower on the sacred hill of Glastonbury Tor." He pointed to a conical hill overlooking the flat countryside. "Eventually all the sacred buildings fell into ruin, but legends of King Arthur still surround this area. For that reason, I thought it might be a good place to meet you—a living midpoint between our worlds."

"Where's Kathleen?" asked Annie, looking around. "We thought she would be with you."

"Well, that is why I called for you," said Teddy. "But first, how much do you know about World War Two?"

Jack gasped. "Did we come to the time of World War Two?"

"I am afraid you have. The war has been going on for almost five years," said Teddy.

"Oh, man," said Jack.

"So you know about World War Two?" said Teddy.

"Some," said Jack. "I know that America fought Germany and Italy and Japan. And a man named

Adolf Hitler was the leader of Germany. And his political party was called the Nazis."

"And we also know that three of our great-grandfathers fought in World War Two," said Annie.

"The people of England are grateful for all the help the Americans are giving them fighting this war," said Teddy. "At this point, Nazis have taken over most of Europe. They have killed countless innocent civilians, including millions of Jewish people."

"That's terrible," said Annie.

"Really terrible," said Jack. "But what does this war have to do with you and Kathleen?"

"When Merlin looked into the future, he saw this frightful time," said Teddy. "He saw how important it was to bring hope to British leaders. So he sent Kathleen and me to London."

"The leaders actually met with you?" asked Jack.

Teddy smiled. "Indeed they did," he said.

"Kathleen used a bit of magic to make us both appear older than we are. We were quite brilliant, wearing the right disguises and using the right manners and speech. We seem to have inspired everyone, including the prime minister, Winston Churchill."

"Really?" said Jack.

"Oh, yes," said Teddy. "In fact, Winston inducted Kathleen and me into the SOE."

"What's that?" asked Annie.

"SOE stands for Special Operations Executive," said Teddy. "It is a top-secret organization that Winston formed. It conducts undercover missions in countries occupied by the Nazis. In the short time since Kathleen and I completed the required training, we have both been sent on many secret assignments."

"Is Kathleen away on an assignment now?" asked Annie.

"Yes. Kathleen left for a mission in France more than three weeks ago. And now . . ." Teddy stopped.

"And now what?" asked Jack.

"Now it seems she has disappeared," said Teddy.

"Oh, no! What happened to her?" asked Annie.

"I do not know," said Teddy.

"What was her mission?" asked Jack.

"I do not know that, either. She could not tell me," said Teddy. "Secret agents must keep their missions secret even from each other. All I know is that two weeks ago, I was asked to fly behind enemy lines to a location in Normandy, France, to pick her up."

"Fly behind enemy lines?" said Jack.

"Yes. I have done that many times," said Teddy. "But when I arrived at the meeting place, she was not waiting for me. I was frantic, and then yesterday I received a message from her, delivered by a French carrier pigeon."

"So she's okay?" asked Annie.

"Well, at least I know she is alive," said Teddy. "The problem is—she wrote her message in a code, in case it fell into enemy hands. But I have had no success trying to make sense of certain parts of it." He pulled a small piece of paper from his pocket and read Kathleen's message aloud:

> Come to me in the darkest time.
> A wand I need, and a magic rhyme.
> Three miles east of Sir Kay's grave,
> Cross a river to find a cave.
> Look for knights, and small, round cows—
> A crack in a rock beneath the boughs.

Teddy sighed. "You see why I cannot share this with anyone in the SOE?" he said. "Even if they could decipher the code, others would not understand her request for the wand and magic rhyme."

"But why *does* she need them?" asked Jack. "Her magic is amazing. Remember when she turned us all into seals?"

"Yes, but these are very, very dark times," said Teddy. "I am not surprised that she may need extra magic. I have found my own powers very limited. That is why I sent for you."

"So . . . do you have something we can take to Kathleen?" asked Jack.

"Oh, yes," said Teddy. "I have the Wand of Dianthus and the rhyme to unlock its magic."

"Great!" said Annie.

"The next two lines of her message I *do* understand," said Teddy. He read on:

> Three miles east of Sir Kay's grave,
> Cross a river to find a cave.

"The secret burial places of Arthur's knights are revealed in one of Merlin's books," said Teddy. "Kathleen knew I would know that the burial place for Sir Kay is Caen, a town in Normandy, France."

"Wait, I'd better write this down," said Jack. He pulled his notebook and pencil out of his backpack. "Spell that, please?"

"*C-A-E-N,*" said Teddy. Jack wrote the town's name in his notebook.

"So we go to Caen," said Annie. "We travel

three miles east, cross a river, and look for a cave."

"Yes," said Teddy. "But I cannot imagine what the next two lines could mean." He read from the note:

Look for knights and small, round cows—
A crack in a rock beneath the boughs.

Teddy looked up. "Do you understand this?"

"Not really," said Jack. "There weren't any knights fighting in World War Two."

"Indeed not," said Teddy. "And small, round cows? A crack in a rock? Boughs? What does all that mean?" He folded the note and handed it to Annie. "Well, I trust you to figure this out. I know you are expert decoders."

"You're kidding," said Jack. "Us?"

"Of course," said Teddy. "When Kathleen and I went with you to New York City, you figured out the secret poem to free the unicorn from the museum tapestry, remember? And Morgan's missions for you were often written as riddles."

"Yes, but—" started Jack.

"We have to find Kathleen," said Teddy. "I cannot lose her. So many people have been lost in this war. It really is the darkest time—truly a terrible time."

"It's okay, Teddy," Annie said. "We'll help you."

"Of course we will," said Jack. "We'll do our best."

Teddy took a deep breath, then smiled. "Thank you, my friends," he said. "I am most grateful, and sorry that I cannot be with you in France."

"You're not coming with us?" Jack asked.

"No, tonight the SOE is sending me on an urgent mission to rescue downed airmen in Holland and Belgium," said Teddy. "I must do so before daylight."

"Wow," said Annie.

"It is the sort of thing the SOE does every day," said Teddy. Then he clapped his hands together. "All right! Let us roll up our sleeves and get moving! It is time you put on your parachutes."

"Parachutes?" said Jack.

"Yes!" said Teddy. "You cannot jump from

a plane without parachutes!" He picked up his duffel bag and strode off.

"Wait, did he say we're going to jump from a *plane*?" Jack asked Annie.

"He did," said Annie. "But don't worry, he said he'd give us some magic." She hurried after Teddy.

"I know. But—" began Jack.

"Come along, Jack!" Teddy called to him. "The moon is rising over Glastonbury Tor!"

THREE

SPY TAXI

A full moon glowed over Glastonbury Tor as Jack and Annie followed Teddy between the hedges. Moon shadows stretched along the ground.

Teddy rounded a tall bush at the edge of the abbey grounds. "There she is!" he said. He pointed to a small plane sitting in an open field.

"Oh, man," said Jack. "Is that real?" He thought the tiny plane looked like a cartoon. A single propeller was attached to its rounded nose, and it had big, clunky tires.

"Yes! We call it a spy taxi," said Teddy. "It was made especially for secret operations. It can fly low under enemy radar and land in tight places."

"How many people does it carry?" asked Jack.

"It is designed to carry only a pilot and one passenger," said Teddy. "But it also has room for supply canisters, which I am not carrying. So one of you can take that space."

"But what about when we add Kathleen?" said Annie.

"Do not worry," said Teddy. "I think we can all squeeze together. And if that does not work, perhaps with the magic you bring her, Kathleen can make everyone fit."

"Good," said Jack. He was eager to get the Wand of Dianthus from Teddy. "And another question: where will you pick us up?"

"In the same place I drop you off," said Teddy. "I have been to that drop zone before. It is a lonely field and, to the best of our knowledge, not under enemy observation. You will have to get back there from wherever you find Kathleen."

"Got it," said Annie.

"But an equally important question is *when* I will pick you up," said Teddy. "And that is a question *you* will have to answer."

"How do we answer it?" asked Annie.

"When you know that it is time to leave, you must send me a secret message," said Teddy.

"By pigeon?" asked Annie.

"No, a carrier pigeon might be difficult for you to find. It would be easier to send a message over a wireless radio," said Teddy.

"What should our message say?" asked Annie.

"In your message, say . . ." Teddy thought for a moment, and then smiled. "Say, *The unicorn is free.* And—"

"Wait, wait," said Jack. He wrote in his notebook:

The unicorn is free.

"And then add the date and time," said Teddy. "Send that message over a wireless radio, and

I will pick you up at that time in the field where I drop you tonight."

"How do we find a wireless radio?" asked Jack.

"As you go about your mission, be on the lookout for members of the French Resistance," said Teddy. "Any one of them will help you find a wireless."

"What's the French Resistance?" asked Annie.

"Throughout France, there are French citizens who are secretly fighting back against the Nazis who have occupied their country," Teddy explained. "They are called Resistance fighters. They live very dangerous lives. If a member of the Resistance is caught by the Nazis, he or she will be imprisoned or killed."

"That's terrible," said Annie. "So how do we find someone in the French Resistance?"

"There are many ways," said Teddy. "The simplest way, though, is to make the *V Is for Victory* sign." He held up two fingers in the shape of a V. "It is a secret way for one Resistance fighter to recognize another. You can make the sign with your fingers, draw it on a piece of paper, scratch it into the dirt, or signal any way you can."

Jack and Annie both held fingers up in a *V Is for Victory* sign.

"Good. But be very careful," said Teddy. "If you give the sign to the wrong person, you could end up in the hands of the enemy."

Teddy reached into his large duffel bag and took out some clothes. "These are your disguises," he said. He handed Jack and Annie each a pair of corduroy overalls and a long-sleeved shirt. They pulled them on over their shorts and T-shirts.

"And these," said Teddy. He handed them each a pair of boots. They took off their sneakers and pulled on their boots.

"And a field pack instead of your backpack," said Teddy. He gave Jack an old-fashioned-looking pack with buckles. "You will have to wear it on your chest. Your parachute will be on your back."

Jack moved his notebook, pen, and pencil from his backpack into the field pack. He left his backpack beside his sneakers.

"And now your flying gear," said Teddy. He took out two leather helmets and two pairs of goggles.

Jack and Annie each pulled on a tight-fitting leather helmet. Then Jack positioned his goggles over his glasses.

"And a torchlight," said Teddy. He handed a large, heavy flashlight to Jack.

Jack put the flashlight into the field pack.

"And now . . ." Teddy climbed up a short stepladder to the door of the plane and pulled out two bulky contraptions. They looked like long canvas backpacks attached to a complicated web of straps and buckles. "Your parachute harnesses!" he said, descending the stepladder. "Come on, I will strap you in!"

One at a time, Teddy buckled Jack and Annie into their parachutes. Then he attached the field pack to the front of Jack's harness.

"So how does all this work?" said Jack. He was fighting to stay calm.

Teddy pointed to a large metal ring on the strap across Jack's chest. "This is your rip-cord handle.

When you pull it, it will release your parachute."

"Okay. But *when* do we pull it?" asked Jack.

"After you step off the plane, you will plunge through the open air," said Teddy. "Count to five, then pull hard on the handle. Easy."

Easy? Jack felt a little sick already.

"Remember, jump quickly, one after the other," Teddy said. "If you do not, you will land too far apart and lose each other completely."

"Got it," said Annie.

"And finally . . . ," said Teddy. He handed them each a printed card with a small photograph. "Identity cards. You now have French names— Jean and Aimée."

"Where did you get our photos?" asked Jack.

"A tap of the wand helped with that," said Teddy.

"Cool," said Jack. He was relieved when he remembered they would have the Wand of Dianthus. He thought their mission would be impossible without magic.

"Climb aboard!" said Teddy. He scrambled up the stepladder. Annie bounded after him.

Jack didn't know how she did it. The parachute equipment felt very heavy and clumsy to him. He climbed awkwardly into the plane after Teddy and Annie.

Teddy was already sitting in the pilot's seat, in front of a control panel. "Position yourselves behind me," he said.

Jack and Annie crouched in the narrow space behind the pilot's seat, squashed by their parachute gear.

"Remember, when you jump, face the earth," said Teddy. "Arch your back, spread your arms out, and count to five. Then pull the rip-cord handle. As you float down, keep your elbows close in. Then roll onto your left side."

"Wait, wait," said Jack. "Can you go over all that again?"

"Easy," said Teddy. "Eight simple steps—"

"Hold on, I'll write them down," said Jack. He pulled out his notebook and pencil from the field pack. As Teddy gave the directions again, Jack wrote:

1. Legs together
2. Face earth
3. Arch back
4. Spread arms
5. Count to five
6. Pull rip cord
7. Elbows in
8. Roll to the left

Annie and Jack stared at the notebook, whispering the steps to themselves.

"Got it," said Annie.

"After you land," said Teddy, "roll up your chutes and hide them. Hide your helmets and goggles, too, and destroy your notes."

"Got it," said Annie.

"All right!" said Teddy. "Gas! Oil!"

Jack peered around Teddy at the instrument panel. There were at least a dozen round gauges. Some monitored oil pressure, fuel pressure, and temperature. There were also compasses, brake controls, knobs, buttons, switches, and levers.

Oh, man, thought Jack. "You must have had a lot of training," he said to Teddy.

"Indeed. A full week," said Teddy.

"A *week*? That's *all*?" said Jack.

"Yes, it was very intense," said Teddy as he started flipping switches. "They said I was a natural." Green lights lit up the panel. Needles swung right and left.

"Air intake control!" Teddy announced. He turned a knob. "It is much easier than learning magic!"

Jack felt a wave of panic. "Teddy, slow down!" he said.

"Engine-starter button!" Teddy shouted, pushing a button.

"Teddy, are you sure you know how to do this?" Jack said. But his voice was drowned out by the sound of the engine as the propeller started to spin.

The big wheels began rolling. The plane shook as it bumped over the grass. Then, rocking from side to side, the spy taxi lifted into the air. As the tiny, cramped plane climbed higher into the moonlit night, Teddy pushed more buttons and pulled more levers and shouted out more information.

His heart racing, Jack tried to focus on the eight steps. He whispered: "Legs together—face earth—arch back—spread arms—count to five—pull rip cord—elbows in—roll to the left . . . What does that mean?"

Jack shook Annie's arm. "What does number eight mean?" he shouted.

"What?" she yelled back.

"NUMBER EIGHT!" shouted Jack, jabbing his finger at the list. "DO YOU ROLL IN THE AIR OR ROLL ON THE GROUND?"

"I THINK ON THE GROUND!" Annie answered.

Jack nodded. That made sense. As the plane rumbled through the night, Jack whispered the instructions to himself again and again.

"We are crossing the English Channel!" Teddy called. "Normandy soon, and your dropping point! Get ready!"

Jack crammed his notebook and pencil back into his field pack. His fingers were trembling so much, he had trouble buckling it.

"We are over France now!" shouted Teddy.

"Oh, no," murmured Jack.

"We are coming to the drop zone!" cried Teddy. "Get ready to jump!"

Jack froze with fear.

"Open the door!" yelled Teddy.

Jack couldn't move. Annie pulled up the latch, slid open the door, and crouched at the edge of the plane. With the door open, the roar of the engine and propellers was deafening.

Jack looked down at the endless dark. *No way I can jump!* he thought. *Not without magic help.* Jack bolted upright. *Oh, no! We forgot to get the wand!*

"TEDDY, WE NEED—" Jack shouted.

Teddy couldn't hear him. "JUMP!" he yelled.

"WAIT! MAGIC FOR KATHLEEN!" cried Jack.

It was too late. Annie leaned out of the plane.

She fell forward, arching her back and spreading out her arms.

"TEDDY! THE MAGIC!" cried Jack.

"JUMP, JACK!" Teddy yelled.

Jack had no choice. He had to jump *now*, or he'd land far away from Annie and they'd never find each other. Jack closed his eyes and hurled himself out of the plane, down into the moonlit, windless night.

FOUR

BEHIND ENEMY LINES

Falling through the air, Jack forgot everything he'd written down. He forgot: *legs together—face earth—arch back—spread arms—count to five*. But miraculously, he remembered, *Pull rip cord!*

Jack fumbled for the cord on his chest strap. He grabbed the metal ring and pulled hard. The parachute popped out from Jack's harness.

As the chute's white canopy opened above Jack, it yanked him backward. The billowing silk slowed his downward plunge. Jack clutched his field pack as he drifted through the night air.

The drone of the spy taxi engine faded into the distance. Teddy was gone. Not far away, Jack could see Annie in the moonlight, floating to earth, too. "Hi!" she yelled to Jack.

Jack was too amazed to answer. He was filled with a strange happiness as they both drifted in a dreamlike fall toward the field below.

Suddenly the earth rose up to meet him. Jack hit the ground with a thud and, remembering the eighth step, rolled onto his left side. He lay in the cold damp grass, trying to catch his breath.

"We're in France! We did it!" Annie called from nearby. She threw off her parachute harness and ran to Jack.

"We did it," he repeated, sitting up. His parachute lay spread on the ground behind him. "We did it!"

"Wasn't it fun?" said Annie.

"Yeah . . . yeah, it was," said Jack in a daze.

Jack wiggled out of his harness. Floating through the night sky actually *had* been fun—

"Suddenly the earth rose up to meet him."

although he had no idea how he'd done what he'd just done. "I have some bad news, though."

"What?" asked Annie.

"Teddy forgot to give us the magic wand for Kathleen," said Jack.

"Oh, no," moaned Annie.

"'Oh, no' is right," said Jack.

"I guess it means we'll have to help Kathleen without magic," said Annie. "But that's okay. We have lots of skills."

"Like what?" Jack asked.

"Well, like—just a lot of skills," said Annie. "Don't worry. We can do this. Let's go."

"Hold on. We have to roll up our chutes and figure out where we are first," said Jack. He and Annie looked around. In the moonlight, they could see trees bordering the field on three sides and a road on the fourth side. A church with a tall white steeple was down the road.

"Let's take that road," said Annie.

"Yep," said Jack. "That should work. But we

have to hide the parachutes before we go."

In the quiet night, Jack stood up and strapped his field pack on his back. He and Annie carefully rolled up the soft silk canopies of their parachutes. They gathered the straps and tangled cords in their arms and started across the field.

"Hey," said Annie, stopping. "I hear a plane."

"Teddy's back!" said Jack. "He remembered that he forgot to give us the magic wand and spell!"

"Yay!" said Annie.

"Wait," said Jack, squinting at the sky. Not just one plane—but *three* planes droned overhead!

"It's not Teddy," said Annie.

"Run!" said Jack.

As the planes dipped down over the field, Jack and Annie ran toward the road, lugging the bundles of their parachutes.

"Get down!" Jack shouted. He pushed Annie into a ditch at the edge of the road. Clutching their gear, they lay in a thick bed of wet and rotting leaves.

The planes roared off into the distance. After a long silence, Jack and Annie stood up. "They're gone," Jack said.

"So what do we do now?" Annie asked.

"We have to find that town," said Jack. He looked around at the moonlit dark. "But we might have to wait for daylight to figure out how to get there."

Jack saw the glare of car headlights coming up the road. "Hide!" cried Annie.

They threw themselves facedown again in the ditch. Jack held his breath as the car rumbled by. Soon all was quiet again, except for the distant barking of dogs.

Jack and Annie lifted their heads. "We have to get away from this road," said Jack, "and find a place where we can stay hidden for a while. Remember, we're behind enemy lines. Nazis could be anywhere. Come on."

Annie didn't say anything. She didn't move.

"Hey, are you okay?" Jack asked her.

"No. I'm scared," Annie said in a whisper.

"You are?" said Jack. He knelt beside her. Annie was never scared. *He* was always the scared one.

"This seems so dangerous," she said. "Hiding from Nazis."

Jack was frightened, too. She was right. Hiding from Nazis seemed much scarier than anything they'd done before. But if Annie was scared, *he* had to act brave. "It's okay," he said. "Think about what you told me earlier—we don't have magic, but we've got skills. And we've used our skills again and again on our missions. Right?"

"Right . . . ," said Annie.

"Well, we'll use them this time," said Jack.

"You think we can?" asked Annie.

"I know we can," said Jack. "First, we need to get to a safe spot." He pulled out his flashlight and pointed it toward the road. The light lit up a sign that said *Biéville*. Not far down the road was the white church. "Okay. Biéville. This is where Teddy will pick us up with Kathleen."

"Right," said Annie. "The field near the sign that says Biéville, near the white church."

"See, we solved that. With our observation skill," said Jack. "So now we'll head into the woods across the road and hide there until daylight. Okay? That's the skill of, um—"

"Being smart," said Annie. She stood up. "Let's bury our stuff here."

"Good idea, I'd forgotten that," said Jack. "See? Skills! We got 'em!"

They buried their parachute gear under piles of leaves and brush. "Don't forget these," said Jack. He pulled off his helmet and goggles and shoved them under the heap. Annie did the same. "And my notes!" Jack ripped his notes out of his notebook, tore them up, and hid the pieces with everything else.

"Okay!" he said. "Onward! Let's go!" With Annie close behind, Jack led the way across the road and into the woods.

Tramping through tangled undergrowth, Jack and Annie made their way deeper into the moon-lit forest. They didn't stop until they came to a wooden fence. When Jack pointed their flashlight toward the area beyond the fence, it shone on neat rows of vine-covered trellises.

"Looks like a vineyard," he said.

"What's that?" asked Annie.

"You know, where they grow grapes to make wine," said Jack. "We shouldn't trespass—"

Before he could finish, Annie grabbed his arm. "Listen!"

Jack listened. From the woods behind them came the sound of a dog barking. Then he heard men's voices.

"They're searching for us!" said Annie.

"Trespass!" said Jack. He turned off his flashlight, and they scrambled over the wooden fence and took off running through the moonlit vineyard. They ran between long rows of grapevines until they saw a small farmhouse ahead. Smoke was rising from the chimney. Not far from the house was a barn.

The barking behind them was getting louder. It sounded as if the searchers had entered the vineyard and were heading their way.

"There!" said Jack. He grabbed Annie's hand and pulled her toward the barn. Jack yanked open a wooden door, and the two of them ran inside.

Jack switched his flashlight back on and shined it around the barn. Horses stood in stalls, swishing their tails and munching hay.

"There!" Annie pointed to a stack of hay bales in the back. They crouched together behind the bales. Jack turned off the flashlight and put it in his field pack. He and Annie waited motionless, huddled on the floor, inhaling hay dust and animal smells and trying to breathe as quietly as they could.

The barking grew louder and closer. The horses moved restlessly. Jack heard men shouting above the barking, but he couldn't understand what they were saying.

Then the door to the barn banged open. "Fritz! Check inside!" a man said.

Jack heard two sharp barks and the sound of a dog sniffing and scratching. The next thing he knew, a German shepherd bounded over to the hay bales! With a low growl, it bared its teeth.

"It's okay!" Annie whispered to the dog. "It's okay."

The dog snorted and sniffed their faces. Jack didn't move a muscle as Annie gently stroked the dog's head and whispered in its ear.

The dog grew calm. Annie whispered again. The shepherd licked her face. Then it barked once and loped out of the barn.

"Nothing in there, Fritz?" the man said to the dog. "Good boy." Then the door slammed shut. The men's voices faded away. Everything grew quiet.

Jack and Annie waited a long moment. Then Jack let out his breath. "What did you say to that police dog?" he asked.

Annie shrugged. "I said, 'Good dog, everything's okay. We're friends.' I just didn't tell him whose friends we were."

Jack shook his head in amazement.

"Let's escape while we can," said Annie.

Jack was relieved. Annie sounded like her old self again. *Calming the dog calmed her, too,* he thought. "Okay, but let's go slowly."

Just as Jack and Annie stood up, the door to the barn creaked open again. Jack's heart pounded as they dropped back behind the hay bales.

The barn was lit with flickering lantern light. Jack heard footsteps on the wooden floor. The steps grew closer and closer. Then a man with a black beard peered over the hay bales. He wore a black beret slanted over one eye.

"Aha! We found you!" he said in a deep, growly whisper.

FIVE

RESISTANCE

Jack was too terrified to speak.

Annie slowly held up two fingers in a *V Is for Victory* sign.

What is she doing? Jack thought wildly. *We don't know who this guy is!*

The man glared at Annie for a moment; then his craggy face broke into a smile, and he held up his fingers in a matching V.

Oh, man, thought Jack. *Did we really just find a member of the French Resistance?*

"Who are they, Gaston?" a woman called from the barn doorway.

"Who are you?" Gaston asked in a raspy voice.

"J-J . . . ," Jack stuttered, terrified.

"Jean and Aimée," Annie said quickly.

Annie's a good spy, Jack thought. He'd completely forgotten their French names.

"Really?" said the man. "Are those your real names?"

Annie laughed. "No, our real names are Jack and Annie."

Oh, brother, Jack thought. *She's a terrible spy!*

"And what are Jack and Annie doing in our barn?" asked Gaston.

"We're hiding from the Nazis," Annie said.

"Well, then," said Gaston, "you are in the right place."

"For the moment, you are safe, children," said the woman, stepping forward. She wore a shawl around her shoulders and a kerchief over her dark hair. "Hello, my dears. My name is Suzette, and this is my husband, Gaston."

"Nice to meet you," said Annie.

"Come with us, back to our house," said Suzette.

Jack and Annie climbed out from behind the hay bales and followed the French couple to the door of the barn. Before they left, Gaston blew out his lantern light. "Silence," he ordered, "until we get into the house."

Gaston and Suzette led Jack and Annie through the dark to the front door of the small stone farmhouse. Once they were inside, Jack and Annie looked around the room. It had a low ceiling. Candles burned on a heavy wooden table. A fire flickered in a large fireplace.

Suzette placed an iron bar over the front door, while Gaston closed the window shutters.

"Sit, children," said Suzette. "We will have apple cider, and you will share our dinner."

Jack and Annie sat at the table near the hearth. A pot hung over the fire. Jack relaxed a little as he smelled roasting potatoes, onions, and carrots.

Gaston poured cider into mugs, and Suzette

prepared four bowls of stew. Then the couple joined Jack and Annie at the table. The fire crackled as they all quietly sipped cider and ate their dinner.

When they were finished, Gaston leaned back in his chair and lit a pipe. "You know," he said, "when the Nazis were here earlier, they were not looking for you."

"They weren't?" said Annie.

"No, they were looking for two paratroopers who'd been spotted dropping into a field near here," said Gaston.

"Oh. Then they *were* looking for us," said Jack.

"No, no—" Gaston stopped and gave Jack a funny look. "Unless you two could be those paratroopers?"

"Yes, we could be," said Annie.

"But no!" said Gaston. "How could two *children* parachute into Normandy? And why?"

"We're working with agents of the SOE," said Annie.

"But no!" Gaston said again.

"Oh, my," said Suzette. "Are things so bad that children are being recruited as spies now?"

"Well, not just *any* children," said Annie. "We were asked because one of our best friends is an SOE agent. We have information that she is three miles east of Caen. We're supposed to find her and get her out of France."

"Then you do not have far to go," said Gaston. "We are only four miles northwest of Caen."

"There is great danger, though," said Suzette. "The city is surrounded by Nazi patrols. You will need the right papers."

"We have identity cards," said Annie.

"Good," said Gaston, standing up. "Come with me. We will hide you here tonight and help you get on your way in the morning."

"Thank you," said Jack, standing up with Annie.

"Thanks for the dinner," Annie said to Suzette.

"It is my pleasure to feed two brave children again," Suzette said.

Why did she say "again"? Jack wondered.

"Come along," Gaston said, waving his arm. Jack and Annie followed him to a room off the kitchen.

Gaston pulled aside a floor rug, revealing a trapdoor. He lifted the door, and then, carrying a lantern, he led Jack and Annie down a staircase to a cellar. Hundreds of wine bottles sat in racks along the walls of the dank, musty room.

"Suzette will bring bedding," said Gaston. "And you can keep the light with you." He placed the lantern on a long table and then started back up the steps. Without looking back, he raised his hand. "Good night!" he said.

"Thank you!" called Jack and Annie.

When Gaston was gone, Annie sat down at the table. "Wow, they saved us," she said.

"For now," said Jack.

"I wonder what these little rubber blocks are for," said Annie. She picked up a small block from the table and held it to the lantern light. "Look—it has the letter *H* on it."

Jack walked over to her. On the table were dozens

of small rubber blocks and several stacks of paper.

"And this one has the letter *S*," said Annie, holding up another block.

"Here's a *D*," said Jack. "*S* and *U*. They're all letters. It must be a printing set."

"Check this out," said Annie. She picked up a piece of paper from one of the stacks on the table. She showed it to Jack.

He read the print on the page aloud:

HOPE AND COURAGE!
FREEDOM SOON!

Annie thumbed through more papers in the stack. "They all say the same thing," she said. "It's a bunch of flyers. Do you think Gaston and Suzette secretly pass them out?"

"Here is your bedding, children," said Suzette, coming down the steps to the cellar. When she saw Annie holding one of the flyers, she stopped.

"Did you and Gaston print these?" Annie asked.

Suzette crossed the room and stood in the

lantern light. "No, we didn't," she said softly. "Our sons did."

"Your sons?" asked Annie.

"Our brave twins, Tom and Theo," said Suzette. "They are couriers for the French Resistance."

"What are couriers?" asked Jack.

"Couriers travel on bicycles, delivering messages from one resistance group to another," said Suzette. "Tom and Theo also printed flyers to give people hope. On their courier routes, they sometimes posted them when no one was looking. Only . . . one day someone *was* looking."

"What happened?" asked Annie.

"Three months ago we received word that Tom and Theo were picked up in Paris by the Nazis," said Suzette.

"So . . . they're in prison now?" asked Annie.

Suzette took a deep breath. "We do not know what has happened to them," she said.

"I'm sorry," said Annie. "Are Tom and Theo children?"

"They are young men. Twenty-two years old,"

said Suzette. "But they will always be our children."

"Are you and Gaston in the French Resistance, too?" asked Jack.

Suzette nodded. "Our job is to gather and send information." She turned away from them. "But *now* my job is to make your beds."

"We'll help," said Annie. She and Jack helped Suzette spread the threadbare blankets on the floor.

"I fear you will not be so comfortable," said Suzette. "But at least you will be safe."

"That's all that matters," said Jack.

"Thank you, Suzette!" said Annie, and she hugged the kind Frenchwoman.

"Try to sleep now, children," said Suzette. "You will need all your strength tomorrow to find your friend." Then she climbed the stairs and closed the door to the cellar.

"That's so sad about their boys," said Annie.

"Yeah," said Jack. He didn't know what else to say. He was amazed by the courage of Gaston and Suzette. Even after their sons were caught, the couple was willing to risk their lives to help others.

"So tomorrow we head to Caen," said Annie.

Jack nodded. "Do you have Kathleen's message?"

Annie pulled the piece of paper from her pocket and read aloud:

Come to me in the darkest time.
A wand I need, and a magic rhyme.
Three miles east of Sir Kay's grave,
Cross a river to find a cave.
Look for knights, and small, round cows—
A crack in a rock beneath the boughs.

"So we've figured out the first four lines," said Annie. "We know Kathleen needs magic—which Teddy forgot to give us."

"Right," said Jack. "And we know we have to go three miles east of a town named Caen—and then cross a river to find a cave."

"Right," said Annie. "And then the weird part." She reread:

Look for knights, and small, round cows—
A crack in a rock beneath the boughs.

Jack shook his head. His brain was getting foggy. "Let's ask Gaston and Suzette in the morning if they have any ideas," he said.

"Good plan," said Annie.

They pulled off their boots and lay down on the ragged blankets.

"We'll figure it all out tomorrow," Annie murmured.

"Yeah, right now, I'm way too tired," said Jack, closing his eyes. He was exhausted from traveling through time to Glastonbury, flying over the English Channel, parachuting into Normandy, running from planes, lying in a ditch, hiding in a barn, escaping Nazis, and making friends with people in the French Resistance—all between twilight and bedtime.

SIX

The Hour of Battle

"Jack! Annie! Wake up!" said Suzette. She stood at the bottom of the cellar stairs. "It is morning. There is news!"

Jack opened his eyes. Where were they? He squinted at the racks of wine bottles against the wall and the table with the flyers and the printing set. Then he remembered: a cellar in Normandy, France. He sat up.

"What news?" Annie asked.

"We just received a message from the London BBC," said Suzette. "It was the message we have been waiting for. The hour of the great battle is coming! Tomorrow, June sixth."

"What battle?" asked Jack.

"The invasion of France," said Suzette. "The invasion by the Allies. The English, Scots, Americans, Canadians, and others will all invade France and drive out the Nazis, starting tomorrow!"

"Really?" said Jack.

"Yes!" said Suzette. "Excuse me, I must get back to Gaston. He is getting more news from the BBC over the wireless." She hurried up the steps.

"Oh, wow!" said Annie. "Did you hear what she said?"

"Yes, the Allies—" said Jack.

"No, the *wireless*—" interrupted Annie. "They have a wireless! Once we find Kathleen, we can come back here and send Teddy a message."

"You're right," said Jack. "But now let's go find out more about that invasion."

Jack and Annie dashed up the stairs, taking two steps at a time. Gaston was at the kitchen table. Smoking his pipe, he was hunched over a small open suitcase. Inside was a radio with tubes and knobs. Gaston wore a headset and was listening carefully.

"Plan Purple!" he shouted.

"Plan Purple!" Suzette repeated.

"Plan Purple? What's that?" Jack said.

"It means all the Resistance must act now," she said. "They must destroy communication lines to keep the Nazis in the south from finding out about the invasion."

Gaston took off his headset and pointed his pipe at Suzette. "Plan Green—and now Plan Purple."

"What's Plan Green?" said Jack.

"We received word of Plan Green a few days ago," said Suzette. "It called upon Resistance fighters to blow up bridges and train tracks to keep enemy troops from traveling here."

"Why would they travel *here*?" asked Annie.

"This is where the Allied invasion will take place," said Gaston. "Here in Normandy! The Allies will come by air and sea. Tomorrow they will land on beaches not far from Caen, and then fight their way across France."

"Oh, man. I get it now," Jack murmured. "*D-Day.* Tomorrow is D-Day."

"Listen to me, children," said Gaston. He pointed his pipe at them. "You must tell *no one* what we have just told you."

"We won't. We promise," said Annie, shaking her head.

"And you must leave France at once," Gaston said. "Now!"

"Leave now?" said Jack.

"Yes, return to England immediately," said Gaston. "There will be terrible fighting here tomorrow. Many bombs will drop."

"But we have to find our friend Kathleen," said Annie.

"Ahh! You cannot worry about your friend now!" Gaston said. "You must worry about yourselves!"

"It is quite possible, children, that your friend has already gone south," Suzette said. "Perhaps she has crossed the Pyrenees mountains into Spain. Many people have escaped that way and found safety."

"*Gaston was at the kitchen table.*"

"We have to at least *try* to find Kathleen before we can leave," said Annie. "That's our mission."

"Then you have only today to find her," said Gaston. "You *must* leave France by nightfall."

"We'd better get going, then," Annie said.

"Wait," said Jack. He turned to Gaston. "We have a favor to ask. Can you send a message by wireless to our contact in the SOE and let him know that we must be picked up tonight?"

"Yes, I can do that," said Gaston.

"And I will prepare food for you," said Suzette.

"And I'll get our stuff," said Annie.

Suzette and Annie left the kitchen. Gaston grabbed a piece of paper and a pencil. "What should the message say?" he asked Jack.

"The unicorn is free—nightfall June fifth," said Jack.

"The unicorn . . . is . . . free . . . nightfall . . . June fifth," Gaston repeated as he wrote down the message. "I like that," he said, nodding. "The unicorn is free. It sounds very hopeful. It sounds like a message I would like to get about my sons someday."

"I'm sorry they disappeared," Jack said.

"Yes . . . ," whispered Gaston. "As am I." He shook his head. "Well!" His voice boomed. "It's wartime! And war is terrible for everyone, is it not?"

"Yes, it is," said Jack.

"Got everything!" said Annie, returning to the kitchen. She was carrying their boots and Jack's field pack.

"And here is a bit of food," said Suzette. She gave Annie a small sack.

"Thanks!" said Annie. She put the sack of food in Jack's pack. Then she and Jack pulled on their boots.

"It is half past eight now," said Gaston, looking at his watch. "It will be dark by eight o'clock tonight. So you have nearly twelve hours to find your friend."

"Oh, we almost forgot to ask you!" said Annie. She pulled out Kathleen's rhyme. "This is the message she sent about where to look for her." She read aloud the third and fourth lines of the rhyme:

Three miles east of Sir Kay's grave,
Cross a river to find a cave.

"So we know we go to Caen first," said Jack, "since that's where Sir Kay is buried. And then we'll head three miles east from there and cross a river."

"The River Orne!" said Suzette.

"Great!" said Jack. "And then we look for a cave."

"Yes, but there are many caves east of the River Orne in Mondeville," said Gaston. "Long ago, they mined limestone rock in that area, creating caverns and tunnels."

"I wonder how we find the right one," Jack said.

"I do not know," said Gaston, frowning.

"Here are the next lines," said Annie. She showed Gaston the message and read aloud:

Look for knights, and small, round cows—
A crack in a rock beneath the boughs.

"Knights?" growled Gaston. "What does your

friend mean? Knights in armor? Knights from the Middle Ages?"

Annie shrugged.

"Small, round cows . . . ?" said Suzette. She shook her head. "That doesn't make sense to me."

"Nor to me," said Gaston.

"It's okay. We'll figure out that part later," said Annie. "You've been a big help just telling us about the River Orne and the caves in Mondeville." She put the note back in her pocket.

"Let's go," said Jack. He took his field pack from Annie and pulled it on.

"Come along, then," said Gaston. He led them out of the farmhouse into the chilly morning. The windy air smelled of wood smoke. The sky was overcast.

"Do you have money?" said Suzette.

"Actually, no," said Jack.

"Gaston?" said Suzette.

Gaston reached into the pocket of his trousers and brought out a handful of coins. "French francs for you," he said, handing them to Jack.

"Thank you!" Jack dropped the francs into his pocket.

"Gaston, they will need bicycles, too," said Suzette.

"Yes, yes. Come along," said Gaston. They all followed him to the barn. Gaston stepped inside and came out a moment later, carrying two bikes. "You can ride these. They belonged to our boys when they were younger."

"Just follow any road to the south," said Suzette, "and you will come to Caen."

"Keep to the back roads," said Gaston. "There are fewer motorcars on them."

"Which way is south?" asked Annie.

"Wait, I will give you something to guide you." Suzette slipped back into the house and returned a moment later. "Take this compass. It belonged to Tom and Theo." She handed a small silver compass to Annie. Then she gave Jack and Annie each a flat black cap. "These berets belonged to them, too."

"Thank you," said Annie. When they put on the

berets, Jack adjusted his to look like Gaston's.

Suzette smiled. "Good. Now you look French."

"If you come to a checkpoint," said Gaston, "act very calm when you pass the sentries. If they stop you and ask for papers, show them your identity cards. Do not give the V sign to anyone unless you are certain that person is on our side."

"Many of our citizens do not belong to the Resistance," Suzette explained.

"In these times, you never know who your friends and enemies are," growled Gaston. "And that is why you must tell no one about the invasion tomorrow."

"We won't, we promise," said Annie.

"But I'll tell *you* guys something," said Jack.

"What is that?" said Gaston.

Jack took a deep breath, and then said, "The invasion will be a success. Tom and Theo wrote the truth: France *will* gain back its freedom."

Gaston gave him a crooked smile.

"Jack's right," said Annie. "It might take time, but we know you'll be free. We know it for a fact."

Sudden tears filled Gaston's eyes. He nodded briskly, and then turned his face away.

"Thank you for your kind words, children," said Suzette, putting an arm around Gaston. "Ride south on the lane running past the farm. Gaston will send your message over the wireless. I hope your SOE contact receives it. And I hope you find your dear friend and take her back to England with you."

"Thanks," said Jack. "Thanks for everything."

Jack and Annie climbed onto the bikes. They rode down the bumpy dirt path away from the farmhouse. When they came to the lane, Annie pulled out the compass. "South—that way," she said, pointing to the right.

Before they turned onto the lane, Jack and Annie looked back. The French couple was still watching them. Gaston held up two fingers in a *V Is for Victory* sign.

Jack and Annie each flashed the sign back at him. Then they turned onto the lane and headed south.

SEVEN

FRIENDS AND ENEMIES

Jack and Annie rode with the wind at their backs. The spring air smelled of plowed soil and freshly cut hay. As their bicycles wobbled down the dirt lane, they passed apple orchards, wheat fields, vineyards, and farmhouses.

"I can't believe it!" Jack called to Annie. "The Allied invasion of Normandy! That was called D-Day! D-Day! Have you ever heard of it?"

"Yes, but I don't know exactly what it was," said Annie.

"I read a book about it," said Jack. "It was one

of the most important military events of all time. Over a hundred thousand soldiers landed in Normandy, France, to fight Hitler's army. It was the beginning of the end of World War Two! I can't believe we came here on the day before D-Day."

"I hope everything doesn't get destroyed by bombs," said Annie. "It's beautiful here."

"Yeah, it is," said Jack. The countryside looked like an old painting: peach-colored farmhouses, apple trees with white flowers, red poppies blooming in fields. Everything was so peaceful and lovely that Jack could hardly believe the battle of D-Day would start here tomorrow. It gave him a strange feeling to know what was coming.

After bumping over ruts and ridges, Jack and Annie came to the end of the dirt lane. Annie checked the compass. "Left," she said.

They turned left and pedaled down the wide road bordered by hedgerows. The hedges were so tall it was impossible to see beyond them.

"Are we on a back road?" Annie asked.

"I can't tell," Jack said.

They hadn't gone much farther when a motor-cycle turned onto the road and headed their way.

Friend? Enemy? Jack wondered anxiously. In case it was an enemy, he called out to Annie, "Act normal!"

"Right!" said Annie. They both smiled broadly and steered their bikes single file along the edge of the road. Jack was glad that Suzette had said wearing berets made them look French. When the motorcycle roared past, the driver didn't even look their way.

The motorcycle disappeared in the distance, but then another car turned onto the road. As it headed toward them, Jack tried to look normal again. Just as the car sped past, he glanced in its direction. To his amazement, a woman driver flashed a quick *V Is for Victory* sign.

Jack grinned and gave the sign back. "Friend!" he called to Annie. The woman's V signal made him feel hopeful. *Maybe this isn't going to be so hard,* he thought.

Coming toward them next was a horse and cart

driven by a young man who looked like a farmer. Seated beside him was a teenage girl. When they saw Jack and Annie, they smiled and nodded.

Definitely friends, Jack thought. When he got close to the couple, he flashed the *V Is for Victory* sign at them, too.

An angry look crossed the man's face. He cried out in alarm. He pulled his horse to a halt and pointed at Jack and Annie. "Couriers! Resistance!" he shouted.

Oh, no! thought Jack. Gaston was right! In these times, you really didn't know who was a friend and who was an enemy!

Behind the horse and cart, another motorcycle was rumbling down the road. The rider wore a gray uniform. The people in the cart flagged him down.

"GO!" Jack cried.

He and Annie wheeled around and raced their bikes against the wind. When Jack looked back, the motorcycle was coming toward them—fast!

"Ditch the bikes!" Annie shouted. They skidded to a stop, dropped their bikes to the ground, and bolted through an opening in a hedgerow.

Scraped by branches and thorns, they pushed their way through the narrow gap until they burst onto farmland. As they ran through a cow pasture, Jack looked around wildly for a place to hide. "Barn!" he cried, pointing. He and Annie ran toward a red wooden building next to a silo. When they drew closer to the entrance, they saw a man in white clothes putting two large milk cans into the back of a white truck.

"Help!" cried Annie.

The milkman looked startled, but as the motorcycle crashed through the hedge at the edge of the property, he seemed to understand everything at once. "Quick! In the truck!" he shouted.

Jack and Annie scrambled into the back of the truck and found a hiding place behind rows of tall milk canisters. Crouching behind the canisters, they covered their mouths so no one would hear them gasping for breath.

The milkman slammed the back door of the

truck shut. There was a panel between the front seat and the windowless back area. Jack and Annie sat in the dark and listened to the motorcycle thunder closer and then stop. Through the closed door, they could hear bits of conversation from outside:

"Yes . . . two . . . boy and girl." "Resistance couriers . . ." "Yes, you are sure. . . ." "Yes . . . good . . ." "Thank you for your help. . . ."

Moments later, Jack heard the motorcycle rev up and drive away.

The milkman started his engine. Then, with the large canisters jiggling in their crates, the truck began bouncing over the road.

"I guess we're going with him," whispered Annie.

"I wonder if he's a friend or enemy," whispered Jack.

"A friend," said Annie. "He must have told the motorcycle guy we went in the opposite direction."

"*Or* he could be taking us to the police," whispered Jack. "Maybe the motorcycle guy was thanking him for locking us in his truck and taking us to the Nazis."

"Oh, no. I hadn't thought of that," Annie whispered. Clutching their berets, they jiggled with the clattering milk cans as the truck continued on.

After a while, the milk truck stopped again. It sounded like the driver was getting out.

Jack froze. He heard the back door handle click. Then the door swung open. The milkman pulled out a large milk canister and whispered, "All clear! Hurry!"

"Thanks!" said Annie.

Leaving the door open, the milkman carried the canister away from the truck.

"Go!" said Jack.

He and Annie jumped out of the back of the truck. It was parked in front of a long building with a sign that said:

CAEN MILK PROCESSING PLANT

"Look! We're in Caen!" said Annie, pointing to the sign. "Isn't that great?"

"Go! *Go!*" said Jack. He and Annie raced across

a street and headed down a narrow alley.

"Wait," Jack said, stopping in his tracks. "We shouldn't run. It will make us look suspicious." They stopped for a moment and tried to catch their breath.

"The milkman *was* a friend," said Annie.

"Definitely," said Jack. "Okay. Let's go. Act normal."

Jack and Annie stepped out from the alley and into a busy town square. In the middle of the square was an outdoor market. Women with children strolled from booth to booth, buying lettuce, peas, potatoes, flowers, linens, and lace. Surrounding the square were cobblestone streets lined with quaint buildings. There was a church covered with ivy, a small train depot, and a sidewalk café with a red striped awning.

Again, Jack found it difficult to believe that a great battle was about to take place. "This is all going to change tomorrow," he said to Annie as they strolled through the market.

"I know," Annie said. "I wish we could tell everyone to leave today."

"Yep," said Jack. He looked at a clock tower in the square. "It's almost ten. We have ten hours left until nightfall."

"Well, we're in Caen," said Annie. "Now we have to go three miles east to the River Orne and the caves of Mondeville."

"Right," said Jack.

"Excuse me!" Annie called to a young woman pushing a baby buggy. "Can you please tell us how to get to Mondeville?"

"It is very easy," said the woman. "Just a short train ride. You get off at the first stop." She pointed to the depot next to the café.

"Thanks," said Annie.

"You're welcome," said the woman. She waved two fingers and kept pushing the carriage across the square.

"Friend," Annie said to Jack.

"How do you know?" he asked.

"She gave me a *V Is for Victory* sign," said Annie.

"Or maybe she just happened to use two fingers to wave to you," said Jack. "Even though the milkman was a friend, we can never be sure who our friends and enemies are. Remember the farmer and the girl in the cart?"

"Yeah, I didn't see *that* coming," said Annie.

"Not in a million years," said Jack.

"I thought—" said Annie

The roar of engines interrupted her. Four open black cars rolled into the square and parked in a line. Each car had a red, white, and black symbol on the side. Jack recognized it as a swastika, the symbol of the Nazis. Soldiers got out of the cars and stood at the edge of the square, watching the shoppers. They wore gray uniforms with black belts and tall boots.

"Enemies," Jack said under his breath.

"Definitely," said Annie.

EIGHT

THE TRAIN

With the arrival of the Nazis, the atmosphere in the square changed. Vendors fell silent. Shoppers lowered their heads and grabbed the hands of their children.

"We should catch that train as soon as possible," said Jack.

"You bet," said Annie. "Look normal."

With their hands in their pockets, Jack and Annie walked as calmly as they could from the market toward the train depot. With quick steps, they crossed the street and entered the small station.

"Tickets," Jack said to Annie. He headed to the ticket window and placed some coins in front of the ticket agent. "Two for Mondeville, please."

The ticket agent counted out some coins, then gave Jack two tickets. "Thank you," said Jack. He and Annie stepped away from the window and walked out to the tracks.

Jack noticed that the waiting passengers were anxiously watching a scene at the end of the station platform. Some Nazi soldiers had stopped an old man. The man had his hands in the air. He looked terrified as the soldiers checked his pockets.

"What are they doing?" Annie asked.

"Don't look," said Jack. He grabbed her hand so she wouldn't hurry to the man's aid.

But he felt fury, too. *Why torment an old man?* he wondered. He wanted to shout at the Nazi soldiers: LEAVE US ALL ALONE! But just like the other bystanders, he was too scared to do anything. He gripped Annie's hand tighter and pulled her in the other direction. "Come on."

To Jack's great relief, he heard the train whistle

blow. Soon the train rounded the bend, puffing steam. The crowd stepped back as the black engine chugged into the station. It let out an ear-piercing shriek and jolted to a stop. Doors slid open and people stepped out onto the platform and headed for the station.

"All aboard!" shouted the conductor, and the waiting passengers moved toward the tracks.

Jack and Annie climbed into one of the rear cars. "Where are our seats?" Annie asked Jack.

"I don't know," he said. He looked at their tickets. "It says 'second-class.'"

"Excuse me, where are the second-class seats?" Annie asked an older woman with a friendly face.

"Follow me." The woman led them up the train corridor and stopped in front of an empty compartment. "You can sit in there," she said, then continued on her way.

Annie and Jack opened a glass door and stepped into a small space with four seats. Jack pulled off his field pack and sat down next to Annie near the window.

"I hate them," said Annie.

Jack knew exactly who she meant.

The whistle blew. The train jolted and began moving. Huffing and puffing, it left the depot and chugged down the tracks away from Caen.

"It's a short ride," said Annie.

"Not short enough," said Jack. "Listen." Even above the roar of the train, he could hear boots stomping down the corridor outside their compartment.

"Ignore them," said Annie.

"Got it," said Jack.

"Oh, Jean! Look! Lovely trees!" Annie pointed out the window.

"Yes, Aimée! They *are* lovely!" exclaimed Jack. "Remember—"

Before he could finish, the door to the compartment slid open. Two Nazi officials stood in the doorway. "Identity papers, please?" one said.

Jack's heart started to pound, but he turned and faked a friendly smile. "Oh! Yes, sure," he said. He pulled out his identity card and showed it to the official. Annie smiled and showed her card, too.

The soldier looked carefully at the cards, then handed them back. "Your bag now," he said to Jack, holding out his hand.

"My pack? Sure," said Jack.

But before he could hand over his field pack, Annie snatched it away from him. "Why do you want it?" she asked the man, grinning.

"I need to look inside it," said the official.

"Really?" said Annie. "There's nothing interesting inside."

Why is she doing this? Jack wondered. He couldn't think of anything in the pack that could get them into trouble—just lunch and Jack's pencil and notebook, with all the notes torn out.

"Give it to me," demanded the official.

Annie didn't move. Her smile had faded, replaced by a look of fear.

What is wrong with her? Jack wondered. He gently pried the field pack loose from her grip. "It's okay," he assured her. "He can look in it."

Grinning crazily, he handed the field pack over to the soldier.

The Nazi unbuckled Jack's pack. He reached in and pulled out the small cloth sack that Suzette had given them. He opened it and took out two apples, a chunk of cheese, and two pieces of black bread. He handed the food to the other official. Then he reached deeper into the field pack and pulled out some papers.

Jack was confused. *Where did those come from?*

The soldier held up one of the papers. It was one of the flyers printed by Tom and Theo!

HOPE AND COURAGE!
FREEDOM SOON!

The soldier put the papers back into the pack. Then he narrowed his eyes at Jack. "So you are working for the other side?"

"What? No!" said Jack. He looked at Annie. "How . . . ?"

"Sorry," Annie whispered. "I wanted to help them. Tom and Theo."

"Stand up!" the official barked at Jack.

"No!" cried Annie. "Please! He didn't do anything! It was me! I did it!"

The Nazi official pushed Annie aside. "Boy, I am placing you under arrest," he said. But just as the man reached out to grab Jack, an explosion rocked the train car.

The sound of screeching brakes split the air. The train ground to a sudden stop. Jack and Annie were thrown from their seats.

The soldiers fell to their hands and knees. Passengers scrambled up the corridor, screaming and yelling: "What happened? What happened?" "Resistance!" "Blew up tracks ahead!"

The two Nazis jumped to their feet. Ignoring Jack and Annie, they hurried away from the compartment.

Jack looked out the window. A few hundred yards in front of the train, black smoke was rising into the air. "Plan Green!" he said. "Let's get out of here!" He grabbed his field pack and started out of the compartment. But more soldiers were running down the corridor, shoving all the passengers aside.

Annie grabbed Jack's arm. "The window!" she cried. "Out! Climb out!"

Jack straddled the window ledge, then swung his leg over and dropped to the embankment below. He reached up and helped Annie drop to the ground, too.

Looking down the tracks, Jack saw train workers and soldiers running toward the billowing black smoke. Sirens were screaming. Passengers were fleeing from all the cars on the train.

"Come on!" said Jack. He and Annie ran down the embankment toward some woods near the tracks. Then they took off through the brush, weaving around mossy trees and pale spring ferns. They pushed back twigs and vines, trying to get as far away from the train as possible.

"Are we heading in the right direction?" Jack asked, panting.

Annie pulled out the compass and looked at it. "Yes! Southwest!"

"Good! Keep going!" said Jack. They ran until they came to the edge of a road. Up the road, a bridge crossed a wide river. A sign next to the bridge said RIVER ORNE.

"That's the river we want!" cried Annie. *"Cross a river to find a cave!"*

"Cross it!" said Jack. He and Annie hurried to the bridge and raced across the river. On the other side was a small restaurant. A sign on the front said SYLVIE'S BISTRO.

"Stop! Stop!" said Jack, gasping. "Before we go any farther, let's stop there—rest—and make a plan—"

"Great, I'm dying of thirst," said Annie.

They caught their breath. Then they straightened their berets, smiled fake smiles, and walked into the bistro. Inside the crowded dining room, the air smelled of coffee and cigarette smoke. Jack and Annie slipped over to an empty table and sat down.

"He reached up and helped Annie drop to the ground, too."

"I'm so sorry," Annie said, leaning toward Jack. "I didn't mean to get you in trouble. I—" Before she could go on, a teenage waitress brought silverware and menus to their table.

"May I help you, sir?" the girl asked Jack.

For a moment, Jack just stared at the dark-haired, rosy-cheeked girl. He was still in a daze both from being arrested and from the explosion.

"Can we have two lemonades, please?" Annie asked.

The waitress nodded and left.

"I'm so sorry!" Annie whispered again to Jack. "When I went down to the cellar to get our stuff, I grabbed a bunch of flyers and put them in your field pack."

"Why?" asked Jack. "Why would you do that?"

"I thought while we were looking for Kathleen, we could do what Tom and Theo did," said Annie. "You know, put up flyers when no one is looking. It seemed like a good—"

"Okay, okay, I get it," said Jack. "But we can't

worry about *their* mission. We have our *own* mission." He reached into his pack and pulled out the flyers. "We have to get rid of these. If we don't—"

"Jack!" Annie said, looking over his shoulder.

Jack turned around. The waitress was standing behind him with their lemonades. When her gaze fell on the flyers in Jack's hand, her eyes widened. Jack clutched the batch of papers to his chest. Without a word, the waitress put down their drinks and hurried to the kitchen at the back of the bistro.

"We have to go," said Jack. "She saw the flyers!" He jammed the papers into his pack.

"Wait," said Annie.

"We can't!" said Jack. "She's gone to tell someone, like her boss. They'll call the police!"

Before Jack and Annie could stand up to leave, the waitress burst out of the kitchen with a tall, stern-looking woman wearing an apron. The woman's heavy shoes clomped on the wooden floor as she headed over to Jack and Annie.

"My mother wants to talk to you," the waitress said.

Oh, no! thought Jack.

The woman pulled up a chair and sat down. She leaned forward. "Tell me, please," she whispered. "How do you know Tom and Theo?"

NINE

CODE BREAKERS

Jack and Annie stared in shock at the woman. Before they could answer, the door to the bistro swung open, and three Nazi soldiers entered. The men ignored everyone as they sat at a corner table not far from Jack and Annie.

The young waitress moved quickly to serve them.

"My name is Sylvie," the girl's mother said softly to Jack and Annie. "I am a friend of the twins. A good friend."

Jack was wary. *Is she really a friend?* he wondered.

Annie did not seem to have the same doubts. "Oh, wow, hi," she said in a low voice. "We know their parents."

"I have never met Tom and Theo's parents," said Sylvie. She glanced at the table in the corner. The Nazis were laughing loudly with her daughter. "In the Resistance, we keep our personal lives secret from each other. That way, other families might avoid punishment if one of us is caught. Do the parents know what happened to their sons?"

"No. Only that they were caught in Paris," said Annie. "They don't know if they're in prison or not."

"Tom and Theo are not in prison. They are safe," Sylvie whispered. "With help from others, they escaped from jail and fled to the south of France. Then they crossed over the Pyrenees mountains into Spain."

"That's great!" whispered Annie.

Jack looked at the Nazis. They were still joking with Sylvie's daughter. Was there any chance Sylvie was working with them? What if this was a trap? Was she making up the story about Tom and Theo?

"Are you sure that's true?" he asked, narrowing his eyes at Sylvie.

"I understand your caution," Sylvie whispered. Then she slowly moved two silver spoons into the shape of a V.

Jack nodded. *Okay,* he thought. He was willing to take the chance that Sylvie was telling the truth.

Sylvie then straightened the spoons. "It is very dangerous for you to carry these flyers," she said under her breath.

"I know. It's my fault," said Annie. "I wanted to help Tom and Theo. We got caught on a train, and Jack was almost arrested. But then the tracks got blown up and we escaped."

Sylvie smiled. "You are brave," she said. "In this time, even children must be brave."

"But helping Tom and Theo isn't really our mission," said Annie. "We're trying to find a friend and help her escape to England."

Jack glanced again at the corner table. The Nazis were studying their menus now.

"Is there any way I can help you?" said Sylvie.

"Yes," said Annie. She slipped Kathleen's rhyme out of her pocket and put it on the table. "Our friend sent us this coded message." Sylvie discreetly looked at the note. "The only lines we don't understand are the last ones."

Jack glanced at the soldiers again. One of them looked up and his gaze rested on Sylvie. "They're watching you," Jack whispered.

Sylvie nodded. Then she laughed. "So you both love apples?" she said.

What is she talking about? Jack wondered. *Is she speaking in code?*

"Yes, we *love* apples," Annie said, smiling.

"What kind of apples do you like best?" Sylvie said.

"Um . . . I like Granny Smith apples," said Annie. "So does Jack."

"Good, good!" said Sylvie. "Well, we have very delicious varieties of apples in this area. They have funny names, such as the Gentle Bishop and Skin of the Dog. But my favorites are the Yellow Knights and the White Calves."

Jack didn't know what to say. He wasn't sure how to play this game.

Annie looked calmly at Jack. *"Yellow knights,"* she said, *"and small, round cows."*

"Oh . . . oh," said Jack. *Apples!* So in her note, Kathleen was secretly writing about *apples*! Not knights! Not cows!

Annie laughed. "And can we find those delicious varieties of apples somewhere near here?" she asked.

"Oh, yes," said Sylvie. "In fact, my bistro is on the Road of Rocks. Down the street is a deserted château with a small orchard. Beautiful Yellow Knights and White Calves grow on trees there. So perhaps that is where you will find what you're looking for." She casually tapped the note. Jack saw that her fingers were pointing to the line *a crack in a rock beneath the boughs.*

"Cool," Jack said. "Thank you."

"You're most welcome," said Sylvie. She stood up and straightened her apron. "Enjoy your day, children. I hope you find the apple of your dreams."

"With your help, I think we will," said Jack. He glanced at the Nazis. The soldier was no longer looking at their table. He was lighting a cigarette and listening to his friends. Jack flashed a quick *V Is for Victory* sign at Sylvie. She smiled, then crossed the dining room back to the kitchen.

"Friend," Annie said to Jack as she put the note back into her pocket.

"Big-time," Jack said. He checked a clock on the wall. "It's almost two. We have six hours left." He took a long sip of lemonade, left some money on the table, and stood up. As he and Annie quietly slipped out of the bistro, he heard the Nazis laughing with each other.

It was still cloudy outside. A damp wind was blowing.

"This is the Road of Rocks," said Annie, looking at a sign. "Now we just need to find a deserted château. What's a château?"

"I think it's like a big, fancy house," said Jack.

"Cool," said Annie. "Let's find it."

"Oh, wait," said Jack. "We have to do something first."

"What?" said Annie.

"Come with me," said Jack. He led the way around the bistro to an open window in the back. Through the window they saw Sylvie in the kitchen. She was stirring a pot on the stove.

Jack looked around to make sure that no one was watching. Then he called in a loud whisper, "Sylvie!"

She looked surprised and came over to the window. "Yes?"

"Could you do us a favor?" said Jack. "Could you send a wireless message to the BBC?"

She nodded.

"Could you have it say . . ." Jack thought for a moment. "Have it say, *Your twin unicorns are free in Spain.*"

Sylvie looked puzzled.

"Tom and Theo," said Jack. "Their parents will

understand what that means when they hear it over their wireless. It will make them very happy."

"Yes," said Sylvie. "I will do that."

"Thanks!" said Jack.

"Good work!" Annie said as she and Jack slipped back around the restaurant.

"Yep," said Jack. "Now, a deserted château with apple trees!"

"Onward!" said Annie.

As they started up the Road of Rocks, Jack and Annie strolled past a couple of houses, a churchyard, and an ancient-looking cemetery. They passed a butcher shop, a bookstore, and a bakery called *La Baguette.*

"I don't get it," said Jack. "Why would Kathleen be hiding in a cave? It seems so safe here. Why doesn't she come out in the open?"

"I was wondering the same thing," said Annie. "And why didn't she just tell Teddy when and where to pick her up and then go there to meet him? You have to be cautious, but you can still travel around. Something's not right."

"Yeah, really," said Jack.

Jack and Annie walked farther up the road and rounded a bend. "Whoa," said Jack. "A deserted château?"

Set against a rocky hillside was a mansion with a sagging roof and broken windows. On its grounds were fallen-down sheds, overgrown gardens, and a scattering of bushes and weeds.

Annie pointed to a cluster of flowering trees in front of the hillside. "Apple orchard," she said. The spring breeze shook their boughs, and white petals floated to the ground like snowflakes.

"Yes!" said Jack. He looked around. No vehicles or pedestrians were close by. "Trespass!"

Jack and Annie walked up the driveway. Their boots crunched over the gravel path as they hurried across the weedy grounds of the château. When they drew close to the hillside, they studied the rocks.

"There," said Annie. She pointed to a crack big enough for a person to slip through.

"Okay," said Jack. "Wait." He reached into his

pack and took out the flashlight Teddy had given them.

"I'll go first," said Annie. She squeezed through the shoulder-wide crack in the rock, and Jack followed her. They stepped into a tunnel, lit only by the shaft of light from the crack.

Jack switched on their flashlight and shined it on the cream-colored stone walls. "This must be one of the limestone tunnels that Suzette and Gaston talked about," he said.

"Listen," said Annie.

Voices were singing deep inside the tunnel—high, sweet voices:

Twinkle, twinkle, little star,
How I wonder what you are.

TEN

HIDEOUT

"What's going on?" Jack whispered.

"Let's find out," said Annie.

Jack turned off the flashlight. The sound of the singing guided them as they tiptoed through the downward-sloping tunnel and into a giant cavern. Across the cavern, candles flickered in a corner. The candlelight shone on a group of small children sitting with a teenage girl. Most of the children were no more than three or four years old. They sat on a pile of blankets, facing the girl as she sang with them:

Twinkle, twinkle, little star,
How I wonder what you are.
Up above the world so high,
Like a diamond in the sky.

The children's bell-like voices were beautiful, Jack thought.

When the blazing sun is gone,
When it nothing shines upon,
Then you show your little light,
Twinkle, twinkle, all the night.

Jack and Annie waited until the children had finished their song. Then Annie called, "Kathleen!"

All the children turned to look. Kathleen let out a cry and hurried across the cavern into Annie's arms. Then she grabbed Jack and hugged him tightly, too.

The enchantress wiped tears from her sea-blue eyes. Her long curly hair was tangled and dirty. She looked tired and thin. "I am so glad to see you!

But what—what are you doing here?" she said. "Where is Teddy?"

"Teddy sent us instead," Jack said, "because he thought we could decode your message."

"Plus he had to save downed airmen in Holland and Belgium," said Annie. "What happened to you? Who are these little kids?"

By now, the children were tugging on Jack's and Annie's overalls, chattering: "Hello!" "Who are you?" "What's your name?" They wore ragged clothes and no shoes, but their small, pale faces were open and trusting.

"Are you taking care of all these kids?" Annie asked Kathleen.

"Yes. I have two wonderful helpers, Sarah and her sister, Sophie," said Kathleen. She pointed to the tallest children in the group. The sisters looked to be about six and seven years old. Their dark eyes shining, they smiled shyly at Jack and Annie.

"These are my friends Jack and Annie," Kathleen said to the children. "They have come a very long way to help us. Jack and Annie, meet Solly, Etty, Daniel, Eli . . ." Kathleen pointed to each tiny child as she said the names. "Pierre, Leo, Marcella and Ella . . ."

Talking over her, the children asked questions all at once: "Who are you?" "Can you stay with us?" "Where do you live?"

"Children, children," Kathleen said in a calm voice. "Hush, please! Go back to your blankets now with Sophie and Sarah, and rest. You can play with Jack and Annie after you wake."

The children did as Kathleen asked. Still chattering, though more softly, they followed the older girls back to their blankets. Sophie and Sarah seemed very grown-up as they tried to settle the younger children down.

"Have you all been living in this cave a long time?" asked Annie.

"This is our hideout during the day," said Kathleen. "After dark, I sneak them into the empty château, and we hide in the attic there. The plumbing still works, and there is fresh well water. I found a supply of candles, thank goodness. Sophie and Sarah are very capable. They watch the others at night while I look for food. I visit gardens and gather old bread from behind the bakery. Before daylight, I lead the children back here. We sing and play games and nap and talk. I don't think they realize that we are in hiding."

"Why do you have to hide them?" asked Jack.

"To keep them safe from the Nazis," said Kathleen. "My assignment with the SOE was to find Sophie and Sarah in a Normandy orphanage and sneak them into England. Their parents had escaped prison and already made their own way to London."

"Why were their mom and dad in prison?" Annie asked.

"Their parents are brilliant scientists. They were both arrested in Paris by the Nazis because they are Jewish," said Kathleen.

"That's crazy," said Annie.

"Yeah," said Jack.

"Yes, it is," said Kathleen. "When I arrived in

Normandy, I found that the orphanage had been abandoned, but there were still children there. Sophie and Sarah were taking care of them as best they could. Because all the children were Jewish, I needed to hide them."

"Oh, man," said Jack. He couldn't understand why the Nazis hated Jewish people so much. He'd read about it and seen movies about it, but he'd never understood it.

"There are too many for me to get them all to safety," said Kathleen. "That is why I sent word to Teddy that I needed magic. I wanted something to make us invisible or something to help us fly. If only I could turn them into little birds, I thought, they could fly across the channel and then become themselves again."

"Right," said Annie, smiling, "like when you once turned us into seals off the coast of Ireland?"

"Exactly like that," said Kathleen.

"Well, why do you need magic from Teddy?" asked Jack. "What happened to your own magic powers?"

"I do not know." Kathleen shook her head. "I—I seem to have lost part of myself here. I fear that sadness and worry have drained me of my ability to perform magic. . . . Perhaps being terrified for the children . . ." She shook her head again. "But you have brought help, yes? The wand?"

Jack took a deep breath. "Actually, no, we didn't," he answered. "No magic. Only ourselves."

Kathleen looked confused. "But in my message—"

"I know," said Annie. "Teddy meant to give us the Wand of Dianthus, but he forgot. He was flying the plane and helping us learn how to parachute and somehow he forgot, and *we* forgot, too."

"I remembered just as we were about to jump out of the plane," said Jack. "But then it was too late."

"He forgot? I cannot believe it. How could he?" Kathleen's voice trembled. "Oh, that is terrible. . . . Only magic can help these children escape harm. We cannot leave France now. We are trapped."

"You *have* to leave," said Jack. "We *all* have to leave France by nightfall. A giant military invasion is starting tomorrow. It's called the D-Day invasion. We heard that bombs will be dropped over this whole area."

Kathleen shook her head. "No . . . I—I don't know how we can leave. . . . No, it is not possible," she stammered.

Jack couldn't believe how much Kathleen had changed, from a joyful, confident person to someone much more worried and fragile. He found his own confidence starting to fail. "I don't know what to do," he said, looking at Annie.

"Well," said Annie, "*I* know what to do. We're going to get all these kids and ourselves out of France by nightfall. We have skills."

"What skills?" said Jack.

"Um . . . skills, you know, you said so yourself. Remember in the ditch?" said Annie.

Jack couldn't think of a single skill that would help their situation.

"Don't worry," Annie said. "We have courage. We have hope. And we have each other. So let's make a plan."

Jack just stared at her.

Annie went on. "First of all," she said, "with all these kids, we won't be able to fit into Teddy's little plane." She turned to Kathleen. "We already sent a message to Teddy telling him to pick us up at nightfall at the same spot where he dropped us off. So now we just need to send a message telling him to bring a bigger plane."

"Sylvie at the bistro can do that," said Jack. Annie's confidence was lifting his spirits.

"Good idea," said Annie. "Next we have to figure out how to get from here back to the drop zone."

"That's the hard part," said Jack. "We need . . . a truck or something . . . like the milk truck that took us to Caen. . . ."

"Right," said Annie. "So the kids can hide in the back."

Kathleen's face lit up. "Oh! Every night I go to the bakery up the street after it closes," she said. "There is always a delivery truck parked in the driveway. It is never locked. I know this because

I gather scraps of stale bread from the back."

"Okay," said Jack. "But there's only one problem: if we borrow that truck, who's going to drive it?"

"*You*, silly!" said Annie.

"*Me?*" said Jack.

"Yes, you!" Annie turned to Kathleen. "Jack's not old enough to have a license, but he learned how to drive an old truck on our great-grandfather's farm. He's only allowed to drive around the pastures, but he's a good driver! That's one of his skills!"

"No!" said Jack.

"Yes!" said Annie. "So all we have to do is gather the kids, use the truck to get them to the drop zone, wait for Teddy to show up with a bigger plane, get everybody on board, and we're all out of here by nightfall."

"Fantastic!" said Kathleen. "We have a plan!"

ELEVEN

THE PLAN

Kathleen's sea-blue eyes were sparkling. "I will go tell Sophie and Sarah to get the children ready!" She hurried across the cavern.

Jack whirled around to Annie. "No, no, no!" he whispered. "This is not a good plan."

"It is! You drove Great-Granddad's truck perfectly just a few weeks ago!" said Annie. "I was there! I wanted to drive it, too, but I couldn't reach the pedals."

"But that—" said Jack.

"You didn't even need a key with that old

truck," said Annie. "Remember? You just turned the starter switch. You learned how to use the clutch and the gearshift. You drove us around the field for hours—around and around and around. You always say you can't wait to drive that truck again!"

"But this is so different!" said Jack.

"It's not *that* different," Annie said.

"Are you crazy? It's totally different!" said Jack. "Stealing a truck, loading it with tiny kids, and driving through a foreign country to try to escape Nazis in World War Two is *totally* different from driving in a circle in our great-grandfather's pasture."

"Okay. It's different," said Annie.

"Thank you!" said Jack.

"It's different because there are lives at stake here," said Annie. "And that's why *you have to do it.*"

Before Jack could say anything, Kathleen came rushing back. She was holding a candle and a folded map. "What was the location of your drop zone?" she asked.

"It's a field in Biéville, next to a church," said Annie. "Six miles northwest of Caen."

"Good," said Kathleen. "I have the Normandy map the SOE gave me. It will help us. Let's go get the truck." By the light of her candle, she led the way out of the cavern and through the limestone tunnel.

Jack's heart was racing. Annie was right. Lives were at stake. But he was already sweating, and they hadn't even started the plan yet! How would he feel when he was trying to sneak a truckload of Jewish orphans past Nazi soldiers?

Jack and Annie followed Kathleen through the tunnel to the crack in the rock. Then they walked into the gray light of late afternoon. The wind blew softly over the grounds of the château as they headed down the driveway.

"Let's refine our plan," said Kathleen. She sounded more like her old self. "Sophie and Sarah will get the children ready. Annie will go to Sylvie at the bistro and ask her to send a new message to Teddy. Jack and I will pick up the bakery truck.

Then we will all meet back here, load up the children, and head for the drop zone."

"Got it," said Annie.

Jack nodded. He was relieved that Kathleen seemed so much stronger. He hoped it meant her magic skills would soon return. Right now he thought they *really* needed a little magic.

When they came to the road, Kathleen turned to Annie. "You should go ahead of us to Sylvie," she said, "so we will not look as if we are traveling in a group. The Nazis do not like groups."

"Okay, meet you guys back here," said Annie. "Good luck!" She started walking up the Road of Rocks toward Sylvie's Bistro.

Jack took a deep breath as he and Kathleen stood together waiting for Annie to get a good distance away. He always felt shy when he was alone with the beautiful enchantress.

"Jack, these have been the two worst weeks of my life," Kathleen said, breaking the silence. "I knew it was possible I could be responsible for the loss of ten children. I felt helpless and sad and angry all at once. I have never felt that way before."

"You're not helpless, Kathleen," said Jack. "You're strong and—and you're good. That's why you were sad and angry."

"Thank you, Jack," she said. "I am very, very relieved you and Annie came to help."

"We haven't really done anything yet," Jack said.

"But you will," she said. "I admire you very much." She looked up the Road of Rocks. "Annie is far enough ahead, I think. We can go now."

Jack straightened his shoulders as he and Kathleen walked together up the road. He was ready to drive the truck. In fact, he was ready to do anything to be worthy of Kathleen's admiration.

The bakery was closed when they got there. No one was on the sidewalk.

"The delivery truck should be in back," said Kathleen. "Come with me." She and Jack slipped behind the building.

An old-fashioned cream-colored truck was parked behind the bakery. The cab of the truck looked just like the cab of Jack's great-grandfather's truck. The back was different, though. His great-grandfather's truck was a pickup, but the back of this truck was box-shaped like a van. The words LA BAGUETTE were painted on the side.

Jack looked at the bakery truck. He took a deep breath. "Okay, this should work," he said, trying to sound calm. "Let's see how she looks inside." He pulled on the handle of the cab, and the door swung open.

Jack stuck his head inside and saw that the truck had a keyless starter switch, just like his great-grandfather's truck. He turned back to Kathleen. "We're in business," he said.

"Wonderful!" Kathleen said. "Do you have a piece of paper so I can leave a note for the baker?"

Jack reached into his pack and gave Kathleen his notebook and a pencil. She wrote on a blank page:

> Thank you for letting us borrow your truck. It is waiting for you near the church in Biéville.

She tore the paper out of Jack's notebook, folded it, and slid it under the back door of the bakery. Then they both climbed into the front seat. "Good to go?" Jack asked.

"Yes!" she said, smiling. "Good to go."

Jack looked at the floor and found the clutch pedal on the left, the brake in the middle, and the gas pedal on the right, just like in his great-grandfather's truck. He put his hand on the gearshift next to his seat. Everything felt familiar. "Okey-dokey," he said. "Let's get this show on the road."

Jack pressed the brake with his right foot and then pushed the clutch pedal down with his left. He moved the gearshift into neutral. Then he turned the starter switch, and the engine rumbled to life.

Jack shifted into first gear. He moved his right foot off the brake and pressed the gas pedal. The truck engine roared. Jack took his foot off the clutch. The truck jerked forward and the engine stopped dead.

"No problem, no problem," said Jack. "It'll just

take me a minute to get the hang of it again."

Jack repeated everything he had done: brake, clutch, gearshift into neutral, starter, gearshift into first. This time, he operated the clutch and gas pedals perfectly, and the bakery truck moved smoothly onto the Road of Rocks.

"Brilliant!" said Kathleen. "We are on our way!"

As Jack headed up the street, he kept all his attention on his driving, not daring to think of their plan. Instead, he imagined he was just driving around his great-grandfather's pasture.

When the truck came to the old château, Annie was heading into the driveway. Seeing Jack behind the wheel, she raised her arms skyward and jumped up and down as if he'd just crossed a finish line.

Jack and Kathleen laughed as Annie ran alongside the truck, waving her arms. Jack brought the bakery truck to a stop near the hillside. Then he and Kathleen climbed out.

"You did it! You did it!" Annie said to Jack.

He shrugged as if it was no big deal.

"Wait here. I will get the children," said Kathleen. "Sophie and Sarah should have them ready by now." She dashed to the rocks.

"Was it hard to drive?" Annie asked Jack.

"Not once I got it going," he said. "It all kind of came back to me. Did you give the message to Sylvie?"

"Yes! I snuck around the back of the bistro and tapped on the window again," said Annie. "I asked her to send another message, one that said, 'Unicorn has ten colts. Need bigger bird.'"

"Good work," said Jack.

"Here they come," said Annie.

Kathleen, Sophie, and Sarah led the small children out of the tunnel. Excited to go for a ride, the little kids raced across the grass to the bakery truck. Jack got out and swung open the rear door. Then he, Annie, and Kathleen lifted each child into the back.

"Is everyone here?" called Kathleen. She called out all their names to make sure: "Ella? Eli? Leo? Daniel? . . ."

"*Seeing Jack behind the wheel, she raised her arms skyward and jumped up and down as if he'd just crossed a finish line.*"

As each high voice rang out "Yes!" Jack climbed into the driver's seat. Soon Kathleen and Annie joined him. Jack could hear the children chattering behind the partition that separated the cab from the back.

"They are so excited," said Kathleen.

"It smells like bread back there," said Annie. "The children found lots of old crusts to eat."

"Really?" said Jack. He could hear their voices saying: "This is good!" "I love it!" "It's hard to chew." "Yes, but it's very good!"

Jack's throat tightened. He wanted only one thing in the world right now—to help these little kids escape from France.

TWELVE

CHECKPOINT

Kathleen opened the map of the Caen area and showed it to Annie.

"Mondeville . . . ," Annie said, pointing. "And Biéville. It looks like we have about seven miles to go."

"All set?" said Jack. He took a breath. He started the truck, shifted into gear, then drove down the driveway toward the road.

"Turn right," said Kathleen, studying the map.

Jack turned right. He drove faster and shifted gears as they moved up the quiet Road of Rocks.

"Left onto Calmette Street," said Kathleen, "then right onto Clopee."

Jack followed her directions.

"Right onto Cabourg," said Annie, "then a quick left."

Jack turned onto Cabourg, then made a quick left—and landed in the middle of a traffic jam!

"Oh, no," Kathleen said quietly.

Up the road, Nazi soldiers were stopping traffic. Two of the Nazis held up spotlights as vehicles crawled toward them.

"What's going on?" asked Annie.

"It's a checkpoint," said Kathleen.

Jack stopped breathing. "What does that mean?" he asked.

"It means officials randomly stop vehicles and check identities," said Kathleen.

The soldiers waved one car through, but they stopped the next. Traffic came to a halt as a Nazi official shined a flashlight into the car that had stopped.

"Oh, man," said Jack. When he saw another

Nazi inspect the car's trunk, he started to panic. He was terrified that the soldiers would stop them, too, and look in the back of the bakery truck.

"Tell the kids to be quiet," Jack said.

Kathleen tapped on the partition. "Quiet, please, children! You must be very quiet now! Not one word!"

The children were silent. Jack gripped the steering wheel to try to stop his hands from shaking.

"Jack, you have to look calm," said Kathleen. "You must look as if you drive this truck every day to deliver bread."

"Yeah, like it's no big deal," said Annie.

"I—I don't think I can—" Jack said in a strangled voice.

"You have to!" said Annie.

"Wait . . . wait a moment!" said Kathleen. She closed her eyes and opened them. "Oh, my!"

"What is it?" asked Jack.

"I just recalled a spell that will keep us safe!" she said.

"Really?" said Jack.

"Yes. Since being with you and Annie, I have grown more hopeful. I think that feeling of hope is bringing back some of my magic!" said Kathleen.

"That's wonderful!" said Annie. "What's the spell you remember?"

"It is a spell to make us invisible," said Kathleen.

"Really?" said Jack.

"Yes, drive on, Jack," said Kathleen. The cars had started moving again. "Do not look to either side—stare straight ahead."

As Jack shifted from neutral into first gear and then second, Kathleen closed her eyes and whispered a rhyme:

Powers of goodness, powers of light,
Shield us now from powers of sight.

When Kathleen started to repeat the rhyme, Annie closed her eyes and joined in:

Powers of goodness, powers of light,
Shield us now from powers of sight.

Holding his breath and staring straight ahead, Jack drove toward the checkpoint.

> *Powers of goodness, powers of light,*
> *Shield us now from powers of sight.*

Kathleen opened her eyes and looked around. "It worked," she whispered. "We are invisible."

"We are?" said Jack. "How do you know?"

"The Nazis are completely ignoring us," said Kathleen. "They see nothing but empty space between the car in front of us and the car behind us. When it is our turn to pass the checkpoint, be calm and drive straight through."

Jack relaxed a little as he imagined being invisible. Kathleen whispered the magic spell again:

> *Powers of goodness, powers of light,*
> *Shield us now from powers of sight.*

The soldiers waved at the driver of the green

car ahead of the bakery truck, giving permission for it to move on.

"Good," said Kathleen. "Now just follow closely behind that car and we will be fine."

Jack fixed his eyes on the back of the green car. Following it, he drove steadily and calmly past the checkpoint. When he glanced in the rearview mirror, he saw that the soldiers were paying no attention at all to the bakery truck. He had no doubt now that Kathleen's magic was working. They were definitely invisible.

"Drive on, Jack," said Kathleen.

Jack drove on. When he looked in his rearview mirror again, he saw the soldiers stopping the car behind them.

"We made it!" said Annie.

"Yes," said Kathleen, looking at the map. "Turn left here, Jack. Then an immediate right and follow the sign to St. Clair."

Jack did as Kathleen said. He turned left, then right, and pressed harder on the gas pedal. The road ahead was empty. He drove faster and faster, shifting into third gear. In the fading light of dusk, the truck glided along the smooth road.

"Yay," said Annie. "I think we'll make it by nightfall!"

Jack said nothing. He was afraid to break the spell of invisibility.

"When you see a sign for Biéville, turn right," said Kathleen.

Jack nodded and kept driving.

"Biéville!" said Annie.

Jack turned right.

"Church!" said Annie.

The white steeple of the church was rising into the darkening sky. Next to the church was the drop zone, the empty field where they had landed with their parachutes.

"That's where Teddy will pick us up," said Annie.

"Good. Drive to the back of the church," said Kathleen, "so the truck cannot be seen."

How can the truck be seen from anywhere? Jack wondered. *Has Kathleen undone her spell?*

He pulled off the road and bumped over the grass to the back of the church. When he brought the truck to a stop and switched off the engine, Kathleen and Annie clapped.

"We're here! We made it!" said Annie.

"You were brilliant, Jack!" said Kathleen.

"Oh, no, you get the credit," he said. "I could never have done it without your magic."

"Yes, you could have," said Kathleen. "In fact, you *did.*"

"What?" said Jack.

"Jack, I fear I did not tell you the truth," said Kathleen. "I still do not have magic powers. I did not make us invisible with a spell."

"You didn't?" said Annie.

"No," said Kathleen. "I knew that as long as Jack felt confident, an ordinary bakery truck would not draw the attention of the Nazis. I felt sure we could slip safely by."

"Oh, brother," said Jack. He took a deep breath. He didn't know whether to be angry with

Kathleen or amazed at himself. In his confusion, he just laughed. Annie and Kathleen joined in. *Well, at least the scariest part of the journey is over,* Jack thought.

Kathleen, Jack, and Annie climbed out of the cab. The countryside was quiet. No vehicles were in sight, and no dogs were barking. The moon was on the horizon.

"I hope Teddy received the messages from Gaston and Sylvie," said Jack, "or else we'll all be stranded here during the D-Day invasion."

"Tell me, what *is* the D-Day invasion?" asked Kathleen.

"Sometime after midnight, more than a hundred thousand Allied soldiers will invade by sea and air to drive the Nazis out of France," said Jack. "It will be the beginning of the end of World War Two."

"That is good. Very good," breathed Kathleen. "All the world is living a great nightmare now. When it wakes, everyone will wonder how this could have happened, and I fear no one will know the answer." She shook her head. "Well, what should we do now?"

"I think maybe we should do a better job of hiding the truck," said Jack, looking around.

"You and I can move it down the road," said Annie.

"While you do that, I will hide the children in the church," said Kathleen.

"Good plan," said Jack. "We'll help you get them inside."

Kathleen, Jack, and Annie walked to the rear of the truck. When Kathleen opened the door, they found the children sprawled all over the back, fast asleep. Even Sophie and Sarah had closed their eyes. "Wake up, birdies," Kathleen sang softly. "Wake up."

Her sweet voice roused the children from sleep. As they began to stir, some reached out and put their arms around Jack, Annie, and Kathleen. Jack gently lifted Leo and Eli out of the back of the truck. Then he clutched their hands and walked with them across the grass. "Let's go inside this nice building," he said. "It's peaceful in there."

"Is this our new house?" Leo asked, rubbing his eyes.

"Can you live here with us?" said Eli.

Jack led his two sleepy three-year-olds into the church, while Annie, Kathleen, Sophie, and Sarah shepherded the others after him.

Inside the dark front entrance, the air smelled of old wood and incense. The last light of day shone through stained-glass windows. After Jack, Annie, and Kathleen got everyone settled in the front pew, Kathleen started to lead the children in song.

"Let's move the truck now," Jack said to Annie. She nodded. As they slipped down the aisle and out of the church, they heard:

Are you sleeping, are you sleeping,
Brother John, Brother John?
Morning bells are ringing,
Morning bells are ringing,
Ding dong ding, ding dong ding.

THIRTEEN

SEARCHLIGHTS

Night was falling fast as Jack and Annie climbed back into the bakery truck.

"We shouldn't drive far," said Jack. "Kathleen left a note for the baker, telling him to look for his truck near the church in Biéville. I hope he's still alive tomorrow and comes to get it."

"You hope he's still alive tomorrow?" said Annie. "That sounds terrible."

"I know," said Jack. "War is terrible." He started the truck, and they bumped back over the grass to the road. Jack drove about a hundred yards, then pulled off the road and parked the bakery truck beside a clump of trees. "I think this should do it," he said.

Annie hopped out of the truck. Jack switched off the motor and rolled up his window. Then he climbed out, too. "Let's hurry—"

"Look, Jack." Annie sounded scared. "Look up."

Jack looked up. Two giant beams of light were sweeping across the sky, crisscrossing each other.

"What's going on?" asked Annie.

"Those lights must be looking for planes to shoot down," said Jack.

"Oh, no!" said Annie. "What if they spot Teddy's plane?"

Jack didn't answer right away. *Maybe the worst isn't over yet,* he thought. "Let's hurry back and tell Kathleen," he said.

Jack and Annie ran up the road to the church. Inside, they found Kathleen still singing with the children.

Row, row, row your boat
Gently down the stream.
Merrily, merrily, merrily, merrily,
Life is but a dream.

Our plan isn't going to work, Jack thought. He felt sure that the Nazis would spot Teddy's plane and shoot it down before he could land.

"Kathleen!" Annie called.

Kathleen told the children to keep singing, and she hurried over to Jack and Annie. "What's wrong?" she asked.

"The Nazis are using searchlights to spot planes," said Jack. "They're sure to see Teddy."

"Show me," said Kathleen.

Jack and Annie led Kathleen outside. The lights were still sweeping across the night sky.

"See?" said Jack, pointing up at the moving beams of light. "How can Teddy possibly—"

Annie gasped. "Look!" she said. "Look at the field!"

Below the dazzling searchlights, a silver plane sat in the dark field. The gleaming plane was much bigger than a spy taxi. It had a snub-nosed cockpit, a long row of windows, and four huge propellers— two on each wing.

"Where did that come from?" said Kathleen.

"I don't know," said Jack, stunned. "I didn't see it when we moved the truck or came back to the church. I didn't hear it fly overhead or land or anything!"

The rear door of the plane swung open. Silhouetted in the doorway was a person in a flight suit and helmet.

"Teddy!" said Annie.

"Oh!" cried Kathleen. She dashed across the dark field. Jack and Annie ran after her.

When Kathleen reached Teddy, she threw her arms around him. Jack and Annie piled on, and they all hugged him at the same time. Everyone was laughing.

"I'm so glad you got our messages!" said Annie.

"So am I!" said Teddy.

"Do you know that D-Day is tomorrow?" asked Jack.

"Yes, I found out today," said Teddy. "With all the preparations for the invasion, I had trouble finding a big enough plane to come for you. But finally I was able to call upon a friend to help me."

"Great!" said Annie.

"How did the plane land without the searchlights spotting it?" asked Jack. "And why didn't it make any noise?"

"I will explain later," said Teddy. "We must act quickly. You have others with you, no?"

"Oh, yes, lots of others!" said Annie.

"This way!" said Kathleen. She grabbed Teddy's hand and pulled him toward the church.

"Kathleen rescued ten little kids from an abandoned orphanage," Annie said.

"That's why she couldn't get out of France," said Jack.

"Oh, no!" Teddy whirled around to Kathleen. "I should have come myself to save you!"

"Do not feel bad," said Kathleen. "Jack and Annie have given me miraculous help, and all without magic. I have lost my powers, Teddy."

"I gathered that from your message," said Teddy. "That is why I sent you the wand and—" He stopped and smacked his forehead. "Oh, no! I forgot, didn't I?"

"You did," said Jack. "But it's not all your fault. Annie and I forgot, too, until just before I jumped. And then it was too late."

"I am so sorry!" said Teddy.

"It's okay," said Annie. "You had a lot on your mind."

"No, it is unforgivable!" said Teddy.

"Seriously, it's okay," said Jack. "We managed."

By then they had arrived at the door of the church. "Get ready to be mobbed by little kids," Annie said to Teddy.

Kathleen led the way inside. "Sarah! Sophie! We are leaving!"

Led by the two sisters, all the children clambered toward the door of the church. They gathered around Teddy, asking questions.

"Hush, children, hush now," said Kathleen. "Everyone grab someone's hand. Etty, take Sophie's hand. Daniel, take Sarah's hand. Leo and Eli, Jack's hands. Marcella and Ella, Annie's hands. Pierre and Solly, Teddy's hands. Come along now. Follow me! We are about to go on a great adventure!"

With little hands tucked into bigger hands, everyone followed Kathleen out of the church into the field.

"Oh, look!" said Leo.

"Pretty plane!" said Eli.

"Yes," said Jack, walking with the two boys. "Let's run! We're going to fly through the air on the silver bird!" Gripping their hands, he ran with little steps so the kids could keep up.

When they reached the plane, Teddy took charge. "Big kids help small kids up the stepladder," he said.

Kathleen lifted two preschoolers up to the rear door. Annie climbed up with two more. Sophie and

Sarah each helped a smaller child. Jack held on to Leo and Eli and led them up the steps.

Boarding last, Teddy squeezed into the passenger cabin with Pierre and Solly. Then he closed the heavy door and latched it. "Sit down. Relax, everyone!" he said. "We don't have far to go!"

The little kids laughed and squealed as they scrambled into seats. Some of them jumped into Kathleen's and Annie's laps. Others climbed onto Teddy, all chirping at once.

"Wait a minute," said Jack. "Teddy, aren't you going up to the cockpit to fly the plane?"

"No. As I said, I called on a friend to help me," said Teddy. "He is the pilot."

"Oh," said Jack. "But how did he land without our hearing him? And how did he get past the searchlights?"

"Explanations later," said Teddy. "I think we are about to take off." He said something else, but his voice was drowned out by kids still asking questions: "Where are we going?" "Who are you?" "Is Kathleen your sister?"

As Kathleen and Teddy laughed and tried to answer the children, Jack thought that Kathleen was completely her old self again. Her eyes were bright; her laughter was lighthearted.

Jack looked out the window. The searchlights were still combing the dark for incoming planes. *So how did the SOE pilot land the plane?* he wondered. *And how will he take off without being seen?*

The large silver plane started moving. It moved across the grass with no bumping and no engine sounds—no whirring, roaring, or rumbling.

This is so weird, thought Jack. *Did they make super-silent spy planes in World War Two?* He would have to look it up, he thought. Before he knew it, the plane had lifted off the ground and was gliding through the night with no vibration, rocking, or shaking.

"Can we open a window?" asked Annie.

"No, silly, not on a plane," said Jack.

"Oh, but on *this* plane we can open windows," said Teddy. He leaned over, undid a latch, and pushed open the glass.

As cool air rushed inside the cabin, Annie grabbed Jack's field pack. Without a word, she pulled out the flyers made by the resistance fighters, Tom and Theo. She showed the printed message to Teddy and Kathleen.

They both grinned and nodded.

Then, one at a time, Annie released the flyers out the open window: one, two, three, four, five . . . ten sheets of paper flapped into the moonlit night.

"That's all," said Annie. "I wish I had more."

Kathleen looked at Annie for a moment. Then she smiled and rose from her seat. She pointed her finger at the flyers fluttering toward the earth below. She whispered some words:

Ain solas keng dural ay du!
Annie's wish shall now come true!

Through the window, Jack saw the flyers begin to multiply . . . from ten to a hundred . . . from a hundred to a thousand . . . from a thousand to ten thousand!

"*Jack saw the flyers begin to multiply . . .*"

HOPE
AND
COURAGE!
FREEDOM
SOON!

Everyone gasped and clapped.

Kathleen's magic was working again! Now that she was with Teddy, now that she was flying home to England, now that she was saving the children, her joy—her magic—had returned!

As the plane crossed the English Channel, the flyers kept multiplying across the sea. Like white petals falling from apple trees, the sheets of paper tumbled and swirled through the air. Tom and Theo's message filled the night sky, gleaming with their bright words:

HOPE AND COURAGE!
FREEDOM SOON!

FOURTEEN

THE PILOT

Soon after the silver plane crossed the English Channel, it landed silently in the field near Glastonbury Tor. Teddy opened the rear door and lowered the stepladder. "Everyone out!" he said.

Once again, the big kids helped the little kids. Everyone climbed down the ladder and stepped onto the dark, dewy grass. The moon was high in the sky now. Jack could hardly believe that he and Annie had only been away from England—and home—for twenty-four hours.

"The SOE has arranged to take everyone to

London," Teddy said to Kathleen. "Motorcars are waiting in the parking lot. This way—"

As Teddy led the group toward the parking lot, Annie carried Daniel and Etty, and Jack carried Leo and Eli.

"Where are we going?" Eli asked him.

"To a safe city," answered Jack. "You'll live in a nice house soon, I promise."

The small boy kissed Jack on the cheek. Then Leo kissed Jack, too. Jack just laughed. "You guys are funny," he said.

"Is Jack your brother?" Etty asked Annie.

"Yes," said Annie. "He's my brother."

"Is he the best brother in the world?" asked the tiny girl.

"Yes, he is," said Annie.

"Are you and Annie coming with us?" Eli asked Jack.

"No, we have to go back to America now," said Jack.

"How will you get there?" asked Leo.

"In a magic tree house," said Jack.

"Can we play in your tree house someday?" asked Leo.

"Absolutely," said Jack. "When you come to America, you can do anything you want."

Three big black cars were waiting in the parking lot beside the airfield. Teddy got four of the children settled in the first car, and Jack and Annie tucked their four into the second car. "See ya, guys," Jack said. "Be good."

Jack closed the door and stood in the dark with Annie and Teddy, as Kathleen guided Sophie and Sarah to the third car in the lot. Before they reached it, the doors opened, and a man and woman climbed out. They were tall and well-dressed.

When the man and woman saw Sophie and Sarah, they both burst into sobs. The man knelt and held out his arms. "My babies . . . ," he said, grabbing Sophie and Sarah and pulling them close. Sophie and Sarah started crying, too. "Papa, Mama! Papa, Mama!"

For a long time, Sophie, Sarah, and their parents all held each other and cried. They were still holding on to each other as they stumbled back to their car and climbed into the backseat together.

Jack felt tears on his cheeks. Kathleen and Annie were sniffling. Teddy cleared his throat and clapped his hands together. "Victory!" he said.

"Victory," said Jack, smiling. Then he held up two fingers.

"What about Eli and Eddie and Leo and all the other kids?" Annie asked Kathleen. "What will happen to them?"

"The SOE will locate relatives and friends to care for them," said Kathleen. "I will go to London and protect them until they are all safely placed in happy homes."

"Thank you for saving them," said Annie.

"Thank *you*, Annie," said Kathleen, "for remaining hopeful and helping make a plan when we were almost ready to give up."

"No problem," said Annie.

"Together, you and Jack saved their lives and mine," said Kathleen. "You are my heroes."

Jack shrugged. "I'm not a hero," he said.

Kathleen took Jack's hand. She looked into his eyes. "You *are* a hero, Jack. Believe me. And you are a wonderful truck driver, too."

Jack laughed.

Kathleen smiled her radiant smile. "Well, until we meet again, farewell," she said. "Teddy? Are you coming?"

"Yes! I will join you for the ride to London," Teddy said. "Wait for me."

"Good." Kathleen blew Jack and Annie a kiss. Then she climbed into the first car.

Teddy turned to them. "If you have a minute before you leave, the pilot of the plane would like to see you," he said.

"Great!" said Jack. He had lots of questions for that SOE pilot—like what kind of plane was he flying?

Teddy, Jack, and Annie hurried away from the parking lot across the grounds of the ancient abbey. In the moonlight, Jack looked back at the landing field. The silver plane wasn't there.

"Where did it go?" he asked, hurrying alongside Teddy. "The plane?"

"Ah, yes. The plane is gone, but the pilot remains behind," Teddy said mysteriously. "Come with me."

Through the misty air, they passed the glistening pond and the sheep asleep in the grass. Just beyond a hedgerow were the ruins of pillars and archways.

"There, on that bench," said Teddy.

Jack could barely make out a person sitting on a stone bench. The person's back was to them, and he was wearing a dark cloak.

"Ohhh," Annie said with a grin. "Got it."

"Got what?" said Jack.

"Got the *whole* thing," said Annie. "I just figured it out!" She hurried to the bench and sat next to the man in the cloak. The next moment, they were talking softly together. The man had a deep voice.

"*Whoa,*" said Jack. Suddenly he got it, too.

He walked over and sat down next to Annie and the man. "Hi, Merlin," Jack said as casually as he could.

"Good evening, Jack," Merlin said. The magician was wearing a black cloak with the cowl over his head. His long white beard shone in the moonlight.

"So Teddy sent for you?" Jack asked.

"Yes," said Merlin.

"And you knew how to find and fly a special military plane?" said Jack.

"No," said the magician of Camelot. "I knew how to *conjure* a special plane to suit your needs, one that could carry fourteen passengers and take off and land without being seen or heard."

"Cool," Jack murmured, still trying to sound cool.

"I know this was an especially difficult mission for you," said Merlin. "You experienced firsthand what it means to live in constant terror."

"Yes," said Jack.

"You know what it feels like to be afraid to

speak or move about freely," said Merlin.

"We do," said Annie.

"You have seen cruel people hunt down the innocent—even children," said Merlin.

Jack and Annie nodded.

"But you overcame your fears in order to accomplish your mission," said Merlin. "Teddy found two excellent recruits in the fight for freedom. There is no way I can adequately thank you. But allow me to try: Thank you. Both of you. And I hope to see you again soon."

"You too," said Annie.

"Anytime," said Jack.

Merlin stood up from the bench. "Well, good-bye," he said. "Have a safe trip home."

"Bye," said Annie.

Jack and Annie watched the master magician walk off into the night and disappear like smoke among the ruins.

"Wow," Annie breathed.

"Wow, indeed," said Teddy, stepping from the shadows. "Now are you ready to go home?"

Jack and Annie stood up from the bench and followed Teddy to the tree house.

Teddy's large duffel bag sat at the base of the tree. Teddy reached in and pulled out their sneakers and Jack's pack. "You can have your things back now," he said.

"Thanks," said Jack. "And you can have your things back, too."

Jack and Annie pulled off their farm boots, overalls, and shirts. Jack shivered in his shorts and T-shirt as he and Annie changed into their sneakers and tied the laces. Then Jack took his pencil and notebook out of the field pack and handed the pack to Teddy. "Thanks for lending this to us," he said.

"You are welcome," said Teddy. "I will have to make up a good story for Winston about how I got all of you out of France. But now I had better catch my ride to London. Until next time— cheerio, chaps."

"Cheerio, chap," Jack and Annie said together.

"Onward!" said Teddy. Then he slung his

duffel bag over his shoulder and headed toward the parking lot.

Jack and Annie watched Teddy march briskly toward the hedgerow. Just before he rounded the corner, he turned and gave them a salute. Then he was gone.

Jack and Annie climbed the rope ladder into the tree house. Annie grabbed the Pennsylvania book. "Ready?" she said.

"Wait." Jack heard the steady hum of planes overhead. He and Annie looked up at the night sky and saw distant lights.

"I wonder if those are D-Day planes," Annie said.

"Yeah, I wonder if they're heading to Normandy," said Jack.

The planes kept moving through the night sky—more planes and more and more.

"It's time for us to go home," said Annie.

"Definitely," said Jack.

Annie pointed to a photo of the Frog Creek

woods. "I wish we could go there," she said.

The wind started to blow.

The tree house started to spin.

It spun faster and faster.

Then everything was still.

Absolutely still.

Frog Creek was warm in the summer sunset. Jack breathed in the smell of dry wood and green leaves. He felt as if he had never smelled anything so good and so safe.

"Nice," said Annie.

Jack just nodded. His heart was heavy, too heavy to talk about all they'd seen and done. He picked up his backpack and climbed down the rope ladder. Annie followed. In silence, they started through the late-summer woods, crossing in and out of dark shadows.

"War really is a terrible thing," Annie said finally.

Jack nodded.

"I don't understand it!" said Annie. "Why would *anyone* want to hurt people like Sophie and Sarah and their parents? Or Tom and Theo? Or the old man at the train station?"

"I don't know," said Jack.

"And how could anyone want to hurt those little kids?" said Annie. "What if the Nazis had caught Leo and Eli and all the others?"

Jack shuddered. It was unbearable to think about.

"Germany, England, France, Italy, and the United States—they all work together now for peace in the world, right?" said Annie.

"Right," said Jack. "They're all good friends."

"And the United States and Japan also fought each other in World War Two," said Annie. "But now they're good friends?"

"Right," said Jack.

"Cool," said Annie. "Let's think about that instead, and let's think about Gaston, Suzette, Sylvie, Tom, Theo, and the driver of the milk truck, all trying to do the right thing. During war, I think lots of people try to do the right thing. Don't you?"

"Yes," said Jack.

Jack and Annie left the shadowy woods and crossed their street to the bright, sunshiny sidewalk. The warmth and beauty of the light lifted Jack's spirits.

"I love our lives," Annie said with a sigh.

"Yeah, me too," said Jack. "Especially our freedom."

"Like the freedom to ride our bikes to the lake and the library," said Annie. "The freedom to watch movies and eat popcorn and play Scrabble with Mom and Dad and cook outside on the grill and visit our grandparents . . . and our great-grandparents."

"Yeah, a million things like that," said Jack. Right now, he had a whole new appreciation for the familiar, ordinary things in life.

Jack and Annie turned into their yard and climbed the steps to the front porch. Before Jack opened the screen door, he looked at Annie. "Hey, did you think the airplane pilot would turn out to be Merlin?" he asked.

"No way. I definitely did *not* see that coming," said Annie. "Did you?"

"Not in a million years," Jack said with a grin. Then he headed inside their house.

TRACK THE FACTS BEHIND JACK AND ANNIE'S MISSION

**Turn the page to learn more
about World War II.**

MORE INFORMATION ABOUT WORLD WAR II

World War II was fought all over the world from 1939 until 1945. The war involved more than thirty countries and 100 million people and was fought between two main groups of powers: the Allied powers and the Axis powers. The chief Allied powers were Great Britain, the Soviet Union, and the United States. The chief Axis powers were Germany, Italy, and Japan.

At the time of World War II, Germany was led by a brutal dictator named Adolf Hitler, who was the head of a political party called the Nazi Party.

Beginning in 1938, Hitler's Nazi forces quickly invaded many European countries, including Austria, Poland, the Netherlands, Belgium, Luxembourg, France, Denmark, Yugoslavia, Greece, and Norway.

In the summer of 1940, Germany's air force attacked Great Britain. But under the leadership of Prime Minister Winston Churchill, the British withstood the attack and defeated the Germans in the Battle of Britain. It was the first defeat for Germany in the war.

The United States did not become directly involved in World War II until 1941. On December 7, Japan bombed Pearl Harbor, a US naval base in Hawaii, and the next day, the United States declared war on Japan. Soon after, Hitler declared war on the United States. The United States joined the Allied powers and fought the Axis powers in many countries all over the world for the next four years.

World War II ended on September 2, 1945, when Japan was the last country to formally surrender to the Allies. The war lasted for six years and one day. It is estimated that during that time, 50 million to 85 million people lost their lives.

D-Day

On June 6, 1944, 150,000 Allied soldiers invaded the coast of Normandy in France to fight Hitler's army. D-Day was the largest land, air, and sea invasion in the history of the world. It became the turning point for World War II.

Spies and the Resistance

During World War II, spies were sent behind enemy lines to gather information for their side. In Great Britain, Prime Minister Winston Churchill formed a highly secret spy organization known as the SOE, which stood for **S**pecial **O**perations **E**xecutive. Both men and women were members of the SOE. They were ordinary people from all walks of life who were willing to risk their lives to defeat the Nazis.

In Nazi-occupied countries, there were also

many hidden groups known as the Resistance, who were trying to fight Hitler's army. Often working with Allied spies, Resistance groups used wireless radios to communicate secretly with Allied forces. They also resisted the invaders through acts of sabotage, such as blowing up rail lines used by the Nazi soldiers for traveling and for transporting weapons.

War Pigeons

During World War II, pigeons were used by both the Allied and Axis powers to carry messages across Europe. The pigeons were known as carrier pigeons or homing pigeons. They were used as couriers because they could fly at high altitudes and find their way home to their handlers many miles away. Soldiers and spies would place a message in a small canister attached to the pigeon's foot. Then the pigeon would carry the message home.

Great Britain had a National Pigeon Service, which used over 200,000 carrier pigeons. One of the most famous British pigeons was named

Commando. Commando flew more than ninety missions, carrying messages from agents in France to soldiers in Britain. He received a medal for his excellent service and today is remembered as one of the bravest creatures to ever serve in a war.

The German Enigma Machine

During any war, military messages are often intercepted by the enemy. In order to disguise their messages, military forces develop highly secret codes. They also train code breakers who try to decipher (or "crack") the enemy's codes.

Germany used one of the most complicated code systems of all time. The Germans created their code with a device called an Enigma machine. (*Enigma* means "puzzle.") The Enigma machine was a complicated typewriter designed to create a code that was nearly impossible to decipher. To make things even more difficult, the codes were changed every day.

Tanks

Tanks were invented by the British during World War I. Soon other countries also began using them. Thousands of tanks were built each month during the war. The early tanks could hardly move faster than a person walking. But by World War II, tanks had greatly improved—they were far more durable than the early tanks and could travel over very rough terrain.

Most countries used their tanks to carry powerful weaponry. But German tanks didn't have strong armor or firepower. This made them lighter and faster. The German tanks helped the Nazis develop a tactic known as blitzkrieg (which means "lightning war"). A blitzkrieg is an attack that uses speed and surprise to encircle and destroy an enemy. Germany was able to win many land battles using this technique.

Submarines and Aircraft Carriers

Much of World War II was fought on the ocean. The battleship had been the most powerful naval weapon in previous wars, but World War II marked the beginning of a new era—the invention of the submarine changed the way naval battles were fought. Both the Allies and the Axis powers used submarines. (German submarines were called U-boats.) The submarine was a valuable war machine, as it could travel underwater for short periods of time. Submarines used an underwater missile called a torpedo to sink large ships.

In addition to submarines, aircraft carriers were also new to naval warfare. These enormous ships carried airplanes that could take off from the ship, as well as land back on the ship. Most aircraft carriers could hold over thirty planes!

Airplanes

Airplanes played a larger role in World War II than in any previous war. Advanced technology made planes faster and more powerful. Unlike a tank or battleship, an airplane could travel anywhere. Taking off from airfields or from aircraft carriers, the plane could engage in combat over any sort of terrain or body of water.

Airplanes could also provide a bird's-eye view of enemy territory to help an army plan its attacks. And they could drop troops, spies, and

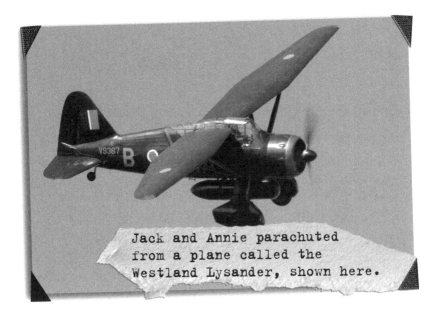

Jack and Annie parachuted from a plane called the Westland Lysander, shown here.

supplies behind enemy lines via parachute.

Fighter planes were especially important in World War II. Instead of dropping bombs like bomber planes, fighter planes faced each other in the air. There were almost 150 different kinds of fighter planes used during the war. One of the most famous of these planes was called the North American P-51 Mustang. It could fly higher and make sharper turns than any other plane.

The Holocaust

The Nazis were extremely prejudiced against the Jewish people. Under Hitler's leadership, the Nazis killed millions of Jewish people, as well as members of many other ethnic and political minority groups. To escape prison and death, some Jewish families went into hiding. They hid in caves or barns or under the floorboards of a friend's house. They had to be very secretive and quiet, often for days at a time.

The Diary of Anne Frank

In the Netherlands, a Jewish girl named Anne Frank and her family secretly moved into the building where her father worked. The price for helping someone wanted by the Nazis was death. In spite of this, coworkers of Anne's father helped the Frank family hide in the back of the building.

When they left their home, Anne and her family wore several layers of clothing because they did not want to be seen carrying suitcases into her father's work building. While they were hiding, they spent long hours every day being very quiet and hardly moving. Anne wrote in her diary to pass the time. She and her family lived there for two years, until they were captured.

Danger in the Darkest Hour

After World War II ended, the whole world was horrified to learn of the full extent of the Nazi persecution of innocent people. People everywhere were deeply moved by the publication of Anne Frank's diary. Perhaps the most famous words from her diary are: "In spite of everything I still believe that people are really good at heart."

World War II greatly affected almost every country in the world, and so many terrible things happened that it is hard to fully comprehend its horrors. But over time, one young girl's diary has helped people to grieve for all those who senselessly died.

Anne Frank, age 12

About the Author

MARY HOOPER is the author of more than 60 children's and young adult books. She has two grown children and lives with her husband Richard in Oxfordshire, England, the same area Anne Green came from.